Forever Yours

~*~*~*~

NICOLE TAYLOR

Table of Contents

Chapter 1

"Why do I have to go with you? I can stay home alone. I've done it before," Nia Carmichael said to her mother.

The response was swift. "Mainly it's because you have lost all credibility."

Nia glared. Deep down she knew she had brought some of this on herself. But that was deep, deep down. At the fore, she just felt resentful of what she perceived as power by adults to oppress their children. It was all because of a mishap at Damon Deverre's birthday party. If she could turn back the clock, she would.

At the time, it seemed harmless enough to accompany her best friend, Bianca, to the nightclub *Zenith* where the rapper and hip-hop mogul was throwing a bash for his thirtieth birthday. Bianca had gained the invite because her father was Damon's accountant. Nia had felt very special to have been chosen from their group of friends as Bianca's *plus one*.

Nia had caught Damon's eye from the moment she walked through the door. She was only seventeen, as her mother took pains to point out afterward. In all fairness to Damon, she had looked a lot older with her makeup, sparkling cocktail dress, jewelry, and stilettos. And, handsome as he was, he'd caught her eye too.

She was aware of his reputation as a ladies' man and was not willing to be just another one of his flings, so she'd stayed clear of him. Then someone had come over to deliver the message that Damon wanted her to join him at his table. Bianca had urged Nia to go, but she had refused politely. Hot-shot celebrity or not, no one summoned Nia Carmichael anywhere. No sooner had the man gone to convey her response than Damon himself appeared beside her, reducing Bianca to a bundle of giggles.

He smiled at her, and if she had thought he was good looking before…*well!* Maintaining her posture of cool disinterest, which as belied by the cartwheels she was doing on the inside, Nia scooted around on her seat to make room for him.

Damon made himself comfortable. He asked Nia countless questions and seemed genuinely interested in her responses. She was flattered by the attention. About an hour later, however, Nia felt someone grab her arm, and yank her out of the seat. She stumbled and before she could right herself was met with a sharp slap across her face.

It took Nia a few seconds to get over the shock of the slap and that her attacker was R&B singer, Sheba. Once she recovered, her response was swift. She balled up her fist and punched the woman in the eye, hard. Sheba lurched backward and then attacked Nia with fury. They fought, and even though Nia had not started it and would have liked it to end, she had no intention of backing down.

She gave as good as she got. By the time Damon had separated them with the help of his bodyguards, Nia had lost an earring, a shoe heel was broken, her dress was torn, and she ached in several places from scratches and blows. She was satisfied to find that the other woman had not fared much better.

The drama didn't end there. Someone had called the cops. Sheba claimed that Nia had assaulted her first. To his credit, Damon came to Nia's defense. Still, the police hauled both disheveled girls to the station for creating a disturbance. By the time Nia's mother had arrived, the paparazzi had also turned up to take pictures of the music star and her daughter. The newshounds managed to capture a few photos of Nikki Carmichael entering and then exiting the

2

precinct with Nia in tow. No charges had been made, and she'd been released to her mother with a warning.

As if on cue, the tabloids picked up the story. Magazines with headlines like "NIKKI'S DAUGHTER IN SHOCKING FIGHT WITH SHEBA OVER DAMON" graced newsstands by the next day.

Her mother had railed at her afterward and given her the cold shoulder for days, but what distressed Nia most about the whole thing was that she was now grounded for a month. This meant that the previous permission granted to Nia to travel to Miami for spring break had been rescinded.

It irritated Nia that her mother didn't want to hear her side of things. Even her father had called from France to ask why she was getting into fights in clubs. At least he had seemed to accept her explanation.

Damon called her afterward and apologized profusely for everything that happened. He explained that he and Sheba, once an item, had recently broken up but she just wouldn't accept it. He also said that he hadn't realized that Nia was only seventeen and that he would like to date her when she turned eighteen, which was almost four months away.

Nia smiled now remembering his deep sexy voice on the phone. Her mother could say what she wanted about him, but the fact that Damon was prepared to hold off their relationship until she was eighteen demonstrated that he seemed to have respect and was not the name her mother had called him.

Nia sighed as she shook her foot. It would be a challenge getting her mother to agree to her dating Damon, but once she turned eighteen, she wouldn't need her mother's permission. Bitterness at the situation almost made Nia laugh out loud. All these years her mother had spent more time either focusing on her career or battling her drug dependency than raising her only child. Nikki had parented between tours and spending time in the studio cutting records. The other half of the year Nia generally spent with her father in France if *he* wasn't busy on location shooting a movie. And when neither of her parents could accommodate her, she would be shuffled off to his mother in Marseilles or Nikki's mother in Atlanta.

Then, soon after Nia turned fifteen, Nikki Carmichael had decided to travel to Antigua to check into rehab for like the tenth time. On the flight there, she met a man who introduced her to God. That experience changed her life. Not only was she healed of her drug habit, but she also fell in love with the man. Soon after, she decided she was ready to retire from singing and settle down to be a wife and the mother she should have been all those years.

Well, maybe she could be a wife, but a mother? It was just too little too late. Because as soon as Nia was of legal age, she had plans to leave California. She was headed for New York City and Julliard. She had already applied and had made it to the stage of being granted a live audition. Based on the expressions on the faces of some of the selection committee members, it seemed to have been well received. In another two weeks, she would know for sure if she'd been accepted, but she felt confident she would gain a place. If there were two things her parents had blessed her with it was a powerful voice and charm. She had used both to great effect.

Nia briefly thought about enlisting her father's help in appealing to her mother to let her go to Miami. She quickly dismissed the idea. Her father was rarely any help when it came to overruling her mother. He was currently on his fourth wife, or was it his fifth? He seemed to be having enough trouble keeping things under control with her without initiating confrontations with Nikki.

Nia searched for an excuse to support her point that she should be allowed to stay at home and forego this trip. She sifted through an assortment of possibilities. She hated long flights. No, that would be easily dismissed as a lie considering she'd been traveling all over the world since she was a toddler and it had become second nature. She hated cold temperatures. Again, that was not a plausible reason. Although she preferred warm weather, like most people who had grown up in cold climates, she was used to it. She couldn't ski. Well, that might work. But her mother would probably argue that lessons were available.

Nia folded her arms across her chest and looked with unseeing eyes on the bedroom floor as she tried to think up a more imaginative excuse. She chewed her gum thoughtfully then decided to say what was really on her mind.

"I'll be eighteen in a few more months, you know. Old enough to vote. Might as well let me get used to freedom. I don't see why I need to travel with you and Thomas like I'm a baby."

Her mother had been going back and forth to her walk-in closet as she packed her suitcase. She didn't pause her stride, but Nia saw her lean her head to one side as if in thought. Maybe, she was making headway.

"Listen, Mama. I've learned my lesson. I swear. I'll be more careful about the kind of parties I attend from now on."

Nia instantly realized it was the wrong choice of words. The word 'parties' seemed to have triggered her mother. She stopped midstride and turned to face Nia. Narrowing her eyes, she wagged her index finger and said in her Georgia accent, "You will not be attendin' another party until you are eighteen, Nia Carmichael. You got that?"

"Fine. I won't go to any parties when you are gone. I'll just stay at home. Promise."

"You are comin' with us, and that's final."

"I can go stay with Dad, then. If you think I can't be trusted to be alone."

"He's shooting a film in Scotland, and he can't babysit you."

"Babysit me? I'm not three years old, Mama," Nia sputtered in outrage.

"Nia, that's enough now! You are coming with Thomas and me to Austria, and that is final! Go and get packed right now, young lady or I swear…"

"I thought you no longer swore."

Nia bolted from her chair the same moment her mother lunged for her. She ran down the hall to her bedroom, slammed the door behind her, and locked it. After a few minutes spent doubled over against the door, she realized that there was no knock demanding that she open. She put her ear to the door and listened. Silence. Very quietly, she unlocked it, eased it open and peeped to her left, then her right. She released the breath she had been holding. Her mother was not in pursuit. She shut the door and locked it again, just in case, and went over to her bed where she threw herself across the middle with a sigh. Ice, mountains, and infernal snow while her friends got to have fun in the sun. Could her life get any worse?

The snow-capped peaks got him every time.

William Lamport IV continued to sweep his gaze across the mountainous Austrian landscape from the cockpit of the Cessna as he guided the plane to its descent. He returned his attention to check the instruments on the panel before him. Satisfied, he turned his head to grin at his father, William III, his co-pilot.

"Have I shared with you just how much I love my new gift?"

Dad laughed. "Only a couple of hundred times."

"I'm just over the moon right now. Being gifted with my own plane and then getting to fly it at the same moment trumps anything else I've received."

"That's what you said about the sailing yacht last year, and the limited edition Aston Martin the year before that."

"Fine gifts both of them, but how can you beat a plane?"

"I'm certainly glad you appreciate it. Your mum and I put a lot of thought into your eighteenth birthday present. It's symbolic. You're coming of age, so we've given you wings to fly."

Liam grinned. "Nicely put, Dad."

As the plane continued to descend, he surveyed the mountainous terrain and felt a thrill of anticipation zip through him. This was another part of the surprise he loved. The fact that they were headed to the ski resort his family owned in Austria. The only thing he probably enjoyed more than skiing was making music.

"I'm going to hit the slopes as soon as we land."

But upon arrival at the chalet, Liam was in for another surprise. The moment he walked through the door three of his closest friends jumped out at him with shouts of happy birthday and chest bumps, thumps on his shoulder, and high fives. Liam was filled with excitement. There was no way this day could possibly get any better.

She grudgingly admitted that the scene before her was picturesque. The snow-capped mountains and pine trees reminded her of that tin of Danish cookies Grandmama Carmichael had given her one Christmas when she was a little girl.

Nia relaxed in the wingback chair beside the unlit fireplace in the living room and took a sip of hot chocolate as she surveyed the white scene.

"Nice isn't it?"

Nia didn't shift her gaze to the owner of the voice, but she shrugged. Suddenly the scene didn't seem quite as nice. The presence of her mother was a reminder of what she'd been denied-- white sand, azure water, warm sunshine, and freedom.

"I'm sure you'll come to enjoy it if you give it a chance."

The voice moved closer as Nikki took a seat opposite her. Nia finally turned her head slightly to the left to meet her mother's gaze and make a comment. "I have to be here. I don't have to enjoy it."

"Your choice, but it would be a waste of a week. It's spring break. You don't have to spend it being unpleasant and acting spoiled."

Nia bit down on her lower lip. "If I'm spoiled it's because of you."

Nikki was silent for a long time.

Nia began to wonder if she had pushed her mother too far this time and tensed for flight. Eventually, though, Nikki sighed.

"That may be true. But at some point, you have to take responsibility for your own actions and your own choices. You have the power to be whoever you want to be. Begin by pouting less and smiling more. Relax a little. Light a fire or somethin'."

Nikki braced her hands on her legs and stood. "Thomas is asleep, and I'm going to join him. I left some food on the stove for you."

Nia nodded and took another sip of her now lukewarm hot chocolate. "Thanks. Enjoy your rest."

Nikki smiled, seemingly heartened. She turned to go then pivoted and came back to Nia. After a slight hesitation, she leaned down and wrapped her arms around her daughter. Nia felt a pang of guilt for her previous conduct and reached out her free hand to briefly rub her mother's back before she pulled away.

"This will be a memorable trip, you'll see," Nikki promised, as she patted Nia's shoulder before she walked away.

Alone again, Nia shook her head. "Memorable for how cold and dull it will be," she muttered under her breath.

She drained the cup, placed it on a nearby end table and reached for her phone. She checked messages, responded to a few and then realized she was hungry. She went into the kitchen, and after fixing herself a plate,-returned to her room. As she ate she messaged her friends, telling them she was already bored out of her mind. Then she saw a response from Bianca asking if she had opened the parting gift she had bestowed on her at the airport.

Nia put down her fork and remembered that the gift was still in her carry-on luggage. She quickly finished her meal and began searching the bag, recalling Bianca's words, with a wink, that the gift consisted of a few things to help her enjoy her trip to the cold region.

Nia found the box, unwrapped it and opened the top. The first thing she saw was the latest CD by her favorite artist. Smiling, Nia peeled off the cellophane packaging, broke the seal and lifted the cover. She scanned the room and saw the radio/CD player by her bedside table. She went over, placed the CD in and pressed play.

She adjusted the volume so that the pop tunes which lit up the room would not wake the chalet's sleeping occupants. Swaying to the music, Nia returned to the box, put her hand in and pulled out a pair of orange earmuffs. Giggling, she slid them over her ears and closed her eyes at the blissful softness.

Next from the box of goodies came purple leggings. She decided she would wear them the next day. She rolled them into a tight ball, looping over the bottom of one to secure it, then, slightly bending her knees, tossed them into her open suitcase on the luggage rack. *Goal!* And who said she was too short to be a basketball player?

Nia smirked as her attention returned to the box. She stuck her hand in and pulled out a tiny book entitled *Ice Cold Jokes*. Smiling in anticipation, Nia sat on the edge of her bed and flipped through the book. She stopped at a random page.

It was so cold, the flashers in New York were only describing themselves, she read. Nia laughed. She flipped to another page. *Why was the snowman sad? Because he had a meltdown.*

She closed the book and placed it on her bedside table. She would read that when she wanted to get to sleep.

Next in the treasure chest was lip balm. Nia pulled off the top and sniffed a fruity and minty scent. She twisted up the bottom of the tube and ran the waxy substance over her lips. It delivered a pleasant tingle. Nice. She peeped in the box. It seemed like she had come to the end of the gifts. She would have to message Bianca and thank her for her thoughtfulness. She was about to close the box when she spotted a thin white tube stuck to the side. Curious, she tugged it free.

Nia's head jerked back in surprise at what she held between her fingers. It was a cannabis joint.

She had never used weed before. A few times in the recent past when she and her friends had been to parties, her friends had smoked, but she had not indulged. Even though they told her it was harmless fun, she was unable to get the image of her mother lying across her bed stoned out of her head while the smoke alarm screamed. Just after that incident, Nia had been sent to live with Grandmama Carmichael so her mother could go to rehab. But it hadn't stuck. A year later, Nikki had started using again.

Nia contemplated flushing the joint down the toilet before she was discovered and was grounded for the rest of her life, never mind a month. Instead, she replaced it in the box and covered it with the leggings, book, and CD case. She would text Bianca and give her a piece of her mind. Crazy chick! Supposed she had been caught by customs officers or something. Maybe her mother was right about her choice of friends. Smoking at a party was one thing. Planting illegal drugs on her was another.

An hour later, Nia, was bored to tears. Her mind drifted to the joint. She thought about trying it. Just once. She didn't have to inhale. She would just get a little puff to find out what the fuss was all about. It was just sitting there. She had nothing else to do. Besides, her mother had told her to relax, unwind, light a fire. She could do all that with the joint in one go…but outside. It would do no good to fill the chalet with the smell of pot. Nia rubbed her hands down her pants legs and reached for the gift box.

An afternoon spent playing indoor games and joking around had culminated in a celebratory dinner outdoors under the stars and near the campfire. Their chef was given kudos. After all, not everyone knew how to prepare vegan food to tasty perfection. Liam assumed the meat dishes were equally good based on the murmurs of ecstasy from his friends and how much they ate.

When they were done with the food, the music replaced the conversation. Like Liam, Sam had traveled with his guitar but to Liam's delight, his mother, Barbara, had arranged for the chalet to be outfitted with a keyboard and drums. He felt a lump in his throat as he thought how fortunate he was. No, not fortunate, but blessed. He was blessed to have parents who showed their love for him at every turn. Not just with material possessions, but more important with their time, affection, words of affirmation and acts of service.

"What song should we play first?" asked Matthew.

Sam jutted his chin towards Liam. "I think we should let the birthday boy decide."

Reinhardt echoed the sentiment.

Liam looked at his friends. There was deep, sensitive, shy Matthew McGregor; cool, laid back, Sam Webber; and logical, standoffish Reinhardt Wolffe.

Liam and Matthew McGregor had been friends since Liam was eight years old, his second year at St. Paul's School. Matthew had landed as a new boy among those who had spent a year bonding. Acceptance may have come easy for some boys, but Matthew McGregor had much going against him. First, he was a small boy who kept to himself and had trouble making friends. He spent more time with his nose in a book than anywhere else.

The next thing was that Matthew McGregor, unlike most of his classmates, was not British, he was Scottish. Because he tended to mumble when he spoke, he was barely intelligible with his Scottish burr. In addition, his people were not rich or even middle class, they were working class--a bus driver and a nurse's assistant. But Matthew was a bright boy, academically and musically. His parents recognized his abilities early and sacrificed so that their boy could have all the advantages they had not. They had even gone so far as to relocate from Scotland to London so that he could attend the premier academic institution for young boys that was St. Paul's.

Liam stood on the opposite side of things. He was popular among the other boys because he was confident, daring, and good-natured. He enjoyed a good joke or playing pranks like the rest of them. The fact that he was extraordinarily wealthy, an aristocrat, and possessed good looks and athletic prowess didn't hurt either.

There was nothing on paper that would put these two together, except that Liam had always had a soft spot for the underdog. He was the one who had brought home strays or gave away his pocket money to the beggar on the street. He would quickly come to the aid of anyone in pain or in danger with nary a thought to his own safety. Matthew, then, presented many opportunities for Liam's nurturing qualities to manifest themselves.

At every opportunity, Liam cajoled Matthew out of his reclusiveness and invited him to join his group of friends. He soon declared war on anyone who attempted to bully or make fun of Matthew. But what really bonded them and moved the relationship from one of benevolence to true friendship was when Liam discovered that Matthew loved music. The boy shyly shared with Liam his collection of '70s music and demonstrated his skill on the drums and piano. Liam was buoyed to have found a kindred spirit. He invited Matthew to his home and taught him to play the guitar. This led to many evenings spent practicing their instruments and listening to music together.

Like Matthew, Sam was a childhood friend. Liam had met him at church. Sam was of mixed blood. His father, the Pastor of the church, was white and his mother was Japanese. As the last born of four brothers and two sisters, Sam felt no pressure to be anything other than who he wanted to be. He was as cool and laid back as they came. Few things fazed Sam, and he seemed to view the world with mild amusement. He and Liam hit it off from the time Sam's father started pastoring their church when Liam was twelve. A trip to Sam's house for a birthday party soon after that revealed that he loved the guitar even more than Liam did. Around that time, Liam invited Matthew to his church, and he eventually became a regular.

Reinhardt was the latest to join the close-knit group. His parents were German expatriates. Reinhardt's father was CEO of an investment company, and they lived on the same street the Lamports did when at their London residence. Even though their families moved in the same circles, Liam had very little contact with the boy.

He had never gone out of his way to befriend him, perceiving him to be arrogant and standoffish. This viewpoint did not change even when both boys found themselves at Eton around the same time, with Reinhardt having been enrolled a year earlier.

Liam's perception of Reinhardt was dispelled, however, after an event that took place at Eton in his second year. One day he was briskly walking past the tennis court on his way to Mathematics class when he heard one boy stoutly defending another before a group of other boys. Liam paused to find out what was amiss and eventually managed to discern that the boy was being bullied and Reinhardt seemed to have come to the rescue.

Defending the underdog was something Liam could identify with so it only took a moment for him to come alongside Reinhardt and challenge the ringleader that if he wanted to start something he would have to take on both of them. After a minute spent contemplating both Reinhardt and Liam's impressive stature and physiques, the ringleader walked away in disgust, taking his gang with him. Liam and Reinhardt had regarded each other for a few moments and then broke out in laughter.

After that incident, they began greeting each other warmly whenever they met. That lead to invitations out, and soon they had formed a friendship. To Liam's delight, Reinhardt turned out to be impressive on the piano. Liam also discovered he had a good voice, not strong enough for solo singing, but good enough for back up.

From this group of musical friends the band, *Redeemed*, was born. After much pleading, Sam's father agreed that they could lead worship singing at church.

Liam now smiled at his friends, his parents and his younger siblings, Leiliana and Benjamin and said, "Since it's left to me, I choose to take songs by request, beginning with my fair mother."

Barbara laughed and turned things right back to Liam by asking for the latest song he'd penned. The guys looked at him expectantly. They had been practicing but had yet to present it to the church.

Liam grinned. "Why not? Let's do it, lads."

Chapter 2

*H*e looked to be around her age. And he sure could sing.

Nia's eyes were riveted to the boy who was singing at the front of the small group of eight people gathered around the fire. He was the one whose powerful baritone voice gave her goosebumps.

She hadn't meant to spy on them, but after she had wandered away from the chalet seeking a safe distance to smoke the joint, she had been drawn to the laughter and the noise at the nearby building. When the music started up, it had beckoned to her.

She had just intended to see what was happening and then move along. But when the guy at the front had started singing, she became rooted to the spot. That was where she remained throughout the song.

She took a pull of the cigarette, resisted the urge to cough again like she had after the first drag, and closed her eyes as she listened. She heard the word "God" and was surprised it was a religious song. It sounded like the type of music she listened to, nothing like the hymns they sang in Grandmama Carmichael's church.

Suddenly, Nia's heart began to race. She placed a hand on her chest and could feel her heart thundering. She remembered reading somewhere that this was a possible side effect of marijuana use. She brought the cigarette up to her line of vision and peered at it as though a list of its side effects were written on the outside. Then she realized the music had stopped.

She lowered her hand and peered through the shrubs again. At that moment the guy, the one singing, called out, "Hey Matthew. What about *Happiness*? Lets' sing that. We haven't sung it to an audience before."

Nia's eyes widened. She had not expected the British accent. She brought the cigarette to her lips and took another puff. This Matthew person agreed and once again Nia was being serenaded by the amazing voice. *So amazing!* She dangled her hands at her side, closed her eyes, and swayed in time with the tune.

"What's that smell?" someone asked.

Nia sniffed the air, wondering what smell they were referring to.

"Smells like marijuana."

Nia's eyes popped open.

"It does," someone else confirmed, and the voice seemed to be coming in her direction.

Nia froze.

It seemed as though everything happened in slow motion after that. Nia released the cigarette, watched as it hit the ground, and saw how her foot moved awkwardly to stamp it out. She could swear the thing moved by itself, and in response, she tried to stomp and twist it into the ground with her boot.

As the voices came closer, she attempted to turn from the evidence and get away from the scene. In her haste to flee, Nia stumbled, lost her footing and saw the ground coming towards her at an alarming speed. She threw out her hand at the last minute which cushioned the impact of her fall but sent a sharp pain ricocheting through her arm.

Before she could catch her breath, strong hands were holding her by the waist and pulling her upright. She turned as she came up against a hard, muscular chest. She found herself staring into the eyes of the young man who had been singing.

"Are you okay?" he asked.

Instantly, floodlights went on. Nia snapped her eyes shut at the painfully bright light. When she dared to open them again, she was struck by the deep blue eyes of the one whose arms were wrapped around her.

Nia grasped her throat. It felt so dry. She would kill for a few sips of water right now. As she began to cough, the arms around her relaxed to allow her the space she needed. Nia doubled over, holding her stomach, as her body was wracked with coughs.

When the embarrassing display subsided, she felt a bottle being pressed into her hand. She realized it was water. She took several sips. Before she could apologize for coughing in the young man's face, an older man came towards them. Based on the resemblance, she figured he was probably her rescuer's father.

As Nia held the bottle out to the boy, movement on the other side of him drew her gaze. She straightened and briefly met the eyes of the other young men who had been playing instruments.

"Hello. What are you doing here? Did you lose your way?" the older man asked.

He sounded suspicious, and Nia resented the questions. As she was clearly outnumbered, though, she decided to be as gracious as possible.

Sweeping a few dislodged strands of curls off her forehead, she allowed her mouth to briefly curve upwards.

She waved a hand to her right and announced, "I'm staying at the chalet over there. I just came outside to get some fresh air."

The man glanced in the direction of her chalet and then back at her.

"Your chalet is a little distance away. Did you venture out alone?"

Now Nia felt offended by the implication of his words. Because she was so petite, there were times she looked younger than she was, particularly, on this occasion. She wasn't wearing makeup and had her hair pulled into a loose ponytail at the base of her neck.

Perhaps attempting to ease the building tension, her rescuer cleared his throat.

"I'm Liam," he said, holding out a hand.

Nia stared at it for a short while as she wondered why her heart was still racing. Could it be a side effect of the marijuana still? Or was it for another reason? She took the proffered hand. It was surprisingly warm, unlike hers which was like ice. He noticed too, based on his next comment.

"Your hands are cold. How long have you been out here? And without gloves. Come by the fire."

"No that's okay," she said, tugging her hand away.

He gestured towards the older man. "This is my dad, William Lamport."

At that moment they were joined by a beautiful woman with lustrous honey blonde hair. For some reason, she looked familiar to Nia, but she couldn't think why.

"Is everything alright?" the woman asked, touching Mr. Lamport's arm.

He nodded. "When you were in the chalet we smelled smoke, marijuana to be precise. We traced the smell to behind these bushes and found this young lady."

He looked at Nia. "Were you smoking marijuana, dear?"

Nia felt the wind come out of her with a whoosh. That effect combined with the racing of her heart made her feel dizzy. Well, this man certainly was direct!

She swayed and instantly was steadied by a strong hand wrapped around her upper arm. Once again, her eyes shifted upwards to meet Liam's as she braced her arm against his chest. There was a questioning look in their depths, and she realized that her audience was awaiting her response. Had he noticed the smell of the drug when she had coughed in his face? Did he know she was guilty or was he waiting to find out?

Nia didn't want to lie to this boy who had already saved her twice in a matter of minutes. But she wasn't about to admit to smoking pot

17

with him and seven other people waiting in judgement of her. So she lied.

"Me?"

She laughed and wondered if it sounded as fake to them as it did to her.

"I don't smoke."

And that was true–to a point. This was her first time smoking and, based on the side effects she was experiencing and the trouble it had brought her, also would be her last.

She didn't dare to meet the eyes of the one who kept the steadying hand on her. When his father spoke though, she lifted her gaze to his.

"Perhaps whoever was smoking put it out. You didn't see anyone else along your stroll?" Mr. Lamport asked, watching her closely, his head tilted to one side.

Maybe this was the lifeline she needed. Yes, she could invent another person to deflect the blame, but she once again sought Liam's eyes. She saw the way he watched her and decided she could not tell another lie in his presence. She stepped away from him, breaking contact as he allowed his hand to drop away.

"I did not."

She stuffed her hands into the pockets of her leather jacket and looked to the ground, hoping she didn't look as guilty as she felt.

"Anyway, I've got to go."

"You haven't told us your name," the woman said, stepping forward. "I'm Barbara, Liam's mother. Today is Liam's birthday, and we're celebrating. We were just about to toast some marshmallows and make some s'mores. Would you like to join us?"

"Thanks, but no," Nia replied, backing away. "I need to get back, or my parents will, well, you know, send in the Calvary."

Liam cleared his throat.

"Cavalry."

Nia frowned. "What's that?"

"It's send in the *cavalry.*"

"That's what I said."

"No, you said *Calvary*. I don't think you want anyone to send you an experience of intense suffering."

Despite the cold night, Nia felt her face warm. She idly noticed that there were groans, hands covering faces, rolling of eyes, and suppressed laughter. Before she could get angry and feel insulted she saw Liam's face suffuse with color. Were those gestures directed at him? Was it possible he also was embarrassed and had *not* intended to make her feel foolish?

She squeezed out a smile. "Anyway, I've really got to go."

"You seem a little…under the weather," Liam said.

Nia almost lifted a brow. That was a polite but thinly veiled way of saying she seemed under the influence. Did she? She felt sure she was doing a good job of looking quite composed and sober.

"At least, allow me to walk you back to your chalet," he continued.

Nia shook her head vigorously. The last thing she needed was to explain to him why she was entering the chalet through her bedroom window.

"No…really. I'm fine. If I show up with a boy, I will really experience Calvary."

There was a tittering of laughter at her joke, from all except Liam. He continued to watch her with narrowed eyes.

Fear that he would insist caused her to quickly turn away with a murmured 'good night' and move as swiftly as her muddled senses would allow. She hadn't gotten too far when she heard a male voice say, "Liam, I think the cavalry dragged her away."

Another voice added insult to injury with his teasing remark.

"Oh, yeah. I bet he feels like *he's* experiencing Calvary now."

"You guys really know how to milk a joke for all it's worth, don't you?" That was Liam's voice.

"Give us a break; we don't get to have fun at your expense too often."

This was followed by more laughter and muted voices.

Nia smiled briefly at their bantering exchange. What an interesting group of people. She wouldn't mind getting to know them better. Perhaps she would have stayed if they'd met under different circumstances. Now there was the embarrassment of the marijuana episode and the lie she had told between them. How could she sit in their midst with Liam's piercing eyes on her wondering if he had guessed she had lied to his face.

Upon reaching the chalet, Nia braced her hands on the ledge under her bedroom window and hoisted herself up. She got off the ledge carefully, well aware she wasn't too steady on her feet, and eased up the window, pausing to listen for noise. All was quiet. Seemed she hadn't been missed. Nikki and Thomas really had been jetlagged. She was only now feeling tired and sleepy herself. Nia climbed through the window and then secured it quietly.

As she moved across the room, she took off her jacket and tossed it on a nearby chair. She decided to just lie on the bed for a few minutes and take off her boots later. That was her last thought before she succumbed to sleep.

"What did you make of that?"

"Of what?" Liam asked as he savored the view of the constellation that this part of the world afforded.

"The girl who was hiding in the bushes."

Liam drew his teeth across his lower lip, slightly annoyed that after he had finally managed to put the girl, Nia, to the back of his mind, Matthew had now gone and brought her to the forefront again.

"At first, I thought that maybe she was a paparazzo, but then when Liam got close to her, I realized she was pretty young. Plus, she wasn't carrying a camera or anything with her," Sam said.

"None that you could see," Matthew countered.

"She snuck away from her parents' chalet to get a forbidden smoke. Isn't it obvious?" Reinhardt chimed in.

"She's quite pretty," Matthew commented.

Sam chuckled low. "Someone's crushing."

"It was just a comment," Matthew snapped.

"If that's *all* it was," Sam taunted.

Liam slanted a glance at the two who sometimes bickered like siblings. A change of subject was needed. Taking a sip of his hot chocolate, he eased down lower in his seat and thrust his long legs before him.

"So, early tomorrow morning we are going to hit the slopes. Okay, guys?"

"This will be my first time skiing," Matthew reminded them, pushing up his black horn-rimmed glasses with his index finger. Liam's gaze traveled over his friend's anxious face. He looked good in the trendy glasses Liam had helped him pick out over a year ago and the fashionable way his black hair was cut suited his narrow pixie face. Though he had grown over the years, he was still the shortest of the three young men at a little over five-foot-eight-inches tall. With Liam's guidance, he had learned to select clothes that were tapered and didn't hang on his small frame.

"Don't worry, Matt. It'll be fun. We'll take the beginner slopes tomorrow," Liam assured him.

The other guys knew how to ski. Reinhardt's family was big into skiing and went to a ski resort at least once a year. Sam was naturally athletic and had gotten the hang of things the first time he had accompanied Liam and his family to the slopes. Matthew, however, was another story.

Though Liam had invited Matthew on several occasions, the young man had always politely declined. Liam suspected he was terrified of the mountainous terrain, so he had not pressed him. He probably had agreed to come this time only because he hadn't wanted to miss out on Liam's celebration. Liam appreciated the sacrifice and sought to put him at ease once more.

"We'll be right there to keep an eye on you and ensure you're safe. We won't let anything bad happen to you. Right guys?"

Sam and Reinhardt readily agreed.

"Sure. It's really very simple. If you've ever skate-boarded or anything, it's kind of like that," Sam said.

"I've never done that. I'm not very good when it comes to activities that require you to keep your balance," Matthew said.

Reinhardt clapped a hand on Matthew's shoulder.

"It'll be fun. You'll get the hang of it. Like Liam said, we'll all be there to back you up."

Liam smiled in gratitude at the exchange. Even though they all bickered occasionally, these guys were like family. Ultimately, they looked out for each other. More important, in spite of being at different stages in their journey, they were all born-again Christians, and that really helped to keep them accountable and on track.

Chapter 3

"The light…it burns!"

Sam's outburst as he shrunk back into the chairlift brought a snort of laughter from Liam's lips.

Liam was not usually an early riser unless there was a slope nearby. That morning he had been up, showered, and dressed before the rest of the chalet's occupants could stir. It had been no small feat getting Sam going, even though Liam had warned the guys the previous night of his desire to hit the slopes early.

As he filled his lungs with the fresh mountain air, Liam surveyed the landscape and acknowledged that it was indeed bright. It was a reflection of the brilliant white snow on everything in sight. It capped the mountains, it sat on the pine trees, it covered rooftops, and best of all it coated the slopes.

Several minutes later, Liam pulled the sunglasses down over his eyes to cut out some of the glare and stepped off the lift. The crunch under his feet brought back childhood memories. Whenever he spied snow through the windows of his home, he would bundle up and beg his mother to allow him to go outside and play. He'd ride his sled, build snowmen, and make snowballs to have snow fights with whoever was willing, or even unwilling. He smiled as he remembered leading his siblings in pelting some visiting cousins from America with snow. It had been so worth the scolding from his mother, particularly since his father hadn't seemed too concerned. He had even caught him suppressing a grin.

Reinhardt and Matthew arrived right behind them on the next chairlift. His parents and siblings had gone to one of the steeper slopes. The ski instructor was soon filling in the young men on the basics of skiing, while Liam allowed his mind to drift. It was only Matthew, really, who needed the information.

He thought about the plans that continued in celebration of his birthday. There was a party organized for him that evening. He didn't know who would be invited, but he suspected it would be his large family, consisting of his mother's siblings, his friends from school, church, their social circle and of course, his father's own large family of Fosters.

He focused as Reinhardt positioned himself to ski down the slopes. His eyes drifted over to Matthew who seemed less tense than he had been at breakfast and who was listening carefully to the ski instructor. The man seemed to know what he was doing. Liam turned his head to see where Sam was and found him a little ways off squatting down on his skis and watching Matthew's training with an expression of pure boredom. Reinhardt disappeared down the mountain, and Sam turned his head to watch him and then threw Liam a deadpan look.

Liam shrugged his shoulders. He too was ready to take off, but he had made a promise to Matthew he couldn't break. He would only leave when Mathew felt completely comfortable with the ski instructor, and that wasn't going to happen in ten minutes. Liam heaved a sigh and reached in his back pocket for his phone to kill time.

"Is it your intention to spend all day on that thing?"

"Sure is," Nia retorted without looking up.

In the next instant, the phone was plucked from her grasp.

"Hey," Nia exclaimed as she jumped up from her seat to stand on tiptoes in an attempt to retrieve the phone which was now suspended above her step-father's head.

After several minutes of futile straining and reaching, during which Thomas calmly kept her away with one hand, Nia dropped back on her heels in frustration. She folded her arms across her chest and glared at the man her mother had married. He was a giant, and she was certain that even if she took a flying leap to get her phone, she would miss her mark.

Nia now noticed the way he was dressed. She took a step back to get a better look. He was outfitted from head to toe in bulky outerwear and looking like the Abominable Snowman.

She turned her head at the sound of her mother entering the room dangling a pair of ugly ski boots from her hand. Nikki's eyes flicked over her husband and daughter just before she sat on a chair and began pulling on the boots.

Nia supposed this meant the two were going skiing. Happy them. But unhappy her if Thomas was going to leave her phoneless.

The young girl approached her mother for help with her unruly step-father.

"Mom," she cried in her most dramatic and distressed voice, "Please tell Thomas to give me back my phone!"

Nikki lifted her head to peer at Nia from under a fashionable beanie. She looked from one of them to the other and then lowered her head once more to tie the laces of her left shoe.

"Thomas is right, Nia. We didn't bring you on this trip so you could sit all day and stare at a screen. You need to get some fresh air and exercise."

Nia closed her eyes as she listed reasons to stay away from the snow.

"It's cold outside. I want to be warm. Or as warm as I can be in a cold country, unlike my friends who are now enjoying the sun and the sea and the sand in…"

Nikki stood and placed her hands on her hips.

"Get dressed."

Nia wasn't sure she heard correctly. "What?"

Her mother looked very serious. "You are coming skiing with us."

Nia's attempts to refuse didn't seem to be working, yet she kept pushing.

"What for?"

"You need to learn a new skill."

"I don't need to learn how to ski. I already know how."

Two pairs of parental eyebrows rose in disbelief.

"Oh? When did you learn?" Nikki asked.

Though tempted to lie that she had learned when she was staying with her dad, Nia knew that Nikki probably would call him to verify and at the very least demand that she prove it. She decided to change tactics.

She turned her face to her mother.

"I didn't learn *per se,* but what I mean is I know how to rollerblade. I'm great at it, as you know. So this skiing thing is no novelty for a girl like me."

"Skiing and rollerblading is not the same thing," Nikki said.

"How do you know? They both involve skating and balancing. I'll bet you they do."

For a minute there was silence. Then Thomas chimed in. "Fine."

"Fine?" The two females both responded at the same time. One sounded hopeful and the other skeptical.

"How about this," he continued. "If you can prove to us that you can ski, from then on your time will be yours to do whatever you want. We won't ask you to join us in any other activities."

"Really?" Nia was surprised by this new turn of events.

Thomas nodded. Nia's eyes shifted to her mother who shrugged.

"How long have I got to prove to you?"

"That's up to you. The sooner you can convince us you can ski, the sooner you get to do whatever you want," Thomas said.

Nia smiled. Great. All she had to do was enlist the services of some ski instructor, and in no time she'd be able to spend the rest of the trip doing whatever she liked.

"Cool."

As they turned to go, Thomas stopped at the door and looked over his shoulder.

"Oh, by the way. Part of the deal is that you can't get any professional lessons."

"That's not fair."

"Remember, you told us you already know how to ski. That means you don't need to enlist professional services. Unless, of course, you want to re-evaluate your comments and agree that you really do need to learn how to ski."

Nia mumbled as she turned to go to her room to get dressed, "Nah. It's fine."

So, they wanted to play hardball? Well, she was all for it. She was an expert at rollerblading. How hard could *skating* down a slope be?

At the top of the run, Nia positioned her skis forward, and with a push of the poles, she was off down the slope. A few seconds later, she began to get nervous. She was moving faster and faster downhill as she gained momentum. How was she going to stop! She could end up breaking her neck!

Nia did the only thing she knew how to do. Just like when she rollerbladed, she tried to bail out by dropping gently to one knee. Only it didn't happen as planned. As she bent her knee, the momentum propelled her head over heels, and she continued to roll like tumbleweed all the way down the mountain.

Her heart was racing as she finally came to a stop somewhere at the base of the slope. After a few minutes of catching her breath, she managed to roll onto her back. She remained like that for a short while before she could get on her side and push to a sitting position.

As she sat with her knees bent, she was thankful for the bulky clothing, certain it had saved her from doing damage to herself. Hair fell into her eyes, and when she patted the top of her head, she realized her beanie, earmuffs, and goggles were gone. In fact, as her eyes caught sight of her feet, she noticed that her skis also were missing.

She turned her head and body to the left, then to the right, sweeping the area with a quick glance to assess the situation. She added her poles to the list of lost items.

Nia ran a hand down her face as her shoulders slumped. It would seem as though her gear had been flung far and wide as she had made her ungraceful descent. How many people had witnessed her headlong tumble? Of course, it really didn't matter since she didn't know any of them. Still, she hoped they hadn't videotaped her and posted it online as people were wont to do these days.

Wondering how she would get back up the mountain without her skis and poles, Nia braced herself to stand when she saw someone coming towards her. Observing the way the skier sliced through the snow with smooth strokes made her both sigh in admiration and prick with envy. A whoosh of cold wind hit her face as the skier came to a graceful, effortless stop directly in front of her.

The broad shoulders and height suggested it was a man but the helmet, sunglasses, and jacket zipped over the lower face made it impossible to guess who he was or even what he looked like. Not that she cared. She needed help back up that slope, and this was no time to discriminate. Before she could open her mouth, however, the skier unzipped the upper part of his jacket, to reveal the lower part of his face and then ripped off his sunglasses.

She found herself staring into a pair of amused blue eyes.

"Nia?"

Liam!

He had barely spotted her downward, ungraceful tumble.

Liam had been encouraging Matthew as he made beginner strides on the slopes. After almost two hours of instruction, Matthew was doing well, which wasn't surprising as he was a quick study. Confident that Matthew was getting the hang of things, Sam and Reinhardt took off for one of the challenging nearby slopes. Liam remained a bit longer until Mathew assured him he would be fine with the skiing instructor.

"I'll be back in about half an hour," Liam promised as he took off to a nearby slope. It was not as challenging as he was used to but he did not want to venture too far away from Matthew.

He was making long strides across the powder when he saw a flash of orange in the corner of his eye. He turned his head and barely caught someone whizzing by him. The skier in the orange earmuffs looked to be a newbie from the way he or she was skiing; no turns, just straight and headlong. He realized that sometimes those who were new to skiing were over eager and didn't take the time needed to get proper lessons or to pace themselves.

Fortunately, this wasn't too steep a slope. Unfortunately, even on a slope like this one, skiers could hit a tree on their way down, or fall at the wrong angle and end up in a world of hurt–or worse. He decided to follow to ensure that the person landed safely at the bottom.

When he arrived at the base of the mountain and found Nia, he was more than a little surprised. She didn't look like she was in pain so much as irritated by the whole thing.

"Are you okay?" he asked, stamping down the desire to laugh at how much she looked like a little girl about to throw a tantrum.

"No!" she said, slapping the ground in frustration. "No, I'm not. I hate skiing! And I lost all my gear."

Liam looked up the mountain. Would it be possible to retrieve her items that were flung here and there all the way down? He would try.

"Can you tell me what you lost?"

She rolled her eyes as if she expected him to figure it out with deductive reasoning. "Everything but the clothes on my back."

He smiled at how cute she looked with the wild curls that had escaped from the French braid gently blowing about her face. A moment later, he cautioned himself to be careful. He would help her as he would for anyone in distress, but he needed to keep his guard up. He could not allow someone he had caught sneaking around at night smoking an illegal drug, and then turn around and lie about it, to get past his defenses.

He gave her a quick once over. She seemed unhurt, and except for her clothing, shoes, and gloves, all the rest of her gear was missing.

"Okay, what color are they?"

"Orange earmuffs, yellow goggles, white beanie, and skis…what do you call that color? Chrome?"

He pulled his goggles down over his eyes.

"I'll be right back. Don't move."

He heard her exclaim as he pushed off, "Where would I go?" That brought a smile to his lips.

He climbed up the slope and scanned the area. Eventually, he found everything except the beanie which probably was camouflaged where it landed. When he returned, Nia was still sitting on the snow but was now covering the sides of her head with the palms of her hands in an attempt to keep her ears warm.

"Here you go," he said, holding out her gear to her. "I couldn't find your beanie." He removed his helmet. "But you can have mine."

Her expression revealed genuine surprise at his gesture. She put up a hand in protest.

"Oh, no. I couldn't!"

He shook his head as he pulled off the beanie.

"It's quite alright."

"No, seriously," she said. "I'll be fine. I've got way more hair than you do."

"Nonetheless," he said, ignoring her protests and leaning over her to fit the cap and pull it down over her ears, "you've been without a warm head covering for long enough."

She closed her eyes for a few moments and caressed the fabric touching her ears.

"Thank you," she said with a sigh. "This beanie feels so good."

"You won't need those," he said, jerking his chin in the direction of the earmuffs lying in the snow beside her legs. He took his helmet and began to fit it on her head.

"Watch your fingers," he cautioned softy as he fastened the helmet securely under her chin.

"Comfortable?" he asked.

She nodded as her eyes seemed to send a message of gratitude. He now realized they were a lighter brown than he initially had thought. Liam was holding his breath, transfixed, and didn't feel like he could break eye contact. A minute later, Nia picked up her goggles and slipped them on.

Liam dropped to a squat and was about to help her with her skis, but she reached for them and began to put them back on by herself. When she was done he straightened and offered her a hand. She took it, and he pulled her to a standing position. She wobbled a little and put a hand on his arm to steady herself, reminiscent of the previous night. He tried to ignore the faint smell of her perfume as he stooped to pick up her ski poles and then hand them to her.

"So what now?" she asked, as she leaned on the poles for balance.

"Back up the slopes. First time?"

"Is it that obvious?"

"Yes," he said, with blunt honesty. "So, are you having lessons?"

"No."

"You should. They are very useful."

"I can't. I have this bet with my mama and stepdad that I can master the slopes without professional lessons."

"Why would you make such a bet?"

She looked sheepish as she shrugged and answered in a quiet voice, "I don't know. I didn't think it through I guess. Sometimes I make rash decisions."

He remembered the scene from last night and wondered if she was one of those people who acted first and thought later. *Like coming out at night to smoke a joint?*

"But I've changed my mind," she continued. "I don't really like skiing after all. It's harder than it looks."

"Most things are hard at first, but they get easier with practice. You weren't that bad for a newbie. I've seen worst."

"Really? That's pretty hard to believe."

He laughed, finding himself drawn to this girl despite his warning to himself to be cautious.

"Once you keep going your confidence will grow, and you'll soon relax and begin enjoying yourself. My friend Matthew was anxious at first as well. This is just his first day, and I already see progress."

She still looked slightly skeptical, but he could see by the light in her eyes that he had inspired her to try again.

She asked, "You sure about that?"

"Yes, everyone feels the way you do at first."

"Did you?"

He wrinkled his brow. "That was a long time ago. I don't remember very much about it, but I'm sure I did."

She nodded thoughtfully. Then her eyes lit up as if she had been shocked by a terrific idea. "Hey, could you teach me?"

The smile on his face froze. Teach *her*? That hadn't crossed his mind. It wasn't at the top of his bucket list for this trip, plus it ran counter to his resolve to keep his distance from her.

Still, some of the most unexpected, impromptu things in life sometimes turn out to be the very stuff that makes the greatest memories. He found himself slowly nodding.

"Sure, why not? But just a few lessons okay? My friends and I have plans and not many more days to fulfill them."

"Oh, no worries. I'm usually a quick learner. I wouldn't dream of monopolizing your time. A day should do it."

He suddenly remembered something she had said previously.

"I thought you told me that part of the deal with your parents was you weren't allowed to be coached."

"No, they meant professional instructions."

"Isn't that just semantics?"

"My stepdad's a lawyer, so I'm sure he would relate to my finding a loophole."

"Well, Nia…what's your last name by the way? I didn't catch it last night."

"Carmichael."

"Well, Nia Carmichael, when would you like to begin?"

"How about right now?"

"Now?"

"Unless you've got other plans."

Since all he had planned to do was ski for the next couple of hours and then snowboard until tonight's party, he couldn't think of an excuse not to start teaching her right then.

He shrugged. "I'm free. Come on, let's go."

Chapter 4

Skiing was actually turning out to be more fun than Nia expected. After a re-introduction to two of his friends, Liam began to teach her some basics. The third one, called Matthew, was a short distance away having professional lessons.

When Sam and Reinhardt began to give her tips, Liam said with a hint of impatience, "I'm the one teaching her here. You two can go find your own beginner to instruct. In fact, go help Matthew."

Nia hoped that Liam wasn't one to lose patience fast, because even though she had bragged she was a quick learner, she wasn't confident that it would apply to this particular activity.

It turned out that Liam was one of the most patient people she had ever met. He spent the remainder of the morning teaching her how to turn, slow down, and stop without falling on her face in the snow. Even though she landed in a heap on the ground more times than she could count, he never scolded or got frustrated with her. He patiently repeated his instructions as though it was the first time he was sharing his tips. It was very encouraging to her as he praised her incremental progress. Eventually, it seemed as though his efforts were paying off.

By mid-afternoon she was finally able to make it to the bottom of the slope, come to a stop, albeit clumsily, on her own and stand for several seconds before falling flat on her face in the snow.

Hunger pangs eventually forced them both to seek sustenance at the ski lodge. They gobbled down their sandwiches and then made their way back to the slopes.

"This is really fun," Nia confessed, laughing. "Even though I keep falling, you've been *sooo* patient."

"You are a good student."

"I am? I feel like I should be wearing a dunce cap."

He threw back his head and laughed.

"Not at all. I love your tenacity and willingness to get this no matter how long it takes. That's what motivates me to keep helping you. That spirit of determination you have."

Nia felt her face light up. Suddenly, she felt self-conscious and very aware of this boy. She reminded herself he wasn't her type at all and that she couldn't wait until she turned eighteen and could start dating Damon.

She decided to change the subject as she unzipped her pocket and pulled out a phone.

"Let's take a selfie so I can post this online and tease my friends about the fabulous time I'm having."

Dutifully, he leaned in closer for the photo.

When she lowered the phone, he said, "How about I take a photo of you going down the slopes? That's sure to make them green with envy."

"Great idea!" she said, head bobbing up and down.

He took several photos that afternoon, but the one she thought was the best was the one at the end of that tiring but exhilarating day. She had just managed a small feat–to stay on her small feet and Liam captured the moment. What a victory!

As they made their way back to her chalet, skis over their shoulders, Nia turned to Liam. "Thanks so much. Now it's time to pay you for your trouble."

"Pay me? No. Not necessary," he said quickly, protesting with a short laugh.

"I don't mean with money. I meant to treat you to a cup of hot chocolate. It's one of the few things I make well."

He smiled. "That sounds great. Regrettably, I have to decline. I'm due back at my chalet. I've got to get ready for a party."

"Someone's having a party tonight?" she asked, brightening at the prospect of partying.

"Yes. Me."

"You?"

"My eighteenth birthday was yesterday."

Nia now remembered Liam's mother mentioning something about that.

"So, it will be a party with your folks and friends then."

"A few more people than that."

"Like who else?"

"About fifty family and friends."

She stopped walking. "Fifty people? Where are they coming from?"

"Various places."

He didn't break his stride, so she had to run a few steps to catch up with him.

"Hey!" she said, grabbing his arm, "Are you a celebrity or something?"

He turned to look at her, his eyes sparkling with amusement.

"Me? Oh no. I'm just an ordinary guy."

Nia lifted a brow. Ordinary guy indeed! Did he think she was blind? Apart from the fact that everything he wore was a luxury brand, the guy simply exuded money and class. Nothing *ordinary* about him at all.

She was now burning with curiosity about a guy who was rich enough to not only have a birthday bash at a ski resort in Austria but also to import planeloads of people from all over the world to celebrate with him. He was good-looking enough to be famous, but she couldn't place who he would be. She began thinking about all the British celebrities she knew. Then a thought occurred to her.

She squeezed his arm and moved to stand in front of him, forcing him to halt his stride. Tilting her head back, she looked him full in the face and squinted.

"Are you royalty?"

He looked stunned for a moment and then he laughed.

"Sure, I'm a prince."

Her mouth dropped open.

"I knew it!"

He laughed again, and then grabbed her by the shoulders to stop her from jumping up and down.

"I am a son of the King of the Universe, Nia. That's what I mean."

She became very still and tipped her head to one side.

"King of the Universe? Who's that?"

"The everlasting God. You know, the King of the Universe."

Nia felt her lips go round. She remembered the song Liam and his friends were playing last night. It *had* mentioned God.

"You're a Christian?"

"Don't look so shocked."

"But you're rich and gorgeous."

She covered her mouth with her hand. She had not meant to mention the last part. He would think she was attracted to him, which she most definitely was not.

His lips twitched. "Why, Nia, are you suggesting that all Christians are poor and ugly?"

She smiled at the absurdity of her statement and waved her hand dismissively in the air.

"Forget I said that. I think I'm tired from all that skiing."

She turned around and resumed her walk. He fell into step beside her.

She continued to probe. "You may not be a celebrity, but you're rich. That much I know. What do your parents do for a living?"

"What do *your* parents do for a living?" he asked, turning the tables on her.

"I asked you first!"

"That doesn't matter. Besides, you owe me for teaching you how to ski. Since I haven't yet collected, that could serve as part payment."

"I thought you said no payment is necessary."

"I changed my mind."

"Fickle…alright, I'll allow you one question."

"Deal. So, go ahead and answer mine."

"What was the question again?"

"What do your parents do?"

She smiled. "My father is a film director and my mother…"

"I thought you said your dad's a lawyer."

"My stepdad."

"Oh, right."

"And my mother is a chanteuse."

"What does she sing?"

"I told you I was allowing you one question. Now it's your turn to answer mine."

"I'd like to extend an invitation to you to my party tonight. If you attend, I will not only tell you what they do, but you'll have the opportunity to ask them anything else you want."

"You're inviting me to your party?"

With comical exaggeration, he looked to her left and then to her right.

"I don't see anyone else around."

Even though her curiosity about his family was piqued and she was excited about attending the party and killing the boredom of being here, she didn't think she could look his parents in the eye after the marijuana incident.

She shook her head and looked down.

"I can't."

"Why not?"

"I've got other plans."

"Like what?"

"I've got to um…wash my hair."

He laughed. It was a full-bodied, rumble-through-the-chest, ultra-masculine laugh that gave her goose bumps. No, it wasn't him. It must be the weather.

"Surely you could have come up with something more original," he teased.

A smile tugged at the corner of her lips despite herself.

"Well, I've got a lot of hair. It's thick…takes a long time to dry…and in this weather. You know?"

He tried to keep a straight face as he answered her wobbly excuse.

"Uh huh. Well, listen. If you change your mind it's starting at 8:00 p.m. I'll leave your name at the door."

That kind of party then. "Nah. Thanks for the invite though."

"So, will I see you tomorrow for our lesson?"

"Tomorrow? But won't you be tired tomorrow morning after partying tonight?"

"I was thinking around lunch time we can practice some more."

"Only if it won't be an imposition."

"No imposition at all. In fact, I'm looking forward to it."

"Who is that cute guy?"

Nia flipped over on her stomach and sent a reply to her *Sistas* group chat. In what seemed like seconds after she had posted her photo with Liam online they'd begun messaging her like crazy.

"Name is Liam. He's teaching me how to ski," Nia typed.

For several minutes Nia continued to respond to questions from her friends about how she had met him and what they were doing together and how her trip was going. In turn, Nia observed the photos they shared of their time at the beach. For some reason, she no longer felt the envy she had earlier.

A little later she got something to eat and then had a warm, relaxing bath.

Feeling tired in a good way, Nia wrapped a thick, terry cloth robe tightly around her body as she contemplated fixing herself a hot chocolate. When her phone gave a message alert, she reached for it, expecting to see one of the girls from the *Sistas* chat. Much to Nia's surprise and delight, the message was from Damon.

"Hi Nia," he wrote.

Nervous energy shot through Nia. She went over to her bed, took a seat on the edge, and with trembling fingers began to type a response. After several minutes spent typing and then backspacing her reply, she eventually settled on, "Hi."

He wrote, "Just saw you online."

Her heart beat faster. "You did?"

"Didn't know you were in Austria."

Nia thought for a moment about saying her mother had dragged her there but then decided against it. She wanted Damon to think of her as a grown up. Someone who was in charge of her destiny, who came and went as she liked.

Flicking damp strands of hair over her shoulder she typed. "Spur of the moment decision to come down here and hit the slopes."

It was partially true, she reasoned. After all, it was a spur of the moment decision made by her mother.

"Didn't know you could ski."

"I've got lots of hidden talents," she typed.

With a groan, she decided that sounded way too suggestive and deleted. Instead, she wrote, "Yeah. I didn't expect to hear from you 'til July though."

She wondered if he'd changed his mind about them waiting until her eighteenth birthday to date.

"I know I promised to wait until you turned eighteen, but I can't stop thinking about you."

Nia's cheeks felt impossibly hot. She turned her face into her pillow and squealed. Good thing they weren't face-to-face or talking on the phone.

After she composed herself enough to type she wrote, "Oh."

"What are you doing tonight?"

Her response was swift. "Why? You asking me out?" That was accompanied by a smirking emoji.

He responded with a laughing face emoji and the words, "Sure baby. I'll be over in my jet in about an hour or so."

In return, she sent him a thumbs up sign and a laughing emoji. For several minutes more they chatted until abruptly he no longer responded.

Nia waited to see if he would return. When he didn't, she got up from the bed, dressed in leggings and a sweater, snatched back her phone and curled up on her bed.

Still, there was no response from Damon.

Concluding he'd probably had to attend to something of pressing importance, Nia decided some face time with her friends was in order. The developments were definitely worth such a level of interaction.

Her palms were sweating as she immediately placed a video call to Bianca.

Bianca's face appeared, and then Marilyn's in the background. "Hi, Nia," they both said. The faces of René and Donna showed up a moment later.

"You will not believe who just messaged me!" she said, barely able to keep the words from tumbling into one.

"Who?" asked Bianca.

"Damon," she squealed in their ears. The other girls squealed too.

"What did he say?" Bianca eventually asked.

When she told them they squealed all the more. They chatted a little while longer until they told her they were about to leave the hotel to go out to dinner.

Half an hour later, Nia was still lying in bed staring at Damon's profile picture and wondering what he was doing at that moment when Marilyn messaged her.

"Don't know how to tell you this, Boo."

"Tell me what?"

"Sheba just posted this Instagram pic."

Nia waited for the image to download and felt her cheeks flame again, this time with hurt, as she saw Mr. *I Can't Stop Thinking About You* getting cozy with Sheba. From the way he was kissing her she was not his *ex*-girlfriend at all. The words Sheba posted, "Me and my boyfriend Damon at the Loft tonight" confirmed what the photo clearly showed.

Nia felt her heart hit the floor like a stone. Then her hurt turned to anger. Just who did Damon Deverre think he was anyway? The swine! The more she thought about it, the more suspicious she became of Damon's motives in messaging her in the first place. She hadn't heard from him in three weeks, and then she posted an Instagram photo with Liam Lamport. Suddenly, he was interested. Might it be that he felt threatened?

She shook her head in disgust. Well, she was not going to sit around and waste her time moping over that low-life. She had been invited to a party, and she was going to attend. In fact, come to think of it, she would do more than just show up. She would go dressed to the nines, and she would take plenty of photos to prove what a great time she was having and post them all over social media. Damon could eat his heart out.

Nia got out of bed and went over to the closet. She examined and dismissed a few choices. She needed something statement-making, eye-catching, something that made people sit up and take notice when she walked into the room.

Her thoughts turned to her mother's own wardrobe. Nikki was always fashionable. Maybe she could find something there to combine with something from hers. Thank God they were the same size and height.

Nia passed Nikki and Thomas where they sat on the floor before a crackling fire playing a board game. From the sound of Nikki's laughter and Thomas' groaning, Nikki was winning.

Nia searched her mother's closet and found a very sophisticated white feather-lined top with tight three-quarter sleeves. She took it off its hanger, draped it over her arm and headed to her room.

She paused to look at the couple.

"Mom, may I borrow this blouse?" she asked, holding it out.

"Sure," Nikki said, her eyes never leaving the board.

On the return to her room, Nia found the perfect pants and shoes to pair with the top. She expertly made up her face then pulled on the skinny black leather jeans laid out on the bed. The pants required a little wiggle and jump to get into, but when she turned around in front of the full-length mirror, she was pleased with the fit.

Next, she carefully pulled the borrowed blouse over her head. It reached the top of her hips. Nia was satisfied that not only was the white attractive against her light brown skin, but the style was so unusual it would be doubtful anyone else would wear a similar top.

Her hair was next. She released it from its messy French braid and applied a squirt of conditioner to it to keep frizz at bay, then she finger-combed it so that her abundance of curls floated around her face and down her shoulders.

Nia hung a pair of triple strand jangly silver earrings on her earlobes and slipped a silver cuff on each wrist and a silver ring on each hand. As she sat on the edge of the bed to pull on knee-high black leather boots, she wondered what Liam's reaction would be when she showed up, considering she had adamantly refused his invitation.

Before she left the room, she liberally spritzed on her favorite perfume and grabbed her coat.

"See you later, guys," she called over her shoulder as she headed towards the front door.

"Hold it right there, young lady!"

Nia paused, praying the reason she'd been asked to halt had something to do with her not wearing a scarf or a hat and nothing to do with her not being granted actual permission to leave the chalet.

She turned, smiling brightly. "What's up?"

"Where are you goin' and in my favorite blouse to boot?" her mother asked.

"You told me I could wear it."

"I don't recall that. But more important, where are you goin'?"

Nia didn't hide her irritation. What, was she twelve?

"To a party," she said, rolling her eyes.

From her peripheral vision, she noticed Thomas shake his head and look down at the board. She gave him the side eye. This was not his business!

"Party?" Nikki screeched, bringing Nia's eyes back around to hers. "We just got here, and you manage to find a party to attend already? You don't waste any time do you?"

"I was invited to a birthday party, okay, *Mother*," Nia responded in a voice rising in concert with her temper.

"No, it is not okay. And don't you get a tone with me! First of all, I'm not letting you go to a party with people I don't know anything about, and second of all, you are still grounded. As promised, you were grounded for a month. That month is not yet up. So, you can return to your room and take off my blouse."

Nia felt her heart rate increase and her throat convulse with anger. Her eyes burned with unshed tears at the injustice of it all. Her instincts told her to throw a tantrum, to tell off her mother and storm from the chateau with a dramatic sweep of her coat. After giving it brief consideration, she decided that it not only would be ineffective given how draconian her mother had become since she'd found God, but also it would likely result in further and worst punishment.

Nia took a deep breath to calm herself, tightened her jaw, pivoted and returned to her room. There she dropped into the first chair, swung her leg over the arm, and dangled it angrily as she contemplated her next move.

Eventually, Nia sighed and unzipped her boots. She took them off one by one and placed them next to the chair. Next, she leaned forward, lifted the blouse up and over her head, and draped it on the chair arm. She stood, wiggled out of her jeans and placed them next to the blouse. As she proceeded to pull her hair up into a ponytail, Nia wondered what time Nikki and Thomas would retire for the night. When they did, she intended to sneak out of the house to attend the party.

Chapter 5

*L*iam had serious doubts that Heidi Wolffe had gained entrance to his party through legitimate channels. He knew without even asking that his mother had not invited her. Barbara Dickson was well aware of Heidi's inappropriate and overt advances on Liam over the last couple of years and had successfully kept her visits to their home short and infrequent.

But Liam knew that a tiny thing like not receiving an invitation would not have deterred Fraulein Wolffe. She had shown up, no doubt having learned about the event from her twin brother, Reinhardt.

She made a dramatic entrance in a full-length, hooded, black mink coat, which she unveiled slowly, much to the delight of several male guests who no doubt enjoyed the view of her mile-long legs in the short, tight black dress.

Liam successfully managed to avoid Heidi for the first two hours of the party. Whenever she came up to him and attempted to glue herself to his side, he would find a way to disengage himself, begging host duties. But the dance could continue for only so long. Eventually, Heidi managed to catch him alone as he was leaving his room after a quick visit to the bathroom.

Liam stopped short as he stepped into the hall and saw Heidi leaning against the wall opposite. He briefly wondered what had prevented her from entering the room and then remembered he had locked the door on entry for that very possibility. He closed the door behind him and frowned.

"Have you gotten lost, Heidi?"

She smiled slowly, and he glimpsed pretty white teeth between the slashes of red. Heidi was an attractive girl. She was tall, slender, bright-eyed, and with blond hair cut in a sleek bob. But she would be so much more attractive if she were less wanton. Her knowing blue eyes twinkled at him as she unfurled herself from her pose and crossed the short distance in two strides.

"I haven't had the opportunity to give you your birthday kiss," she said in a throaty whisper.

As she reached for him, Liam instead caught her by the arms and pulled her briefly in for a quick peck on her cheek. He immediately stepped around her and held her upper arm as he led her down the short corridor.

"How was your trip?" he asked.

"Uneventful. Liam, I don't bite you know."

"You don't?" he said, laughing low and holding her arm firmly as she once again tried to turn her body towards his and halt his progress. She strained slightly, but he continued to take deliberate steps forward and lead her towards the party noise. He was prepared to drag her if necessary.

She eventually sighed in defeat and relaxed her body as the other guests came in view and the music and noise greeted them full force.

"I wanted to talk to you alone," she said turning her mouth to his ear and raising her voice slightly so he could hear.

He leaned down. "About what?"

"I don't want to say right now, Liam. But maybe if we could speak privately."

His curiosity was not even mildly piqued. This was a different version of the same game Heidi had been playing since he turned fourteen and her school girl's crush had, like her body, taken on a more womanly shape.

"Not now, Heidi. Perhaps we can speak over the phone. Leave your number with me, and I'll give you a call." He patted the back of her hand and gave her a sympathetic smile.

Pretty female laughter drew Liam's gaze to the entryway.

He took in a sharp breath. Nia Carmichael had just walked into the room. And she looked stunning!

Lustrous black curls tumbled down her shoulders and framed an exquisite face. As Matthew took her white coat, she revealed a white top and black leather pants that disappeared into thigh-high black boots. He almost forgot that Heidi was at his side until she tightened her grip on his arm.

"Who's she?" she asked scornfully.

"A guest I need to greet. Excuse me, please. Duty calls."

The possessive way she was holding on to his arm suggested she was his girlfriend.

Nia's eyes skimmed Liam and the long-legged ice-cold beauty queen glued to his side. Her first thought was that they made the perfect couple. Equally statuesque, both blond, blue-eyed, gorgeous. She turned at a touch on her shoulder.

It was Matthew. He offered to take her coat. Smiling her thanks, she shrugged out of it and darted a gaze at Liam. He was releasing the blonde and making his way towards her. From the look on his girlfriend's face, she wasn't too happy about his destination.

"Well, well. You made it after all," he said holding out a hand…for what? A handshake? She almost laughed. Did he think it inappropriate to hug a girl he'd only met a night ago? Too bad, that wasn't the French way. She placed her hands on his chest and tipped her head up to kiss first his right cheek and then the left.

He appeared momentarily dazed but recovered quickly with a laugh.

"Thank you," he said as she settled back on her heels.

"For what?"

"For coming tonight. I didn't think you would show up."

"It turned out my hair didn't need washing after all."

He chuckled and took her hand. "Would you like a drink?"

Nia nodded, thinking it would be good to have something to do with her hands to hide her nervous excitement at being in a room full of a whole bunch of rich, classy looking people she didn't yet know.

When they arrived at the bar, Liam asked what she would like to drink. After she told him, he gave the bartender the order. Nia was about to say something when a female voice called, "Liam."

Nia turned her head as the girlfriend came up to them and slid her hand over Liam's shoulder.

"You haven't introduced me to your friend," she said.

If Nia hadn't been watching Liam, she would have missed the way his mouth tightened before it thinned into a smile.

"Nia, this is Heidi Wolffe, Reinhardt's twin sister. Heidi, this is Nia Carmichael, a friend of mine."

Nia wondered at that introduction. Was it possible Heidi was not his girlfriend, then? She couldn't be sure because in the next instant Heidi's smile widened and she leaned towards Nia, well-manicured hand extended.

"Pleasure to meet you, Nia. We're so happy you have joined us for Liam's celebration."

Now it was impossible to miss the way Liam's whole body went rigid. He turned to Heidi and opened his mouth and based on his expression Nia was sure whatever he was going to say would not be pleasant. But suddenly, he snapped his mouth shut, breathed in deeply through his nose, turned his back on Heidi, and directly faced Nia.

He glanced at the drink she had just received from the bartender. "Let's find my parents," he said. With that, he took her free hand and stepped around Heidi.

Nia felt eyes on her and looked over her shoulder to see that Heidi had dropped the false smile and was now staring daggers at her back.

Liam still seemed annoyed. For a moment, Nia got a feeling of déjà vu. This seemed like a repeat of events at Damon's birthday celebration.

"I don't think you should have left your girlfriend alone. I really don't need a jealous female trying to scratch my eyes out at their boyfriend's party. Been there, done that."

He stopped abruptly and turned to her, dropping her arm.

"She is not my girlfriend," he said through clenched teeth. "Why would you think that?"

She took a step backward and held up both hands.

"Whoa there, defensive much? I guess I assumed she's your girlfriend 'cause when I walked in you two looked pretty cozy. Then her comments just now, you know 'we're so happy to have you join us.' Well, I just assumed. No reason to bite my head off."

He went silent for a few moments then he sighed deeply as his rigid bearing relaxed. His features had softened slightly when he met her eyes again.

"I apologize. That's a sore point with me, I guess. Heidi has been a bit of a thorn in my side for a little while now, and the only thing that keeps me from telling her off is that Reinhardt is one of my closest friends. I fear that it could affect our friendship."

"Why?"

"The two of them are very close. Heidi takes advantage of his relationship with me."

"How?"

"Like her entrance to this party. I'm quite sure my parents didn't want to invite her or maybe didn't invite her at all, but she would have used Reinhardt to get here. Sadly, he would have played right into her hands."

Nia looked back to where she had left Heidi. The girl was no longer there. A search with her eyes revealed Heidi was now in a corner chatting with some other guests.

When Nia turned to face front again, she almost bumped into Liam who had stopped at the entrance to a large living area where groups of people were scattered huddled together talking and laughing. Music was playing in the background.

Nia's eyes zeroed in on the couch in the corner where some adults sat talking. The ones who instantly stood out were the man who looked like Liam's father if she could remember correctly from last night and the woman his arm was draped around. Most likely, based on the long honey blonde tresses, she was Liam's mother.

Nia took a nervous sip of her drink, her throat suddenly dry. She forgot why she had allowed Liam to lead her to meet his parents. A lapse in judgment for sure. There was no way she was going into that group and instantly become the center of attention.

She ran a hand down her throat and gulped.

"Listen, Liam…"

"Have I told you how pretty you look tonight?"

She almost forgot what she was going to say and couldn't stop the silly grin from spreading across her face.

"Thanks," she breathed out.

She gave him the once over. Of course, she had noticed from the moment she saw him how good he looked. He was wearing fitted dark blue jeans, white vee-neck tee shirt, and Navy designer blazer, sleeves pushed up to the elbow. He reminded her of a lead singer in one of those boy bands.

"You don't look so bad yourself," she replied.

He tilted his head towards the room.

"Now I'm going to take you over to my parents, as promised. My father, William, is CEO of Lamport Holdings and my mother, Barbara, is a former actress and film producer."

Nia nodded. "Okay, thanks for the info. I don't need to meet them."

His eyebrows met. "You don't want to say hello to my parents?"

"No. Please?"

His frown deepened. "Why not? It's their party. It would be rude if guests arrived and I didn't bring them to meet my parents. They would scold me about it and deservedly so since they've raised me better."

He looked quite insulted and annoyed with her. Nia groaned inwardly. She didn't want to offend him.

"Listen, it's not that I don't want to say hello to them. It's just that their first impression of me wasn't that great."

Perplexed, he shook his head. "What makes you say that?"

Nia shifted uncomfortably to the next foot and diverted her gaze. She was instantly sorry she had referenced the previous night. She had hated lying to his face about the marijuana joint, and she really didn't want to have to do so again. She wanted it to disappear from her past.

"Well, you know they caught me in the bushes and mistook me for a prowler. That's not exactly the best first meeting, right?"

She smiled weakly, silently willing him to accept her explanation and not ask her about her lie and the joint.

He placed a hand on her shoulder. "This gives you the opportunity to make a great second impression then."

She began to protest, but Liam gave her a knowing look.

"Why don't you tell me why you are really so uncomfortable."

Nia froze. Decision time. Should she confess everything and risk his scorn or feign ignorance and risk his suspicion. She decided to just tell the truth and let the chips fall where they may.

"Okay, I did have a joint. But I barely smoked the stupid thing. It wasn't even mine. A friend slipped it into my luggage. It was the first time smoking, I swear. I didn't mean to lie, but I was so intimidated by the bunch of you staring at me. I'm so sorry," she blurted in a low voice.

He stared at her, and she wouldn't have been surprised to hear the words, "You need to leave." She was surprised, though, when he said, "Apology accepted but no more lies, Nia. I can't be your friend if you lie to me. If it happens again, I'll have to end things."

Nia nodded eagerly, grateful for his forgiveness and the opportunity to make wrong things right. Even so, she was distantly aware that whatever friendship they managed to form in the next several days would surely end forever when they returned to the real world on two separate continents no less.

The tall, handsome man who was Liam's father intimidated her initially when he viewed her with his intense blue eyes that seemed to search her very soul. But then he smiled, and the condemnation she searched for wasn't there. She sighed in relief when his big warm hand closed around hers. His voice rang with sincerity as he greeted her by name and welcomed her to the chalet. Liam's beautiful, classy looking mother gave her a quick hug, told her she looked 'lovely' and asked how her skiing lessons with Liam had gone.

Nia looked across at Liam and saw his eyes fixed on her with a slight smirk on his lips. He raised an eyebrow at her.

"Very well, ma'am. Liam's a great teacher. He's very patient. I've improved a lot."

It was clear by the time she and Liam made their way across the room that he was adored, not just by his family but by his friends. It was easy to see why. He was genuinely warm and amiable. The questions he asked about developments in the personal lives of those they interacted with suggested he kept in touch and honestly cared. He was unlike the self-absorbed boys she knew.

He embraced a redheaded woman who he introduced as his aunt Prudence and her husband, Stavros. When they moved away, he pointed out that the redheaded twin boys who she'd seen poring over video games earlier were her sons.

Liam asked her if she wanted something to eat and it occurred to her that she was indeed hungry. Nia glanced around and counted six food stations set up across the room.

"This is quite a spread. I don't know if I'll be able to eat from every station." She patted her stomach as they headed to the first one. "I've got a tiny tummy."

He glanced at her midriff and smiled. "I'd be worried if you didn't. The stations will be here all night. You can sample anytime you want; you don't have to try to fill up on everything now."

Nia took up a plate and passed it to Liam as she surveyed the selections from the pizza buffet bar. She loved pizza but didn't want to take too much knowing that five other buffets awaited her. The selection was extensive, ranging from vegetarian varieties to meat-lover specials.

She chose a small slice of Margherita and pepperoni pizza and placed it on her plate. She glanced at Liam's plate and saw that he took two small vegetarian slices, one with mushrooms, olives, corn and jalapenos and the other with pesto and artichokes.

"What, no meat?" she asked, looking across at him as they walked towards the next station.

"I don't eat meat," he said.

Nia's eyes widened. "Really? Wow. So you're a vegetarian?"

"Vegan actually."

Her eyes roamed his muscular frame. "But I thought vegans were supposed to be skinny," she blurted.

A corner of his mouth lifted. "Full of stereotypes aren't we? All Christians are poor and ugly. All vegans are skinny. What's next, all Brits are emotionally stunted?"

She elbowed him in the side. "Alright. You made your point."

They took food from the salad, sushi and taco stations. Nia decided to leave the dessert stations for later.

"Come let's sit by the pool while we eat," Liam suggested.

When they reached the pool room, Nia was surprised at how intimate and romantic it looked with its soft lighting casting a glow over the water. Instrumental music played low in the background, and a movie was showing on the large TV screen on one wall.

Nia settled herself against the back of the chair, stretched out her legs and placed her plate in her lap. Then she lifted the slice of pizza off her plate and took a huge bite.

Liam positioned his food on his legs, closed his eyes and bowed his head.

As Nia chewed, she watched him pray and felt increasingly uncomfortable. She remembered saying grace over her food when she was with Grandmama Carmichael. She looked down at her plate and decided she should give thanks. There were many people around the world with nothing to eat and certainly not fabulous gourmet food like this. She closed her eyes briefly and said a prayer. When she opened them, she found Liam's eyes fastened on her.

She pried a slice of pepperoni from her pizza, nibbled on it and gave him a sidelong glance. "What?"

"Did you just pray?"

She nodded.

"To whom?"

Her mouth dropped open. "To God of, course. Who else?"

He sheepishly shrugged.

"Why would you ask me that?" she asked.

"I didn't know you were a Christian," he replied.

Nia shifted in her seat. "I'm not," she said softly, looking away from him once more. "But I do know about God. My grandmother was a pastor, and she taught me a lot."

She moved a taco to one side of her plate and took up a few vegetables that had dropped out of it and chewed them.

"I may not exactly be living the life, but I do have morals." Why did she sound so defensive? She did not have to justify herself to him.

When he didn't respond to her comment, she returned to her plate and popped a sushi roll into her mouth.

"This food is really delicious."

Liam nodded. "We've got a great chef. How come you changed your mind about coming to the party?"

For the first time since she had arrived at the party, Nia remembered Damon and the reason she had decided to attend. She was tempted to lie to Liam again but remembered his threat and her promise. But she couldn't speak the bald truth either. She came to a compromise.

"Well," she said, "I got some bad news today. I felt like I needed to forget my troubles, and this party seemed like a good way to do that."

"What bad news?"

She shook her head. "I don't want to talk about it if you don't mind." She looked around her again. "This place is really nice," she said.

"Your chalet is not the same?"

"No. I think you guys got the penthouse version," she smiled. As she ate, her eyes drifted to the movie on the screen. "Hey, what movie is this?" she asked suddenly.

"*Joan of Arc.*"

"I thought it looked familiar." She turned to him excitedly, jabbing her finger at the screen. "My dad directed that movie," she said proudly.

Liam's mouth dropped open. "Your dad? Jacques Annuad is your father?"

Nia nodded. "Um hmm."

His focus returned to the screen.

She continued, "He's very talented–very good at what he does. He's won three Oscars; one of them was for this movie. He's been nominated for countless more. This year he was nominated for one, but he didn't win even though I thought he should have…"

It was at this point Nia noticed she was doing all the talking. Liam wasn't answering. His gaze was still fixed on the screen.

She took a bite of her taco and looked at the television. It was a scene featuring the lead character. Nia stared at the actress, and then tilted her head to one side. She chewed and swallowed quickly.

"Liam, she looks a lot like your mother. Doesn't she?"

Then she remembered Liam had said his mother was an actress and her name was Barbara.

"Hey, is your mother, Barbara Dickson?"

Liam slowly nodded.

"But you said…didn't she introduce herself as Barbara Lamport?"

"Formerly Barbara Dickson."

Nia looked back at the screen. She now understood why Liam's mother had seemed so familiar the first time she met her. She had watched all her father's movies, and Barbara Dickson had starred in two of them: *The Lady* and *Joan of Arc*. True, it had been almost three decades ago, but she looked the same, though a little older. But if Barbara Dickson was Liam's mother, then that meant…

"Your mother was married to my father!" Nia blurted out, sitting forward abruptly and upsetting her plate.

Liam caught the plate just before it hit the floor.

She took her plate from his hands. It only now occurred to her that he didn't look surprised at her statement.

"Liam, how long did you know?"

A corner of his mouth hitched but he did not look amused.

"From the moment you said your father was Jacques Annuad."

Chapter 6

*W*hat is mum going to say?

That was all Liam could think of when it hit him that he was sitting next to Jacques Annuad's daughter. His next thought was *why does mum even need to know?*

This trip would end in a week's time when he and Nia would go their separate ways, so there was no need to risk upsetting his mother with the news.

He corrected himself. She might be surprised, curious, even amused, but upset? Hardly. It was, after all, almost three decades since Barbara Dickson had divorced Jacques Annuad, her first husband. He had been the one, from her account, into whose arms she had run on rebound after her relationship with Liam's father had ended unceremoniously the first time around.

It surely couldn't matter now that the man Barbara Dickson had been married to for less than two years, the one whom she had caught in bed with another woman and served with divorce papers shortly after, was the father of her son's new friend.

Still, even though he might mention it to her after they returned home, he didn't want to do it now and perhaps prejudice his mother's view of Nia. He didn't know why it was important to him that his parents approved of Nia. It just was.

"Nia, I ask you not to reveal this to my mother. I'll tell her when I'm ready." *If at all,* he thought.

"Sure. No problem," she agreed as she leaned back. Then she sprang forward with a bark of incredulous laughter.

"Liam, can you believe it? We could have been siblings."

He didn't find that thought as amusing as she apparently did, but he played along.

"Well, I'd be much older than you then. Considering my mother married Jacques Annuad when she was twenty, and she's now forty-nine."

He did a quick mental calculation. "I'd probably be maybe twenty-eight now if they had had a child together."

Nia shook her head. "Twenty years old! Imagine marrying that young."

She laughed out loud. It was uninhibited joyous laughter. And Liam found himself attracted to the sound. He remembered her laughter yesterday on the slopes and how drawn he was to her exuberance. Was that what the attraction was? Was that all there was to it?

"I'll be twenty in two years. I can't imagine myself married at twenty."

She shook her head fiercely. "Uh-uh. No way do I want to be tied down that young. I want to be free."

He didn't know why he found that remark irritating. "How does marrying young prevent you from being free?"

She sobered when she looked at his face. "Because instead of being able to pursue my dreams I'd be tied down to a man and probably nursemaid to a baby."

Liam looked at his food. He took up a toothpick carrying a feta cheese covered olive and placed it between his teeth. He slid out the toothpick and put it carefully on his plate. Why was he with her? He and this girl were poles apart when it came to many things including their outlook on life and values they had. Her sparkling personality couldn't overshadow that truth.

"So, do you have siblings?" he asked, finally allowing his eyes to meet hers again now that his emotions were under control.

She nodded. "I've got an older half-sister, Anaïs, she's twenty-two and a brother Louis who is twenty, and I now have a baby brother, Alessandro. He's two."

She smiled, and her beautiful brown eyes lit up.

"He is so cute. He's the most beautiful baby ever!"

Before Liam knew what was happening Nia was retrieving her phone from her bag. After tapping it a few times, she turned it to face him. Despite himself, a small laugh escaped his lips at the image of the smiling fat-cheeked toddler with floppy brown hair and twinkling brown eyes not unlike Nia's. She kissed the picture, and then she sighed.

"I miss him when I'm away. Thank God for video chat."

Liam found himself perplexed. These actions seemed at odds with a girl who had just declared she had no wish to get tied down to a man and play nursemaid to a baby.

He couldn't help commenting, "I almost thought you didn't like children based on your comment earlier."

"What comment?" she asked as she returned her phone to her bag and zipped it up.

"About not wanting to get married and playing nursemaid to a baby?"

She backhanded the air between them. "I just meant I didn't want to get married and have kids right away. I'd like to establish a career and name for myself first. But sure I want to have kids, someday. Are you kidding?"

She pointed to her face. "These genes are too good not to pass on."

Then she sucked in her cheeks and crossed her eyes. Liam laughed. It was becoming very difficult not to like this girl no matter what he told himself.

He swung his legs around so that now he was sitting directly in front of Nia. Their knees brushed, and she moved back slightly at the unintentional contact.

"How many times has your father been married?" he asked, curiosity getting the better of him.

She screwed up her bow-shaped mouth, and then pressed her index finger in the middle of her lower lip drawing his gaze to it and making him feel stirrings that he should not. She leaned forward.

"I think his current wife is number five."

He gave a low whistle. "He sure gets around."

He immediately regretted his comment certain she would take offense at what in retrospect sounded rather judgmental. He was surprised to find her shake her head and sigh.

"He sure does. I hope this current wife is his last. I want them to stay together for the sake of Alex. The rest of us didn't get to have both our parents living with us as we grew up. I want that for him. Dad seems to be trying, I think."

"Trying?"

"To make things work. To stay committed. They have had counseling, his wife tells me."

"She confides in you?"

She shrugged. "She's closer to my age than Dad's. She's twenty-seven."

Liam tried not to look shocked.

"Sometimes I think it's easier for me to understand her than it is for my father. That's when I have to play the role of the intermediary."

Liam shook his head. What a life. Imagine having to be the mediator between a parent and their spouse. No wonder Nia had issues.

"Does he go to church?"

She looked stunned for a moment. "Church? Dad? No."

"How is he going to change then?"

She shrugged. "If he wants to change I think he can."

"Why would he want to change?"

"I think because he's tired of broken relationships and instability and having to start over with new wives. He's not as young as he used to be you know. He'll be sixty early next year..."

A sixty-year-old man with a twenty-seven-year-old wife. Liam told himself not to judge, but it was hard.

"...I think he's getting tired and just wants to lead a peaceful life."

"And his wife?"

"She can be a little high strung, but she was raised Catholic, so I don't think she will take divorce lightly."

"Hmm...does she go to church?"

"Not really. Maybe sometimes on religious holidays, you know?"

"God can help them both if they will let him. He can help them to find peace as individuals and as a couple."

"You're really religious aren't you?" she asked.

"I prefer the terms *redeemed, saved*, and *Christ-like* to the term *religious*."

"What's the difference?"

"The word 'religious' implies following a set of man-made rules and rituals. The other terms connote relationship."

He sat forward abruptly capturing her gaze and feeding on the tiny sparks of curiosity he saw in her eyes. Trying to ignite them he said, "How would you feel if someone had died a terrible agonizing death to save you?"

She laughed nervously, played with the edge of her blouse.

"I don't know. Grateful."

"That's all?"

"Really grateful. Like I'd be forever singing their praises."

"Precisely. That's how I feel about Jesus Christ. He saved me, Nia. And I'm showing my gratitude by making my life a living sacrifice to Him."

"What do you mean by making your life a living sacrifice?" she asked tentatively.

"What I mean is I have decided I'm going to live for Him. I'm going to tell others about Him so they can experience His saving grace too. I'm going to be obedient to Him and His commands. I'm going to seek to model my life after His and every time I fall short I will ask Him to forgive me, and I will seek to do better."

She took her bottom lip between her teeth. "Is that what those songs I've heard all night are saying? It's Christian music, right? 'Cause I don't recognize any of those songs, though they're nice."

"It's Contemporary Christian music."

"That's what you were singing last night by the fire. You've got a great voice by the way."

"Thank you."

"Is that like your hobby, singing?" she asked.

Liam nodded thoughtfully. It occurred to him that seeing she had noticed the songs must mean she was receptive to music. Perhaps he could minister to her this way. Not only to her but to others who were present tonight. This night did not just have to be about him. He could use the opportunity of his captive audience to use his God-given talents to spread the Good News.

In the meantime, Nia awaited a response to her question. He sat up.

"It's the thing I love doing most in the world. So, yes, I guess you can call it a hobby."

He pushed to his feet and held out a hand to her. "Come let's rejoin the others. There's something I need to do."

When Liam left her in the main room where people were still eating, laughing, talking, and just enjoying the party, Nia felt lost. She hadn't realized how completely at ease she had felt with him at her side until she was left sitting on a sofa in the living room watching others interact. Suddenly, she felt like she didn't quite fit in. None of them looked like her kind of people and even Matthew, Sam, and Reinhardt had disappeared with Liam too.

She shook her head and took a tiny sip of her lemon squash. Maybe it was time to leave.

"How are you enjoying the party?"

Nia looked up as Liam's sister sank into the vacant seat beside her.

"Oh, it's going great," Nia said, forcing cheerfulness into her tone and nodding appreciatively. "You people really know how to party in style."

"What's your accent? I was trying to narrow it down, but I feel as though it may be a combination of accents."

Leiliana's smile was genuine, and Nia found herself relaxing. She placed an arm on the back of the seat between them and angled her body towards the other girl.

"What combination would that be?"

"Hmm, let me see. I hear a bit of French, Parisian I'd say, American, um…American south, I think, and then more urban like New York."

Nia laughed and clapped, noiselessly.

"Paris, yeah. Outskirts but that's fine. South, yeah. Atlanta, Georgia, and Los Angeles, not New York. I don't speak fast enough to be a New Yorker, girl."

Leiliana laid a hand across her pretty amber eyes. "My mother would kill me. She's a New Yorker, born and bred."

"You're good. Don't be so hard on yourself. Are you like a linguist or something?"

"I've always had a keen ear for languages. I find them fascinating. I actually speak three languages fluently and two conversationally."

Nia leaned towards her, impressed. "I speak French and English, and I thought I was accomplished. Look at you."

Leiliana laughed, and Nia felt as though she had made a friend with Liam's more reserved younger sister.

"My fluent ones are French and of course English and also German. The conversational ones are Spanish and Mandarin."

Nia's head tilted. "Mandarin? That's Chinese right?"

Leiliana nodded.

"Wait, so Liam is multi-lingual too?"

Leiliana twisted her palm from side to side. "He knows French and Mandarin pretty well. That's mainly it."

Nia leaned back in her seat and beamed without knowing why. Why did it warm her to her toes that Liam knew how to speak the same two languages she did? That and the fact that they both loved to sing was literally the only two things they had in common.

As she pondered this, her gaze was drawn to the far left of the room where something seemed to be happening. Other people seemed to have noticed too and were drifting over in that direction.

Leiliana touched her hand. "I'm going to see what's going on. Coming?"

Nia nodded and followed Leiliana, craning to see over the crowd gathered. Even in her boots, she couldn't see over some heads. She pushed her way through until she reached the front where she discovered what all the commotion was about.

Liam and his friends were taking their places behind several musical instruments. There was a guitar strapped across Liam's torso, similar to last night. Then he stepped forward and took the mic in his hand.

"I've been thinking of a way to repay all of you for being here this evening. For celebrating with me…"

He scratched his head and glanced back at the band members, "…and the only thing I could think of, besides the really cool party favors, of course…" There was a ripple of appreciative laughter, and Liam waited for it to die down before he continued, "…was to share with you a few of our songs."

The instrumentals began first. Reinhardt on the keyboard, Liam and Sam each strumming the guitars. Matthew was on the drums. Then Liam opened his mouth and out flowed his incredible voice. It washed over her like a warm bath. That amazing, grainy voice caught her in its grip at its first syllable. The next thing Nia knew she was pulled into the music.

The song was called *Rescuer*. She remembered their conversation about Jesus rescuing him. Had he chosen the song for her? She dismissed her idealistic notions as fanciful. Then his eyes met hers and the way he focused on her as he sang made her once again question if it was indeed a personal performance.

She idly noticed that the other guys were skilled, but Liam was obviously the star of the show. His voice was phenomenal and his stage presence palpable. That song was followed by another, and when Nia glanced around, she realized with surprise that the area was so packed with guests that she could not find an empty space in the throng.

As Nia listened to the third song, her eyes drifted closed, and she began to move her head. Before she knew it, she was waving her hands over her head, and swaying her hips to the beat of the music. Liam's passionate rendition fueled her own excitement. She caught the fever, and suddenly it wasn't enough to move, she wanted to be there beside him, singing.

As soon as Liam's set was finished and before she could talk herself out of it, Nia pushed past the person ahead of her at the front and made her way towards him. The surprise written on his face almost caused her to falter, but she had come too far to turn back now. Raising her chin a notch, she went up to him, placed a hand on his shoulder and tilted her head upwards. He leaned his ear down to her.

"I want to sing," she said, so close her lips grazed his ear.

Liam straightened, his eyes searching her face. She could almost see what he was thinking. What was she going to sing? Could she even sing? Could he depend on her not to create a spectacle? She stood on her toes once more.

"Trust me," she whispered. "I won't do anything inappropriate."

His chest rose and fell, and then he shrugged. "Do you want this?" he asked, tapping his guitar.

She shook her head. "Strictly vocals."

"What will it be then, Nia?" he asked.

Nia vaguely noticed that the crowd was buzzing with curiosity.

"Do you know the song *Winning*?" she asked.

Liam shook his head. He looked around at the group. They didn't seem to know it either.

"Follow my lead, then," she said and turned towards the mic.

Liam caught her shoulder. "Do you want me to introduce you?" he asked.

"No." She stepped forward, encircled the mic with her hand and swept her gaze over the crowd.

"Hey, y'all."

There was no response.

"I said hey, y'all," she said louder. There was a low rumble of "Hi."

Nia smiled. She was getting somewhere. This was not her first rodeo. What Liam did not know was that she had been performing since she was a toddler. She had been the star of countless home videos shot by her father; accompanied her mother a few times on stage over the years. Also, she sang for Grandmama Carmichael's church. The crowds had been bigger too.

Once, the crowd had been in the tens of thousands when her mother sang the *Star Spangled Banner* at the Super Bowl, and Nia had been there right beside her. Her mother had bent over and allowed her to sing the last stanza. When the crowd had roared at the end, Nia had felt such a surge of triumph she had known that the stage was where she wanted to be.

Just as her mother knew how to lay on the charm with her Georgia peach accent, Nia would too.

"I met most of you tonight, so you know that I'm Liam's friend."

She paused, her gaze once more surveying the audience.

"What you might not know is that we two only met last night."

She had their attention now.

"…and since then, this kind gentleman has rescued me–twice. I won't tell y'all how he rescued me 'cause that's a story for another time, but not only did he rescue me…"

She paused again, observed the interest sparked in several pairs of eyes and the smiles on many lips. "…he also spent the day teaching me how to ski."

Nia placed her hands on her hips and glanced over her shoulder at Liam, then back at the crowd. There was now open curiosity on many faces.

"…and if *that* weren't enough, he invited me to this party, which I've just gotta say is *epic*!"

Rocking back on her heels, Nia laughed as cheers and claps rang out. When the merriment settled down to an excited buzz, she said, "And I know y'all folks will agree with me that Liam is completely deserving of such a celebration in his honor."

This was followed by a ding of voices cheering once more. Laughing, Nia held on to the mic and turned her head to look at Liam. He was staring at her as though he was seeing her for the first time. In some ways he was. He was seeing Nia, the performer, for the first time. She threw him a wink, and when he raised an eyebrow, she smiled and turned around.

"So…in tribute to the one we have come here to honor I want to sing a song called *Winning*. I chose it because Liam Lamport is a winner."

Again Nia waited for the cheers that erupted to die down before she leaned forward.

"But I'm goin' to need your help with this song. Every time I say 'hands' I want you to push your hands up in the air like so and sing 'winning!' Do you think you can do that?"

There was loud agreement. "Let's go ahead and try that then. Hands!"

There was some confusion as a few hands went up but most didn't. Some in the audience mumbled "winning," and others sang the word a few moments later.

Nia laughed. "Okay, slow start. But you'll get it. Don't worry. Let's go."

When she opened her mouth, the tune rolled off her tongue as smooth as silk. She was singing acapella at first, but soon she heard the guitars followed by the keyboard and finally drums as Liam and his friends found the beat.

The crowd discovered their groove, and soon most were singing 'winning' at the appropriate time, and most hands went up in the air together. Still, it needed perfecting, so when Nia was done, and the crowd began to clap, she held up her hands.

"I think we need to do that one more time properly, y'all. What do you say?" They were all for it.

When Nia finished the song this time, the applause was almost deafening.

"How about a duet by you two," a loud British-accented voice called from the front of the crowd. It was Liam's brother, Benjamin.

Nia turned to Liam. "I don't know any of the types of songs you listen to," she said to him apologetically.

He grinned. "You knew that one gospel song. Was that the only one you knew?"

She thought for a moment and then shrugged. "My Grandmama taught me *Amazing Grace*."

"Let's do that then."

"Together or alternate verses?"

"Alternate verses. Chorus together."

He held up his hand for a high-five, and she didn't leave him hanging. When their palms connected, Nia felt a thrill go through her, which she immediately blamed on the excitement of performing. She broke eye contact.

"You going to begin?"

"Ladies first," he said low.

Just in time, Nia remembered social media. She searched for Leiliana in the crowd and beckoned for her to come over. When she reached her, Nia leaned toward her ear and said, "I need you to record this. Use my phone. I left it in my bag on the couch."

A few minutes later the instrumentals to the song began.

As Nia sang *Amazing Grace,* unexpected memories washed over her. Sitting in her grandmamma's little church. Going up to the altar and accepting Jesus into her heart when she was six. Going back when she was eight because she thought she had sinned so badly since then that she had to be saved all over. And then, she went back to be saved when she was eleven. That was the last time she went. Grandmama had died the next year.

The emotions were real, and she poured them into the rendition of the song so much that she forgot she and Liam were to sing alternately. When he joined her at the microphone and started the second verse, she did not draw back but sang on. The song indeed became a duet.

Nia didn't know why her eyes were closed, but when she caught herself the song was over. She opened her eyes and startled slightly to find Liam's head bent low and so close to hers she could see the flecks of gold in the depth of his eyes. She looked out at the audience. They seemed enraptured, and then applause erupted. She felt Liam's arm at her shoulder as he pulled her into a side hug. She turned her head towards him once more, her eyes roaming his face.

He smiled at her and after a final squeeze, dropped his arm and reached for the mic.

Liam's voice rang out behind her.

"Give it up for Nia Carmichael. And remember, you saw her perform here first."

Chapter 7

When Nia had asked Leiliana to video record her and Liam singing *Amazing Grace,* she didn't know the girl would also play photographer with her phone for the rest of the night. Nia didn't even remember that Leiliana still had it until near the end of the event.

Nia's performance had broken the ice with Liam's guests. Suddenly, she was Miss Popular. People kept coming over to compliment her. All except Heidi Wolffe who Nia noted kept her distance from both Liam and her. It occurred to Nia that maybe the reason Liam had stuck so close to her all night was to repel Heidi.

This thought so deflated Nia that she moved to a corner of the living room and sat alone, absently watching as guests began to dwindle and say their goodbyes.

"Well, well, well."

She barely spared Liam a glance as he sank down in the seat beside her.

"Who knew that such a big voice was wrapped up in such a petite package? And where did that Southern belle come from?"

When she didn't respond, Nia could feel Liam's questioning gaze on her. A minute later, she startled when Liam held both sides of her head between his hands and turned her head to his. She reached up to remove his hands but stopped when her palms made contact with his.

She looked into his eyes and sighed deeply. Was it possible for eyes to be any bluer?

"What's wrong?" he asked.

"Did you spend the night with me by your side to make Heidi Wolffe jealous?"

His brow furrowed. "Heidi is simply my friend's sister. That is all she is to me. I spent time with you this evening because I enjoy your company."

His gaze drifted to her mouth, and all she could feel was her pulse begin to race. He dropped his hands and glanced around, conscious perhaps, that they were now an object of curiosity for those looking on.

"Did you have a good time?" he asked low.

She nodded. "Did you?"

When he smiled his whole face lit up. He really was beautiful to behold.

"Yes, it was an epic party as you pointed out. And you certainly played a major role in that. You were brilliant! Is that what you want to do with your life, be a singer?"

She smiled and bobbed her head.

"Yes. You should be. You were born for the stage."

"You too, Liam. You had me going when you began to sing. Your voice inspired me."

She didn't know what she said, but his expression lost a lot of its joy, and his eyes became serious. "No, I'm not meant to have a singing career. You were right the first time. It's just a hobby."

She touched his arm, "But no, you…"

"It's getting late." He braced his hands on his legs and stood. "It's almost 1:30 a.m. Most guests are leaving for their chalets. Do you want to get anything to eat or drink before you go?"

She snorted a laugh. "Wow, is that your inelegant way of telling me to get lost."

His lips curved and the seriousness in his eyes receded.

"Of course not. I'm beginning to feel a little tired, and I want to have enough energy to walk you back to your chalet, that's all."

Nia sobered. Just like she hadn't wanted him to walk her home last night–actually, two nights ago–she didn't want him to take her home this morning and realize she was entering by an irregular route, her bedroom window.

How did she do this? She eased to the edge of the couch.

"No, I'm fine. You shouldn't leave your guests."

He looked around. "The guests are dwindling."

He braced his hands on his thighs and leaned toward her so close she could see his deep blue irises.

"I'm not letting you walk home alone again like I did last night, I mean, two nights ago. So, are you getting something to eat or drink, or are we leaving now?"

Nia thought about letting him get a drink for her and then disappearing. That wouldn't work unless she had no intentions of seeing him again for the rest of the trip. He would feel betrayed. She was still trying to win his trust after that lie. Mercy, what a dilemma. Eventually, she shrugged. She'd just have to play it by ear.

She shook her head. "No. I want to leave now."

"Okay, I'll just let my parents know where I'm going."

As Nia waited for Liam, Leiliana came over and held out her phone.

"Liam told me he's taking you home and I needed to return this."

Nia took the phone and began thumbing through it. "What were you doing with it for so long?"

"Taking loads of photos," Leiliana said with a grin. "I want to show you one in particular." She dropped down in the seat next to Nia and scooted close. Reaching for the phone, she asked, "May I?"

Reluctantly, Nia released it. Leiliana's hand closed around the phone. After a few seconds, she held it in front of Nia as she tapped a nail on the screen.

"Look at this."

Nia gasped and stared. It was a photo of her and Liam. She recognized it as the moment when he held her face between his hands and looked into her eyes and when she reached up to remove them. But the photo conveyed more than that. The way his hands curved around her face, the way her own hands covered his, and the way they gazed into each other's eyes, made them look like lovers.

Nia gulped.

"What are you two gawking at?" a voice asked.

Nia blinked and blushed guiltily. Liam was standing over them, hands on his hips.

Before Nia could lock the screen, Leiliana snatched the phone from her hands and held it before Liam's face. Covering her hand with his so he could steady it, he peered at the image for several seconds before he looked at Nia. Their gazes held and locked.

Eventually, he said, his eyes not leaving Nia's, "Send that photo to my phone won't you, Leia."

Leiliana preened. "Doesn't it look great?"

He finally shifted his gaze to his sister. "Yes, very good job." He turned to Nia. "I'm going to get our coats. I'll be right back."

As she awaited Liam's return, Nia posted the video of them singing *Amazing Grace* and a few photos of her with Liam and his guests on her social media sites.

"All set," he announced when he came to stand in front of her, holding out her coat.

After quick goodbyes to his parents, and a few select guests, Nia left with Liam. She noted that Heidi Wolffe was still there and told herself that it didn't bother her that when Liam returned to the chalet, she probably would be there waiting for him.

They walked in silence for a little while. Nia couldn't say the silence was comfortable because the image of that photo was still stamped in her mind and she could recall how she had felt with Liam's hands on her skin as she stared into his beautiful eyes.

"Oh, I almost forgot," Liam said, breaking the silence. When she looked at him, she realized he was holding out a gift bag. "Party favors," he explained.

"Thanks," she said. Their fingers brushed as her hand closed around the bag handles. She peeked inside. "What's in here? Is it like the Oscar nominees gift bag of goodies?"

He laughed, stuffing his hands in the pocket of his coat. "Not quite."

Nia looked up and realized they were now in front of her chalet.

"I'm here. Goodnight. Thanks for the company."

Nia turned to go and was tugged back around to face him. Her lips parted in surprise. For a crazy moment, she was sure he would kiss her. Then he cleared his throat and said, "So, I'll be around at noon okay?"

"Noon?" she asked but then remembered his promise to take her skiing again. For a moment she allowed herself the feeling of excitement at the prospect of seeing him again, then reality seeped in. It made no sense getting too close to him. It was best to keep her distance.

"I'm starting to feel the effects of our workout on the slopes. I don't think I'll be in any condition to ski later."

He shook a stern finger in her face. "No excuses and no cop-outs. We made too much progress today for you to quit now."

"Yesterday," she corrected him.

He smiled as his gaze drifted to her lips. Was he finally going to kiss her? A moment later he released her and took a step backward.

"Goodnight."

She waved and stepped up to the front door. But he continued to stand there. Her smile froze. She cleared her throat.

"Um…you can leave now."

"Not until I see you through the door safely."

Nia almost groaned. What to do? Thank God she had walked with the cabin key. She retrieved it from her handbag and, as quietly as she could, inserted it into the lock and turned. The door gave, and with a hand on it she looked back at Liam and mouthed, "Don't want to wake the folks."

That wasn't a lie. She really didn't want to wake them. He nodded in understanding and backed away with a wave.

Nia slipped through the narrow space. She eased the door closed and peered through the peephole. As soon as he strode away, she released a breath in relief, turned away from the door and gave a little scream.

Her mother stood there, hands folded beneath her chest, glaring.

~*~*~*~

Nia had known that the punishment to be meted out to her would be severe but this was beyond harsh, it was torturous.

"No media time whatsoever," her mother had declared and then confiscated all her devices, her Smartphone, her tablet, her laptop. That meant Nia couldn't call Liam and tell him not to expect her this afternoon. So the poor boy was probably waiting on her and wondering what was causing the delay or, worse yet, thinking she had stood him up.

Even Thomas had felt it necessary to weigh in, telling her how disappointed he was in her--like she cared. Nia made a face. Okay, maybe she cared a tiny bit. But they were both overreacting. Hadn't they ever been young? And hadn't they ever made mistakes? She knew for a fact her mother had. One wouldn't think so the way they carried on.

She curled around her pillow and sniffed. What was a girl to do when all she could do was read a dumb book? Her mother wasn't even allowing her to go outside for fresh air.

Nia rolled onto her back and looked up at the ceiling. The third day in this miserable place and her life was already a nightmare. She couldn't even check her social media sites to see if her posts early that morning had roused any interest. Life totally sucked.

Nia shifted and began to punch her pillow. Hearing the sound of a strange voice somewhere beyond her bedroom door, she paused mid-punch and strained her ears. Silence greeted her. As she began to relax she heard the sound again. Was that a British-accented male voice? Her heartbeat began to race. Holding her breath, Nia sat up, pushed off the bed and tiptoed her way to the bedroom door.

She pressed her ear against the door. The voice was a little clearer now. It was Liam! Nia couldn't hear what he was saying, but she heard her mother's voice in response, followed by Thomas'.

Nia felt as though she would die. What were they talking about? She needed to creep into the corridor and eavesdrop some more. She slowly opened the door, her heart missing a beat when it creaked, then slipped into the hallway. Easing her face from behind the wall, she saw Liam sitting on the sofa directly opposite. He looked his usual confident, cool self, not flustered in the least.

Sitting down in front of him, and with backs to Nia, was her mother and Thomas. The three were conversing.

Not a bad sign but not necessarily a good one either.

When he had turned up at the slopes around noon, and Nia was nowhere to be seen, he wasn't alarmed at first. After all, not everyone was punctual. He normally struggled in that area. However, thirty minutes later, he became concerned she had forgotten or was still wrapped up in bed. That was when he had called her number. It went straight to voicemail, so he had left a message and waited another ten minutes.

Then he started to get annoyed. Had she stood him up? He recalled she had seemed reluctant to come this morning. He hoped she wasn't the type to just not show. That would be plain rude. He decided he would go to her chalet and find out what was really going on.

On his way to the chalet, he had wondered what kind of reception he would receive. He didn't have to wait long to find out. When the door was opened he looked into a face he immediately recognized and then almost kicked himself for not making the connection. Nikki Carmichael.

Nia had told him her mother was a singer. Nia was a Carmichael, and the girl had clearly inherited her mother's musical talent. He could now see the resemblance.

Nikki Carmichael was a beautiful black woman, petite like Nia. She watched him with mild curiosity when he introduced himself, but she instantly scowled when he explained he had come to see Nia. Then she began firing questions at him.

"Were you the guy Nia went partying with last night?"

"Were you the one who helped her sneak out of the house?"

"Were you the reason she got home at two o'clock this morning?"

Liam was momentarily at a loss for words. When they were joined by a man with light brown skin, tall and broad enough to be a bouncer, he realized he needed to defend himself and fast. The man stood with his feet apart and hands folded in front of a chest that looked like a wall of solid muscle. Liam sensed that he seemed very annoyed with him.

He flashed his most charming smile.

"Ms. Carmichael, I think I need to explain what happened. If you just allow me to come in, I'll be happy to do that."

After a long considering silence, Nikki Carmichael waved him in and led him over to a nearby sofa. Liam took the seat and sat perched on the edge as he contemplated what he should say.

He thought of beginning the conversation speaking about the night he met Nia but decided against it. He instinctively felt that bringing up the marijuana episode or even the fact that she had been out alone that night would do more harm than good.

He cleared his throat and began.

"I first met Nia yesterday on the slopes. She had gotten into a bit of difficulty, and I helped her out. Then I spent the afternoon giving her some skiing lessons. My birthday was the previous day, and my parents were throwing a party for me, so I invited Nia to attend. She initially said she couldn't come but, to my surprise, she showed up, albeit late."

A look passed between Nikki Carmichael and her husband. Liam pressed on.

"I want to assure you that my party was not some rowdy affair. My parents and a few other adult relatives and family friends were present the whole time, so we were well chaperoned. Furthermore, no alcohol was served as there were minors present. The celebrations officially concluded around midnight, but people lingered. It was around 1:30 a.m. that I insisted on seeing Nia back home to the chalet. We reached here around two. I saw her safely inside, and then I left. That is the entire story."

"Why are you here now?" Nikki asked, eyes narrowed.

"Nia and I made a date to ski some more today."

At the climbing of one dark eyebrow on Nikki's face, Liam realized maybe the word 'date' wasn't the right choice.

"What I meant to say was that Nia and I agreed to meet at midday because she wanted additional tips on improving her skiing techniques. After I didn't see her and her phone kept going to voicemail, I decided to come over to see if everything was okay."

"Well, for your information, Liam, is it?"

At his nod, she continued.

"Nia was told last night that she couldn't attend your party since she is being grounded. I woke early this mornin' with a cough, went to the kitchen to get a glass of water and saw her sneakin' back into the chalet. Needless to say, we are very disappointed and angry at her actions, and there is no way she is goin' out with you or anyone else durin' our remaining time here."

She rose and continued to speak. "I'm sorry things had to happen this way. I do apologize. After all, she is my daughter, and her actions are a reflection on me and the way I raised her. I have made some mistakes, many mistakes, in the past, but I'm seekin' to rectify 'em now. It was nice meeting you despite the circumstances. You seem like a nice boy. Happy belated birthday, by the way."

Liam didn't stand. He hoped he wasn't being rude, and he silently prayed that he was doing the right thing, but something in him propelled his next words.

"Ms. Carmichael, forgive me, but I would like to appeal to you regarding Nia."

Nikki put her hands on her hips, and he saw from the corner of his eye how her husband straightened in his seat. Liam almost bowed out, yet the memory of Nia, all they had shared the previous night and early that morning inspired him to press on.

Yes, Nia was rebellious, clearly, and there were many issues she had to work through, but last night he had seen something, not only during their conversation but during her rendition of *Amazing Grace*. He didn't think it was fake. It appeared that a seed had been planted some time ago and even though they only had a short time together he wanted to continue the watering begun last night.

"Ms. Carmichael, I understand exactly why you have punished Nia. I'm just asking you to entrust her to my care for the remainder of the trip."

Shock covered her face, and for a moment Liam thought she would explode with outrage. Instead, her body went limp with laughter. She doubled over, held her belly and laughed until tears streamed down. She stumbled to the sofa and collapsed against her husband. She tried several times to speak but was overtaken by laughter each time and became incoherent.

Thankfully, Thomas Wilson seemed to understand what Nikki wanted to say. His gruff voice belied the merriment in his hazel eyes, "Young man, are you saying you want us to entrust our teenage daughter to the care of a teenage boy?"

Put that way, it did sound quite absurd. But Liam was in way too deep to back out now. He sat forward eagerly.

"Not just any teenage boy, Mr. Wilson. And understand when I say entrust to my care I just mean allow her to hang out with me and my family and friends during the day. I'll ensure she's back by 6 p.m. every evening."

Liam took a deep breath and looked at the woman who had recovered sufficiently to direct her attention to him, though her lips did continue to twitch.

"Ms. Carmichael, Mr. Wilson, when I say I'm not just any teenage boy I don't mean that in a boastful way. What I mean is I'm very responsible, I'm a Christian, and I'm committed to living a Christ-centered life."

"Well, this is new," Nikki drawled, but Liam was encouraged by the interest that lit up her eyes. He caught a movement in the corner of his eye, turned his head slightly and saw half a face looking at him. Nia. He suppressed a smile and redirected his attention to Nia's parents.

"My friends and I are members of a group called Teens for Sexual Purity. It's a youth ministry at our church."

He fisted his right hand and raised it so the two adults could get a close look.

"I made the purity pledge when I was sixteen. This was the ring I received."

They leaned forward to peer at the ring. Nikki got up and took his hand in hers. She traced the words of the platinum ring and read them out loud.

"True love waits. Timothy 6:11."

She looked back at Thomas. "What verse is that again, honey?"

After rubbing his chin for a moment, he replied, "But you, Man of God, flee from all this. And pursue righteousness, godliness, faith, love, endurance, and gentleness."

Liam was impressed. It seemed there were others in Nia's home who were doing some watering. All was not lost.

When Nikki released Liam's hand and reclaimed her seat, he continued.

"This is just a symbol of my commitment to Christ and to living a life that is pleasing to him. I will never do anything to devalue or degrade your daughter. I would like the opportunity to talk to her some more about God's love for her and His sacrifice. When we started speaking about it last night, she seemed interested. I wouldn't like to lose that ground."

As they silently watched him, he felt compelled to add, "My parents are Lord and Lady William Lamport. They can vouch for me if you want. I would be happy to arrange for you to meet them."

Nikki and Thomas looked at each other, and a slight smile appeared on her lips. Then she spoke.

"There is more to it than Nia not being allowed to go out. We also have banned her from social media. It would be difficult to prevent her from visitin' those sites she frequents if she's not here for us to monitor her movements."

Liam thought about this for a moment. He didn't think it would be an easy thing to control Nia Carmichael based on what he had seen for the last two days, but he had never backed down from a challenge before.

He squared his shoulders. "I promise she won't have access to social media. If she attempts it all bets are off, and I return her home to you."

He saw more movement in his peripheral vision and looked up to see Nia standing in the corridor glowering and shaking her fists at him! When Nikki followed his gaze, Nia dove behind the wall.

Nikki turned back to Liam and raised a brow. "You are ambitious. I'll give you that."

She looked over at Thomas and squeezed his leg, nodding slightly. Thomas placed an arm around his wife's shoulders and leveled his gaze at Liam.

"Well, Liam, it seems you have succeeded in convincing us to give you a chance. However, if we don't like what you two are doing or if you in any way renege on your agreement to have her home by 6 p.m. and to keep her off social media then the deal is off."

To add emphasis to his point, his eyes hardened as he leaned forward, forearms on his thighs.

"And know this. It doesn't matter who you are or who your parents are. If you harm our daughter in any way, you will rue the day you came into this world."

Chapter 8

"You rescued me!" Nia giggled as she tugged on her skis. She stood up with hands over her heart. "I am forever in your debt!"

Liam smiled, but it was guarded. It was not the open smile he'd had last night.

"Forever is a long time," he said. "Let's go. We've already lost a lot of ground."

After his speech and appeal on her behalf, she had been summoned and asked if she wanted to go out with him. At first, she had screwed up her face and glared at him, still annoyed at his promise to keep her from social media like she was a child.

It didn't take her long to realize that what he offered was far more appealing than being holed up in a chalet with naught but a book for entertainment for the next four days. So, she had agreed. For effect, she had plastered on the most submissive face she could muster as she listened to the rules of her parole from her parents. Finally, she was allowed to get dressed and leave with him.

There had been awkward silence between them for a while as they walked over to the lifts. She realized that she owed him more than gratitude. She also owed him an apology.

"Sorry," she mumbled.

"For…?"

"For putting you in an embarrassing position with my mum and stepdad."

He stopped walking and stood still while he stared at her with his intense eyes.

"Why do you do that?"

"What?" she asked, slowing her stride.

"Refer to him as your stepdad all the time."

"What do you want me to call him, Dad?"

"Sure, why not."

"I already have a dad. Soon you will want me to call Alessa mom. How absurd. Listen, everyone doesn't have a perfect nuclear family like you. So keep your judgments to yourself."

She saw his face tighten and immediately regretted her outburst. She took a step toward him, but before she could apologize, he shook his head and spoke between clenched teeth.

"There is no such thing as a perfect family but I am blessed to have a great family, and I'm not going to be made to feel guilty for it. And for your information, I don't live in a bubble. I know many people who have blended families. Some of them have chosen not to let their parents' choices determine their behavior. You should do the same."

Soundly chastised, Nia felt her face heat despite the chilly temperature. In response, she wrapped her arms around herself and bowed her head.

"Are you cold?" he asked, drawing her closer and lifting her chin with a finger, his exasperation with her replaced with concern.

She nodded. She wasn't about to confess to him the real reason she felt the need to hug herself. She knew if she didn't, she would ask him to hold her instead.

"I'm sorry. I keep messing up don't I?"

He looked off into the distance. "No. You're right. I can't relate to your situation. I have no right telling you what to do. Just out of curiosity though, how come you don't have your father's surname."

Nia looked down at her shoes. How embarrassing to have to share her parents' problems with someone she'd just met. "I did have it once. But after my parents divorced my mother changed my name to hers."

"Your father didn't protest?"

She shrugged. "Not as far as I know."

"How did that make you feel?"

"Not too good, but I had no say in the matter. After a while I accepted it."

He nodded and jammed his hands in his pockets.

"Back to your original apology. I accept it, but I have to say I'm disappointed that you never saw fit to say at any time during our conversation yesterday that you were attending my party without permission."

She kicked a pebble. "I didn't think it was something you would support."

"You're right. I wouldn't have. I probably would have appealed to your parents to let you attend, though."

"I couldn't possibly have known that."

He took a deep breath. "Let's put it behind us."

Now they were here on the slopes putting it behind them. With each new tip shared by Liam and with each climb and successive trek downhill, Nia's skiing improved. They hung out with his friends and his siblings for lunch and then hit the slopes again. Nia gloried in her freedom and her newfound friendships. It seemed Liam hadn't told them that she had snuck out and attended his party because no one mentioned it or acted strangely towards her.

When they asked why she wasn't joining them for dinner, Liam kept his gaze averted and allowed her to answer. She explained that her parents had asked her to return by 6 p.m. and she was just obeying. When she glanced at Liam, she saw the way the edges of his mouth twitched.

The next day Liam shared a few final tips with Nia. He had plans to go snowboarding with Reinhardt, Sam, and Benjamin. Nia felt a sense of loss when he said he was confident she had gotten the hang of things and would leave her in the capable hands of Leiliana and Matthew. She didn't realize how much she missed him until he rejoined them at lunch and her heart soared at the sight of him. Was she crushing on this boy? But how was that possible?

She and Liam couldn't be more different. He was so good, so well-mannered and conscientious while she was used to having her own way and rebelled when she didn't. It would be a disaster if the two of them ever got together.

She knew it intellectually. And yet, she found it hard not to be drawn to Liam and his cozy group of family and friends. She looked forward to seeing them every day and dreaded leaving them in the evenings. They skied and participated in other snow-based activities during the day.

In the late afternoons, she sat curled up on the couch when the guys practiced their music, even lending her voice a few times, much to their pleasure, until a quarter to six, when Liam would leave to take her home.

Before Nia knew it, six days had passed with just one more to go when the unthinkable happened – she reneged on their deal.

The group had been sitting at a café having hot chocolate and pastries after an exhilarating day spent on the slopes. Nia excused herself to go to the restroom. On her return, she spotted the Internet café. It occurred to her she hadn't had the opportunity to check her social media sites or communicate with any of her friends for days.

Curiosity began to build as she wondered what the reaction had been to the video and images she had posted the morning after Liam's party. Nia glanced at the free computer table and then glanced behind her. The area was secluded from the main area of the café. Liam and the others wouldn't be able to see her, and she would be very brief.

With a final scan of the area, Nia quickly took a seat, shook the mouse and connected to her sites. In a few minutes, she saw that her postings from Liam's party had generated a large number of responses from her followers! As she checked her messages her heart rate shot up when she saw the one from Damon.

"Wow, babe! What a voice! Didn't know you could sing like that! Can't wait for you to get back to L.A. We gotta talk!"

Nia felt her temper flare. The nerve of this man.

She quickly typed. *"I have nothing to say to you, DD! You and your GIRLFRIEND Sheba deserve each other! Never contact me again!!"*

She posted it, sat back and felt good. Almost instantly there was a response. Did this guy live on his phone?

"Baby! What are you talking about!! I swear to you me and Sheba are HISTORY!"

She leaned forward abruptly and began to pound the keys, lips taut, nostrils flared. "LIAR! You–"

Then the screen went blank.

"Wha–?" Had the electricity gone off? Nia looked up to discover she had been caught. Liam was standing there with the computer plug in his hand and fury in his eyes.

But he couldn't be angrier than she. How dare he?

She jumped to her feet and shoved her hand in his face.

"Hey! Why did you do that? I was in the middle of something."

"So I saw. Contrary to your parents' rules."

"Who do you think you are? My bodyguard? Listen, you have taken this whole thing way too far, buddy. You cannot tell me what to do!"

"I made a promise to your parents."

"Well, too bad for you, you should never make promises you can't keep."

She moved towards the next computer determined to finish her communication with Damon, but she was brought to an abrupt halt when Liam grabbed her arm. She swung around and brought her hand against his rock hard chest.

"Release me right now. I am not your property."

He grabbed both her arms and brought her up to face him, so she was now on her toes.

"We are leaving now! And I am taking you home to your parents. Either you will walk or be carried over my shoulder. You decide."

She had never seen him this angry. His irises were now almost dark blue. A muscle spasmed in his jaw. His chest rose and fell rapidly. And she had never found him more attractive. The close proximity of his body, his hands around her arms fueled her next actions. She leaned forward and closed the few inches of space between them as she fitted her mouth on his.

Liam told himself to resist. He told himself this wasn't the time. He told himself this wasn't the place. And finally, he told himself this certainly was not the girl. Yet, his body had a mind of its own. And when his lips felt the soft flesh beneath them, he wanted more. The hands that held her drew her closer, and he deepened the kiss. Nia pressed into him as his hands went around her back and pulled her closer still. But when she released a soft moan and his body tightened in response, he realized he was in dangerous territory. Pulling back, he ended the kiss.

When he stared down at her, at her pouting, softly bruised lips, her closed lids with their long lashes, her flushed cheeks, he felt such a magnetic pull to move downward again, he physically set her away from him. This seemed to jolt her back to reality. She opened her eyes, stared at him as if through a haze, and blinked rapidly.

"Let's go," he said huskily and stepped around her. As he made his way back to his friends, he didn't even check to see if Nia followed.

When they came into view, Reinhardt immediately commented, "Where have you two been? We were just about to send in the cavalry."

Sam released a loud guffaw, "You sure that's not Calvary?"

Liam reached across the table to gather up his things. "Nia and I are leaving. I'm taking her home."

He saw the way Matthew watched him. No doubt he noticed something in Liam's body language that signaled all was not right. Even Sam and Reinhardt exchanged a look after he didn't react to their attempt at humor.

He didn't look at Nia, but he could sense her displeasure. He still refused to look at her. She had made him feel things he didn't want to. He had lost control of his emotions twice on her account. First, in anger, then, in desire. If he weren't careful, this girl would ruin him before the end of this trip.

They didn't exchange even a single word during the walk over to her place. When they reached the chalet, she turned to him.

"Thanks for seeing me home."

"I need to speak with your parents," he said, feeling enough in control by now to meet her gaze.

To his surprise, her eyes widened in alarm.

"Please don't tell. We're leaving tomorrow evening. There's no need to make what happened an issue."

"I promised them."

She took a step towards him. He retreated a step. Her brown eyes were pleading. He told himself to remain impassive because she was trying to manipulate him.

"Liam, I'm sorry for how I behaved. I know I was wrong and that you were right. I won't do it again, I promise."

He tried to stand resolute and would have insisted he tell her parents, but then her next words gave him pause.

"I won't apologize for kissing you though. That's one thing I'm not sorry about."

He felt every muscle in his body tense. When she touched his cheek, instead of turning away as he should, he turned his face into her hand, closed his eyes and savored her touch. And when she leaned close, he whispered, "Why aren't you sorry?"

"I enjoyed it too much," she murmured, eyes on his. His own eyes drifted down to her lips. They beckoned him, and he would have answered, except at that moment, the door to the chalet swung open. Liam and Nia jerked apart as Thomas Wilson called out, "It's early. Decided to call it an evening, guys?"

Liam felt guilt flow through him. He avoided the man's gaze as he said his goodbye to Nia.

"Wait," he heard her call.

He stopped but didn't turn around. "Will you come to collect me tomorrow morning?"

He hesitated briefly. "Of course. Nothing has changed."

"Nothing has changed," Nia mimicked as she shifted her body on the armchair and moved the book in her hand to the opposite side, a book whose page had remained unchanged since she picked it up an hour ago.

Something *had* changed that was for sure.

She touched her lips as fire rushed through her body. Was this what it was like? What all her friends had been talking about? That feeling of desire and passion? How come she'd never felt it for anyone before, not even Damon. And Liam Lamport of all people. Beyond attractive, no doubt, but too nice and too religious.

She got up and went to stare unseeingly at the pine trees. Why did this have to happen to her now? What sense did it make to go and develop feelings for a boy who she would never see again?

In disgust, she turned from the window and regained her seat. Tossing the book across the floor, she leaned against the back of the chair and moaned. If only there were someone she could talk to about her feelings. She didn't have her phone, so she couldn't reach out to any of her friends. She and Leiliana had formed something of a friendship, but Nia certainly couldn't confide in the girl about her feelings for her brother; it would be too awkward. That left Nikki or

Thomas. She sighed. Perhaps it was time to have a mother-daughter moment. She leaped to her feet and went in search of her mother.

"Mama."

Nikki looked up from her tablet.

"Yes, honey?"

"Got a minute?"

She patted the seat beside her. "Sure. Come and sit."

Nia lowered herself beside Nikki. She reached back and pulled a throw cushion from behind her and hugged it to herself as she settled back in the seat.

"So, Liam…" she began.

Nikki smiled as she placed the tablet on the empty cushion beside her.

"He's a nice boy. I like him."

Nia swallowed. "He's not my boyfriend or anything. You know that, right?"

Nikki didn't answer her daughter's question. She had her own.

"Something happen between the two of you today?"

Nia shifted uncomfortably. "We had a fight."

"About what?"

"Some little misunderstanding. But the thing is, Mama, we kissed."

Nikki's eyes widened. "Oh."

"It was my first kiss."

"Oh!"

"It was really something."

"Why did you come home so early?"

"I don't think he was happy about what happened. I think he regrets it."

Nikki tilted her head to one side and briefly frowned. "Maybe it wasn't so much the kiss as the timin'."

"What do you mean?"

"You know that you two only met days ago. He seems to have very strong values about that kind of thing. He seems like the type who would ask parents their permission to court their daughter. I don't think he would feel too good about kissin' you when he promised us you were just friends, and that nothing sexual would be involved."

"You think that's what it is?"

"Sure do. What else could it be? I can see that he really likes you."

"Really?"

Nikki laughed. "Trust me, Nia. I've been around a long time. I know these things."

Nia felt more at ease by the time she returned to her room. Perhaps she needn't worry. Things would settle down soon. If Liam regretted the kiss for reasons of honor, then he wouldn't be interested in her for the same reason. She had nothing to worry about. She was just crushing on the first boy to show her kindness. Plain and simple. Soon they would be apart forever. Things would return to normalcy. She leaned back against her pillows and told herself that was exactly what she wanted.

"What do you think of this?" Liam asked Nia, dangling the delicate chain in front of her. It was a lightweight gold necklace with an Austrian crystal snowflake pendant.

She touched it gently. "Very nice. Are you purchasing it for someone?"

"You think it would make a nice gift?"

She nodded and turned away to reach for a ceramic photo frame. "I was thinking of getting this for my mama and Thomas."

He raised a brow. Too old fashioned looking for his taste.

"You don't like it," she concluded.

"Do you?"

"Not really," she said with a sigh and put it back on the shelf.

He laughed as they moved down the aisle. "Never buy something for someone you wouldn't buy for yourself."

She took up a key ring with the word 'Austria' on it. "Perhaps I should be safe, hmm?"

He shrugged. "Can't go wrong with a key ring, I suppose. Although…"

He snatched up a scarf off the rack and held it out to her.

"…something practical might be of more use. People have loads of key rings."

She took the plaid scarf from his hand.

"I like this. In fact, I'm going to buy one for everyone on my list. Thanks for the idea."

"Any time."

Even after the word left his mouth, he was jolted. Time was something that was not on their side. They would both be leaving Austria that evening.

That morning when he had arrived to take her skiing, there had been no reference made to the kiss by either of them. He had told himself that suited him perfectly, but increasingly, as the hour of their separation drew near, he found it harder and harder to keep his thoughts away from her.

He couldn't stop himself from the attraction he felt for her no matter how often he prayed, or how often he reminded himself that a relationship with her didn't make sense on any level. For one thing, she lived in another country. Even more, she wasn't a Christian.

Was he developing feelings for her? Matthew had suggested this yesterday as Liam sat brooding by the fire. Conversation swirled around him, but he didn't care because Nia wasn't there with them. If Matthew hadn't looked so concerned for him when he had questioned his feelings for the girl, Liam might have asked him if he wanted to fight.

Now, on their last day, he and Nia were truly alone because she had asked him to accompany her into the village to choose souvenirs for family and friends.

I'll be happy when tomorrow comes, and I don't have to think about her and stress about her anymore.

What a lie that was. He was already missing her, and he hadn't even left Austria yet.

The week had come to an end much too soon. Nia felt a strange sadness settle over her. Curious. She hadn't even wanted to be here in Austria. She had railed to be with her friends in Miami, but now she couldn't bear to leave the wintry clime. She knew it had more to do with Liam Lamport than anything Austria could offer.

The Lamports were leaving first. She went over to their chalet to see Liam off. She wanted to hug him but wasn't sure if it was the right move. Instead, she stuck out her hand.

"It was great meeting you."

To her surprise, he swept her into a hug that went on for a long time. She sunk into it, into him, inhaling the smell of him. She filled her nostrils and her heart in the hope that would sustain her in the days ahead.

"Call me," he said in her ear before they moved apart.

She nodded. "I will."

He gave her chin a soft jab. "Atta girl."

She giggled.

"Enjoy your L.A sunshine and smog," he teased.

"Enjoy your grey skies and chilly breeze."

He made a face. Then he pulled something from his coat. It was a flat, square shaped gift. "Don't open this until after I'm gone."

She took it with surprise, immediately regretting she hadn't gotten him anything. How could she have been so thoughtless after all his hospitality? She quickly slid off one of her silver rings and grabbed his hand and slipped it on his pinky finger. It didn't go all the way down.

He laughed. "Don't worry I'll put it on my chain," he said, removing it and pushing it into his pocket.

"Don't lose it," she cautioned, "That's my favorite ring."

He nodded. "I'll remember that."

She hugged his family and friends in turn, waved to them as they disappeared into the limousine, and then she jogged back to the chalet with Liam's gift clasped tightly in her hand.

Butterflies in her stomach, Nia went into her room and closed and locked the door. She wanted to savor whatever Liam had given her alone. She tore off the wrapping and stared. It was a framed photograph of the two of them. It was the same photo Leiliana had taken the night of his party as Liam clasped her face between his hands and they stared into each other's eyes.

When had he gotten it printed and why had he gone to so much trouble to have it framed? A lump formed in her throat as she ran a finger along his profile. They'd had so much fun together; gotten to know so much about each other.

She angled the beautiful gift and now noticed the words he had scribbled on the wooden frame in black permanent marker.

"Though miles may lie between us, we are never far apart for friendship doesn't count miles, it's measured by the heart."

Nia rolled over to her back and clasped the framed photo to her chest. Then she felt something on the back. She turned the photo over. Taped to the other side was the necklace Liam had shown her in the gift shop.

She took a deep breath to calm the emotion in her heart as she stared at the necklace. Blinking back tears, she prayed her first prayer since she had been a little child in Grandmama Carmichael's church.

"Jesus, please don't let Liam forget me."

Chapter 9

Four Years Later

"*R*emember tone, Nia. Remember lift."

Nia recalled the words of her first vocal arts teacher as the makeup artist put the finishing touches on her face. Mrs. Hillman had said those words during her third year *Opera Chorus* class, a requirement for all singers.

"*Miz Carmichael, three words you would do well to always remember: phrasing, phrasing, phrasing,*" Mr. Mark would say during her voice training in the second year. "*Knowing how to phrase your words as you sing is a huge part of being able to deliver a song with feeling. It's one of the techniques that really sets great singers apart.*"

"*The voice of the performer coupled with the music and the words creates an effect on the audience that cannot be topped.*" That one had been from Professor Montrose during the fourth year course *Acting for Singers.*

Louise Everard would often say during the first year *Movement* class, "*Stand up straight, push your shoulders down and back, hold your head up high. Good posture is a dancer's friend.*"

Now it was almost over. The amazing roller coaster ride that had signaled Nia's four-year Bachelor of Music Degree at Julliard was practically at an end.

Even though there had been a few times she had been tempted to throw in the towel and take up the offers made by music labels, she was now glad she had stuck with her studies. Julliard had not only been a great place to train with some of the best vocal coaches in the world, but it had also taught her the business side of music. Nia believed that she was now more than equipped to embark on a singing career. All her life she had yearned for independence, the opportunity to make her own decisions and steer her own ship. She was looking forward to putting all her training to use and conquering the music world.

Nia looked up at the clock. Ten minutes until show time. She felt a rush of excitement. This night, two weeks before graduation, would be her last performance at Julliard. More important, Liam Lamport would be in the crowd. She would be seeing him in the flesh for the first time in four years. Damon Deverre also would be there, but that was of less significance because Damon showed up from time to time.

Ever since he realized she could sing that spring break when she had posted her performance online at Liam's party, Damon Deverre had hounded her. In fact, he had featured most prominently among those who had tried to entice Nia away from school with offers of a lucrative contract with his recording company. Eventually recognizing that he could not dissuade her from her course, he had grudgingly agreed to wait until after she graduated.

The stagehand appeared. "Time to get into position," he said.

Nia followed him backstage to await her cue. She took a deep breath. Now the usual nerves before a performance were kicking in. She knew she would put the adrenaline to good use. She put a hand to her chest and exhaled slowly. This was the night she would give it her absolute all; put all the advice from her teachers to good use. Liam Lamport was here tonight. She needed no greater motivation than that.

Joining in the applause, Liam caught his breath as he watched Nia take the stage. She was even more beautiful at twenty-one than she had been at seventeen.

The four years since he had last seen her seemed to have made subtle differences that had bridged the gap between child and woman. She now looked leaner, more toned, her features more refined, her carriage more statuesque. And she simply exuded confidence.

The tickets she had sent him were good ones. He sat right down front, near enough to see the sequins in her sparkling white dress and the way her long lashes swept over her beautiful eyes. He was near enough to notice she seemed to be searching the front row for someone. Then her eyes landed on him. The way they lit up and her lips curved slightly seemed to signal that he had been her target. Liam's body flooded with warmth despite the coolness of the theatre as he met her smile with his own.

A moment later music filled the air as Nia looked out into the crowd and began to sing. It was as though she was transformed to the realm of the angelic. Her voice flooded the amphitheater, flowed over him, through him, into him and filled every pore in his body. His breath suspended. His nerve endings tingled. He felt the drumbeat in his bones.

Soon he was sitting forward, eyes riveted, lips parted in awe. He always knew Nia could sing but how had he missed how phenomenal she was? Was it possible that these four years had refined more than just her physical appearance, that her voice had also undergone a stunning metamorphosis?

Emotion poured from her mouth, her eyes, her body. She flirted with the audience, seduced them, and won their hearts and their minds. Her voice was so rich and soulful, her expression, so captivating. She moved in fluidity with each note. Her performance left him mesmerized.

She was joined by others: dancers, singers, musicians, but she eclipsed them all. They were like minor satellites orbiting the star. Then she broke free. She danced. She turned, leaped, was lifted and spun around. Each move was perfectly choreographed.

Eventually, the supporting actors receded into the background. Once again Nia was alone on stage. She was the bright, intoxicating, spellbinding star!

After she sang the last verse and the music ended, the crowd surged to its feet in a crescendo of deafening applause.

At the end of the show, Liam hustled out of the theatre. He tried to step around the crowd of bodies but was forced to wait due to the number of people filing out, some at an excruciatingly leisurely pace.

Finally, he was in the lobby. His eyes immediately zeroed in on their agreed meeting place. To his disappointment, Nia had not yet arrived. He quelled his anxiety. Of course, she was delayed. After all, she had been the star of the show. There probably were people backstage talking to her, congratulating her. She would be receiving flowers too, like the ones he had sent her.

He glanced across the crowd again and spotted her coming his way. He started forward to greet her when someone crossed his path and in the blink of an eye the usurper enveloped Nia in a hug.

"That was amazing, baby! Wow! You are amazing!" the man said.

Baby? Liam's steps slowed. Had he made a mistake? Was it not him who she had been expecting? Was this her significant other?

But before he could allow his thoughts to run further amok, he caught her expression. It did not signal pleasure. It reflected annoyance with the one who was holding her much too close, much too tight. She was not enjoying this embrace. The moment she was set back on her feet she was slapping the interloper's arm and shoving him in his chest.

"You didn't have to squeeze me so tightly, Damon," she scolded. "You nearly broke me in half."

Liam recognized who it was the moment she said the name and caught a look at the man's face. It was Damon Deverre, one of the world's best-selling music artists, known for his edgy, hard-core rap music. He was also a leading music producer as the founder and president of Double D Records. The man had managed to distinguish himself as an entrepreneur with a business empire that spanned not only his recording label but also real estate, clothing, and sports teams. Under normal circumstances, Liam would be an admirer. After all, this was a man who had lifted himself out of an impoverished background to become hugely successful.

The problem was that Damon Deverre had essentially accumulated the majority of his riches by packaging, marketing and selling entertainment that preyed on man's most primitive desires. His message was clear: life was about money, power, and sex. He used highly sexualized images of women to help emphasize his point. Worse was how he appealed to cultural stereotypes of blacks as loudmouths, gangsters, hos, baby mamas, and party animals. He represented everything Liam stood against. Why was Nia hanging out with such a man?

"I got carried away. I'd like to carry *you* away tonight to celebrate your success. We can leave right now," Deverre said.

"No, I'm meeting someone," she said. As she strained to look around the man's broad shoulders her eyes widened when she caught sight of her long-anticipated date.

"Liam!"

She pushed past Damon Deverre, and a moment later she was in Liam's' arms. She stood on her toes and pressed her mouth to his cheek.

His hands went around her. She felt so good. He could get lost in this embrace, but they were not alone. When he pulled back, Liam caught a whiff of her perfume. She smelled as good as she looked, as she felt.

Nia turned her body away from him, her hand still clasping his arm. She extended the other arm in a sweeping gesture.

"Liam, this is Damon Deverre, singer, record producer, entrepreneur. Damon this is Liam Lamport, heir to the Lamport dynasty, and my friend."

Upbringing dictated that Liam should offer his hand, but as suspicion crawled through him as to Damon Deverre's motives, all he could manage to do was incline his head.

The way Damon Deverre responded, nostrils flaring, eyes scornfully traveling over Liam's form as though he was about to do battle with him, suggested that the man liked Liam as much as Liam liked him.

Deverre turned to Nia with a smile. "Let's go celebrate," he repeated, clearly dismissing Liam.

Nia smiled patiently. "I just told you, I have other plans. Liam and I have some catching up to do. I haven't seen him for years. So, sorry. I can't tonight. But call me tomorrow, and we'll discuss that other thing."

"But I had a dinner party all planned for you," Deverre boomed.

Nia shook her head. "You should have discussed it with me first. I made plans already," she repeated firmly.

Damon Deverre's lips thinned, and his jaw hardened.

"But, Nia, I've got the limo waiting."

She took a deep breath and closed her eyes briefly.

"I am not your property, Damon Deverre. Goodnight."

She tugged on Liam's arm as she turned away. He was stunned. What was going on? Why did he have the distinct impression that there was more to this relationship than a music contract in the wings? With a final look at the enraged Damon Deverre, Liam moved away, but he was far from pleased.

Outside the building, he pulled Nia up short. "What was that about? Is there something going on between the two of you?"

"Just business. Forget him." She grasped his hand. "This night is about us. Liam Lamport and Nia Carmichael catching up on each other's lives. Please?" she implored with that winning smile, and eyes sparkling with delight and anticipation, so much so that he couldn't remember why he was mad.

In the cab, she sat very close to him and ran a hand over the jacket of his tux.

"Very spiffy," she smiled playfully.

For an instant, he was transported to their teenage years.

"So what did you think of my performance?" she asked.

He regretted that she even had to ask. It had been his intention when he left the theatre and went in search of her to congratulate her at once on her amazing show. But, of course, he had been sidetracked.

He turned to her and again got a whiff of her flowery perfume that stirred something in him.

"You were wonderful. God has blessed you with the voice of an angel. I was riveted throughout the entire performance. I didn't want it to end."

She placed a kiss on his cheek. When she drew back, she rubbed a spot on his face with the back of her thumb. "My lipstick," she explained.

His eyes drifted down to her lips. Ruby red. Beautiful. Sensuous. He took a deep breath and looked away. He reminded himself that he had accepted Nia's invitation strictly out of his interest in renewing their friendship and because it happened to coincide with a series of business meetings he had in New York. He was not about to be enthralled all over again with a girl who, still, was all wrong for him.

Nia didn't think Liam had a true appreciation of how much his presence meant to her. Even now, hours later, she was still buzzing from the feeling of pure happiness that had exploded in her soul the moment she picked him out in the audience.

"Four years. Hard to believe all that time has passed," Liam said, taking a sip of his Caffè Americano and settling the mug back on the table.

"I know, right?" Nia said, twisting a lock of her hair around her finger.

He was even more attractive than she had remembered, and the way he was watching her, his intense blue eyes not missing a thing, made her feel tingly all over.

"We had great intentions to keep in touch didn't we?" he said.

"I tried to keep in touch. You're the one who only had great intentions it seems."

He had the grace to look sheepish.

She continued, "Yes, I remember a certain someone giving me a photo frame saying, "Though miles may lie between us, we are never far apart for…"

He finished, "…friendship doesn't count miles, it's measured by the heart."

It was a lofty sentiment, certainly. The reality had been different. It seemed as though the miles between them had made it difficult for Liam to sustain their friendship. At first, they had communicated often but soon months would go by without a response from him until eventually, he stopped responding altogether. She had been disappointed, but in time her feelings for Liam receded in the background of her busy life. Or so she had thought.

A few months ago, she had been at a New Year's Eve party when someone found a video she had posted singing *Amazing Grace* in Austria with Liam all those years back. She and her friends had a good laugh over the whole thing, but after the laughter had died down, she was left thinking about Liam Lamport and wondering what had become of him. She decided to message him.

The words were brief. "Though miles still lie between us, you are still in my thoughts, and I wish you everything wonderful this coming year."

She didn't even think he would respond. To her shock, however, he replied. He thanked her, wished her the same and asked how she was. She had eagerly replied and then spent the remainder of the party texting him.

They had kept up messaging each other in the coming weeks and months. Then a couple of weeks ago, Liam messaged Nia and said he was going to be in New York on business and would love to have dinner with her. She had excitedly told him she would be performing in her last show at Julliard just before his visit and would be delighted if he would plan his trip so he could attend.

Since she had just placed her emotions on the line, she had held her breath as she waited for his response. His answer would determine how much she meant to him if he would be willing to arrive in New York three days earlier than his meetings just to see her perform.

When he had said yes she hadn't known what to do with herself though she had managed to sound quite nonchalant in her reply.

Now here they were staring into each other's eyes for the first time in four years. Nia was as happy as a clam at high water.

"That really meant a lot to you, didn't it?" he asked.

"You mean the photo frame?"

"The words."

She didn't want to let on how much both the photo and the words meant to her. "Why do you say that?"

"When you messaged me at the beginning of this year, you used the quote. It suggested you'd taken it to heart."

"Shouldn't I have?" she almost cringed at how needy she sounded. But just the thought that she had read more into them than intended made her feel very foolish.

He stared at her for a while, took another sip of his drink and slowly placed his mug on the table. Then he leaned towards her and nailed her with his gaze.

"I meant those words, Nia. At the time I meant them with every fiber of my being."

She was almost taken in for a moment then she caught herself. She blinked and shook a finger at him.

"At the time you meant them, but that sentiment changed once you got back to your life as King of the Hill, didn't it?"

"Why would you say such a thing?" he asked with a curious expression on his face as though her conclusion was completely irrational.

"Because you stopped responding to my messages."

He stayed silent, watching her like a shrink might watch his patient. His hooded gaze made her feel nervous and unsettled. It wasn't a feeling she was used to, and she wasn't sure how to respond.

She was relieved when their meals came and allowed her time to gather her composure.

Liam bowed his head over the meal. She waited until he was done and began to eat her food.

"Honestly, Nia, I'm not a social media or a telephone person. I prefer more direct communication," Liam said picking up his cutlery.

"Hey, you're the one who made me promise to call you when I returned to L.A., and now suddenly you tell me you're not a phone person?"

He began to eat quietly and didn't reply. In the intervening silence, Nia started to feel insulted. Why wasn't he responding? Might it be because he had no defense for his actions? She sat back and regarded him with a frown. She was beginning to think it was a mistake assuming they could just pick up where they had left off four years ago.

"Why did you even come tonight?" she muttered tersely.

His eyes flew to hers. He looked shocked. "Because I wanted to be here...I wanted to see you."

"Why? For years you ignored me. Ignored my messages and my emails as if I meant nothing to you despite your profession of everlasting friendship."

She was conscious she was laying herself bare, but she was just going to be completely honest. What did she have to lose anyway? He had disappeared from her life before, and if he intended to do it again, there was nothing she could do about it.

He reached across the table and grasped her hand. Though she told herself to move out of reach, she couldn't. When he lightly skittered his thumb over the inside of her wrist, she felt her whole body go limp in response.

"There was never any way I could forget you, Nia," he said softly. "I've remembered those days in Austria more and more lately."

She held her breath for a second. So, it hadn't just been her. She hadn't imagined the feelings that had developed between them. She started to smile, and then stopped. Maybe he hadn't forgotten her, but it hadn't stopped him from distancing himself for the past four years. Clearly, the depth of his feelings did not match hers. What a fool she had been to think his coming tonight signaled something.

Well, perhaps it signals he's looking for a little fun during his stay in New York and thinks you are easy prey.

Nia took it back the moment the thought formed. No, not Liam. Damon would think like that, but not Liam. Unless he had changed drastically over the last four years, he was a man of honor, one who knew how to respect a woman. Which reminded her, did he still wear his...Nia's eyes drifted down to Liam's ring finger.

The purity ring was gone!

She sat forward abruptly and grabbed his left hand. Without thinking she blurted, "Liam, what happened to your purity ring?"

His face grew red as he glanced at his finger. "Embarrassing story," he mumbled.

Nia's heart fell. She released Liam's hand and fell back against her chair. So, there had been someone else in his life. Someone who had so enraptured him, he had been willing to break his vow. She had been disillusioned in many ways.

He continued to speak. She was no longer listening, but dwelling on her dashed hopes.

"…and so now I need to get a new ring."

"What did you say?" she blurted, jolted back to the present by the implication of his words.

He quirked a brow at her.

"I was explaining that on a road trip in New Zealand a few months back, a grasshopper flew into the jeep and landed on my chest. I grabbed the thing and tossed it out the window, and my ring along with it. When I realized what had happened, I stopped the vehicle and searched high and low for that thing. I was still looking when it got too dark to search any longer. When I told the guys, they thought it was hilarious. I didn't. It's not like I'm scared of grasshoppers, you know. It's just that it was as big as a locust and it had startled me."

He took a sip of his drink and met her gaze. "And I can see you also think it's funny. Thanks, Nia, I really appreciate it."

True, she did think it was amusing, but that wasn't the reason for the grin that she couldn't stop. It was how happy she was to see no woman had gone where she hadn't. But of course, she couldn't confess that. She covered his hand with hers.

"You've got to admit it's a pretty funny story. I think the grasshopper must have just taken it. His motives, no doubt, were pure."

"Oh, Nia! That was bad. That was so bad."

He smiled at her. His eyes twinkled. Her heart took flight once more.

They resumed eating their meal. After a while, Nia returned to their unfinished business.

"Tell me something. If our friendship did mean as much to you as you claim, why did you disappear?"

"I got busy," he said quietly, averting his eyes. In that instant, she knew there was more to the story than he was telling her.

As soon as she opened her mouth to say that, he leaned forward. "Where are the flowers?"

"Flowers?"

"The ones I sent you tonight. You got them, right?"

"Yes. The red roses. Thank you. I forgot to say that when I saw you tonight. Forgive my manners. Oh, I left them in the dressing room seeing we were going out. I'll collect them tomorrow."

As she picked at her cheesecake pie, she said, "How long will you be in New York? You indicated in your email that you'll be here for a few days to conduct some business."

"I'll be in your hair for at least a week. I hope I get to see you during that time."

She squealed happily. "I would be thrilled. I won't wash my hair."

His face went blank for a moment, and then he threw back his head and laughed. He pointed his two index fingers at her.

"The hair. That's going to be a running joke between us, I see."

Chapter 10

*H*ow could he tell her?

Liam sat in the darkened penthouse apartment, armchair positioned before the wall of windows so he could watch the stars. But he hardly saw them now as he replayed every moment of his night with Nia. He paused at the scene where she had questioned him about why he hadn't called or messaged her for all those years.

He heaved a sigh and rubbed a hand over his face. While he knew that telling her he had just gotten busy was a cop out, he wasn't sure she would speak to him again if he revealed the truth.

After he had left Austria, they had frequently messaged each other. Even though it had been in no way suggestive or romantic, the constant communication was doing something to him. It was making him feel close to her. He had realized with growing dread that he was digging a deep pit for himself by continuing along that road.

They were so different. They resided in two different countries, across two continents. They had different backgrounds and different values. For the next few years, they would each be immersed in their studies. Studies that reflected the divergent paths they would take through life; hers a life in the arts, his a life in the business world.

And most significant of all was the fact that Nia was not a Christian. He realized that should he continue as he was going it would lead to a romantic relationship, and he couldn't let that happen. After much prayer and agonizing thought, he had made the only decision he could. He had chosen to let their relationship die.

It had worked – for the most part. His studies at Cambridge were rigorous. Because he had chosen to do a double major the work was intense. Most days were spent in lecture halls, study room, or in the library. He lived and breathed his studies; immersed himself in it to the point where friendships became distant memories and social functions more so. Even break from schools, instead of bringing much-needed relief meant internships at Lamport Holdings to prepare him for the role as a director at Lamport Holdings right after graduation.

Then, out of the blue the first day of this year he received a text from Nia that set him straight back to brooding on the girl he had tried to forget. Like a recovering opium addict who had tasted just one drop, he responded to her message and couldn't stop. In the coming months, even though he tried hard to restrict contact, he would eventually succumb to the temptation to pick up the phone and reply to her messages and then send her queries of his own.

Now after four years they were face to face again. The attraction he felt was undeniable, but he assured himself that he would be in New York for only a week. What was the worst that could happen in a week? He had always been self-disciplined. This would just be another opportunity for him to grow stronger emotionally and spiritually.

Liam took another sip of his tea and glanced at his watch as he thought about the hours until he would see Nia again.

Nia was going to die.

She was sure she would die if Liam didn't stop.

She rolled off the couch, toppled to the floor and hugged her side. Tears were coursing down her cheeks.

"Liam," she said weakly, "No more. Please."

He showed her no mercy and kept going with his story. He was laughing too and yet he continued.

Nia pulled her legs up, hugged them to her chest and rolled from side to side. "No...I'm serious," she stammered. "Stop...you're killing me."

Literally, her sides were aching from the convulsions of laughter that had seized her when he began to tell the story. Finally, he stopped and flopped down beside her. Eventually, their laughter subsided, and they went quiet. Occasionally, Nia's giggles would punctuate the silence and Liam would join her in laughter again.

"Oh...my...gosh! I haven't laughed like that in a long time." Nia propped up on one arm and gazed down at Liam's smiling face. "You are not a nice person. I begged you to stop."

He laughed, and she began to laugh too. She shook her head and got weakly to her feet.

"Uh-uh. Not again." She resolutely made it to the kitchen and called over her shoulder. "You want me to reheat your burrito. I'm sure it's gone cold again."

"Sure," he replied from the next room. "Why not?" Then he began to laugh again.

Suppressing a giggle, Nia popped open the microwave and touched the burritos. They hadn't gone cold, but they could use a little heat. She closed the door and decided to nuke the food for half a minute. Then she went over to the refrigerator.

"Water for you, right?" she called before she pulled open the door.

"Yes, thank you," he replied.

The smile that spread across her face revealed pure joy she thought, as she caught her reflection on the front of the stainless steel fridge. How was it possible for four years to just disappear as though someone had taken an eraser to them? It was as if a day had not passed since that week in Austria.

She discovered that for all his additional responsibility and occasional pensiveness, Liam Lamport was the same, easy going, fun loving, amazing guy he been when they had first met and she was enjoying every minute of his company. She kept pretending that the days were not ticking by and that he was not returning to London for God knew how long before she saw him again.

"So, you're leaving tomorrow," she said as she entered with the food.

He was still lounging on the floor. He sat up abruptly and then vaulted to his feet.

"Let me help you with those," he offered and took the plates, allowing her to return to the kitchen for their bottles of water.

When she came back with their drinks, he was holding out the chair for her. Without thinking, she popped a kiss on his cheek. The air became charged as he stared into her eyes before breaking eye contact.

She sunk into her seat and he took the one opposite.

"Didn't I tell you? It turns out I need to have more meetings with some of our people here. There are some things I didn't quite get around to discussing with them."

He met her eyes and threw her a wink. "Go figure. It looks like I'm going to be in your hair for another week."

Nia's heart pounded. She was so overjoyed she almost didn't realize it was her cue. Then she recovered sufficiently to say, "Another week without washing my hair. Oh my. What would my mama say?"

The delay of Liam's return to London enabled him to attend Nia's graduation.

As he entered the halls of Julliard, he remembered that his mother had once shared with him that before she had left high school, she had dreamed of attending the prestigious institution. Instead, she had answered the call of Hollywood.

He found his seat and soon after spotted Nia's mother and stepfather seated down front. He searched the crowd but couldn't identify her father. He hoped sincerely for Nia's sake that Annuad was just running late. It would disappoint Nia if he didn't show up and Liam didn't want her to be disappointed. He realized that he was coming to care for her more than he should and he didn't know how he could stop it. Honestly, he didn't know if he *wanted* to stop. She wasn't the rebellious teen he had met before. She was more mature, more focused. She also seemed open to Christianity and had even attended church with him last Sunday. That had to mean something.

The music of the orchestra began, and the graduating class was welcomed. As the students filed in, he rose to his feet and waited to spot Nia. He didn't have to wait long as they entered by alphabetical order. Even in the shapeless gown, she looked exquisite.

The featured speaker at the commencement ceremony spoke of how entrance to Julliard was not determined by financial ability or academic prowess, but by the applicant's potential in the chosen area of study. Liam glanced at Nia across the row of seats. She sat in the center of the room with the other graduands and from the expression on her face she was paying rapt attention.

Liam turned his attention to the front. The speaker had gone on to explain that the applicants had to be able to first convince the selection panel, based on their essays, they were worth an audition. Having been granted an audition date, they were then required to impress sufficiently to gain entrance into the college.

Again Liam looked at Nia, this time with pride. She had not only impressed enough to gain entrance into the college, but she had so mastered the courses over the last four years that she was graduating valedictorian. She took great pride in her craft and was determined to succeed. She had shared with him the many offers to launch a career she had received during her years at Julliard. Instead, she had chosen to expand and elevate her gift; to deepen and enrich it.

Even his mother had not managed to delay her own gratification enough to do that. Nia, for all her seemingly cavalier attitude, had the patience and tenacity to do things the right way. Even if it meant her dream would be delayed by years. His admiration and fondness for this girl just grew.

Liam enthusiastically applauded Nia as she mounted the stage to accept her scroll. He knew his original plan to not develop feelings for her had gone up in smoke.

Two weeks became three weeks as Liam found further excuses to stay in New York.

"I'll be spending another week in New York, Dad."

"Doing what, Liam? There is work here for you to do. There's a project coming up that I want you to oversee."

"I actually need to take a holiday. I'm past due."

There was a pause. "Who is she?"

Liam felt his heart thunder. Then he felt relief. "Nia Carmichael."

"Nia? You told me you were going to watch her performance at school. Are you two now dating?"

The words stunned him. Was that what he was doing? He hadn't put a name to it but what else could it be?

"Yes, I guess you could say so."

Though they had not shared even a kiss these past two weeks, that seemed like a minor detail considering the erotic dance and heat charged moments between them every time they were together. He was treading dangerous territory, and he knew it. His father seemed to read his mind.

"Liam, remember your purity pledge."

"Of course, Dad. What are you thinking of?"

"That I was just a year older than you are now when I met your mother, and I understand the battle between the flesh and the spirit very well."

Liam bit his lip and glanced at his bare ring finger.

"Liam, is Nia a Christian?"

There it was up in his face. That critical detail that he had managed to push down every time it threatened to make an unwelcome appearance.

"No, she isn't," he admitted softly.

The sigh from his father was heavy with meaning. "Son, please be careful. You don't want to end up falling for someone who is not a believer because it would be a mistake to be unequally yoked."

"I know. I talk to her about God, Dad. She attends church with me on Sundays."

"Just be careful. Remember, Christianity is a personal decision. Going to church is not the same thing as accepting Christ to be your savior and the Lord of your life."

"I know. I'm not forcing her." He couldn't stop the annoyance from resounding in his voice.

His dad ended the conversation with, "I'll be praying for you."

Liam rubbed the faded white line on his finger. Past due time to get another ring. Dad was right. Nia wasn't a Christian. He had to be careful with his heart.

"You got a new ring," Nia said swiveling on the stool at the ice cream parlor to take Liam's hand in hers. She traced the words on the ring.

"True Love waits," she read out loud. "Its design is a little different from the first one, but I like it. Very nice. You mustn't let any bugs take it from you this time."

He chuckled as he took a lick of his ice cream cone. "You think you're really funny, don't you?"

Nia licked her own ice cream but couldn't help the smile that covered her face as she watched him. Sitting astride the bar stool in his blue jeans, red slim-fit motorcycle jacket, and white V-neck tee shirt, he just exuded masculinity and strength even while eating an ice cream cone, even while wearing a purity ring. She found him outrageously attractive, and it went beyond physical attraction. Though they had never shared a kiss, she knew she was in great danger of falling in love with him.

And that would be a terrible mistake. She turned the cone at an angle and licked some of the cream escaping down the side. She glanced up and caught Liam's gaze fixed on her mouth as she licked the cone. She swallowed. Yes, it would be a terrible mistake to fall for him. Not only had he not even hinted at having any romantic feelings for her, but she would be returning home to L.A. to embark on a singing career. There would be no chance of them attempting a long distance romance if he was so inclined. They hadn't even been able to pull off a long distance friendship.

The ice cream parlor was not heavily patronized, and they sat at a corner of the bar in relative seclusion. She smiled when she thought that for their myriad of differences she and Liam were discovering that they had a lot in common. They had known they shared a love of music. They also had found over the last few weeks that they shared a love of other forms of artistic expression, like art, theatre, dance, even gastronomical experiences like eating gourmet ice cream.

"What did you think of the singing last night?" she asked as she munched on her cone.

He shrugged. "It was okay. But I kept thinking to myself that Nia could do better. Heck, I could do better."

It was true; she hadn't been terribly impressed by the quality of the singing. At several points in the production, she wanted to leap on stage and show them what it was about.

"You really like my voice don't you?" she asked Liam.

"Love it," he admitted, and the gleam in his eye told her it was true.

She sat forward and lowered her voice. "What else do you love about me?"

His eyes flickered. Clearly she had caught him off guard. He finished up his cone and then wiped his hands in a napkin. When he was done, he swiveled the stool so that he was now backing the counter. Then he turned and watched her with the intensity of a surgeon about to make a critical incision.

"I love your passion. I love your tenacity. I love how real and unpretentious you are. I love your optimism about life, your hope for the future. And I love your courage in the way you're not afraid to experience new things even though you don't know how they will turn out."

"Like soy ice cream?"

He laughed his full-bodied, masculine laugh that sent shivers racing up her spine.

"Yes, like that."

She'd made a joke so he wouldn't see how his words had impacted her; how they had reached out and wormed their way into the crevices of her heart. This was the first time in her life someone had taken the time to tell her what they admired about her character, but it was a bittersweet sensation. Even though Liam thought she was all these wonderful things, he had never once made a move towards her. She needed to understand why not.

"I get the impression I'm off-limits for you," she said cautiously.

He swallowed. "Alas, you are."

"Why?"

"You're headed to L.A. to become a pop star are you not? There's no room in your life for me."

"You mean there's no room in *your* life for me. It doesn't matter how stellar my qualities are, does it? You're not attracted to me."

He slowly swiveled in his stool until he was now facing the counter. He reached out and began folding the napkin in front of him. She reached forward and snatched it from his hands.

He straightened and glared at her. "That was rude."

"Answer me," she said in a fierce whisper.

He said slowly, "I've never said I'm not attracted to you, Nia. I simply believe it's best we remain just friends." He looked at his watch. "I think we should leave it's getting late."

Stretching his long legs before him, Liam clasped his hands behind his head and watched Nia through his sunglasses as she fed the ducks in Central Park.

He sighed with contentment and wondered idly if he was bewitched. Despite his firm resolution that he and Nia would remain friends only, it seemed his feelings for her were spiraling out of control. Had Nia Carmichael bewitched him? And, if so, why was he ecstatically happy about it?

Nia came briskly over to the bench and plunked down beside him.

"That was fun." She slapped him on the leg. "You were back here sitting in record time."

"I had no more bird seed left."

"You didn't distribute it properly."

"Is that so? And how would you know that?"

"Because proper distribution takes time."

He reached out and squeezed her nose. "You're just jealous because I got through faster than you. It's all in the wrist, my dear. Next time watch and learn from the master."

She threw back her head and laughed. "You are so conceited."

"Not conceit, just the truth. I was feeding birds at our pond when you were still nursing at your mother's teats."

Her jaw dropped open. "You do realize you're only a few months older than I am, right?"

"I stand by my assertion."

She grinned at him and shook her head. "What am I going to do with you?"

"Accompany me to Barbados."

Her eyes widened, and her breath caught. "What did you say?"

Nia had told him of her plans to return home to California as soon as the lease in her apartment was up, which would be the next eight days. It meant their time together was limited. It occurred to him that to take a trip with Nia to the Caribbean would allow him to savor these last precious moments with her before they returned to their individual lives.

"I want you to come with me to Barbados for a week. My family has a villa there."

"Are you sure that's a good idea?" she asked carefully.

She had him there. He couldn't say he was entirely sure it was a good idea. The proposal was fraught with moral difficulties. Flying down to the Caribbean with Nia in the absence of a chaperone presented a minefield of temptations. But he reasoned that it was no different to what they were faced with now in New York. If he could manage all this unchaperoned time with her now, what difference would a change of setting make?

"I am sure."

"I'm not."

The irony wasn't lost on him that the reckless one was being cautious and the cautious one was being reckless.

"Why not, Carmichael. I thought you loved adventure."

She turned serious eyes on him. "I do, but I don't love nursing a broken heart which is what I may end up doing if I go to a romantic Caribbean destination with you. I'll look into your dreamy blue eyes, get swept away and then get the cold shoulder for the next four years when you get busy again."

He was stunned. Not only by her forthrightness but also by what her words revealed. She was hinting that, like him, she was in danger of falling into a place of no return. She feared for her heart. And rightly so. He could not guarantee her that he would not walk away after this. As much as he felt for her, he still could not marry her.

Their lives were going in two different directions. He knew it. During that week she had admitted that a contract with Damon

Deverre's company was one of the offers she was considering when she got to Los Angeles. He had cautioned her against linking up with the likes of that man, but she seemed undeterred.

In spite of all this, he still wanted to spend the next week with Nia. He wasn't going to let her, his father, or his own conscience derail him from that course of action.

He wrapped his arm around her shoulder and drew her to his side.

"Falling in love with me would be a very bad idea, so you're not going to let that happen are you?"

"But Liam–"

"Shh." He placed a finger over her lips to silence her. "We've got a great friendship going, and we're not going to sabotage that. Are we?"

He stared into her eyes with intensity.

She glanced down at her hands and took a heaving breath. "Of course not."

"Good. We can take a trip as friends to Barbados. Nothing untoward is going to happen. We'll have a great time and wonderful memories to sustain us when we are once again miles apart, even if we don't see each other again for four years. Deal?"

She smiled weakly and took the hand he offered.

"Deal."

Chapter 11

"It will soon be over," Nia muttered, gazing up at the stars as they lay side by side in front of the pool at the villa in Barbados.

The one week vacation Liam had planned had become two weeks. He didn't dare try to extend it. He was so close to the fire he was being singed by its heat.

"It'll be okay," he said soothingly, "We'll always have Barbados, right?"

She shot upright. "Is that the best you can do?"

He looked up at her in alarm and then moved to a seated position.

"We can call each other. We can talk on the phone..."

She cut him off. "That's what you said last time and look how it turned out."

She drew her knees up and rested her chin on them. "No. You're returning home to your life as heir to the Lamport Dynasty and the most eligible bachelor on the London circuit. Just as you intended, I'll just be the girl you knew way back when."

Perhaps she had meant it to sound matter-of-fact, but when her words caught, it revealed her heartache.

Never," he said firmly as he struggled not to get swept up in the picture she was painting. He was determined not to spoil things by giving in to the identical thoughts he had been battling for days now. He was afraid that once she returned to L.A., she would become

Damon Deverre's star and heaven knew what else and forget him. And *he* would just be the guy she knew back when. While that should have been a comfort considering that he couldn't marry her, it was not.

His gaze ran down the curve of her back. The way her skin glistened in the moonlight tempted him to just touch, to give in to temptation just this once. He twisted the ring around his finger.

She straightened her back and swiped her eyes. Then she leaned forward and began playing with the water in the pool. Suddenly she threw a handful of water his way.

He jerked in shock as the water hit him full in the face. "Hey, what was that for!"

"For setting me up."

"Setting you up? What are you talking about?"

"I warned you this would happen and you insisted we come here. And idiot that I am I agreed."

"What are you harping about, Nia," he asked, annoyed at how she was ruining their penultimate night here with her theatrics. He stood and began drying his face and chest with a towel.

"I love you, you fool!" she roared. "I've fallen in love with you."

Liam's eyes widened as his heart pounded. He lowered the towel in his hand and stared into Nia's blazing eyes.

Love.

Was that what he felt as well? He was incredibly attracted to Nia. He wanted to be with her every waking moment. He felt intense feelings of pleasure and happiness when they were together and missed her like crazy when they were apart. He spent times thinking about her and caught himself smiling. He had been thinking more and more lately of a future with her, even though he told himself it was impossible.

He hadn't put a name to what he had been feeling. But was this it? Was this *love*? Of course, it was love. He really was a fool.

He snapped out of his musing when Nia suddenly shoved him.

"It's not fair. It's not fair you should make me feel this way and then up and leave me."

He reached out a hand to touch her hair, and she ducked out of the way.

"I'm going to pack now. I'm going to leave here tonight. Why prolong the torture for one more day."

"Don't be ridiculous, Nia. There aren't even any flights available to L.A. right now."

"Well, I'll find somewhere else to stay, then."

He caught up to her before she could get too far and grabbed her arm.

"What has gotten into you?"

She swallowed hard.

"You have. I can't bear this anymore, Liam. How can you not care that by tomorrow this will be over?"

He crushed her to him. "Who says I don't care?" he whispered into her hair. "I care very much, silly girl. My heart is breaking too. Can't you hear it?"

"Then why…"

"Because the next step from here is marriage and how can we make a marriage work when we are being pulled in separate directions, Nia. Number one, you are not a believer, and you know how important Christ is to me. How can I be married to a woman who doesn't share my faith?"

"I'm not quite where I should be yet, Liam, you know that. But I believe in Jesus."

Liam took a deep breath. She believed. That was more than so many. That meant something, didn't it? Maybe they could build on that.

He touched her cheek and trailed a finger down to her mouth, running it gently over her bottom lip. Nia began to lean into him. Suddenly her phone started to ring. They both glanced at it. He saw the name Damon before Nia snatched up the phone and silenced it.

She slid a hand to the back of his head. "Where were we?"

"Damon Deverre. Reason number two."

She shrugged. "He means nothing to me."

"Nia, don't play games with me. You know I'm not talking about that."

"What do you have against his record company?"

"His reputation precedes him."

"He's a self-made man. Very successful. It's admirable how he was able to start up his own label and now is a multi-millionaire."

"His success is built on Blaxploitation."

She quirked a brow.

"Yes, Nia. Back in the 70s, there was a genre of film known as Blaxploitation. They played to the stereotypes of black people in the culture. That's what Damon Deverre does. This man has built a music empire based on stereotypes of black people as thieves, gangbangers, and party going lushes. That's why I say his music and others like it fuels a new era of Blaxploitation."

She stepped back and folded her arms. "I know what Blaxploitation is, Liam. Yes, critics argued it played to stereotypes, but many black people rose to prominence in these films. People like Richard Roundtree and Pam Grier. For the first time, black people were the stars in films playing heroes and not chauffeurs and mammies. The genre actually went a long way in reshaping race relations in America. It got black folk into people's homes in a way nothing else could."

"So, is that what you think Damon Deverre's motivation is? Assisting with race relations?"

He was vaguely aware that he sounded old, parroting his parents, in particular, his mother who had black heritage, although it was often said she passed for white.

"I'm not going to argue with you about this, Liam. I see things differently than you."

"Clearly," he said turning away in disgust.

"I'm going to bed," she said. He noted the fatigue in her voice. It had been an emotional night. She looked weary and defeated. She was not her usual energetic and bubbly self. He felt guilt prick at him that this was his doing.

"Don't leave yet," he said softly. "Please come and sit beside me a little longer."

She squeezed her eyes just before he caught the tears glistening in them. He crossed the distance between them in an instant and gathered her to him. When she opened her eyes, he kissed the tear that trailed down.

"I love you," he whispered. "I love you so much," he said, embarrassed when his voice cracked with emotion.

She wrapped her arms around his waist and cried quietly against his chest. He had made his strong little warrior cry, and he took no pride in it.

In that instant, Liam knew it was too late for him. He could not let Nia leave him and go back to L.A. Come what may, she had captured his heart as surely as if she had placed it in chains and no matter the arguments, he could not let her go.

"Nia?"

She sniffed and then tilted her head to look up at him.

"Marry me."

~*~*~*~

"What did you say?" Nia whispered as her breath suspended in shock.

Liam held her gaze. "You heard me."

She was distantly aware that she was shaking her head. "This is not funny, you know."

He looked mildly outraged. "You think I'm joking?"

"Aren't you?"

He glanced away for a moment, giving her that time to breathe, but then his eyes were on hers again as intense as ever.

"I'm perfectly serious."

"You're really proposing to me?" she asked barely above a whisper now, pulse roaring in her ears.

"Yes, I am."

"Just like that?"

"What do you mean 'just like that?"

"I mean, you were just explaining to me why you couldn't marry me...weren't you?" She was beginning to question her sanity. Or should she question his?

He answered, "It just occurred to me that love covers a multitude of sins. I believe we can make this work if we love each other enough."

She ran a hand up his chest, felt it quiver beneath her touch.

"And you're not going to regret your decision?" she asked softly.

"I swear you are the most trying woman. First, you berate me for not wanting to marry you, now you're asking me if I'm sure I want to marry you. Nia Carmichael, are you trying to drive me crazy?"

She shook her head, now laughing. "No, I'm not. I promise. I just want you to be sure."

"I am sure. Now answer my question."

"What question?"

He glanced heavenwards. "Will you marry me?"

"Oh, that question." She tilted her head to a side placed a finger on her chin.

Liam pushed his face right up to hers. She breathed deeply of him, and suddenly it didn't matter whether he was sure or not; or whether he'd come to regret his hasty decision or not. All that mattered was that Liam loved her and wanted to marry her. Everything else would fall into place.

"Yes," she breathed out.

A relieved laugh burst from his lips. He crushed her to him and then picked her up off her feet and whirled her around. They collapsed into a nearby lounge chair, legs and arms wrapped in each other. They began to kiss. Nia felt as though she didn't want to stop.

"Let's get married tomorrow," Liam said moving to rain kisses down her neck.

Her heart beat like a pounding drum in her chest. "Tomorrow?" was her breathless response.

He lifted his head to look into her eyes.

"This will probably go down in history as the most spontaneous night of my life, but I'm fine with that. Tomorrow we marry. Just the two of us, and the minister of course. No fanfare. No wedding to plan. Just you and me."

Warmth flowed out from her heart as she caught the vision. "Yes, I love it. Let's do it."

He released her hand and reached for his phone. He searched the internet and found guidelines on what they needed to do to get married in Barbados.

It says we can go down to the marriage license office, then connect with a minister or go off to the courthouse and get hitched. Does that sound acceptable?"

Nia nodded vigorously because she was too choked up with emotion to utter a coherent sound.

How had a chance meeting between two teenagers one night in Austria, followed by a week-long friendship, and then four years of silence, followed by a renewal of that friendship and what could only be described as a whirlwind romance, lead to this – marriage in a little church in Barbados.

After completing the necessary forms and acquiring the marriage license, Nia and Liam stood before the minister holding hands and repeating vows.

Nia's heart was so full that even after the beautiful ceremony ended in the evening, she could only manage the tea at the nearby restaurant. She knew she couldn't eat the dinner laid out even though she usually loved red snapper.

She was still digesting the fact that she was now Mrs. William Lamport IV. She looked down at her ring. The two-tone gold ring selected in a jewelry store that same morning was breathtakingly beautiful. She placed her cup back in its saucer and gently traced the blue diamonds which encircled the center – the same shade as Liam's eyes. Her rings perfectly matched his though hers was the thinner version and narrower to accommodate her slender fingers.

She glanced across the table as he sipped his own tea. In a gesture that had been symbolic in so many ways, she had been the one to slide off his purity ring and replace it with the wedding ring. She thought about what awaited her back at the villa. She and Liam would finally be going all the way after weeks of restraint that she was sure would drive her mad. She felt excitement grow in her belly.

When she looked at his face, she was startled to find him intently watching her, a smile playing around the corners of his mouth, his eyes twinkling. Was it possible he was reading her thoughts just now?

"I think true love has waited long enough. What do you think, Mrs. Lamport?" he said huskily, his meaning clear.

Her breath caught as she realized he had indeed followed her train of thought. She felt her face grow warm. She gave a little nod and reached for her bag.

One of the first things Liam found out about his new wife, apart from the fact that physically loving her was beyond anything he ever could have imagined, was that she loved to shop.

He sat in the fourth store at the Limegrove Lifestyle Centre with Nia, tapping his feet to *Happy* playing through the stores piped in music, and wondered how it was possible for him to be happy watching a woman shop. As he felt the smile on his face, he knew it wasn't that he enjoyed what he was doing; rather it was with whom he was doing it.

He glanced at the Hublot watch on his wrist. It revealed that they were now two hours and fifty minutes into their shopping expedition and she gave no indication of running out of steam any time soon. As much as he didn't mind watching her "ooh" and "aah" over shoes and bags and dresses and jewelry, she had promised that they would spend at least part of the afternoon watching the latest superhero movie in the theatre.

As she walked out of the changing room in a pretty summer dress, he felt his body tighten in response. One wouldn't believe that he had seen her unclothed for a few days now and seeing her body clothed should do nothing for him. Amazingly, it still did. And right now the way the dress fit her curves inspired him to ditch the movie and return to the villa.

When his wife did a little dance to Ray Montagne's *You Are the Best Thing*, and when those light brown eyes zeroed in on his with their seductive glint, for a moment, Liam couldn't think straight.

"So what do you think?" she finally asked, coming to a stop in front of his legs.

He cleared his throat. "Very nice choice. I like it." He glanced at his wrist and tapped the face of his watch. "Let's pay for the items and leave."

She made a face at him before she started back for the changing room.

"I know. You want to see your movie."

He followed her inside, bolted the door, and just before he kissed her said, "Actually, we need to return to the villa. There's an urgent matter we need to address."

Chapter 12

"*I* can't believe we're really married." Nia giggled, holding onto Liam's hand tightly as they boarded the Cessna 206. "Oh, my goodness. What will everyone say?"

For the first time in the five days since they were married, Liam felt apprehension creep in on the edges of his bliss.

What would everyone say? He could think of at least two people who would be disappointed and hurt. He was not looking forward to the conversation with his parents.

He took a deep breath and resolutely pushed those feelings down. He told himself that what they said or thought did not matter because, in the final analysis, he was a grown man. He was twenty-two years old. He was an adult, and so was Nia.

"Who cares?"

"Do you mean that?" she looked at him in surprise as she took a seat.

"Of course," he lied.

The phone rang. The phone he had deliberately shut off and successfully ignored for days. The phone he had only just turned back on.

He slid it out of his pocket and looked at it. After a moment's hesitation, he answered.

"Hi, Dad." He met Nia's gaze as he took the seat opposite her.

"I've been calling you, Liam. I left you a voicemail message. You didn't respond."

"I thought I was on holiday, Dad."

There was silence then his father said, "On holiday from being a son? Your mother was worried. She was the one who called you first. After you didn't respond to her, she asked me to give it a go."

Liam sighed and ran a hand over his head. He stepped out of the plane and stood outside, leaning against the side. Why was he so defensive? His parents were not his enemy, they were only concerned.

"I'm sorry I didn't return your calls. My phone was turned off for a while."

"Why? Is something wrong? Are you okay?"

"Yes, Dad. I'm alright."

"Are you sure?"

"There's news I've got to share with you, but I'd rather do it in person."

"Does it concern Nia Carmichael?"

It was Liam's turn to be silent.

"Liam!"

The urgency in his father's voice made him regret he'd answered the call. But he might as well say it and get it over with.

"Nia and I got married on Saturday."

"You did what?"

"Why do you sound so shocked, as though I just confessed to committing a crime? This is my life, Dad. I'm a grown man. I can make my own decisions. I don't need you to sanction everything I do."

"Of course you don't, but courtesy would dictate you'd at least tell those closest to you what you're doing."

Liam glanced into the plane at Nia. Her head was bent over a magazine, but he knew she was imbibing every word.

He walked around the plane and got into the cockpit. The aircraft was small, so the distance from Nia still was not significant.

Lowering his voice, he said, "I meant no disrespect. I just didn't want anyone trying to talk me out of my decision."

"Well, if you were in danger of being talked out of it, maybe it wasn't the right one."

"Goodbye, Dad."

He clicked off the phone. It was just as he had feared. He had been so right to marry Nia without telling anyone. He knew he would have received no support from his parents. Had he called it or what?

"He's not pleased, I take it?"

He angled his body so that he could look back at Nia between the cockpit seats.

"Doesn't matter. It changes nothing." He saw the uncertainty in her eyes. "Nia, I love you. I hope that's enough."

She smiled sadly. "Is that why you asked me to marry you here? 'Cause you knew they wouldn't have approved."

Did he want to begin his marriage with a lie?

No. But perhaps total honesty wasn't necessary at this moment.

"Come up here," he said.

She got out of the plane and came around to the cockpit. He leaned over and opened the door for her. When she was seated next to him, he took her hand in his.

"Mostly it was because I didn't want to wait. I saw no reason why we should. And hasn't it been wonderful?"

She blinked away the moisture he saw glistening in her eyes, the sight of which tore at him. She turned to him and buried her face in his shoulder.

"Yes, it has. I just don't want to ever feel as if you regret marrying me, Liam. I couldn't bear that."

"Darling, I won't. I don't. I know we did the right thing."

~*~*~*~

Nia looked around the lobby of the Waldorf International Hotel & Tower London with huge eyes. To think that this would be her home, at least until she and Liam found a house of their own.

As they passed the guards, Liam inclined his head. Nia noticed the interest in their eyes at the sight of them, hands clasped, making their way into the elevator.

She nudged him. "What's up with them?"

Liam followed her gaze as the guards discreetly shifted theirs.

"I have never brought a girl here. They must be quite curious."

She smiled in pride. It felt good to know she was his first in so many ways, just as he was hers.

At the elevator, Liam released her hand to insert a gold card into a machine beside the elevator.

"What's that?" she asked.

"It gives us special access to my penthouse. It prevents any unauthorized person from gaining entry."

As soon as the green light turned on, he pulled the card out, and the doors slid open.

"Very high tech," Nia commented as she stepped through the doors Liam held open for her. He followed, wheeling the two suitcases behind him. He propped them to one side of the elevator and reached for Nia and tugged her close.

"I'm going to arrange to get one for you tomorrow," he said as she watched the elevator numbers change rapidly.

"How far up are we going?" she asked on a yawn. Suddenly she felt very tired. She was looking forward to collapsing in bed.

"100th floor," Liam replied.

"Good thing I'm not afraid of heights."

The elevator doors opened right into the foyer. A few steps later Liam swiped the keypad again and pushed open double doors. Nia froze mid-yawn.

"Wow!" she exclaimed as her head slowly turned from left to right. The view was breathtaking. Floor to ceiling windows framed a black leather sectional. A baby grand piano sat in the corner of the room.

"If you think this is something wait 'til you see our bedroom," he said dropping a kiss on her neck and wrapping his arms around her waist. He seemed to hear her stomach rumble. "Hey what's that? Do you want me to get you something to eat?"

She shook her head and turned in Liam's arms. "I'm dead on my feet. *Our* bedroom sounds very good right now."

He chuckled and took her hand.

When they reached the bedroom, she saw what Liam meant. Her eyes were immediately drawn to the king-sized bed which took center stage in the large room. It was flanked by side tables in the same dark walnut color and directly faced an accent lime green wall covered with a large television. In one corner of the room was a two-seater couch next to a coffee table. On another side of the room, she spied a walk-in closet and the ensuite bathroom. But it was the floor to ceiling window that framed views of the London skyline and the River Thames that made it most magical of all. Nia fell in love with the room instantly.

"You've got great taste," she said, throwing herself on the bed and sinking deep in the ivory and chocolate coverings. It felt as good as it looked.

In the next instant, the bed shook as Liam landed beside her. He propped up on one elbow and positioned his face over.

"Of course I do. I married *you* didn't I?"

She smiled happily at him and then turned to gaze around their bedroom.

"This place is great, Liam. I'm so happy I don't have to decorate it or anything. It's just wonderful."

"You're a study in contradictions. A woman who loves to shop but doesn't like to decorate."

"I love to shop for clothes, shoes, bags, and jewelry. Not much else. I probably should have warned you, Liam, but I'm not very domesticated."

He slapped his forehead. "Shoot! If I'd only known."

Nia was about to respond to his teasing statement when she caught a glimpse of a photo on Liam's bedside table. Scooting to the side of the bed she reached for it. It was a replica of the one he had given her as a parting gift that spring break in Austria.

She looked over her shoulder at him where he now sat at the edge of the bed tugging off his boots.

"I didn't realize you had printed one for yourself."

He looked around at her. "Do you still have the one I gave you?"

"Of course. It's in the luggage I sent to L.A. before we left for Barbados but I'm going to have mama forward my things here."

She looked down at the photo once more.

"I'm surprised you kept this photo considering that you stopped communicating with me."

She swung around.

"Hey. What about my ring? Do you still have it?"

He bent over and finished taking off his boots. After he straightened and stood up, he turned to face her. She noted he looked a little uncomfortable.

"Suppose I said I lost the ring. Would the one I gave you on our wedding day make up for that?"

She jumped to her feet and placed her hands on her hips.

"You lost my ring? I entrusted that ring to you! You promised to wear it on a chain. How could you have lost it?"

He shrugged helplessly. "I never got around to putting it on a chain. Soon after I returned from Austria, I placed it in a drawer at our family home. When I moved here a couple of years ago, I didn't even remember to look for it."

"I see." So he really had not been thinking about her over the years. That shouldn't have come as a shock considering he hadn't made contact.

It particularly hurt since from time to time she still wore the necklace he had given her. She had also taken the photo with her to college. Even though she placed it in her drawer after communication between them had ceased, she had never even deleted the image from her phone. Well, at least he had kept that as well, so that must mean something.

"You kept the photo on your phone, so I can't be too mad at you," she said smiling as she walked towards him with outstretched arms. But his next words stopped her cold.

"I did delete the image, Nia," he said quietly.

She took in a sharp breath as her arms dropped to her side. "B-but, it's there. You had it printed."

"You sent it to me earlier this year, remember?"

She gulped. Yes, she remembered now. She had attached it to a message to him a couple of months ago with the words, 'Remember this?' The implications of his confession deflated her.

With slumped shoulders, she asked, "Why did you delete it?"

From the way he guiltily glanced away, Nia knew she wasn't going to like his response. And she was right.

"I didn't want to be in a relationship with you. I felt you were all wrong for me. I was determined to forget you."

He spoke the words reluctantly, as though they were being dragged out of him.

Nia felt as though she had been kicked in the gut. She felt that if she didn't sit she would fall. On rubber legs, she made it to the nearby couch and dropped on to it heavily.

She knew she was finally getting insight into the reason why Liam had stopped communicating with her during those years at Julliard. Funny how she had thought at the time that getting to the bottom of things was so important. Now she wished she had never learned the truth. Somehow, it made her feel diminished as if he had chosen her against his better judgment, which meant that one day when he became wiser…

When a hand touched her, she flinched and jerked back.

She raised her head to stare at him, wondering how it was possible to feel so close to a man one minute and so distant from him the next.

"In essence, then, you married me *despite* your feelings about me not *because* of them?"

He groaned and ran a hand through his hair. When he reached for her again, she lurched to standing and went to stare out the window into the bright lights of London. She was angry. She was hurt too, but she was not going to give in to that because it might make her weep. She would not allow him to see how his words had wounded her.

She felt it when he closed the distance between them, but he didn't touch her.

"Nia..."

"Leave me alone, Liam."

There was silence. A minute later when he placed his hands on her shoulders, she tried to wiggle away, but he wouldn't let her. He held her firmly. Eventually, she stopped struggling but still kept her body as rigid as she could.

"Nia, darling. I adore you. Whatever I thought four years ago does not matter because look where we are now. Do you think we're the first couple to have tried to deny our feelings for each other and then realized it was futile?"

He lifted her chin. "I felt our situation was impossible because we lived so far apart, had different goals in life, different values...but I realize that none of that matters. Without you, I'd be miserable. I don't want to go through life without you by my side."

The way he said it, with such heartfelt sincerity, lifted her spirits and made her want to believe again. "Really?" she breathed.

"Really." He raised her left hand and kissed her wedding band. "This is for life. Forever. I'm forever yours. The past is of no consequence."

She embraced him tightly, burying her head against his chest.

Forever. She liked the sound of that.

Chapter 13

He saw through her ploy and was having none of it.

Nia had figured that if she kept busy long enough, she could delay the trip to meet Liam's parents at their country home.

She had made excuses for a week that she had to sort out her documents; she had to inform friends back home of her new status and address; she had to traverse her neighborhood and get comfortable with living in a new city, and finally, she had pleaded fatigue from doing all of the above.

Once Liam realized that the incessant delays were a willful dragging of her feet, he made the arrangements for them to leave that coming weekend and even proceeded to pack for her.

Nia sat on the bed pouting as Liam carefully folded her tops and placed them in a suitcase.

"You are a real tyrant. How come I never noticed this side of you before?" she asked plaintively.

He looked her squarely in the eyes.

"What are you concerned about, Nia?"

"That they will hate me," she wailed.

He rolled his eyes and returned to packing a cardigan. "My parents liked you when we met in Austria, why would they suddenly hate you?"

"I wasn't their daughter-in-law then, Liam. Are you trying to be deliberately obtuse?"

"Well, then it stands to reason that they will love you even more now that you're family."

She heaved a sigh and flung herself back on the bed.

Liam offered a suggestion. "Okay, here's what I propose. If they hate you as you say, then we will leave immediately and never darken their door again."

She sat up abruptly and looked at him in shock. "Do you really mean that?"

He stared at her grimly and then his mouth began to twitch.

"Of course not, because that will never happen."

She snatched a pillow from behind her and tossed it at his head.

He caught it, laughing, and came to sit beside her on the bed.

"Darling, I keep telling you my parents are not like that. They aren't hostile people. They are kind and warm. They will come to love you as much as I do, I promise."

Still, Nia remained unconvinced. She had recently conducted an Internet search on the Lamports, and now she felt more intimidated than ever. Lord and Lady Lamport were labeled among the world's most powerful couples. Lord Lamport was a nobleman with distant ties to the British throne. With a net worth of over $70 billion, he was also listed among the top five wealthiest men in the world.

It didn't stop there. Through the work of their foundation, William and Barbara Lamport were also considered among the world's most generous couple, giving away billions of dollars to charitable causes each year. How did she begin to fit into their world? Why had she never considered how being Liam's wife would change her life?

When Liam kissed the corner of her mouth, it shook her from her reverie.

"Listen, I was joking earlier about not darkening their door again if they hate you, but I promise you, Nia, if at any time you're uncomfortable and want to leave, we'll do that, okay?"

She nodded and squeezed out a smile, praying that the next weekend would come and go very quickly.

Belfield Manor was truly a beautiful place. The River Severn flowed north of the property. Undulating fields and hills covered the lands. As it was still summer, the gardens were filled with a spectrum of colorful, lush flowers. Liam had many wonderful childhood memories of this place.

They drove a few minutes up a long winding driveway before they reached the large electric gates. He glanced at his wife and felt so happy to be able to share this with her. He was glad he had insisted they come.

As the Rolls Royce swept past the formal front gardens to a turning circle, he asked, "What do you think?"

"This place is huge, Liam. I had no idea." She looked at him with wide eyes. "You grew up here?"

He nodded as they came to a stop opposite a water fountain.

"This is our country home. We spent weekends and holidays here."

"Country home? My goodness, this place looks like a museum or a palace or something." She looked at him in awe. "I was right about you the first time. You really are royalty."

~*~*~*~

Nia had expected a very old-fashioned interior to match the exterior of the manor. She was surprised to find that the furnishings were altogether modern and supremely elegant.

Upon entry into the reception hall, she was greeted with a spectacular cantilevered staircase rising to the upper floors and marble stone flooring. The furniture was an eclectic mix of modern and traditional, resulting in a classy decor.

As impressive as the hall was, it was nothing compared to the reception she received. She mused that perhaps the delay in London had given Liam's parents the time they needed to adjust to the idea of her as their new daughter-in-law. That was the only explanation Nia could come up with for why instead of the guardedness, suspicion, aloofness or downright anger she had anticipated, she was instead greeted with seemingly genuine warmth and affection.

Over the next few days, Nia still struggled to get used to her in-laws and her surroundings. Even though both her parents were well-off, neither of them was insanely wealthy like the Lamports. Liam took her on a tour of the manor. She discovered that among the nine-bedroom house's many rooms were a gymnasium, an extensively stocked library, a magnificent drawing room, a large dining room, a spacious kitchen, and an entertainment room.

When Liam took her on a walkabout of the property a few days after they arrived, she discovered that the interior was nothing compared to the exterior. The property was surrounded by beautiful, well-maintained lawns and gardens including a magnificent walled garden area which could be viewed from the kitchen. Then she spotted the stables.

"Horses?" she asked in a suspicious voice as they approached the facility.

A man was rubbing down a horse as it neighed and flicked its tail. Liam called the man by name and introduced Nia as his wife. The man doffed his hat and smiled.

"Would you like to go riding?" Liam asked as they moved away.

She looked at him in alarm. "Absolutely not!"

He burst out laughing. "You should see the look on your face. Like I asked you to go bull riding."

Her eyes widened. "Don't tell me you raise bulls too?"

He threw back his head and laughed all the more.

"What's funny?" she asked, annoyed that he was laughing at her.

He took one look at her face and instantly grew serious.

"Sorry, I thought you were kidding."

She pouted, feeling quite stupid.

He reached out a hand and wrapped it around her shoulders.

"No, we don't raise bulls. We have a few dogs and one or two lazy cats. You'll see some meerkats from time to time, and we have horses because Dad loves to ride. Polo is his favorite sport."

"Do you play Polo too?" she asked, realizing that there was still a lot she had to learn about her husband.

He shook his head. "I play on the odd occasion. But I can't honestly say it's my thing. You know what I love?" he said watching her with a twinkle in his eyes.

"Skiing!" she answered.

He pumped a fist in the air. "Bingo! I love skiing, and I hope you'll come to enjoy it too."

"You know, I didn't really like the cold until I met you and discovered that it is possible to have fun in freezing temperatures."

"So glad you said that. It means you'll settle right into our climate. Because, my love, England is cold for most of the year."

"So I heard," she responded dryly. "Why is it called 'jolly old England' then?"

"Because we have to keep our spirits up to stay warm."

He made a drinking motion with his hand when he said the word 'spirits,' and she instantly understood what kinds of spirits he was talking about.

She doubled over with laughter.

When they came upon a body of water, she stopped walking. "Hey, is this the pond you bragged about where you fed ducks when you were a baby?"

He laughed. "The very same. While we're here, I'm going to teach you the art of feeding birds as you are so truly terrible at it."

She jabbed him in the ribs with her elbow.

"Ouch," he said, holding his side. "I'm going to get you for that."

She took off running with him chasing her and didn't realize until she stopped to catch her breath that they had run straight into a thick woodland. She looked around her and suddenly felt overwhelmed by the enormity of it all. This property was huge. No way could one family own all of this.

She turned to Liam. "Are we still on your land?"

He nodded and dragged her over to sit on a bench with him.

"Your parents are extremely rich aren't they?"

She noticed that he looked flushed and uncomfortable. It could be the bit of exertion from chasing her, but she didn't think so. She got the impression he didn't like talking about his money.

"Are you embarrassed about your wealth?" she asked.

He cleared his throat. "I don't like to discuss money if that's what you mean. We've taken the position that everything belongs to God and we are just stewards. God has a say in how we spend it, and that includes using it to help other people."

"Yes, I was reading that the Lamport Foundation donates one billion every year to fight poverty worldwide. Is that true?"

He turned to watch her with his head tilted to one side. "You've been reading up about my family?" he asked quietly.

"I just wanted an idea about what I had gotten myself into."

"You could have asked me."

"I guess."

They lapsed into silence for a while. She gazed up at the majestic trees in the woods and wondered how many hundreds of years it would have taken them to grow this tall. She watched as the leaves swayed in the breeze and the sunlight streamed through spaces in the forest. It smelled like rich dirt and moss. She could hear the birds singing and other wildlife scurrying around. She could feel the wind on her face as it rustled through the leaves. It was a lovely, peaceful place. A person could forget that there was an outside world with important decisions to be made just sitting here. Regrettably, though, there was no escaping from life or its responsibilities.

"I was also researching the role I'll be expected to play as your wife."

"What do you mean?"

"I was curious about what I will have to do so I looked it up on the Internet. I learned that I'll have to host parties and do charity work."

He looked very somber and nodded. She was startled when laughter suddenly burst from his mouth. Liam apologized, schooled his expression and stared ahead again. When another bark of laughter escaped, Nia jumped from her seat and chucked him on the shoulder.

"What's so funny?"

Instead of answering he continued to laugh. When she chucked him again, he grabbed her by the waist and tugged her into his arms. He kept chuckling as she rained down her fists on his back and tried to wriggle away. Eventually, he managed to pull her into his lap and wrap his arms around her to keep her still.

"If you don't want me to laugh at you, stop making such ridiculous comments. Listen, darling, you can do whatever you want. The only duty that comes with marrying me is keeping your vows to have and to hold me."

He kissed her neck, "…for better or worse."

He kissed her jaw, "…for richer, for poorer."

He kissed her cheek, "in sickness and in health."

He kissed her temple, "to love and to cherish, till death us do part." And then he kissed her mouth.

Nia felt a comforting warmth flood her entire body as she stared into her husband's eyes. She clasped her hand on his cheek.

"And you will support my singing?"

"Of course, I love it when you sing. In fact, you can start by singing at our church. I heard our worship team is looking for a new leader."

Nia's smile thinned. Didn't Liam understand that she was talking about having a singing career? Did he know that she still had every intention of pursuing the contract with Damon's company? Or was he merely pretending ignorance of the whole situation?"

She was about to open her mouth to remind him when he tenderly kissed her. At the feel of his mouth on hers, she sighed and relaxed in his embrace. The discussion on her career needed to take place and soon, but not today. Not when she was getting to know Liam better; not when they were enjoying each other's company so much. She would pursue it when they returned to London the following week.

Unexpectedly, Liam and Nia's return to London was delayed after Liam's parents suggested to them that there should be a celebration to introduce Nia to the family, friends, and associates of the Lamports.

Nia had no objection to the event. It was when Barbara suggested that Nia's parents and their spouses be invited to spend the weekend so she could get to know them better that the drama began.

The first moment they were alone, Liam dropped into a chair and placed his head in his hands.

"What is it?" she asked, alarmed.

"I never told my parents who your parents are."

"What? Why not?"

"Honestly, I didn't think it was important that they know when we were in Austria. And since we got married, I haven't really had the opportunity to sit down with them and have a proper conversation."

"So, they never asked?" It seemed unlikely that people as protective of their children as the Lamports would not have asked such an important question.

"They know who your mother and stepfather are. I mean they don't know who your father is and I don't think my mother made the connection between Jacques Annuad and Nikki Carmichael. Anyway, Jacques and Mother were married for such a brief time."

"Not that briefly," Nia muttered.

She had been six when her mother had left her father. She remembered how he had knelt down before her at the door as they were about to go and said that things would now change between them.

He had told her that she would spend half the year with him and half with her mother, but that didn't really happen because it often depended on whether he was shooting a movie or not. Many times, when he was supposed to keep her, he often foisted her off on his mother – her cold French grandmother who didn't seem to like her very much.

"I'll need to tell them as soon as possible," Liam said.

"Yes, you do. Do you need me to be there?"

"No, that's okay. I'll speak to them alone."

That night after dinner Liam asked his parents to join him in the drawing room. They sat before him on a two-seater couch and looking from one to the other, Liam said, "Mum, Dad, there is something you need to know about Nia's father."

"What?" William asked with his usual dry wit. "Is he an ax murderer?"

"No, actually he is a French film director."

Barbara's eyes narrowed. "Which French film director?"

"One you know very well, Mum."

"Liam?" his father growled, "You have never been one to beat around the bush. Just say it."

"Jacques Annuad."

Barbara Dickson gasped.

William Lamport's face hardened. "The man I just agreed should spend a weekend in my home?"

Liam shrugged helplessly. "Sorry. I should have told you. It slipped my mind."

"How long have you known?" William asked.

"Since that year I met Nia in Austria. It didn't seem important that you know since I wasn't planning on seeing her ever again. But now…well."

Barbara nodded slowly.

"That explains why her brown eyes have always looked so familiar to me. She has her father's beautiful eyes."

When William raised a questioning brow, she patted him on the leg for reassurance.

"It doesn't matter. Sure Jacques and I parted on acrimonious terms and have never spoken since but it is all water under the bridge now. I owe him no malice. In fact, honestly, I'm glad things turned out the way they did, and I found my way back to my true love again."

His father smiled broadly in return. "Okay. I'll allow him to come, but I'm going to be keeping a close eye on him."

Chapter 14

*N*ia didn't know how to interpret the fact that her father could not seem to stop laughing upon learning that his daughter had eloped with Barbara Dickson's son.

"This is too good," he said between fits of laughter that began to make her blood boil. "I could not have orchestrated this myself, *ma chérie*. I eloped with his mother over three decades ago, and he comes now and does the same with you. I'll bet *Monsieur* and *Madame* Lamport are thrilled."

"Of course they are!" Nia said reasoning it was not a lie since they had never said they weren't thrilled. But she just wanted to rub that smug look her father was no doubt wearing off his face. "Why wouldn't they be?"

This stopped his laughter for a moment.

"You cannot be serious. No matter what they say, they are *not* thrilled. Do not forget I was married to Barbara once. I know her very well. She is quite judgmental, that one, and when she became a Christian, she became more overbearing than ever. Her husband is no different. I have heard his views on a number of things like same-sex marriage and abortion. They are quite conservative. I don't know how you will manage. They will no doubt attempt to convert you, but stick to your guns, *ma petite fille chérie*. Do not let them change you."

"Stick to what guns, Papa? And what would they be changing me into? Why would they even need to change me? Am I not perfect as I am? You are acting as though this is a remake of *Stepford Wives*."

"Now there is a classic. Hmm…I have been thinking of doing a remake."

"Papa!"

"*Pardon, ma chérie*. What I am saying is that you, my delightful daughter, are a free spirit. You are an independent thinker. You take after me that way. You are not bound by societal rules or conventions. A family that has such staunch views about right and wrong, well, it may be at odds with your own view of life, *non*?"

"Papa, I also have views about right and wrong. I am not a heathen, you know." *Like he was.*

He went very quiet. "I didn't mean to imply that you were. Congratulations, nonetheless. You know, I can't help but think your William could have been my son. Now he is my son-in-law."

She had thought the same thing. When she and Liam had first discovered the connection between his mother and her father she had found the notion they could have been siblings amusing. Not so any longer. In fact, this whole picture her father was painting of her being so different from Liam's family was making her stomach churn.

Was she really likely to be at odds with her in-laws' worldview? What about Liam's? They had not discussed any of these issues in depth. She had been to church with him a few times, but during the services, none of these real-life issues had come up. The minister had said that to love God meant being obedient to him.

Nia knew she wasn't at that point, and that she didn't consider God when she made decisions. She just went with what felt right to her. She worried that Liam's parents would see right through her. She didn't want to be a hypocrite but could she truly be her real self around them? Her father was suggesting that if she were herself, it would have deleterious effects.

Nia rubbed the back of her neck. She wasn't so sure about this reception anymore. It seemed to be a potential minefield. It presented so many opportunities for her to commit a faux pas, not to mention her father's presence to roil things. Perhaps she should talk Liam and his parents out of it.

"I agree with the Lamports that they should present you to their society." Her father's voice returned her to the present. "Let them see who has come to shake things up." He burst out laughing.

Nia had to find Liam fast and put an end to this idea.

A twenty-minute search found him in the exercise room running on the treadmill. She waved her phone in front of his face.

"I was calling you. Why didn't you answer?"

He pulled wireless headphones down to dangle around his neck. "Sorry. I put my phone on silent…needed to concentrate on my workout. What's up?" he asked breathlessly.

She took a seat on a nearby window seat and watched Liam's muscles ripple as he slowed to a jog.

"I'm beginning to think this reception is not a good idea."

"Why not?"

"Dad is not acting mature. He was full of jokes about the irony of you and me eloping two decades after he did the same thing with your mother."

"Three," Liam said, slowing the machine so that he was now walking briskly.

"Three what?"

"Three decades not two. What else did he say?"

Nia swung one leg back and forth. "He said they won't accept me as I am."

She didn't realize how hurt she was until she felt her nose burn unexpectedly and her eyes prick with unshed tears. She didn't allow them to fall. She had had enough of this. She was weepier than an expectant mother, which was possible given her period was now late. She didn't want to consider the implications of having motherhood suddenly thrust upon her given her immediate plans for a singing career. She instead prayed that her period was just late because of the recent changes in her routine.

"Nia, do not let your father upset you. My parents have accepted you. Remember this reception was their idea. If they didn't feel that way about you why would they want to have a party and introduce you to all their family and friends?"

She shrugged, somewhat comforted but still doubtful. "Maybe because protocol dictates they should. Liam, I'm sure they would not have chosen someone like me for you."

He frowned, stopped the machine and got off. When he came over and wrapped his arms around her, she buried her face in his sweaty vest, inhaling the musky scent of him, relishing it, wanting to get lost in his embrace and forget her troubles.

"I chose you for me, and they respect that."

He eased her hand from around him and dropped to a knee in front of her. He reached for her hand and kissed it.

"I agree with my parents. I want the world to know the beautiful, amazing woman I married. I'm so proud and excited to show you off. Please don't deny me the pleasure. And it's fitting that your parents be there. No matter how irascible your father might be, if you don't allow him to be a part of this I fear you will regret it for years to come."

Nia sighed. She just hoped Liam was right and that she didn't regret *inviting* him for years to come.

"Will you allow me to assist in the planning?"

Nia redirected her gaze from the lovely view of the walled gardens to Barbara as she came to sit beside her in the first-floor living room.

Barbara followed Nia's gaze.

"Beautiful aren't they? I really enjoy summer. By fall they will be gone."

Nia shifted her body towards her mother-in-law.

"Yes, the gardens are beautiful. Very well maintained."

"I was asking if you'd like me to assist with planning for the reception."

"I am so glad for your offer. In fact, honestly, I'm not that great at planning parties. I'm a whole lot better at picking out the great outfit and providing the entertainment though," Nia said with a self-conscious laugh.

Joining her laughter, Barbara patted her leg. "Don't despair, darling. I'm no great party planner either. That's why I rely on professionals. We'll hire someone to do all the heavy lifting, and all we'll have to do is to make the final decisions on décor, the menu, stuff like that."

Nia nodded. "I'll also need your guidance there. You'll find I'm very easy when it comes to those things."

"I realize that. Some women would have insisted on a wedding with all the works. Instead, you allowed my son to convince you to elope."

Nia's eyes widened. "Bar…Mrs.…Lady…"

"Mum will do just fine, Nia."

Nia swallowed. "Mum, I hope you're not angry at us for eloping."

"Angry is not the word I would choose," she said carefully. "But it wasn't my choice to make. Liam has to live his own life," she said diplomatically.

"It must have brought back memories of what happened with you and my father," Nia blurted out, then wished she could take it back. It wasn't exactly a light topic.

Barbara Dickson shifted her body, and a corner of her mouth hitched. "It did. It struck me as ironic."

"That's what he said."

Barbara glanced at her sharply. "What else did your father say?"

Nia looked down at her hands folded in her lap.

"Well, he was surprised. I never told him about the connection between Liam and you. In fact, he never even met Liam. He agrees that a reception would be a great opportunity to do that and he's looking forward to it."

Nia swallowed and kept her head down. She didn't want her mother-in-law to probe further. She might just give in and confess his negative comments about them and ask if it was true that they thought she was a bad choice for their son.

"Well, I want you to know that I'm available to discuss anything you want. I look forward to getting to know you better, Nia."

With a final squeeze of Nia's clasped hands, Barbara stood to leave.

"Bar...Mum, may I ask you something?"

"Sure." She sat back down.

"When you married Liam's father did you get the impression he didn't want you to continue your acting career."

Barbara Dickson answered slowly.

"No. I didn't get that impression. When William and I married, I was well into my career. I continued for a little while, but soon after the children came along, I chose to be a stay at home mother and let other people manage the film studio and production company. Tell me, Nia. What do *you* want to do with your life?"

"I studied Vocal Arts at Juilliard. I'm going to become a professional singer. The thing is, I'm not sure how it will fit into my life as Liam's wife."

Barbara studied her. "Have you and Liam discussed this at all?"

"He knows I love to sing. I just don't think he wants me to pursue a singing career."

"Why wouldn't he?"

"I was offered a recording contract, and he doesn't want me to accept it."

"Tell me more about that. Who made the offer?"

"Damon Deverre."

Barbara's eyes flickered, and the corner of her mouth tightened slightly.

"I see. Is this the reason Liam doesn't want you to pursue this contract because of who offered it?"

"I think so. But whenever I try to discuss it, he just shuts down on me. He doesn't seem to like Damon."

And neither did his mother based on her non-verbal cues.

Barbara Dickson looked off into the corner of the room and nodded thoughtfully.

"You should discuss this with Liam, Nia. It's important that you and Liam are honest with each other. You can't build a relationship by closing off yourself from each other. You need to discuss everything, even the uncomfortable bits. That's how intimacy is developed. Tell him what you want. Share how it makes you feel when he refuses to discuss it and tell him you're seeking dialogue so that you can agree on a way forward together."

She stood. "I've got to go make some calls, including the one to the event planner, but I'll keep you in prayer."

"So, Nia, has been offered a recording contract?"

Liam paused mid-stride as he was about to mount the staircase with the steaming mug of coffee. He turned to watch his father as he approached from the drawing room.

"She told you about that?"

"Not me. Your mother."

"Did she also tell her it's a contract with Damon Deverre?"

"Is that what you're afraid of?"

"Me? Afraid? Who's afraid of Damon Deverre?"

"Liam…"

"Dad, I do not trust that man one iota. And, yes, I am afraid my wife will get caught up with him and his unsavory troupe. If she's going to sing something let it be wholesome and I will happily pave the way for her to do that."

Shaking his head his father placed a hand on his shoulder. "That's not your decision to make, Liam. If you don't let her make her own choices, she will feel like a caged bird."

"Is that how mum felt when she married you, Dad. She gave up performing for a long time. Did she feel caged?"

"No, because it was her decision to give that up. I never told her I wanted her to give up anything. I never even hinted that she should become just Lady Lamport. I supported her in whatever she wanted to do."

"Yeah, but knowing Mum, her choices would have been positive."

"Liam, you are not Nia's father. You are her husband."

He dropped his hand and looked off into the distance for a moment.

"Look, your mother and I would not have chosen a non-believer for you. But the deed is done. You made a vow before God to honor her, cherish her, and protect her. By disregarding her interests and telling her what to do you're not honoring her, and you're not cherishing her, and you're not protecting her–"

"But I *am* protecting her!" Liam protested vehemently, causing his hand to shake and a little coffee to slosh off the side of the cup.

Didn't his father understand that what he was doing was in Nia's best interest? He was motivated by love and a desire to protect his wife from things that could harm her. How could that be wrong?

"No. You're trying to control her. And based on what I've observed about Nia, not only is that *not* going to work, it will push her away from you and from the very God you are trying to lead her to."

Liam felt shock reverberate through his whole body. He could not believe that the father who had taught him these very values was now saying this to him. He didn't get it. There was no point in continuing this conversation.

He ground his teeth. "Thanks for the advice, Dad, but I think I can manage my own affairs. In fact, Nia and I are returning to London tomorrow. We will come back next weekend for the reception."

He turned when he reached the third step. "If she wants to record an album, Christian or secular, I will arrange that, but she's not going to join Damon Deverre's company."

William looked after his son as he stalked away and said a prayer that God would show him the way before it was too late.

~*~*~*~

"Look at this. Isn't it beautiful?" Nia exclaimed as she ran the pads of her fingers over the satin smooth gold embossed invitation. She held it out to Liam as he entered the bedroom.

He took the invitation as he passed her the cup of coffee. Nia took a sip and instantly made a face. "This is lukewarm."

He lowered himself beside her on the bed as he scanned the invitation.

"Sorry. It was hot when I left the kitchen, but Dad waylaid me," he muttered. "How did you get this?"

"Your mother dropped it off a few minutes ago."

"It's nice," he commented. She agreed. The words were on point. They said:

*"**William and Nia are married!***
William and Nia were married on July 21st in a private ceremony.
Please join the newlyweds and their parents at a reception to celebrate.
Hosted by Lord and Lady William Lamport

All the arrangements like food, entertainment, decorations, and favors had been decided. Barbara was right. Hiring an event planner had made the entire ordeal almost painless.

Liam's face softened slightly. "William and Nia are married," he read aloud.

He looked over at her. His eyes ran over every inch of her face. Then he leaned over and kissed her cheek, her nose, the corner of her lips.

"Nia, my precious wife."

She felt her heart leap at his soft words. Would she ever get used to hearing such sweet sentiments?

He ran his fingers over her bare arms, sending chills down her spine. He nibbled the side of her neck.

"I've been thinking," he murmured, "I can start a music label with you as my first artiste."

Nia's eyes widened. She had to look away for a moment to process the words. Try as hard as she might though she could still feel herself stiffen. Liam seemed to notice.

"Did I say something wrong?"

"What about my contract with Damon–"

"Forget Damon Deverre!" Liam ground out, slamming a fist on the bed.

Nia was so angry she jumped up and moved to the other side of the room. She needed to distance herself from Liam right now.

Liam watched Nia stalk across the room and didn't try to stop her. Why hadn't he followed his gut instinct not to say anything to her just yet? To instead gently steer her toward his plans for her.

His heart skipped a beat as he acknowledged his train of thought. *His* plans for *her*? That didn't sound right. Was his father correct? Was he trying to control her? And if so, why? And then it struck him. *Fear*. He was afraid of losing her, of losing his life with her.

In fact, that fear had manifested itself just that morning a little before he had gone down to fetch Nia a cup of coffee because period cramps had kept her in bed. Nia's period had been late by about four days, and he had begun to think she was pregnant. Then this morning it came.

The relief with which she relayed the news had annoyed him. As he had tramped down the stairs, he had considered why he was annoyed. It wasn't as though they didn't have time. Nia was only twenty-two. It struck him that he had hoped she was pregnant so that she would be consumed with motherhood and lose interest in Double D productions.

But acknowledging his fear didn't mean it wasn't legitimate.

"Why should I forget him?" Nia asked from across the room.

He looked up at her as she stood with her back to the window, framed by a halo of sunlight streaming through. He was struck for a moment by how captivating she was, even dressed as simply as she was now in tights, and a cardigan with her curly hair falling loosely around her shoulders. But when she folded her arms beneath her chest and glowered at him, it got his hackles up.

Why was she angry? Damon Deverre was a misogynist who aided and abetted in the objectification of women. Why did Liam need to justify his opposition to him? He refused to be placed in that position.

"I give up, Nia. Do whatever you want. We're leaving here tonight, by the way, so you need to get packed." With that, he sprang to his feet and left the room.

Chapter 15

ow could he be so loving and tender on the one hand and so hateful and disrespectful on another? Was he threatened by Damon? Could that be it?

Nia pondered these things as she shopped with her mother-in-law for the perfect dress for the reception. Truth be told her heart was no longer in the whole thing. It was difficult to look forward to a party at a time when she and her husband were at odds with each other.

Even though she had initially looked forward to returning to London to be alone with him, that feeling no longer held. She was very hurt by his childish behavior and for days after their return to the penthouse suite the tension between them was so thick you could cut it with a knife. This morning would make the third day he would coldly kiss her cheek and leave to go off to work and return home late in the evening when she was already asleep.

Now here she was shopping with Barbara who had come into the city to help her find a dress for the reception. Nia welcomed the distraction. Shopping still had the effect of calming and de-stressing her.

Fight number two and they'd been married just four weeks. Was this normal?

Nia discovered an exquisite champagne gold sequin and rhinestone dress. It was reminiscent of the era of the thirties in the way the fitted silhouette flared into a mermaid skirt that grazed the floor.

"I'm going to try this on," she told Barbara.

The fitting confirmed that the dress was perfect. Then, of course, Nia had to find the perfect shoes and accessories to go with the gown.

After they left the store with their purchases, Barbara suddenly addressed the invisible elephant in the room they had managed to avoid all day. She was straightforward and blunt.

"Don't you think it's about time you and my son make up?"

Nia glanced at her mother-in-law in surprise.

"How did you guess?"

Barbara gave her a wry look. "I'm old, Nia, not demented. You two left here acting cold with each other and days later you still look glum."

"I don't know what to do to make things right. He won't even talk to me."

"Go to him at his office. Tell him you want to resolve things."

Nia looked at Barbara in alarm. "Why me? He started it."

"Because it's your marriage too, my dear. Someone has to take the first step towards reconciliation. There's nothing wrong with you being the bigger person."

Nia took her sweet time walking to Liam's office after the elevator stopped at the floor. She'd never been there before, so when his secretary looked at her curiously, she almost bailed.

"Uh, Nia Lamport to see William Lamport IV."

The woman instantly smiled and said, "Mrs. Lamport, welcome to Lamport Holdings. Mr. Lamport is taking a call right now, but you can go right in."

Nia was trying to figure out how the woman knew who she was. But then she realized that their marriage was big news. It must have been talked about within the corridors of Lamport Holdings.

When Nia got to Liam's office, she took a deep breath then eased open the door. There was her husband with his back to her. He was speaking to someone on speaker phone as he stared out the windows. His sleeves were turned up to the elbow, and he was gesticulating as he spoke. Then he turned and saw her, and his words trailed off. Their eyes met.

"I'm going to have to call you back," Liam said to the person on the other end of the line. Without breaking eye contact, he ended the call. Then he walked around the large desk and came to stand a few feet in front of her.

He pushed his hands in his pockets. "I didn't know you were coming."

Nia realized he wasn't sure, despite her presence there now, if they were still fighting. She would have to hold out the olive branch. For a moment she resented it. Wasn't it enough she was there? Shouldn't he pull her into his arms now?

She closed the distance, reached out, and took his face in her hands.

"Let's not fight. I hate it when we fight."

He sighed, and his hand curled around her back as he drew her close.

"I'm sorry. So sorry." He leaned in and eagerly she received his kiss.

The weekend of the reception had arrived.

Nia had spoken to her father on the phone just that morning to get his flight details so that she could send a driver to collect him from the airport.

"Is Alessa coming with you?" she asked.

She had to ask. It seemed as though trouble was brewing between them. Alessa had recently called Nia and complained that she suspected her father was having an affair with his personal assistant. Last she had heard the P.A. had been let go at Alessa's insistence. Things had settled down a bit, but it seemed terrible to be married to a man you could not trust. Still, this was a record for her father. For the first time, his marriage had lasted for as long as seven years. She knew this was in part because Alessa was doing all the compromising. This did not seem fair.

"*Bien sur, ma chérie.* She's excited for you. Thinks it is so cool you eloped with my ex-wife's son." He snorted a laugh.

"Papa, please be civil."

"Nia, I am insulted. I would never be ungracious to my hosts."

Based on his promise, Nia relaxed her guard. It turned out to be a mistake to think her father could be anything but who he was.

Jacques Annuad had been born into privilege. He was the first son of wine producers in the South of France. He had been groomed to run the business one day, but that was not where Jacques' interest lay. He was attracted to the arts, film in particular. His father sent him to Paris to attend university and to major in business studies. That was the worst place he could have sent Jacques.

The temptations Paris offered were too much for him to resist. The city provided a veritable feast of cultural and artistic delights. Soon, unbeknownst to his father, Jacques changed his degree to film studies. By the time his courses were completed he had informed his parents that he would not be returning to run the family business but instead would be remaining in Paris to become a film director.

His father had been enraged and threatened to cut him off without a cent. His doting mother had intervened and offered up her second born, Jean-Paul, to be the one to take over the vineyard. His father appeased, Jacques had been allowed to continue his lifestyle. With the financial support of his family, Jacques had been able to launch his film-making career. Eventually, he gained a reputation as a brilliant film director and was able to support himself.

His mother, despite indulging his every whim since birth, was not always happy with his choice of wives. In fact, she seemed to have only liked one of them, the mother of Anaïs and Louis. She was a beautiful French ballerina who had died while in childbirth with their third child. The baby had died with his mother.

It was a tragedy from which Jacques had spent months trying to recover. He had eventually done so in the arms of a beautiful black songstress whom he met on a friend's yacht a year later. From Nikki's account, when Jacques had shown up at his parent's chateau with her so soon after his wife's death, *Madame* Annuad was not too happy. When she later found out about Nikki's dependency on drugs, her mother-in-law despised her all the more.

While Nia remembered her grandfather as being a reserved man, though pleasant, she remembered her grandmother as being very stiff and aloof. Nia would often catch the woman watching her with thinly veiled disapproval as if the child was somehow to blame for her mother's transgressions. Still, *Grandmére* Annuad found it impossible to refuse any request from her oldest son and accepted the responsibility of caring for his offspring when it was really his responsibility to keep them.

Due to such an upbringing, Jacques walked the earth with an air of entitlement. Nia was sure he felt the world revolved around him. He had never once acknowledged that any of his failed marriages were his fault. 'If only my wives had been more understanding,' he had once said to a reporter.

On the evening of Jacques arrival at Belfield Manor, he strutted into the house smelling of expensive cologne, with arms outstretched as though he was the long-awaited hero. Even in his early sixties Jacques was still very good looking and exuded charm. He folded Nia into a hug and kissed her.

"Nia, *ma chérie*. You are a sight for sore eyes."

He shook Liam's hand and clapped him on the shoulder. "Finally, I meet the young man who has stolen my daughter's heart."

Alessa stood to one side smiling shyly. She was a leggy Italian supermodel with long straight black hair, parted in the middle and framing a pretty face. Nia embraced her, and they kissed each other on both cheeks.

"Where's Alex?" Nia asked. She rarely saw her little brother, now six, and had been looking forward to spending time with him.

"Mama is watching him for us," Jacques declared. Nia frowned. Some things never changed. Jacques still enjoyed foisting off parenting duties on his mother.

She opened her mouth to speak to him about it, but something, or was it someone, had caught Jacques attention.

"Barbara," Jacques said on a low growl that made Nia cringe. He strode towards her mother-in-law with open arms, making it impossible for her to avoid his kisses on both cheeks without being rude.

That wasn't the crime, though. The crime was when he allowed his gaze to slowly run down her still beautiful and well-toned figure and muttered, "*Mon chéri*, you look absolutely stunning. Those curves. Mmm…how well I remember the feel of them."

Nia gasped. She felt Liam stiffen beside her. Her eyes flew to her father-in-law who had entered the room as Jacques addressed his wife. The way his nostrils flared and his back straightened made it obvious he was in no way amused by Jacques little trip down memory lane.

The bone-crushing grip in which Jacques' hand soon found itself was proof. Nia would swear, the only thing that kept her father from crying out and dropping to his knees was pride.

Would her father never learn?

Nia felt embarrassment wash over her. She glanced at Liam for assurance that he didn't lump her with her father, but she only saw annoyance in his eyes as he glared at Jacques.

When Nikki Carmichael and Thomas Wilson showed up an hour later, Jacques didn't miss the opportunity to attempt to flirt with his ex-wife. Nikki was quite disenchanted with Jacques, however, and gave him the brush off.

Neither Nikki's cool reception nor Lord Lamport's threatening glare prevented Jacques from making a remark at dinner about it being a historic moment to have three of his wives together. The company descended into uncomfortable silence. Nia felt like crawling under the table.

~*~*~*~

"Well, that was quite the disaster," Liam said as he shrugged out of his jacket.

Nia took a seat at the vanity table. While she took off her jewelry, she watched Liam in the mirror as he undressed.

"I felt in my gut that this would not go well, but you convinced me it would work." She placed her jewelry on the table and met Liam's eyes in the mirror as he squeezed her shoulder.

"I should have listened to you," he said.

"Yes, you should have. I hope you don't make that mistake again," she said as she picked up a make-up wipe and swiped it across her forehead.

Liam gave a short laugh. "Well, if tonight was this bad, what is tomorrow going to be like?"

Nia balled up the wipe and tossed it under the vanity table into the wastepaper basket. She removed another wipe from its package.

"I don't think things can get any worse than tonight. Perhaps, the worst is behind us." She smiled weakly and looked up hopefully. "Yes?"

"At least tomorrow we won't all be stuck at a table. It will be a cocktail reception and I can move away from anyone I find offensive."

"Do you find my father offensive?"

Liam realized he had to choose his words carefully. While he couldn't claim to be an admirer of Jacques Annuad, the obnoxious man was still Nia's father.

"There are some things he says that bother me. I find it hard to relate to his view of life and relationships. There are certain values that I hold dear that he doesn't share. That could be a problem, but I've resolved to accept him for who he is while we're together and pray for him."

To his relief, she smiled in understanding.

"You know for a long time I made excuses for him or made light of his actions, like when he didn't show up for my graduation from Julliard even though he promised he would. I also find some of his actions offensive, and I don't feel that I want to tolerate them anymore. But then I feel guilty like I'm disloyal."

"You are not. Loving someone doesn't mean we have to like their conduct or embrace it. There are some members of my family who, while I love them, I don't agree with their lifestyle."

"Do you try to change them?"

"No, I realize that doesn't work. That's the Holy Spirit's job, not mine. All I do is strive to live life honestly. In other words, be true to my values as I try not to be a hypocrite, nor be ashamed of who I am or who I aspire to be. I have at times faced ridicule for not participating in certain activities or for having an unpopular viewpoint on topics of the day. But I've accepted that I can't be both true to myself and be popular. I've got to choose the most honest way to live."

Liam was glad to be able to share these things with his new wife. He continued with a fresh boldness.

"Loving God first for me means honoring Him first whether others consider me loving or not. It means that by loving Him first, I can love others in the true sense of the word. Not in a superficial way or not in the way they perhaps interpret love either. But love them enough to tell them the truth even when a lie would be easier."

"Is that how you love me?"

He paused. "Why do you ask?"

"I think you've tried to be honest with me about your feelings even when a lie would have been easier. Is that your way of showing me love?"

He thought of this for a moment before he took a seat opposite her on the edge of the bed.

"I don't know any other way to love. Sometimes I think I may come over as harsh and judgmental and I'm sorry if I do. I want to love you in the First Corinthians 13 way. Though I may not always do that perfectly, I want you to know that's my benchmark."

"What does that verse say?"

"The critical verses for me say, love is patient, love is kind, it does not envy, it does not boast, it does not give up."

He paused, smiled and reached for his phone. "I should know it by heart, but I don't quite. So, let me find the exact words."

With a few swipes on the screen, he found what he wanted.

"Love does not dishonor others, it is not self-seeking, it is not easily angered, and it keeps no record of wrongs. Love does not delight in evil but rejoices with the truth. It always protects, always trusts, always hopes, and always perseveres."

He lowered the phone to his leg, raised his head and stared at Nia. Did he really love her this way? Love was not easily angered; it did not keep a record of wrongs. He was guilty of both of those things recently when he had allowed his anger to fester for days and not seek reconciliation.

It had been Nia, the one who wasn't a Christian, who had sought peace first. What did it say about him? It said that there were some aspects of his character that he still needed to work on. It challenged him to reevaluate his relationship with her in light of what he had just read.

Lord, help me to be the husband you created me to be. Help me to love Nia like this.

Was she aware of his failings? He pondered this as he watched her appear to absorb the words. Eventually, she sighed and said, "That's beautiful. Something for me to aspire to for sure."

When she met his eyes, it was without judgment, and he felt relieved.

Chapter 16

*I*t was so like a wedding reception Nia almost forgot that it was not.

In the beautiful champagne gold dress she wore and Liam in his dark suit, they did indeed look like a bride and groom. They moved as one, greeting the hundred-plus guests that ranged from their family and friends to some of the world's most influential people.

Her mother had helped her to put on her makeup and style her hair so that her long curls framed a halo around her face with one side pinned back in a way that made her look quite feminine and coquettish.

In true marriage tradition, she hadn't allowed Liam to see her until the night of the reception. She had spent the entire day at the spa with her mother, Barbara, Leiliana, and Alessa. When she stood at the top of the stairs that evening awaiting her husband to escort her to the bottom, she felt her chest swell with happiness at the awestruck look on his face when he spotted her.

He ascended the stairs in record time. When he reached her he whispered, "You look amazing."

She smiled shyly in response, but before she could reply they were asked by the photographer to pose for a picture, to which they obliged.

The front hall was crowded with elegantly dressed men and women. The men wore crisp formal suits and the women fabulous evening gowns in jewel inspired colors. They all clapped as the butler introduced the newly married couple and they slowly descended the stairs arm in arm.

Nia managed to keep her smile in place even though she felt as though her heart was a beating drum in her chest. She wasn't ordinarily nervous around crowds, but all these upper-class people staring at her made her feel as though she should rush back upstairs and check to make sure everything was still in place.

Liam must have sensed her tension because he whispered out the side of his mouth, "You're going to be great. I'm right here, and I'm not going to leave your side."

Nia felt her tension drain away. She might not have the approval of all these people, but she did have the love of the wonderful man beside her. She met her mother's eyes and the love and pride that she saw there made her relax all the way.

The event planner was to be commended. The rooms were exquisitely decorated with fresh flowers. The hors d'oeuvres were excellent. Based on the laughter and flowing conversation everyone seemed to be enjoying themselves. Waiters wove in and out among the well-heeled guests with trays of crab salad canapés, gravlax with mustard-dill sauce, Swedish meatballs with gravy, and chicken liver pâté with bourbon and cranberry gelée; and bearing crystal champagne flutes of Moët & Chandon.

A string quartet played classical music on the terrace. It was a perfect accompaniment to the summer evening breeze as it wafted through the open doors. Nia felt herself swaying to the music.

"Steel yourself, the speeches are coming," Liam whispered in her ear as his father stepped up to the podium in front of the quartet holding a champagne glass and a pewter spoon.

The music stopped, and there was the sound of the tinkling of a glass struck gently with a spoon to get attention. A quiet settled over the crowd as all eyes swiveled to the front. Nia felt nervous excitement at what was about to happen. She still was not absolutely sure how Liam's father felt about her but now would be the moment of reckoning. She had never found him to be an insincere person and was certain that his comments would be heartfelt--for good or bad.

Liam squeezed her hand as Lord Lamport began to speak and she knew he was as nervous as she was.

"Liam and Nia, you are now a married couple. We all know the official deed was done a few weeks ago, but this is the first opportunity for us, your family, and friends to gather in one place and congratulate you."

He looked directly into Nia's eyes as he spoke the next words.

"Nia, I hope you feel the outpouring of love and support for both of you that is in this room today. The two of you are surrounded by people who have been waiting for this day for a long time."

There was a ripple of laughter and noises of agreement. Lord Lamport continued.

"We never knew who Liam would marry. We never dared consider making that choice for him. All we prayed for was that he would find the right woman. A woman God chose for him to spend the rest of his life with. Liam has determined that you are such a woman. Proverbs 18:22 says he who finds a wife finds a good thing and obtains favor from the Lord. While finding a good thing is important, even more important is keeping it good. What I'm saying is that love, as beautiful and amazing as it is, has to be nourished in order to grow and thrive."

He looked over at his wife and held out a hand to her. When she reached his side, he kissed the back of her hand.

"Twenty-five years ago I made a commitment to this woman to love and cherish her for as long as we both should live. I've tried to keep that vow. I may not have done it perfectly. I'm sure she would tell you I haven't."

Laugher filled the room. Lord Lamport smiled and then grew serious once more.

"But she would also tell you that I have spent all this time trying to be the best husband I can. It meant learning from my mistakes. It meant saying sorry when I was to blame. It meant saying sorry when she was to blame. The point is that love is a constant act of asking for forgiveness and granting forgiveness."

He turned to Liam and Nia.

"Do not allow unforgiveness, anger, or petty arguments to drive you two apart. Remember that perfection only exists in heaven. Do not demand it from each other. Love each other as Jesus loves us. Love always protects, always hopes, always perseveres."

Lord Lamport came up to her and kissed her cheek. When he said, "Welcome to the family," Nia felt her throat constrict. She blinked back tears as her father-in-law moved away to embrace his son.

It was hard to top that toast, so when her father stepped to the podium to speak, Nia held her breath. Her father could be charming, but he also could be provocative. She said a prayer that on this occasion he would choose the former and not embarrass her in front of Liam's family.

"I pulled the short straw, so now I have to follow that act. Go figure."

There were quite a few chuckles. Nia smiled nervously. Not a bad start.

"Okay, so here's what I propose. I wish them the best, we all toast them, and then I go sit down. Yeah? No. Got you didn't I, Nia? I know she's over there saying, 'Papa, don't embarrass me.' I promise I won't – not too badly anyway."

When he laughed, Nia felt her palms begin to sweat.

"Seriously, though. All jokes aside, this is my little girl. The moment I saw her I just fell in love. She is like a work of art. So beautiful. She has made me so proud over the years. She's bright, passionate, headstrong and feisty too. So, Liam, uh, I agree with your father. You need to say sorry when you're wrong *and* when she's wrong."

He laughed along with the guests. "An asbestos suit, I'd keep handy."

Then he got serious. "But she's got a big heart too. She's sweet and loving and kind. Honestly, it's not easy to hand your daughter over to another man. But since I don't have a choice here, I'm glad it's you, Liam. From what I've observed so far you're the sort of man a father would feel safe entrusting with his daughter. So, please join me in a toast to my daughter, Nia, and my new son-in-law, Liam. May this be a happily-ever-after tale."

Nia looked at Liam. She had never heard such words coming from her father before and for the first time in a long time she began to feel that he did love her in his own way. When Jacques embraced her, she sank into her arms.

"Thank you, Papa," she whispered.

"I didn't do too badly then?" he asked low with a twinkle in his eyes.

"You did great."

A moment later she heard the tinkling of a glass again and looked up in surprise to see that Thomas Wilson now stood at the front of the room. He looked so tall and handsome. Funny how she once found him imposing and annoying. Now she regarded him with new eyes. He was a big-hearted man, who loved her mother fiercely. He was one of the tallest, buffest men in the room and looked as fierce as any warrior, but he also had kind hazel eyes.

She looked around and noticed the glances of female appreciation on several faces. She knew, though, that Thomas only had eyes for one woman, the petite black woman with the flowing tresses at the front who still looked like she was in her thirties even though she was forty-six.

"I couldn't let this night end without making a toast on Nia's behalf. I only entered her life six years ago, but over that time I have watched her grow from a typical rebellious teenage girl to a sensible woman with strong ambitions and clear direction. I proudly witnessed her graduate from Julliard as valedictorian, and I am proud today to celebrate her marriage to a young man I both admire and respect. Nia and Liam, I wish you the best."

He took a breath and continued in a strong and loving voice.

"As Lord Lamport put it so eloquently, love has to be nurtured. I would also like to add that love is a decision. It is the choices we make every day to put the other person ahead of ourselves that make or break a marriage. I pray that you two will choose each day to put the needs of the other above your own. A toast to my beautiful daughter and my new son."

Nia didn't even realize she was crying until Liam wiped a tear from her eye with the back of his thumb. She had not always been loving to Thomas, but through it all, he had remained loving to her.

After the toasts, the reception resumed with dancing. Matthew shyly invited Nia to dance with him, and she accepted. Soon her dance card was full. She danced with her father, Thomas, Liam's brother, Benjamin, then Reinhardt and Sam and two other guests. When another guest tried to gain a dance, Liam tapped him on the shoulder and declared that he would like to have his wife back.

Holding her in his arms as they swayed to the music, he kissed her on the corner of her mouth and said in her ear, "Instead of promising not to leave your side, I should have made you promise not to leave mine. You have really been working the room tonight."

She chuckled. "I guess I feel really relaxed. People have been so warm and kind. I feel accepted and welcomed."

She didn't mention that this didn't extend to all people. Heidi Wolffe, in particular, kept glowering at her whenever Liam was out of sight. She had seen Heidi dancing with Liam while she was dancing with Benjamin. She didn't like the way the woman was clinging to him. In the intervening years since she'd last seen her, Heidi had grown even more attractive. Towering, shapely, and with endless blonde hair she was quite the head turner.

Nia resolved not to let Heidi faze her, however. This was her night. It was she who was wearing Liam's ring, not Heidi, and she had nothing to fear.

In fact, she was so happy she felt like singing. It occurred to her that she *could* sing. It was her night after all.

"I'll be right back," she whispered to Liam. Without awaiting a response, she made her way over to the quartet. Following a brief exchange with them, she took the microphone in her hand.

"Good evening everyone."

Heads turned in her direction. She smiled. "I want to dedicate this song to my husband. It's called *No One*."

It was the first time she was singing along with a string quartet, but it did not alter the effect of the words. As they poured from her mouth, she met and held Liam's gaze, and he became the only one in the room. Every word was meant for him. She promised to be with him through the days and nights. She vowed that though people might try to divide them no one would come between them. She hoped he understood she meant the Heidi Wolffes of this world and any other interlopers or naysayers.

Liam stared into his wife's beautiful eyes. His heart warmed at the words of her song. She was making a promise to him that no one would come between them. Not the Damon Deverres of this world or anyone else. He humbly accepted her commitment, and when she was finished, he felt an overwhelming desire to serenade her too.

As the applause rang out for Nia, he signaled to Sam.

"Go fetch me your guitar," he whispered. He knew without a shadow of a doubt that Sam had his guitar. He went everywhere with the thing.

Sam disappeared, and Liam went over to stand beside Nia and took the mic from her hand.

"I have not sung or written music for the last four years, but a month ago something happened. I was reunited with Nia, and it seemed as though all I wanted to do was sing and write poetry."

A tittering of laughter rippled through the audience. Liam threw Nia a wink.

"I finished this song just last night. I wondered about the right time to sing it to her. There will never be a night more perfect than tonight."

There was nodding of heads and clapping of hands.

"What I find remarkable is that the song she just sang echoes the sentiment of the song I wrote. If that's not divine, I don't know what is. To summarize, this song, which I call *Forever Yours*, describes how things will change throughout life. We'll grow old, we'll get busy, we'll have conflicts, disagreements, but my prayer is that through all that our love for each other will grow. I believe that's what God intended. I am humbled beyond words that He has chosen me to be the man to love and cherish her forever. So here we go."

Just then, Sam pushed through the guests and held out the guitar. Liam positioned it and began to play. Then he serenaded Nia as she had just serenaded him. The way she watched him, with fat tears spilling down her face, made it all he could do not to stop singing and start blubbering too.

At the end, one fisted arm across his chest, head bowed, he genuflected in a gesture of deep respect for his wife. Standing, he wrapped his arms around her and kissed her tear-stained face.

"That's the most beautiful song I've ever heard." She sniffed, and a tremor ran through her. "I love it when you sing. I wish you'd do it more often. You seem so happy when you sing. It looks like you are in ecstasy."

He smiled and crushed her to him once more. "*You* make me feel ecstatic. Come on, let's bid our guests goodnight and retire for the evening."

Chapter 17

*I*t didn't take long for Nia to realize that putting Damon Deverre on hold while she pursued her own interests had not been without consequences. She had taken Damon's interest for granted. Now, she was paying the price for her naiveté.

Damon had a reputation as a ruthless businessman. Everyone knew that "El Honcho", as he was known, was not patient and that he didn't suffer fools gladly, if at all. She hadn't known at the time that it had been a departure from business as usual when he had agreed to wait until she completed her degree at Julliard to accept his contract; but when she had further delayed things to run off to Barbados with Liam Lamport, that had been the last straw.

The moment she messaged him with the news that she and Liam had gotten married his pursuit had stopped – stone cold. He simply had not responded. At the time she didn't care. She was caught up in the euphoria of being married to Liam. That was swiftly followed by the excitement and anxiety of a new life with him. She had assumed that plans for her career would fall into place when she was ready.

Weeks after returning to London after the wedding reception she was growing anxious as she sent message after message to Damon Deverre and he continued to ignore each and every one as though she didn't exist. She felt like tearing out her hair in frustration. What made it worse was that Liam was completely unsympathetic.

She remembered the first time she had messaged Damon and after a couple of days had received no response. She had complained to Liam that night at dinner that it seemed as though Damon was ignoring her.

"He was so confident I would be a star. Now he's not responding to me. It's depressing."

Liam chewed on a forkful of pasta. "What do you care about Damon Deverre? I told you before I can arrange for you to record your songs. You don't need Deverre or any other record producer for that matter."

"Are you going to acquire a recording studio for me too? Are you going to market and promote me?"

Liam shrugged. "Sure, if that's what you want. Money can buy anything."

She shook her head. "That's not what I want. I want to have the satisfaction of making it on my own. I don't want my husband buying a recording studio for me. I want to know that the person promoting me did it because they thought I was that good and were willing to take a chance. Nepotism isn't a motivator for me."

She saw hurt reflected in Liam's eyes a moment before he wiped the corners of his mouth with his napkin and threw it down beside his plate in anger.

"You seem to take it for granted that I'm willing to give you what you need. I do it because I believe in you, Nia."

She hadn't intended to offend Liam. She just wanted him to understand her position. She would never be taken seriously as an artist if it was seen as vanity recording. She reached across the table and covered his hand with her own.

"Don't get defensive. I didn't mean it like that. I'm just saying that it's different when someone who has everything to lose invests in you."

"You're saying I have nothing to lose? You think spending millions to promote you is a small thing."

"Liam, you are looking at this the wrong way. This isn't about you at all. It's about me. If I want to be taken seriously in this business, it can't be because my husband helped me to get my record out there. Look, Liam, I'm not saying that I don't appreciate your gesture, it means a lot to me to know you're trying to make things better. It's just not the way I want to go about this."

After a couple of weeks had passed and there was more of the same, Nia made the decision to pursue other options. Damon Deverre was not the only producer out there. While at Juilliard there had been a few others who had heard her sing and had shown interest. The trouble was that she had not kept any of their cards. In her naiveté, or was it arrogance, she had assumed that Damon would always be waiting.

The next morning after Liam left for work Nia sat down in front of the computer and took a deep breath. It was time to go searching for all those producers and jog their memories of who Nia Carmichael was.

How was it possible to be married and still feel as though he wasn't settled?

Liam pondered the question as he sat in a planning meeting with contractors and architects and various other players at a project management meeting for a Lamport Holdings business complex. He tried to solve work-related matters with one part of his brain while the other part struggled to solve what was wrong with his marriage.

Nia just did not seem happy. Perhaps it was the change in culture; the fact that she was living in a new city among people she didn't know with a way of life different to her own. While it was true that Nia was bright and adventurous and few things fazed her, it was also true that she was a rebel and an iconoclast. She might not be very eager to be immersed in a life that called on her to tame her wild spirit and conform to certain social mores.

This cultural shift coupled with being far away from all her friends and family must be exacerbating things. Maybe she felt isolated. At this point, all her friends were his friends. Matthew, Reinhardt, and Sam had dropped by once or twice, but apart from them, Nia hadn't taken to anyone else.

Heidi Wolffe was the closest thing he had to a female friend these days, and Nia seemed inherently suspicious of her. Whenever Heidi invited them out, Nia found reasons to decline. He couldn't understand what Nia had against Heidi. Admittedly, Heidi had been romantically interested in him when they were young, but she had gotten over her crush. She was a confident woman, pursuing a career in banking and engaged to the son of a brewery giant.

He had questioned Nia about all those things, but she always responded that she was fine. She didn't miss anyone from home, she was used to being on her own, and she had been raised in different cultures and was adaptable.

But something was eating at her. Not even shopping seemed to be bringing her any comfort these days. All she could think about was getting a recording contract. All she wanted to do was talk about Damon Deverre and how he was not responding to her messages. And now this past week every time Liam came home, she spent the whole evening talking about calling producers, leaving messages, and how they were either not returning her calls or the calls she did receive were not the types of deals Damon had offered her.

The pen Liam was tapping against his leg stilled. How could he have been so blind? That was it. Nia was frustrated and depressed because the one thing she wanted more than anything was out of her reach. He remembered when he had first met her she had declared she was going to be a star. She had said it with such conviction he had believed her. This was Nia's dream, and this was why she was wilting.

He stood abruptly. Conversation stopped, and the others in the room looked up at him curiously.

"I've got to go. I'm sorry. There's an urgent matter I have to deal with. You lot carry on the meeting. Harry will fill me in later."

He hurriedly made his way over to their penthouse. As soon as he entered the apartment, he knew something was up. Nia was packing.

He was stunned. "What are you doing?" he blurted.

She looked up at him with a mixture of surprise, determination, and excitement. "I've just decided what I'm going to do. If Mohammed will not go to the mountain, the mountain must go to Mohammed."

"What are you talking about?" He watched her snatch some things off the table and toss them into her open suitcase.

"I'm going to see Damon."

Liam felt as though a weight had just crashed into his chest making it difficult to breathe. He found a chair and sat.

He wanted to explode with outrage, but he knew that was not going to be helpful. He considered the situation before him as though it was a crisis event that occurred in business. He examined it, analyzed it and selected the most effective response needed at this time to diffuse the situation.

Finally, he cleared his throat. "When will you be back?"

Her back was to him, but she turned and stared at him. "What did you say?"

"When will you be back?" he repeated, forcing his tone to be casual as though she had told him she was going to the theatre with friends instead of traveling miles away to meet up with a man he despised.

Her face lit up. She came over and threw her arms around his neck.

"Thank you."

"For what?"

"For understanding. I was so sure you'd be angry and not want me to go."

He *was* angry, and he *didn't* want her to go, but what good would it do to say so? He chose to accept her gratitude graciously and allow peace to reign for whatever moments they had together before she took off. This was his Nia, impulsive, passionate, headstrong, and he loved her, even at times like these when she infuriated him.

"I only have one request," he said.

"What's that?"

"That you return home in time to accompany me to the upcoming charity ball at Windsor castle."

"That's easy."

~*~*~*~

But what if the mountain went to Mohammed and Mohammed still refused to see the mountain.

Whoever had come up with that saying apparently hadn't thought it through.

This crossed Nia's mind as she faced off with the receptionist in the lobby of Double D Productions in her attempt to gain entrance to see his highness himself.

After she had made the decision to fly to L.A. to see Damon, she had called Bianca and begged her to find out what Damon's schedule was like. She had reasoned that it wouldn't make sense to turn up at his office to find he was in another part of the world.

Here she was, very close to his business inner sanctum, and still, admission was being denied. Not that it hadn't occurred to her that this would happen. The eight-hour flight from London to L.A. had given her plenty of time to consider that simply showing up would not guarantee entry. She had formulated several backup plans, including sneaking into the elevator and barging into his office, but now faced with the reality of armed guards posted strategically in the lobby, she wasn't sure it would work so well.

Come to think of it, Damon was always surrounded by armed guards. Probably had something to do with him having created many enemies over the years. She couldn't think why.

"I understand you are saying that you do not have an appointment? Is that correct?" the woman asked as she eyed Nia from behind a glossy white desk.

Nia smiled brightly. "I don't need an appointment. Damon and I go way back."

The woman didn't miss a beat. Nia was guessing she heard versions of that claim every day. "I am afraid Mr. Deverre is in a meeting right now."

"I can wait."

"That is not possible, ma'am. Mr. Deverre frowns on people lingering around in his waiting area without an appointment. I would suggest that you call his assistant and make one."

Nia thought wistfully of the times she took for granted when she would call Damon and he answered on the first ring. Now here she was and was being treated like some pushy wannabe trying to catch a break.

"If you would just call him and tell him I'm here I'm sure he will see me."

"Like I said, he's in a meeting."

"Well, ask his assistant to do it. It's urgent."

The woman raised a perfectly waxed brow. "May I ask, what is the nature of your business with Mr. Deverre?"

"Mr. Deverre has offered me a recording contract, and I have come to accept his offer."

There. She hadn't wanted to say it, but the woman had forced her into a corner. To Nia's chagrin, the woman's expression didn't even budge an inch.

Still, she asked Nia to have a seat and spoke to someone on the phone in low tones. After a few minutes, she called Nia back.

"Mr. Deverre's assistant says that he's unable to fit you in and she asks that you call her so she can set up an appointment."

"An appointment!" Nia shouted.

The woman' eyes widened in disapproval. Nia lowered her voice.

"Listen, do you know how far I've traveled to see him. I just came straight from London. I'm only booked into my hotel for one night. My return flight leaves tomorrow morning. I have to see him today. Can't she interrupt his meeting? I promise it won't take long."

"Interrupt Mr. Deverre's meeting, ma'am?"

"Did you hear me? It's critical I speak with him today! So tell his assistant that I'm not leaving until he gives me ten minutes of his time."

Nia returned to the leather couch and sunk into it. She heard the receptionist on the phone again. During the conversation, two men and one woman entered the building.

Nia watched them speak to the receptionist. Apparently, *they* had an appointment because in no time, they were signing in and being whisked away.

She contemplated racing to the elevators behind them but again dismissed the idea as completely harebrained.

Eventually, the receptionist beckoned Nia over. "Mr. Deverre's assistant, Cassandra Dear, will see you."

Nia was still seething when she got off the floor. She pushed through the double glass doors and was met with a surprise. The woman who greeted her had platinum blond hair pulled up into a high ponytail, jet black eyebrows, and black eye makeup. She didn't wear any jewelry and wore a micro floral black chiffon dress with Doc Martins. She was holding a tablet and typing something on it when Nia walked in. This was Cassandra Dear.

Somehow she had expected someone dressed in a black power suit. She liked her style. A throwback to the grunge era for sure, but the woman was clearly confident enough to wear what she wanted and not conform to some image of what a personal assistant for a high-level businessman should look like.

Nia began to speak but was immediately silenced by Cassandra Dear's index finger.

"No. That is unacceptable. Damon is not going to agree to that. He is traveling in two weeks so I would suggest you set up an appointment with him as soon as possible to discuss this issue. I've got a half an hour opening next Thursday at 4:00 p.m. That's the best I can do for you."

Nia was about to ask her what she was talking about when she realized that the woman had a Bluetooth device attached to her ear and was speaking to someone on the phone.

She gestured to Nia to sit as she continued to speak, walking around while tapping and swiping her tablet.

Nia glanced around the office. It was decorated with modern white and chrome furniture. White walls were littered with photos of Damon and all sorts of people. She stood and went up to one with him posing with one of the football teams. She remembered that he had his fingers in many pies and owned a sports team.

Despite herself, Nia smiled. It was hard not to admire someone who had begun life in abject poverty and had managed to reach the pinnacles of the entertainment industry. It was easy for Liam to dismiss him. Liam had led a privileged life from the moment of his birth. Damon was the opposite, and yet he had made it.

Not that she didn't have great admiration for Liam. He wasn't the spoiled rich boy he could so easily have become. He worked hard and gave of himself to others. It was just that she had difficulty seeing Damon in the light that Liam did.

"Miss Carmichael."

Nia was about to correct her when she recalled that was the name she had given the receptionist.

"You wish to see Mr. Deverre about a recording contract I'm told."

Nia nodded. "Yes, you see, Mr. Deverre offered me–"

"Do you have it?"

"Pardon me?"

"Do you have the contract with you?"

"Oh, no. It was never in writing. It was just a promise he made to me."

"Right. Miss Carmichael, you're a pretty girl. Mr. Deverre may have said something to you in the heat of the moment that you somehow misconstrued to be an offer of a recording contract. Such, uh, misunderstandings have been known to happen."

Nia wasn't so dumb that she couldn't read between the lines. Cassandra Dear thought she had been one of Damon's floozies who he had promised the moon and the stars to get her into bed and while he'd grown bored and moved on, she still believed the fairy tale.

"It wasn't like that at all!" she denied vehemently. "There is nothing going on between Damon and me. In fact, I'm a married woman."

Cassandra's eyes drifted down to Nia's ring. Her expression softened a bit. "I see."

"Please. I've traveled a long way to see him. I'm sure he's interested in seeing me. If you'll just tell him I'm here."

She cut her short. "He knows you're here."

"Oh."

Gently she said, "And he says he can't see you right now."

"When you say right now…"

"He says to set up an appointment for three months from now."

"What!"

"Yes."

"That…" Nia grabbed her things. "You know what? Damon Deverre can go straight to hell. Tell him that for me. I don't need him or his stupid contract. Furthermore, I *will* become a star, and when he comes crawling to me begging me to come over to this company, I will remind him of how he treated me this day. Good bye!"

Chapter 18

The annual charity gala hosted by the Duke and Duchess of Cambridge was considered to be one of the premier events on the London social calendar. The Lamports always supported the ball by purchasing at least one hundred tickets for distribution among family, friends and managerial staff of the company and its United Kingdom subsidiaries.

Liam observed his wife as she glided around the ballroom with him, interacting with and charming everyone she met. He was struck by three things. First, how resplendent Nia looked in a red full-length gown that showcased her beautiful figure and contrasted delightfully with the diamond and blueberry tanzanite gems around her throat and ears. Second, the distinctive quality Nia had that dazzled and drew people to her; a certain *je ne sais quoi* as the French would say. Third, the fact that unless one looked very close and very hard there was no trace of the tremendous disappointment and blow her pride had suffered when Damon Deverre had refused to meet with her.

Liam recalled how she had returned home to him two days ago, completely enraged but also extremely hurt by Deverre's treatment. He had done his best to comfort her but had felt a pang of guilt in doing so because things had turned out exactly as he had hoped they would.

Perhaps in the coming weeks, Nia would come to reconsider his offer to help launch her career. Unlike her, he couldn't pursue his dream. His birthright and sense of responsibility weighed heavily on his shoulders. He had schooled his thoughts and desires to accept his future role as the head of Lamport Holdings. In the meantime, he would be content to live vicariously through Nia by helping her achieve all she was meant to be in this world.

Nia stared at her reflection in the illuminated vanity mirror as she ran a hand down her neck. She didn't feel quite herself, and she knew why. Even though two days had passed since her return from Los Angeles, she still felt humiliated, hurt and angry.

Her hand trailed down to the necklace Liam had given her. It was undeniably beautiful, and she knew it was a peace offering, but she couldn't help feeling resentment towards him right now. Even though he tried to conceal it, she knew he was glad Damon had not met with her. In all fairness to him, though, he had never made any pretense about his feelings for Damon and all he stood for. It just would have been nice if he was genuinely sympathetic to her plight instead of faking.

As she exited the bathroom, she decided to find Liam and tell him she was ready to go home. The formal event was over, and dancing was taking place. She was not in the mood for any of that. In fact, the only reason she had attended the gala at all was that she had promised Liam she would.

Nia scanned the area where she had left him earlier. He wasn't there. As she began to move past the dance floor, she spotted someone who looked like Liam leading a woman in the waltz. She stopped and stared. She blinked twice, but still, Liam was dancing with Heidi Wolffe. She resolutely made her way over to them, jostling dancing couples who were obstacles in her attempt to reach the blond couple ahead.

As she neared, Heidi looked up and Nia saw triumph spark in her eyes before it was veiled. Nia grabbed Liam's arm and tugged him away. He could have resisted she reflected afterward, but he probably wanted to save her the humiliation. Still, he was far from pleased. The moment there was some distance between them and Heidi he stopped and jerked his arm away.

"What is the matter with you? Are you trying to cause a scene?" he asked in a furious whisper.

"Why were you dancing with her as soon as I turned my back?"

"Turned your back! That's a rather offensive statement particularly coming from a woman who left me not too long ago to go meet with a man whom I'm convinced has a romantic interest in her."

Nia turned and stalked away to avoid creating the scene Liam had just accused her of wanting to cause. She kept walking and eventually found herself alone in the gardens of the castle.

She felt hurt and betrayed. Did Liam not see what Heidi was doing or was he just pretending not to know? Like her father had cheated on so many women and told so many lies over the years, was this what he was doing? Was she being taken for a ride?

She was so lost in her own thoughts she didn't realize she was no longer alone until she felt a hand on her arm. She startled and turned her head to stare into the insipid gaze of a viscount she'd been introduced to earlier in the evening.

"Sorry to scare you, my dear. But I came for a smoke and saw you out here all alone. Are you okay?"

Nia gave him the once over. He was holding one of those e-cigarettes in his hand. He was young and not bad looking in a milksop sort of way. She turned away from him.

"I'm great," she said monotonously.

"You're William's wife."

"And you are?"

"Viscount Halifax. We were introduced earlier this evening."

Nia wanted to be alone. She didn't want to make small talk with this man who was watching her in a wolfish way she didn't appreciate. She remembered also being introduced to his wife who, based on the size of her baby bump, was expecting any day now.

"You're very beautiful," he murmured, his gaze skimming her body. "Very exotic looking."

Nia wanted to roll her eyes. The man was acting as though she was some rare bird. Had he never seen a light-skinned black woman before?

"I think I've had enough of the outdoors," she said. "If you'll excuse me…"

She tried to move past him, but he stepped into her path. Quickly glancing around, Nia realized she was fairly isolated in the garden. She was suddenly conscious of her vulnerable position. This man was big, not as tall as Liam, but broader.

"Is there something I can help you with?" she asked frostily, hoping her tone would discourage him.

He grinned. "As a matter of fact, there is. I saw the way you looked at me when we were introduced. I want you to know that I'm also interested."

Nia stepped back in shock. What was this man talking about? Yes, she remembered smiling at him. She had been charming to everyone, wanting to create a good impression. Had she laid it on too thick? Even so, this was inappropriate. Whatever he might have thought, he was married and so was she.

"Listen, you are mistaken. I'm happily married."

"Are you? I witnessed the exchange between Lamport and yourself before you came out here. It looks like all may not be well in paradise."

He ran his hand down her arm. She jerked away.

"Hey, don't touch me!" she exclaimed.

But he continued unabated.

"You look as though you were created just to pleasure a man. If I had a wife like you, I'd spend all day in bed. But I remember

Lamport from school days." He gave a snort of degrading laughter. "The man wore a purity ring for heaven's sake. Maybe he has no idea how to satisfy a red-blooded woman like you."

He pocketed his e-cigarette and closing the distance between them grabbed her by both arms and hauled her to him. Nia felt anger and effrontery blaze through her. She felt violated by his very words never mind his touch. When he tried to kiss her, her response was instinct coupled with rage. She brought her leg up between his and landed a blow that sent the man on his knees and howling with such pain that it brought several people running to see what was happening.

Among them was Liam who perhaps had been on his way to find her given that he was among the first to arrive. He looked from her to the man on his knees holding his private parts and moaning incoherently.

She awaited his reaction and felt relief when he seemed to assess the situation correctly and asked, "Are you okay?"

She nodded.

"What happened?"

"He tried to assault me."

Halifax looked up at them through watery eyes. He seemed to have recovered sufficiently to point a shaky hand at Nia.

"You lying little b…"

She never knew what name Halifax would have called her because in the next moment Liam landed a fist to his mouth. He stumbled back and fell into the bushes. A shocked murmur rushed through the small group of witnesses.

Liam stood over Viscount Halifax.

"How dare you touch my wife!" he said.

The offending man's pregnant wife appeared and looked like she was about to give birth then and there. Nia felt humiliated at suddenly being the focus of such unwelcome attention.

She felt someone at her shoulder and turned to find Heidi Wolffe standing there, her face covered in disapproval.

"What an embarrassment you are to poor Liam. You don't belong here," she whispered. She took Nia's arm, "Why you don't you go back to America."

It was likely Heidi had misjudged Nia. Perhaps she expected her to dissolve into tears or maybe she had hoped that Nia would react badly and disgrace herself further. If so, she would have been right although it would come with a hefty price.

Nia knocked away Heidi's hand, took a good look at her, and then punched her straight in the eye.

When she felt someone take her by the arm, she turned on them expecting it was Liam but found herself staring straight into a familiar pair of amused dark brown eyes. Her mouth dropped open. Forgetting Heidi, she blurted the words, "Damon! What are you doing here?"

The ride home with Liam seemed to go excruciatingly slow. Nia and Liam entered the house in silence, ascended the stairs in silence, got ready for bed in silence, and lay in the dark in silence.

When she couldn't take it anymore, Nia said, "Are you going to just lie there like a lump of coal without saying anything?"

More silence. And finally, "What do you want me to say?"

"You didn't ask me what happened."

Silence descended again like a cloud.

"Are you speaking about with Viscount Halifax or with Heidi or with Deverre?"

"All three."

"Tell me then."

She sat up and looked down at him where he lay.

"Maybe you should sit up, so I feel as though I'm conversing with a living person and not a corpse."

After a pause, he moved to a seated position beside her. She couldn't make out his features in the semidarkness, but certainly could tell by the way he kept to his side of the bed, arms folded across his chest that he was brimming with anger.

Nia felt like screaming in frustration that she should have to defend herself but refused to give in to the pointless emotion. She needed to suck it up and deal with this head-on.

Taking a deep breath, she began.

"After our confrontation when I separated you and Heidi, I went to the garden to clear my head. I was alone for some time before I realized I was no longer alone. Viscount Halifax appeared. I immediately felt uneasy the way he was watching me. I felt like prey. We exchanged a few words, and I made to leave. Then he told me I looked like I was created to give a man sexual pleasure and he grabbed me and tried to kiss me."

She heard Liam's sharp intake of breath. She glanced at him across her shoulder and could see by the way his chest rose and fell rapidly that his anger had increased exponentially. This time it was clearly directed towards Viscount Halifax. She couldn't help the way her hope leaped at that. Surely it meant that he didn't blame her for what transpired that night, and that he was in her corner and once more her defender. But would his outrage remain when they got to the subject of Heidi or Damon?

"What happened next?" Liam asked.

"It was at that point I kneed him in the groin."

"He deserved it, sick bastard."

"Do the two of you have a history? He alluded to going to school with you, and he ridiculed you for your stance on sexual purity."

"Halifax has never been a friend of mine. Let's just say we clashed more than once at Eton over his bullying others he perceived as weaker than himself. We also came to high words over remarks he made about members of the opposite sex. I often called him out for many of the crass jokes he made and asked if he would want to have his mother and sister discussed in those terms. He and I actually came to blows once, and he got the worst of it. He has had it in for me since then. When I started wearing the purity ring, it became a source of endless humor for him. Unfortunately for him his jokes never caught on the way he hoped and often my comebacks ended up making *him* the laughing stock. I think his attack on you tonight was his way of getting back at me."

"After all these years?"

"It was just four years ago really. Some people can hold on to a grudge well into eternity never mind four years."

Liam's tone had now softened. Encouraged, Nia scooted closer to him and pressed her palm to his bare arm, noticing how the muscles flexed beneath her touch. She felt her body sway towards his. He turned his head and stared into her eyes.

"What about Heidi? Why did you hit her?" he asked.

Nia took a deep breath. Would Liam believe her? He seemed to be taken in by Heidi's false charm. Well, it was time for him to face the truth about his friend.

"After you hit Halifax, she came up beside me and told me that I was an embarrassment to you. Then she took my arm and told me I should leave and return to America."

Liam looked at her in shock. "She told you what?"

She swallowed. "She's not what you think she is, Liam. I keep telling you she's not a nice person."

He was silent for a while. "She had no right to say that to you. I'm going to speak to her."

Relief washed over her that he had unquestioningly accepted her explanation.

"I know I shouldn't have done it, but I was so angry and tired of being abused."

"Remind me never to make you mad," he observed dryly.

"You make me mad all the time."

He laughed a little, and then grew quiet. "What about Deverre? Did you invite him to the gala?"

"Of course not! I didn't even know he was in London."

"I'm quite sure he wasn't at the gala by chance."

Nia perked up. Was it possible Damon had come just to see her? She thought back to the gala. He had asked her to have dinner with him tomorrow night so they could talk. Before she could even respond, Liam had returned to her side, and considering how he seethed with anger she was sure he was about to wage war on Damon. To prevent a confrontation she had immediately told Liam she wanted to leave. With one threatening look at Damon, he had taken her hand and they had left.

"You think he came because he knew I would be there?" she asked excitedly.

She felt Liam's body tense. "I wouldn't presume to know what goes through Damon Deverre's mind."

"He asked me to have dinner with him tomorrow."

Liam didn't even speak, but his nostril's flared.

"It's just business, Liam."

"And you're still interested in conducting business with him after the way he treated you?"

"I'll at least hear him out."

"Fine. I'll accompany you to meet with him. We'll discuss what he's planning."

"But you're going on a business trip tomorrow, aren't you?"

"I'll postpone the trip."

"Why does that sound like you don't trust me to make a decision on my own?"

"I'm sorry if it came over that way. I just see protecting you as part of my role."

"I do not need or want your protection, William Lamport."

That hadn't come out quite the way she had intended. She could see by his sharp intake of breath that he was hurt by her words.

"Liam..." she reached for him, but he was already throwing off the bed covers.

"Where are you going?" she asked, her voice rising in alarm.

"I need a little space to think. I'll sleep in the guest bedroom tonight."

Nia leaned back against the headboard. She really was making a mess of things. Maybe Heidi was right. Maybe the best thing she could do for Liam was to leave.

Chapter 19

"*Y*ou look beautiful," he said. "But then you always do."

Nia narrowed her eyes on Damon Deverre where he sat opposite her. She wondered if he thought she was there for his flattery. It was the last thing on her mind. Thinking that it would be excellent if he would focus on the point of their meeting, she began to tap her nails on the table.

He followed the gesture with his eyes and with an amused smile, settled against the back of his chair.

"You really are a piece of work. You do everything in the world to get my attention, and when I finally show up, you act like you're doing me a favor by meeting me. You realize that I bought an overpriced ticket to attend that gala to see you. I mean do you think I could ever eat a £1000 worth of food? Ridiculous."

She sucked in a breath. He really had come to see her. She flattened her palms against the tablecloth and smiled.

"Thank you for coming, Damon. I don't mean to appear obnoxious. I'm just excited to hear what you have to offer me."

He threw back his head and laughed.

"Girl, you are precious. There is something about you. Anyone else I would have written off long ago. But you just do something to me. I figure if I feel that way then mere mortals don't stand a chance. Let's get down to business, then. I'm ready to sign you to my label right now. Your voice is phenomenal. You're gorgeous. You've got extreme stage presence. The stage is where you belong. You were born to shine. You don't belong here with these stuffy upper lip people."

It was on the tip of Nia's tongue to say "stiff upper lip," but she thought better of it. She hadn't met with Damon to correct his grammar. She wanted him to keep talking about the details of a contract. She was happy he still wanted to sign her. The question was, what kind of deal was he willing to negotiate? She had been offered some real doozies by two of the recording companies she had approached. That's what had sent her back to Damon, but was his previous offer still on the table?

He probably believed he had her over a barrel given that she was the one now on the hunt. This was why she had to play it cool and act like she had options. If worse came to worst she could try things Liam's way. She just didn't want to go that route unless it was absolutely necessary. She folded her hands on the table and just continued to smile as Damon spoke.

A waiter delivered the tea he had requested. The scent of peppermint reached her nostrils. It never ceased to amaze her that he only drank herbal teas. She would have expected someone like him to drink alcoholic beverages or coffee at the very least. He never touched alcohol. He had confessed to her one night that his father had been an abusive drunk. Because of the effects of drinking on his family, Damon had determined that alcohol was to be avoided at all cost.

Maybe that was one of the reasons she could relate to him. She too had had a substance abuser for a parent and also vowed to stay away from drugs. Except for that one foolhardy incident with marijuana in Austria, she had kept her vow.

Regrettably, Damon's admirable stance did not extend to his parties which were known to be wild events where huge quantities of alcohol and drugs were available. She'd witnessed it once with her own eyes. It had been during her third year at Julliard when she had gone to L.A. and attended a party he hosted. She had watched in something like bemusement as the night had worn on with Damon's friends getting more plastered by the hour, making fools of themselves, losing control, while he remained sober and in control.

As he took a sip of his tea, she took a sip of her tonic water, and her eyes traveled over him. He reminded her of T'Challa from the Black Panther movies. He did look like a powerful African Prince with his smooth brown skin, buff physique, trim beard and mustache, trendy haircut, and expensive suit. Even the rhinestone studs in both ears only succeeded in making him look dangerous and sexy. But when she stared into his shiny, chocolate-colored eyes, she couldn't help but feel that he was cunning and crafty, like a fox.

Nia picked up her fork and just as the food was almost on her lips, she returned it to her plate and bowed her head. She heard Damon ask if something was wrong and didn't respond as she asked God to bless her meal and for good measure to also guide her interaction with Damon.

She didn't meet Damon's eyes when she raised her head and reached for her fork, but she did hear him say.

"Sorry. I didn't realize you were praying. Why didn't you ask a blessing over my meal too?"

She took a bite of her salmon and chewed thoughtfully as she contemplated her response. "I didn't know you were a believer," she said finally allowing her gaze to rest on his.

He grinned and picked up his own knife and fork. He sliced the steak, and as the pink watery substance ran out, Nia felt her stomach convulse. She glanced away and reached for her glass of water.

"Are you suggesting *you* are?"

When she didn't respond, he chuckled and continued. "I guess you came looking for me because you've gotten tired of languishing here in England and are ready to bless the world with your amazing voice. Am I right?"

She kept her head down as she carefully stabbed penne pasta with her fork. "I'm not languishing. I quite enjoy my life here."

"Stop lying," he burst out with a derisive laugh. Her eyes flew to his in surprise.

He did not stop his barrage.

"Save that for your in-laws. I know you. You and me, baby, we are the same." He waved his hand around the restaurant at the diners. "We're not like these people."

Nia glanced around. It was an upscale restaurant, and the diners looked like high society people based on the way they were dressed and their mannerisms. It was very likely there were a few noblemen among them. As much as she hated to admit it, Damon was right. Even though she tried to fit in with Liam's extended family and their circle of friends and associates, she still felt like an outsider. She knew that she wasn't really accepted by many of these people. They were polite and very careful to be politically correct in her presence, but she knew that deep down they didn't welcome outsiders like her.

Barbara Dickson had confided in her that the British upper classes could be vicious. She had said she had only managed to survive in their world because she had the support of the Royal Family. They were very close to her in-laws, the Fosters. Without that, she felt that her social calendar would perhaps have been very bare over the years. While Nia couldn't say she had the support of the Royal Family, she knew she had Lord and Lady Lamport's public blessing, and that seemed to mean something. However, she still had to prove herself. What happened at the gala last night had done nothing to help her case.

Her mind drifted to the argument with Liam last night. He was ice cold this morning when he had left for his trip to New York. Was that part of the reason he was still angry at her? Because she had been the center of a scene and embarrassed his family? She knew he would be furious now if he knew she was meeting with Damon, but she had to do what she had to do. She just hoped he would come around to her way of thinking sooner rather than later.

Damon was watching her with interest. She hoped her emotions weren't playing out on her face. She straightened in her seat.

"What are you offering me Damon Deverre?"

His face instantly took on the hard veneer it did whenever he talked business.

"An exclusive contract for an initial period of two years during which time Double D Records will pay for your recordings, album cover design, and promotion. All such costs will be charged against your royalties."

It was all standard. The question was how much of the royalties was he keeping for himself?

"What's the percentage that goes to you?"

He watched her with calculating eyes.

"I would have expected you to ask what's the percentage that goes to *you*."

"The outcome will be the same. But since it's my voice and image you will be capitalizing upon I consider that I'm giving a percentage to you and not the other way around."

He laughed and sipped his tea leisurely as he continued to stare at her. As the minutes ticked by, she began to lose patience.

"Please answer my question. What will be your percentage of the royalties? Your response will determine if this meeting needs to continue."

He remained silent until he had drained his cup. "Ten percent for you."

Her jaw dropped. "That's all? What happened to your original offer of twenty percent?

He examined his trimmed buffed fingernails then met her eyes. "It expired. This is a new deal."

"A worse deal is what it is! I'm not accepting it."

A corner of his mouth lifted. "Like I said, a real piece of work. As beautiful and talented as you are do not forget that you are an unknown. Generally, the people I take on are those who have proven their worth. They are people I poach from other labels because I know I can make even more money for them and myself."

"I don't care what excuse you come up with. I'm not accepting that deal. It's twenty percent or nothing."

He sat forward abruptly and slapped the table. A muscle in his jaw jerked.

"Do not get on your high horse with me, little girl, or I will reject you and blacklist you and no one in the business will ever touch you," he said in a menacing voice.

Nia's heart jolted in terror. She felt intimidated by this version of Damon she'd never seen before. Here was the ruthless businessman, not the suitor. Had things changed because she had married Liam? Was he punishing her for her decision?

She didn't know. But one thing she did know was that if she had even a hope of coming out of this encounter successfully, she could not let her fear show. She lifted her chin and leveled her eyes at him.

"Ten percent is ridiculous, and you know it. You are a shrewd businessman. Sentiment is not what got you where you are, so I know that if you didn't feel deep in your gut that I was worth investing in you wouldn't even be here. Don't waste both my time and yours by insulting me with an offer like that. It's twenty percent, Damon, or no deal."

He shook his head. "Unheard of."

"Nothing has changed. I'm the same person I was a few months ago when you were offering that to me."

Anger flashed in Damon's eyes. But then he shrugged, and it was gone. Rubbing a hand thoughtfully along his jaw line he replied, "That was before you decided to go and become a missus."

She had been right. This was payback.

"It's easier to promote you as a fresh young single thing than someone's wife," Damon continued. "If you get what I'm saying."

"That makes absolutely no sense."

"Maybe not to you. But as you just said, I'm a shrewd businessman. I've been in this long enough to know what works and what doesn't."

Nia wished she had accepted Liam's offer to be here with her now negotiating on her behalf. This was the sort of thing he did with his father's company, negotiating with suppliers and contractors and clients. And he was good at it too from all accounts. But even as she thought it she dismissed it.

A meeting between the two men would not go well. Liam couldn't stand Damon, and the feeling was mutual. She couldn't envisage them sitting opposite each other and having a cordial conversation. No, if she wanted to negotiate with Damon, she was on her own. In the next breath, she recalled that her stepfather was a lawyer, so she really wasn't on her own at all. Maybe Thomas could provide her with some guidance.

After several sips of her water, she said, "Damon, as you mentioned, I'm a married woman now. I have a life here. If I sign with your label, how is returning to L.A. with you going to impact that?"

"That's your problem, baby."

He signaled to the waiter to refill his teapot.

For some reason, she was thrown by his rudeness. She was too stunned to react for a moment. After a few minutes, she realized she should have expected no other response. It wasn't realistic to believe that Damon would want to support her marriage when he clearly hadn't approved of it in the first place. She dragged her teeth across her bottom lip. It was amazing how he had changed. There was a time he never would have treated her with such disrespect. She began to wonder if she really wanted to put her career into his hands.

Maybe he sensed her distaste because his gaze softened slightly and his tone was more conversational.

"Nia, I can't tell you how to balance your career and family life. That's something you'll have to work out. What I can tell you is that I'm prepared to give you everything. I'm prepared to use every means at my disposal to make you a star."

He put down his fork and abruptly grasped her hand before she could return to her own meal.

"Sacrifices must be made to achieve greatness, Nia. I'm not going to lie to you. It won't be easy. It may mean a long distance marriage for a while but the moment I met you I sensed that you were the type of girl who would do whatever it took to succeed. Make any sacrifice necessary. Was I wrong about that? About you?"

"Do you think I really will become a star? Like a superstar."

He nodded. "I strongly believe that. I have seen you in action. You have tremendous star power."

She sat back. "Twenty percent is only fair then."

His eyes widened, and then he cursed. "Are you back on that again?" he growled. "I told you I'm not budging."

"Well, then, I'm not signing. This was a mistake," she said softly. "You made me believe I had worth to you and now you treat me like a punk."

She reached for her bag. "I'm leaving. I have other offers you know."

"And those offers do not even amount to ten percent.

She froze. How did he know?

He leered at her. "There is nothing that goes on in this business, in that town, that I don't know about."

She felt like screaming in frustration. This was not going the way she had hoped.

He sighed. "Baby, why are you fighting me on this? I think you're glorious, but I've got a business to run. I can't be swayed by every pretty face that walks into my office. If I did, I wouldn't have a business and then where would all my precious artists be. Trust me that what I'm offering you is fair. And in two years and you're making me millions we can re-negotiate."

"Twenty percent or I'm walking, Damon."

He slammed his fist on the dining table making the cutlery jump. Nia could see a few heads swivel in their direction. She cringed. It was likely that tongues would be wagging about this meeting by the next morning.

"You are a stubborn little thing aren't you? Okay, here is what I'm willing to offer you. Twelve percent, against my better judgment."

She tilted her head to the side. "Eighteen percent."

He stared at her for a long time before he said firmly, "Fifteen percent. My final offer. Take it or leave it."

Nia looked at her hands. Fifteen percent was a lot less than she had expected, a far cry from twenty percent, but Damon seemed unlikely to budge. It had already taken everything out of her to push for this. It was probably time to accept.

"My lawyer will still have to look over the terms of the contract. I may have questions before I sign."

"Does that mean you accept my generous fifteen percent offer?"

She mumbled her agreement.

"I can't hear you, Nia," he said holding a hand to his ear.

She gritted her teeth. "Yes, Damon."

"That's better. I've already got four great songs lined up for you. One of them is a duo with Byron on his new album. I think I'd love to launch you that way."

Nia's interest piqued. She leaned forward and felt her nose tingle as the scent of peppermint wafted up her nostrils.

"Byron Brown?"

"The same."

"He's great."

Bryon Brown was a mega recording star. It would be mind-blowing to start out with him. The only thing was that the lyrics of his songs could be quite suggestive.

Nia sat back. "I don't know about some of his songs though."

"He's versatile. He has his popular pop music, sure, but he can do romantic. He can even do inspirational. His song *Shine* landed at number two on the Billboard charts when it first came out. That was an inspirational one."

Something Damon said suddenly dawned on Nia. "You've got songs written for me already? But I haven't even signed the contract yet. Aren't you getting ahead of yourself?"

He smiled wryly. "I assessed you as an intelligent woman. One who would act in her best interest." He shrugged. "However, if I was wrong there are plenty of women out there ready and willing to take what you don't want. The food you reject will become food for someone else."

Again, Damon reached out and this time ran the back of his hand down her bare arm. "But you won't let that happen. Will you?"

Nia suppressed a shudder. Didn't he know she was strictly off limits now? She shifted her arm and leaned far back in her chair to prevent him from easily reaching for her.

He regarded her with dark hooded eyes and slight amusement played around his lips as though he knew he had made her uncomfortable and enjoyed doing so. Then he drained his teacup and resumed eating his steak in silence.

Nia was grateful for the pause in conversation. It allowed her to think as she picked at her meal. She wanted to become a star but would she be doing the right thing if she signed up with Damon. A part of her felt uncomfortable, but she chalked that up to resistance to change and fear of the unknown. No, she had to face her fears. She had to be confident. There was nothing that should scare her.

It wasn't as though Damon was an unknown quantity. His reputation preceded him. Everyone knew he was a hit-maker, a star maker. He was a mogul. Most of those who signed to his label were superstars. She had nothing to fear from him. She wasn't naïve or a dunce, and if he thought so, he'd soon find out the truth. He would not be hand-picking his own team of zealots or spies for her. She would choose her own people to look after her own interests. She would begin by having Thomas carefully peruse the contract to ensure it was to her best advantage.

"I'll get back to you by the end of the month."

"One week."

"But my lawyer has to see it."

"I will email the contract to you tomorrow when I return to L.A., and I expect you to get back to me with the signed copy or any proposed changes within one week from today."

"But Damon…"

"One week! I've waited for you long enough."

Nia blinked at Damon's words. They reminded her of what Liam had said on the day of their wedding: 'True love has waited long enough.' How she missed him. What would become of them if she signed this contract? But if she didn't sign it, what would become of her.

Nia returned her attention to the man before her. "One week it is."

Chapter 20

ia listened to Liam's muffled voice talking to someone on his cell phone as she brushed her hair into a ponytail. She touched her lips. They felt dry. She proceeded to the vanity with the intention of smoothing on lip gloss and stopped midway.

She was delaying meeting with Liam. They had not spoken since that night. During his two day trip to New York, he had not called, just sent her a text message saying he had arrived safely. Now she was concerned over what his greeting would be. But avoidance was not her style. She pivoted and made her way out of the bedroom.

He stood near the entryway, bag at his feet and shuffling through the mail. Then he looked up. His beautiful eyes pierced to her very soul. Nia could only stare as her heart pounded so hard she was sure he could hear it.

He tossed the mail on the nearby table and hastened toward her. Before she could react his hands encircled her waist and his mouth descended on hers. Nia's gasp was swallowed in a kiss that seemed to go on forever.

He placed his hands beneath her knees, lifted her up as if she weighed nothing, and headed to the bedroom. She sighed into him and sagged against his body. Sometime later, husband and wife lay entangled amidst sheets and pillows, satiated.

About the same time, they both realized words were still needed.

"I'm sorry," Liam and Nia said almost together. They looked across at each other and laughed, then sobered. Nia propped on an elbow and stared down at Liam.

"I didn't mean what I said about not wanting or needing your protection. I'm sorry for my disrespectful words."

He trailed a finger down her cheek. "I'm also sorry. I shouldn't have insisted that I accompany you to meet with Deverre. You are quite capable of making your own decisions." He dropped a kiss on her shoulder.

"I missed you. Every night in New York without you was so lonely."

She smiled slightly. *"Comme on fait son lit, on se couche."*

Liam raised a brow. "As you make your bed, so you must lie?"

She nodded and with a mischievous grin replied, "It's a French proverb meaning you must put up with the unpleasant results of a foolish decision."

Liam began to tickle her and despite her squeals and pleas refused to stop.

"Comme on fait son lit, on se couche," he said.

~*~*~*~

She signed the contract.

Thomas had laid out for her, via video conferencing, what every clause would mean. She understood that she would be the property of Double D Productions, but according to Thomas, this was standard in the industry. He did confirm that the fifteen percent was a good deal for a beginner. He felt it suggested that Damon was quite confident of her abilities. With the deadline due she signed the document and sent it to Damon just that morning.

Nia thought about how to break the news to Liam and decided that it was probably best to do it over lunch rather than wait until he got home from work. She asked him to meet with her at a restaurant a few blocks away from his office. To overcome her nervousness, she decided to do a little shopping first.

When she met up with him, her hands were laden with several purchases made at Harrods. She was pensive as she awaited their order. Liam noticed.

"What's wrong, Nia?"

She looked up at him as though startled from a reverie and for a moment didn't respond. Then she said, "Did you mean it when you said you trust me to make my own decisions."

"Yes," he responded carefully, "Why do you ask?"

"I met with Damon when you were away."

She saw Liam stiffen. It was an infinitesimal movement, but she noticed.

He stayed silent, so she went on.

"He offered me a contract. I sent it to Thomas to look at."

Liam took a sip of his water and waited.

"I signed it today."

The way his nostril's flared and his eyes hardened was a preview of his negative response to her news.

"Without discussing it with me."

It was a statement, but nevertheless, she nodded.

"Only because I didn't think you would be very supportive considering your stance regarding Damon."

He sat back in his seat and looked off into a corner of the room.

"It doesn't have to affect us, Liam. I've been thinking about it. I will have to be in L.A. for a few months working on the new songs, but during that time you can move there. You can commute to London as necessary. We can do whatever it takes to make it work."

He reached for his napkin, carefully dabbed the corners of his mouth, draped it back across his lap and said nothing. 'Stuffy upper lip' Damon would say. Stiff or stuffy, it was driving her crazy.

"Are you going to sit there and say nothing," she demanded.

"What's the use? My opinion clearly does not matter to you."

The arrow found its mark. Nia winced. But he wasn't finished.

"But if you really want to know what I think I'll tell you. I believe that Deverre will exploit you. He will take your beauty and your talent and use it to advance himself and his empire. I believe that you will become his slave. You will march to the beat of his drum. And the irony is you won't even know it's happening. He will ensnare you in his lifestyle, woo you with all the desires of the flesh and you will lose yourself to him. You will forget who you are and become just another foot soldier in his army; another cog in his machinery. He will rape you, plunder you, and when there is nothing left, he will discard you."

He was scaring her. She couldn't afford to listen to this. Not now. She didn't want her doubts fueled, she wanted them extinguished.

"You sound like some crazed preacher. That's a whole lot of nonsense. He is not the devil you make him out to be. You shouldn't resent him. There is room in my life for both of you."

"Not in mine."

"What are you saying?"

He leaned forward and stared at her. His blue eyes were like fiery balls.

"I am not going to share you with him. If you choose Deverre, if you leave here and go to him, don't bother coming back."

Her breath caught. She could feel tears burn the back of her eyes.

"I can't believe you would threaten me in this way. You are a selfish man. You accuse Damon of wanting to control me, but you're no better. You want to mold me into your image, and because I have desires of my own, you resent it. But I'm not going to live my life trying to be your perfect woman. I know who I am and I'm going to embrace it. Unlike you who pretend to be someone you're not."

"What are you harping about?"

"Does your job make you feel fulfilled?"

His gaze flitted away then returned to hers. "I believe this is where I'm supposed to be right now."

She sat forward, eyes bright. "That's not what I asked you."

He narrowed his eyes at her. "Don't try to distract me. This isn't about me it's about you."

She grasped his hand. "The real reason you don't want me to do this is that you have spent years suppressing your true passion and convinced yourself that it was the right choice. Well, I can't do that."

His voice went up a notch. "When did I ever ask you to give up your dream? All I asked was that you be careful who you align yourself with. I thought that was my role as your husband--to be your protector."

He pulled up short. "But, oh right. That's not what you want, is it? You can take care of yourself. In effect, I'm just getting in your way aren't I?"

Nia swallowed. That wasn't how she viewed him at all, but she was beginning to question whether they had made the right decision to get married. She had ignored the voice that suggested it was too rushed; that they hadn't ironed out the kinks first. In typical Nia style, she had acted first and thought later. Now it looked like the kinks might not be so easy for them to iron out. It was becoming more obvious that they had different expectations of each other.

Liam seemed to want her to fall in line with his plans. He had a view of her career, his way. She, on the other hand, wanted a partner who would be there for her, supporting her emotionally as she paved her own path. She had thought Liam was that man. Maybe she was wrong about that. Liam was not fulfilled, but he was content to live a safe life. She, on the other hand, was not cut out for safety. She had broken her arm at the age of five because she had wanted to climb a big tree with a view of the ocean. She had caught a glimpse just before she came tumbling back to earth. Even though she was in pain and had to wear a cast for weeks, she never regretted her decision.

"You're not the boy I met in Austria. The boy who made such an impression on me I couldn't forget him no matter how hard I tried."

She saw him flinch. She hesitated for a moment. It wasn't her intention to hurt him, but it had to be said.

"You go through the motions. You do your job to perfection like the good son, but the joy you once had is gone from your life. You know why?"

He held up a hand. "Stop," he whispered in a ragged voice.

"Your music brought you joy."

"Joy is not found in doing things. It's found in a life devoted to serving God in whatever area He has placed you," he retorted.

She shook her head. "How do you know this is what God wants? You have let fear keep you from discovering what He wants for you. Fear of disapproval, of opposition, of…I don't know…failure."

She threw her napkin on the table and stood. "I'm going to L.A. to record the demos for the songs."

"I see."

"What do you see?"

"I see I made a mistake. I believe we both made a terrible mistake."

She blinked back tears. "Seems like we did," she rasped.

He shook his head. "Go then. It's probably for the best."

She began to speak then halted, covered her mouth with her hand, pushed away from the table and ran out of the restaurant.

Liam just sat there. He was still quivering with anger. How could Nia be so insensitive? Did she think that he was made of stone? That he had no feelings? The fact that she could deride him for his choice to join his family's business instead of selfishly pursuing his dreams had struck him to the core. She had no right to look down on him. She only cared about herself and her own interests, no matter who got hurt in the process. With great power came great responsibility. He did not answer to himself or his desires as she did. What had ever led him to think he could make a life with such a volatile, immature girl?

As time marched smartly on without a care to his personal crisis, Liam's rage began to recede. He drank two more cups of tea, his things were cleared away, and regret slowly replaced anger.

Why had he said the things he had to Nia. He had given her an ultimatum; he had told her their marriage was a mistake. Could he have said anything more devastating?

He signaled to the waiter and requested the bill. When he had completed the transaction and stood, he noticed that the bags from Nia's purchases were on the floor. She must have really been upset to leave her shopping behind. As he gathered up the bags, it suddenly occurred to him to wonder how Nia had left. Had their driver taken her home? He reached for his phone.

"Mr. Lamport," the chauffeur answered.

"Giles, did you take Mrs. Lamport home?"

The man sounded surprised. "I thought Mrs. Lamport was with you, sir."

Liam stepped out of the restaurant and looked down the street.

"You're still parked?"

"Yes, sir."

"I've just left the restaurant." He hung up as he saw the Benz rolling towards him.

He called Nia's cell phone. While he would prefer to apologize in person rather than on the phone, he still wanted to know that she was safe.

The phone rang for several times and then ended abruptly. He redialed. This time it went straight to voicemail.

He sighed deeply as he embarked the vehicle.

"Nia, where are you?" he whispered.

~*~*~*~

Nia just walked with no particular destination in mind. She was hurt and angry right now and walking just seemed like a great way to help to clear her head.

To think that Liam would have given up on her and their marriage so casually, and if that wasn't bad enough, he had told her it had been a mistake marrying her. That had really gutted her. She had been the one to try to warn him that maybe they were rushing things. She had been the one to say she hoped he would have no regrets. And now to hear him say this. Did he not have any heart? How could she have been so wrong about him? She had thought he loved her. How could she have been so blind?

She stopped for a moment and leaned against the window of a store as she struggled to gather her composure. Her phone began to ring. She pulled it out of her handbag. It was Liam. He was the last person in the world she wanted to speak with. She rejected the call and turned the phone off for good measure and dropped it back into her bag.

An old lady walking a small white dog passed and gave her a sympathetic smile. Did she look so pathetic? She ran a hand over her face and turned around to peer at herself in the show window. She really did look tragic with her tear-stained face and windblown hair. She found a used tissue in her bag and wiped her eyes.

It wouldn't do for her to walk the streets of London looking like something the cat dragged in. Some paparazzo hoping to catch a break would be only too happy to snap her photo and put a negative spin to it. Probably something scandalous like her marriage was on the rocks. The irony was that this time the negative spin would be correct. Her marriage was in a wreck.

She turned and resumed her walk and thought about what it would mean to leave behind everything she owned. But if she returned to the apartment, Liam would most likely be there. She did not want to see him much less talk to him. She had two options then: return for her things when she knew he would be out or ask him to post her things. The former seemed like the better option. It would be cleaner, require no contact with Liam, and would likely produce the desired results.

Chapter 21

She was back!

Immense relief blew through Liam as he noted that the doors were not double locked and the alarm system was no longer armed as he had left them that morning. No one else could get up there without the gold keycard that only Nia and he possessed.

He was going to fall to her feet and beg forgiveness the moment he saw her. He had just spent the worst night of his life. It was a wonder he'd been able to make it to work. The only reason he had gone was that he realized it was either that or go insane waiting for Nia to return his calls.

After he had left the restaurant, he had spent the remainder of the evening calling and leaving several messages on Nia's phone for her to call him. Then he had become annoyed at her insensitivity and immaturity in not even messaging him and letting him know she was okay. This was followed by worry as the night wore on and she didn't turn up. Swallowing his pride, he had called friends and family and asked if they knew where she was and finally prayed and asked God to keep her safe.

Now he called out her name as he moved from room to room and wasn't ashamed of the eagerness in his voice. He wanted his wife. He wanted to kiss her all over; nothing else mattered. They could work things out by God's grace, find a middle ground somehow.

Liam continued to look for signs of life but as he entered their bedroom something struck him as odd. It was the eerie silence that filled the apartment. Nia craved noise. Even when she wasn't speaking or humming or singing, she had on the TV, radio, or the Internet.

It was the mess. While Nia was not the tidiest person in the world, the bedroom was in quite a disarray. Drawers were left open, clothes were on the floor. It looked as though someone had hastily packed.

Liam took in a sharp breath. He raced to the walk-in closet. Nia's clothes were missing, so were several pairs of shoes. A quick check revealed that her suitcases also were gone. His further search revealed that her important documents were absent too. A whole drawer had been emptied as though she had just upended it in the suitcase. Her jewelry was gone, and her electronic equipment. Liam sat on the edge of the bed and held his head in his hands.

And then he saw it. It was an envelope placed to stand against a small vase of orchids. Liam opened it with trepidation. It contained Nia's gold keycard and a letter. He regained his seat and began to read.

Dear Liam,

You told me if I left not to come back. I guess this means goodbye then. I'm sorry things had to end this way. I was hoping we could have been a team. You and me against the world. I see now that I'm on my own as I have always been. Please don't hate me. I don't hate you. I think this is just one of those things. We tried. It just didn't work out. I wish you the best. I hope you find someone who suits you better than I do.

The paper fluttered to the floor as pain sliced through Liam like a knife. He screamed, but no sound came. Only agony.

~*~*~*~

Liam sent his father a message.

"Dad, something has come up. I need to take emergency leave. We will talk when I return."

He did not go to Los Angeles, although it crossed his mind. He decided that there was no point to it. Nia had left him. She no longer wanted to be his wife. Her message had been crystal clear.

He flew to Austria, returned to the chalet on the mountain, and channeled all his anger into the physical exertion of extreme sports. With every difficult slope he said to himself, if this is what she wants, she can have it. She can go ahead and pursue her dreams. And when she realizes that it wasn't all it was cut out to be, that Damon Deverre is the devil, then she will come crawling back to me begging for forgiveness. But it's not going to happen.

For days he moved from being angry at Nia, and then God, and then Deverre, and finally himself. He felt stupid for rushing into marriage. He was so gullible to think she was the one; to believe she truly loved him.

In one angry moment, he tugged off his wedding band and flung it with all his might down the mountain. When the horror of what he had done hit him, he pushed off and skied in the direction where he had thrown it. He fell to his knees and frantically dug around in the snow with his bare hands. It was futile. He dug for what seemed like hours and never found it. He returned to the chalet exhausted and more depressed than ever.

In the days that followed, the pain did not go away. If anything, it got worse. Soon the physical exertion, combined with him not taking care of himself found him laid up in bed with the flu.

Heidi Wolffe stood at the door of the chalet knocking for several minutes, but no one answered. She knew that Liam was there. A rental jeep was parked outside, and Reinhardt had told her he was there a few days ago. She had asked if he knew where Liam was after several unsuccessful attempts to reach him. Reinhardt had apparently called Liam's parents and gotten his whereabouts.

Then she heard a rumor that Nia had left Liam and returned to the States. It was very likely that the woman was just being her usual melodramatic self and had every intention of either running back to Liam or trying to manipulate him into chasing after her.

Interestingly enough, the latter hadn't worked thus far. Perhaps whatever had caused the break had been so bad that Liam wanted nothing more to do with Nia. Maybe it had to do with that good looking black man who had shown up the night of the gala. Maybe Nia had had an affair with him. Or better yet, run off with him.

The more Heidi thought about it, the more she knew that she had to take full advantage of this opportunity. It wasn't every day that she got to help Liam when he was at his most vulnerable.

Heidi had been in love with Liam for years. He had viewed her as a nuisance when they were younger but, after college, she had managed to win his friendship. She had accepted that role because she knew that it was all that was available to her. She didn't understand why Liam seemed immune to her charms. Most men found her very appealing. She never failed to turn heads wherever she went.

She and Liam had similar family backgrounds, moved in the same social circles. They also had similar educational backgrounds. She had pursued a degree in accounting while his studies had been in finance and management. And of course, they both worked in the corporate world. When they got together, they always had something to talk about. As far as she was concerned, there was no one better suited for him than her.

And then he had gone to New York this year and met up with Nia Carmichael, and all Heidi's hard work in winning his friendship and trust had gone up in smoke. For the life of her, she could not fathom what Liam saw in that brash, common, American girl. It was true that Liam's mother, Lady Lamport, was also American and had been an actress, but Barbara had poise and class, something that Nia did not.

Maybe Liam had been going through a rebellious phase by marrying her. Maybe he was acting out or visiting his wild side by marrying the bad girl. Heidi ran a hand absently over her eye. She still could not believe Nia had dared to attack her. And to think, far from coming to her aid, Liam had simply taken the woman's hand like she was a recalcitrant child and led her away. Fortunately, the bruising around her eye had cleared, and she now looked normal.

It had been humiliating knowing people were talking about her behind their hands but it had been worth it to prove to Liam what a low-life he had married. She had given the marriage one month before Liam came to his senses. It had lasted a little longer than that. This small victory could not be taken for granted. She had to move in for the kill now.

As she stood banging on the door and getting colder by the minute as it went unanswered, she began to have doubts that he was there at this moment. Maybe he had gone skiing or something. She dialed his phone, and this time instead of going straight to voicemail it mercifully rang.

But it rang and rang. She went around the chalet to peer in a window. She saw signs that someone was occupying the place, but there was no sign of Liam. She banged the door again and then decided to try the phone. Just as she was about to hang up a second time, she heard a voice answer. But that couldn't be Liam. It sounded like a grizzly bear. Then he gave off a thunderous sneeze.

"Liam, is that you?"

Another sneeze rumbled through the phone, and then his muffled voice.

"Who is this?"

"It's me, Heidi."

"Can't talk right now…phone kept ringing so I answered…but I'm not feeling well."

"What's wrong?"

He sniffed. "…flu I think."

"You need to open the door. I need to come in."

"Door? Are you outside?"

"Yes."

"Why?"

"Liam, please open the door. I'm freezing out here."

"Okay…give me a few minutes."

It was more than a few minutes. Just as she was about to ring him again, she heard the door crack open.

When she looked around at him, the smile on her face died. Liam looked like death warmed over. Shrouded in a blanket, he peered at her through watery, red eyes. His nose was red and bulbous, and it was clear that a razor had not gone near his face in the past couple of weeks. It looked like she had arrived just in time.

She felt his forehead with the back of her hand. "You've got fever," she said.

"What are you doing h…" he broke off to sneeze loudly.

She pushed past him, wheeling her suitcase in with her.

"Did your cleaning lady go on strike?" she asked looking around her.

The chalet was an absolute mess. It looked as though it hadn't been cleaned since Liam arrived there.

He didn't respond. He seemed to barely make his way over to the couch before he collapsed on it and curled himself into a ball. The sight of someone like Liam who was always so strong and confident reduced to a helpless invalid filled Heidi with concern. She conceded in the next breath that it could prove a blessing in disguise. Wouldn't Liam be eternally grateful if she nursed him back to health?

She dropped to a squat beside him and ran her hand down the arm that covered his eyes.

"Where hurts, Liam?"

"Everywhere," he moaned.

"Have you taken anything for the pain?"

He nodded. "Two Tylenol…a while ago, though….think the effect is wearing off."

She stood. "Don't worry I'll take care of you."

Heidi found him the pills and gave him two more with a glass of orange juice. She went into his room and changed the sheets which stank of sweat. When she returned to the sitting room, Liam's eyes were closed, but she didn't think he was asleep based on the way he kept twisting around as though trying to get comfortable.

"Come let me help you get settled. You'll feel better in a comfy bed."

As sick as he was it was a burden trying to get him into bed. She had to coax several times. When he eventually rose, he leaned heavily on her as she guided him to the bedroom. She was almost as tall as he was but his body was a wall of muscle. It was no easy task, but eventually, they reached his room. With obvious relief for both of them, he dropped into bed.

"I'm going to make you some soup," she said as she smoothed back a damp lock from his forehead. She realized he had dropped off to sleep based on his even breathing.

"I'm going to take good care of you and prove I would make you a great wife," she whispered to his sleeping form.

~*~*~*~

Nia watched Damon Deverre in barely suppressed anger.

"You cannot tell me what to do with my hair."

"I'm telling you what will sell."

He picked up a strand of her curly hair. "And this natural look, baby, is not going to have worldwide appeal."

"It's about my voice, not my looks," she responded, swatting his hand away.

He guffawed. "It's about your voice *and* your looks. It's a package. Our role is to make you your best you. This hair is cute, but we can do better; make you even more gorgeous."

"By making it straight?"

"That's right."

She couldn't believe what she was hearing. It had taken her years to accept herself and her looks. She was not Caucasian like her other siblings, and her *Grandmére* Annuad had never let her forget it. She would tug the comb through Nia's thick locks and complain bitterly that she didn't know how to manage the wild, wooly hair as she called it.

It turned out her hair wasn't that wooly after all. Grandmama Carmichael had known the right products to use so that it was soft and shiny like it was now. Her white grandmother, though, hadn't taken the time to learn how to care for her type of hair, so she merely brushed it and left it. When it inevitably got all tangled she would then curse and criticize when she couldn't comb through the knotted mess. Nia could still remember the feelings of humiliation as her half-sister and her cousins with their light, straight hair snickered as *Grandmére* Annuad carried on.

"That's outdated nonsense!" Nia protested.

"I get it. You're black, and you're proud, right? Only you're not that black." He ran a hand along her bare arm. "You look like one of those Frappuccinos."

"Drop dead."

Another thing she hated. The kids in her mother's hometown of Georgia hadn't been too kind when they peppered her with terms like cookies 'n cream, caramel, domino, zebra, or any other derogatory label to punish her for having skin so much lighter than theirs. Although her grandmother told her the kids just envied her good looks, Nia didn't understand why anyone would envy looks that made her stick out like a sore thumb on two different continents.

"That was not an insult," Damon protested holding up both hands. "You are such a feisty thing. My, my, my. No wonder poor Will-eee-um couldn't handle you."

She wanted to cover her ears with her hands. She did not want to hear Liam's name mentioned. She was already finding it hard enough trying to discipline her thoughts not to drift to him every hour of every day.

She turned away. "Leave me alone."

Damon grabbed her arm. Nia reared back her fist to hit him, and he caught her hand.

"Do you really think you can fight me, little girl? I grew up on the mean streets of Harlem. I was eating guys twice my size for breakfast by the time I was half your age. Calm down and listen up. This is just an experiment. You let these people do your hair, and then we'll monitor the response. If it's not positive, we can go back. What do you say?"

She shook her head. "You're going to straighten my hair and then make it natural again? By doing what…waving a wand? I don't think so."

His expression hardened. "You signed a contract with Double D Records. That contract says that you will participate in all marketing promotions."

"That did not include my appearance."

"Didn't it? That lawyer of yours must not be advising you right."

He tilted his head to one side. "I am quite certain there is a clause in there that says, and I quote *'so as to ensure the artist looks and appears the same as she did at the date of this agreement she will not cut, color or alter in any way her teeth, hair, eyebrows, skin, body size or general physical appearance including, without limitation, becoming overweight, underweight or piercing, or tattooing any visible part of her body without the prior written consent of the producer,'* that's me…"

"Exactly…"

He held up a finger silencing her. *"...and she will allow the producer to cut, color or otherwise style her hair so as to meet the requirements of the role and of the production provided that at the end of the period of service and if requested by the artist, the producer will return the artist's hair to its original condition and if this is not possible to such reasonable standard as agreed between the parties.'* End quote."

Nia stared at him in awe. Had the man memorized the entire agreement? How had she missed that part about her hair? Probably because she hadn't considered that the first thing he would want was for her to change it. She thought of Sheba with her flowing honey blond hair extensions. No doubt he wanted Nia to be a clone of her. Good thing the contract was only for two years with an option to renew.

She relaxed her body. "Release me."

He did. First her arm, and then the hand that had been about to strike him. His eyes remained watchful.

She turned away, running a hand over her head as she did so.

"Fine. I'll let them straighten my hair. You may go."

"Listen." His voice took on a persuasive tone. "I promise you, Nia, whatever we do will enhance your looks. Not detract. What do I have to gain by detracting from your appeal? I'm investing a lot in you, baby. Remember that. I stand the most to lose here. Trust my judgment. I've been in this a long time. I know what works and what doesn't."

Nia was sure he did. But it didn't make her feel better. She felt as though instead of being herself she was shaping herself once again into someone's idea of who or what she should be. At least Liam had liked her hair. She remembered that time in New York when he had taken her to Curlfest, an event that allowed people of color to embrace their curls, kinks, and coils, and he had not been concerned that he was one of the few white men there.

She squeezed her eyes closed. Why did she have to think of him so often? She was sure it would have gotten better by now. It had been three weeks since she had left. But he had been the love of her life. How did a person overcome such strong emotions?

She took a deep breath. By willpower, that was how--willpower and working hard and focusing on her career.

"Are you even listening to me?" Damon's angry voice broke through her thoughts.

She blinked and turned to him. "Can you repeat what you were saying?"

He heaved a sigh.

"I was saying that I will leave you to the capable hands of your stylist and her team." Those who were waiting on the outside after having called Damon following Nia's fiery outburst upon discovering their intentions for her hair.

"You will fully cooperate with them. Because if I have to return here over this, you will not like it, Nia Carmichael."

"Lamport," she corrected automatically.

"Nia Carmichael," he repeated through clenched teeth. "Are you about to fight me on this too?"

She had forgotten for a moment her agreement with him that they would use her maiden name as her stage name.

She folded her arms and scowled at him. "I forgot, okay?"

He rudely sucked his teeth. "You've got two weeks before we begin promotion and recording simultaneously. Use the time to get your head in the game. You are no longer with Will-eee-um. You are no longer a high society princess. You are mine now. I will not tolerate your tantrums. I am a very busy man and getting called out to deal with things like this is a waste of my time. Comply, or I will drop you from my label, and you will never work in this town again."

Before she could respond, he had already turned his back to her and was striding toward the door. As he swung it open, it banged against the wall. Nia slammed it behind him and slumped against it.

Was it possible she had made a big mistake? Damon was turning out to be a handful. It would take every ounce of strength she possessed to stand up to him when she needed to. She slid down the door onto the floor and placed her head in her hands. Liam had tried to warn her that Damon was not all he appeared, but she hadn't listened.

She groaned. Liam again. Why couldn't she stop thinking about him? It didn't matter if she had made a mistake or not. She had walked out on him, and he had told her if she did she was not to come back. It was too late for them.

Her head came up. Or was it? Liam had left messages for her weeks ago when she had first stormed out of his life. She hadn't listened to them because she hadn't been interested in what he had to say at the time. Now she felt a deep desire to know.

She crawled over to the coffee table where her phone lay. She took it up and for the first time listened to his messages one by one.

"Nia, call me."

"Nia, it's Liam. Please call me."

"Nia where are you? Please call me the moment you get this message."

"Nia, why are you doing this? I'm worried sick about you. Call me back."

But it was the final one that gave her hope.

"Nia, my darling, I'm sorry for what I said. Please call me back. I know we can make things right."

Nia's breath hitched. He had said they could make things right. Perhaps it wasn't too late after all. She frantically dialed his number. It was ringing. Her heart thumped in her chest in anticipation of what she would say when he answered.

"Hello?" said a female voice.

Nia's heart missed a beat. She glanced at the screen to see if she'd dialed the wrong number.

"Who is this?" she demanded.

"Who would you like to speak with?"

"William Lamport. This is his phone."

"Who may I ask is calling for him?"

Nia was barely able to keep her voice from shaking. "Nia Lamport, his wife."

"Hello, Nia."

"Who is this?" she repeated frantically.

"Heidi."

Nia felt her breath catch. "Why are you answering Liam's phone?" she squeaked.

"Because he's in bed, asleep."

Nia's blood ran cold.

"We're in Austria at his chalet," Heidi continued cheerfully.

"Is…are his parents there? I'd like to speak to his mother."

Heidi laughed. "His parents aren't here. We're quite alone. It's over between the two of you, Nia. I'm sorry you had to find out this way. Liam wanted to tell you himself."

Nia felt as though she'd been punched in the gut. She disconnected the call.

She now noticed Liam's profile picture. It was a cozy image of him, and Heidi snuggled up together. His eyes were closed, but hers were wide open as she smiled at the camera. It even looked like they were in bed. She couldn't believe Liam could be so brazen. It was so out of character for him. They were still married. How could he flaunt his affair with Heidi for all the world to see?

Nia dropped her head in her hands as her body wracked with sobs. Yes, she had left him but to think he had moved on so quickly. It suggested that his feelings for her hadn't been very deep. She had no choice now but to proceed as she had been going. No knight was going to show up on a white steed to rescue her. *As she had made her bed so in it she must lie.*

Chapter 22

Liam was sure he was going to be sick. Some time ago, he had stumbled out of bed and locked himself in the bathroom. He stared at his reflection in the mirror.

How had it come to this? At what point had he made the decision that he was going to walk away from all the values he'd been taught and had stood for. As he drew the back of his hand across his mouth his ring finger caught his eye. That was the point of no return – the moment he had taken off his wedding ring and flung it in the snow in anger. He had dashed away his ring in an emotional outrage the same way he had dashed away his wedding vows the night before.

The night played out before him, and he retched.

Heidi had been there for him these last few days, caring for him, meeting his every need. He had been so grateful he had begun to see her in a new light. He had never even known Heidi had such nurturing qualities. She'd always struck him as cool and detached. But all that had changed.

She was like an angel come to minister to him. For the next few days, she had made him soothing lemon teas and other herbal concoctions, cooked him nutritious vegan meals, fed him, and played board games with him when he got cabin fever.

He had even confided in her what had caused Nia to leave and that she had left to go with Damon Deverre. She had shared his outrage and suggested that it called for something stronger than tea.

She had brought him some coffee and then poured some whiskey into their cups.

"Irish coffee," she'd said with a wink.

They had drunk two more cups, and before he knew it, Heidi was curled up against him with his arm around her shoulder. It was a short step from there for her to turn her face to his in expectation and for him to meet his lips with hers. Suddenly, it felt good to just feel pleasure again. Even though it would be easy to claim he'd been drunk, he knew that a part of him made the conscious decision to seek pleasure first and deal with the consequences later.

And now he was dealing with the consequences, and the consequences were dire.

Liam slid down beside the bathtub, holding his head in his hand. It wasn't just the hangover that made him feel as though his head had been split in two. He wished with all his heart that was all. No, it was the guilt, the guilt that was eating him alive from the inside. How could he face Heidi after he had used her body for his temporary pleasure? What about Nia? How could there ever be a chance for reconciliation between them after this? How about his parents' disappointment if they ever found out, or his friends, his church? His image as this virtuous role model would be shot if this became known. How could he head the Purity Pledge Ministry any longer? He was no better than a Pharisee.

Liam pressed his fist to his mouth as his stomach heaved again. All those years of being pure were in vain. He was worse than a fornicator now. He was an adulterer.

He heard a rap on the door and Heidi's voice.

"Liam, are you alright?"

How was it she was so chirpy? Had she not drank as much as he had? He remembered being awoken that morning by her kisses and her hands caressing his body. At first, he had thought Nia had come back to him. He had sighed with contentment and then a moment later it had hit him like a ton of bricks that it was Heidi. And the events of the previous night had descended on him like a shroud.

Oh God, what have I done?

There was another knock at the door. "Liam." Heidi's tone was more urgent this time.

He had to get himself together. He cleared his throat.

"I'm fine. Make me a cup of strong black coffee, will you? My head aches something awful."

"Oh, right on it, Liam," Her cheerful voice came through the door.

"No alcohol this time."

She laughed. He wasn't kidding. At this point, he didn't know what she would do.

"We need to talk," Liam said.

Heidi looked at him over her shoulder.

He had taken a cold shower to help wake him up. When he had come out of the bathroom, she was waiting with his cup of coffee and two painkillers. Now, half an hour later he was feeling a little better. Well enough to have the conversation that couldn't be delayed a moment later, he realized, as Heidi turned to him and pressed her lips to his jaw.

"Mmm…you smell good," she murmured.

He stepped away and poured himself a second cup of coffee. This conversation would require him to have his wits fully about him.

Heidi moved past him and began stirring something in a pot on the stove.

"Porridge?" she asked.

"No," he replied and observed her as he took a large mouthful of the coffee.

She was dressed in a black turtleneck sweater and white slacks. Her hair fell across her face as she leaned over the stove and she pushed it behind one ear. She was quite a beautiful woman. Too bad he had no interest in her beyond friendship. And that friendship was now spoiled forever.

She looked up at him and smiled. "I enjoyed last night," she said.

He gulped. "About that…"

"I know what you're going to say."

"You do?"

"Yes. You'll say it was a mistake. You'll say it shouldn't have happened. Aren't I right?"

He drained his cup and placed it on the kitchen counter. This conversation was going to be harder than he thought. Heidi knew what he was going to say but didn't seem to care.

"That's right. Heidi, what we did last night was wrong on so many levels. First of all, I'm still married. Whether Nia and I are separated is not the point. The vows I made to her are still in effect, and I broke them."

"For all you know she broke them too. Running off as she did with this Deverre character."

Liam went over to the window and looked out at the snow-covered terrain. Somewhere out there his ring was hidden under all that snow. It was gone, along with his vows.

"Again, that does not exempt me from doing the right thing."

"Oh tosh, Liam, she made her choice. She left you. You can't be blamed for moving on with your life."

"Heidi, just stop! I *can* be blamed. I was wrong. Wrong for committing adultery and wrong for sleeping with you. You're not my wife."

But she didn't seem to be listening. "I'm not your wife right now but you can get a divorce from her, and we can be married. That way we can make every wrong thing right."

She was now ladling porridge into bowls. Had he not told her he didn't want any porridge? She was ignoring him on all fronts.

He took her by the shoulders and stared into her surprised blue eyes.

"Heidi, I am married. I'm not planning on getting a divorce. I'm sorry for what we did, but it ends here and now."

She looked confused. "Why wouldn't you get a divorce from a woman who left you? What's the matter with you? Did she cast a spell on you or something?"

As Liam stared at Heidi, she went out of focus, and Nia's face appeared. He saw her heart-shaped face, her shock of thick curly hair, her light brown eyes twinkling with mischief, her bow-shaped mouth and high cheekbones. He could swear he even heard her husky laugh. His heart contracted. How he missed her! Perhaps she *had* cast a spell on him because in spite of everything he still wanted her back.

"You need to leave, Heidi."

She looked shocked. "Leave…but Liam I just got here. I've been taking care of you…"

"And I appreciate that. I really do, but it was a mistake allowing you to stay here with me alone. I don't know why I did that. I'm still a married man, and it's inappropriate to be up here alone with you. I apologize for taking advantage of y…"

"Stuff your apology!"

She wrenched away from him. Her eyes darted between him and the bowls. He could swear for a second that she was contemplating dousing him with the steaming contents.

"I would have made a better wife than that trash you hitched yourself to."

He stared at her in horror. The fact that she had called Nia trash reminded him of something. How had he forgotten what Nia had told him of Heidi?

"That night at the gala did you tell her she was an embarrassment to me and that she should leave?"

She lifted her chin and looked him squarely in the eyes.

"Yes, I did because it's the truth. She made a fool of you at the gala in front of the Royal Family, Liam. She attacked Viscount Halifax and then me for no good reason. She is wild and erratic.

Everyone can see it except you. And now she runs off with one of her kind…"

He sucked in a breath at the vitriol pouring from the mouth of the one he had considered a friend. How wrong he had been.

"One of her kind? Are you forgetting that I am also one of her kind?"

Her eyes widened. "You think I mean about her being black? I was speaking about the thug she was with, Deverre. Besides, no one would describe you as anything but Caucasian."

"I identify with both races, Heidi…"

She shrugged.

"…and for your information, Nia has never been an embarrassment to me. I love and accept her for who she is."

"What about me?"

"What about you?"

"I've been here for you all these years. You have taken me for granted all this time. You ran off and married someone you barely knew and rejected the one who has always been here. The more I think about it, I have no sympathy for you. She was right to treat you as she did."

He told himself Heidi was lashing out in hurt and rejection and that he shouldn't respond in kind.

Resolutely, he took a deep breath. "Heidi, I need you to pack your things. I'll go call you a taxi."

As he turned away, she raised her voice. "That's right. Use me and then discard me like a dirty Kleenex. Nice. I wonder what the parishioners of your church would think of that."

The barb found its mark. Liam spun around.

"Don't play the victim, Heidi. You were a willing participant in all of this. You're the one who took it upon yourself to hop on a plane and come all the way up here uninvited knowing I was alone and vulnerable. You were the one who served me alcohol, and come to think of it, how much of it did you drink yourself?"

She glanced away, confirming his suspicions.

He marched up to her. "You deliberately got me drunk! I'll bet you put more whiskey in that coffee than necessary to reduce my inhibitions." He pushed his face into hers. "So I'll say you got exactly what you came for and now you're getting no less than you deserve."

The silence was punctuated a second later by the sharp sound of flesh on flesh as her palm connected with the side of his face. Liam's adrenaline was racing so much he barely felt the pain.

He straightened as Heidi pivoted and left the room.

Liam immediately made the call for the taxi. She would be leaving if he had to lift her and put her in the vehicle himself. He went into the living area and sat on the couch, listening to the sounds of her moving around. Heidi emerged several minutes later pulling her little suitcase behind her, as cool and composed as ever.

"Your taxi is here," he said.

She slanted him a gaze. "I'll give you some time to think about your actions. When you come to your senses, I'll be here…maybe."

He shook his head. "What I'm going to do is seek reconciliation with Nia."

"Good luck with that. She may not be as eager to let sleeping dogs lie as you are," she said with a mysterious smile. With that unsettling comment, she was gone and he was left with a funny feeling in the pit of his stomach.

Liam deleted the images on his phone and could only conclude that his drunken stupor the previous night had allowed Heidi to take advantage and save selfies of the two of them as his profile picture. The woman was completely delusional. He didn't understand how he had missed that. It occurred to him to wonder what had happened to her fiancé. He hadn't even thought to ask.

He shook his head. How had he managed to be so gullible? How had he, in fact, lost his way to the point where he had no discernment? In as much as he had preached to Nia about living a godly life, he had left himself wide open to the enemy. He had neglected to put on the full armor of God over the years. Had it happened when he was at college?

He had gotten so bogged down in his studies he hadn't really been as committed as he had been earlier. That was around the time that his songwriting had also stilled. He had turned his back not only on God but also his God-given talent. He had rushed into marriage with Nia to fill a void only God could.

For the first time in weeks, Liam opened his Bible. He felt immediately led to go to the passage in the first chapter of James that spoke about a double-minded man being unstable in all his ways. He read the remainder of the verses and closed his eyes.

Anyone who listens to the word of God but does not do what it says is like someone who looks at his face in a mirror and after looking at himself goes away and immediately forgets what he looks like.

Liam leaned back against the wall as tears ran down. That was him. He was a double-minded man. He had spoken a good game all these years, but when it came down to hardcore decisions in his life, he was being led only by what he felt was best. Decisions that would please his parents, like running the family business. Decisions that pleased him, like marrying Nia. He hadn't consulted God. No wonder his life was slowly unraveling.

"Lord, please forgive me. Forgive me for being double-minded and unstable in all my ways. Forgive me for leaning unto my own understanding. For sinning against you and for not living out my faith. For withholding some of myself from you. Help me, Lord. Please help me to be who You created me to be. Please remove all fear and doubt from my heart. Oh, Lord, help me to be strong and courageous. You have promised me that by your power I can do anything. That with faith even as small as a mustard seed I can move mountains. Lord, I don't need to believe in myself and in my abilities. I only need to believe in You. Please grant me the faith to

move, to go where you send me. Please reveal to me clearly, so there is no doubt about your plan and purpose for my life."

He poured out his heart and soul before his Father.

"Lord, please restore me. Lord, restore my joy. Lord, please renew my zeal, my passion, my desire for You and Your way. Let me return to You dear loving Father. Please, God. I need to feel You. I want to be on fire for You, Lord. I surrender to You. From here on in, I want to be on fire for You, dear Lord."

It was a dark day. It was a struggle, but in the end he felt the joy that no one else could provide. He felt God's touch bringing him closer and His hand healing what was broken.

Hours later his heavenly Father said, "Rise, William."

"I hear you call my name, Jesus. I'm coming," Liam said.

For the first time in four years, he wrote a love song to God. When he was done, he knew what he had to do. He had to pursue his dream.

Chapter 23

"I am resigning from the company."

Liam's father stared back at him, the blue eyes, identical to his, registering shock.

"What on earth for?"

"To pursue a career in Christian music."

His father rocked back in his office chair and swiveled slightly so that he was now staring out the window of the skyscraper into the London sky.

Liam had imagined this scenario and spent a great deal of time all last night thinking about possible reactions from his father and playing out what his own response would be to each one. He loved and respected his father very much. This had not been an easy decision for him.

While it was true that he was not in danger of ever becoming a starving artist given that he inherited a small fortune when he turned twenty-one, what had given him turmoil had been the duty he felt to his family.

He did not want to pursue his dream at the expense of those who had raised him to put commitment to others above one's own personal wants or desires. So much had been invested in preparing him for his role, not only formal training but all those times his dad had taken him on business trips and groomed him.

That was what had sent him on his knees for days petitioning God to guide him and assure him that this was what he really should do. God had revealed to him during that trial that his sense of duty was a part of his identity which was why he was struggling. God replaced that with the truth that first and foremost, Liam's identity was found in who he was in Christ.

It was with that in mind that he had finally felt the peace to make the choice to walk away from Lamport Holdings Inc. and pursue his calling.

Now there was no turning back. Regardless of the outcome, regardless of whether or not he had the support of family and friends, he knew he was doing the right thing.

"Why not just take a leave of absence," William III asked.

"I thought of doing that at first, but I realized that I would just be trying to appease you if I did. This is what I need to do. I'm going all in."

"You don't need to quit to pursue your music. You just need some time away. A lot has happened in your life over the past year, and you need to process and analyze that. Your job here will be waiting for you once you've sorted that out. Don't turn your back on your future."

Liam swallowed. This was hard, but it had to be done. The words had to be said. He looked his father squarely in the eyes.

"That's just it. I don't believe being CEO of Lamport Holdings is my future."

His father's face seemed to be full of sympathy and understanding. He thought he was giving wise advice.

"This is probably a result of your separation from Nia. I think it has shaken your confidence in yourself and your choices."

"Actually, I think the opposite is true. Our break-up challenged me to consider the choices I have made and recognize that many times I really didn't consult God. I did my own thing and asked Him to sanction it. That includes marrying Nia, and it includes following along in the career that was chosen for me."

When his father's eyes narrowed, Liam realized how accusatory that sounded and hastened to add, "I'm not blaming you, Dad. It was my own assumptions at play here. I've always loved music and singing, but I just didn't feel like it was possible for me. I was told for so long that I was to take over Lamport Holdings, I never considered I had a choice. When I entered university, I buried my talent and moved on. I told myself that it was time for me to grow up. But deep down I always felt a part of me was missing."

He looked at his father more intently and asked, "Didn't it strike you as odd that I had gone from writing songs and playing music almost daily to not showing any interest?"

His father shrugged. "I figured you'd just outgrown it. When I was young, I also loved to sing. In fact, your mother always said you inherited my singing voice."

"You do have a great voice."

He smiled wryly. "When I met your mother one of the first things I did was serenade her with *Let's Stay Together*."

"Still one of your favorite songs, as I recall."

"Of course, because it's our song." The boyish smile told Liam his father was taking a nostalgic trip. "Anyway, even though I enjoyed it, I never considered it beyond something fun to do."

"Yes, but was it your passion?"

William III considered this. "Can't say it was."

"What *is* your passion?"

"This business. The wheeling and dealing. Growing it. Diversifying its offerings. I enjoy every aspect of it. I guess I just assumed you did too."

"You know who else in this family feels that passion?"

His father waited.

"Leiliana. She loves this company. She reads *Forbes* and *Fortune* when other girls have their noses stuck in *Vogue* and *Glamour*. She confided in me recently that she challenged one of her professors on his theory of product diversification. He apparently got annoyed and told her to write a paper and present it to the class by the next morning or he was going to fail her. Using examples from our own company, she presented her paper and not only proved her point but impressed him so much with her knowledge of global diversification strategy that he begged her to return and be a part-time tutor next year after she graduates."

Liam noted the pride that lit his father's eyes at his words. "You should seriously consider her as your successor, Dad."

William III nodded thoughtfully. "Your mother told me recently that I have a daughter with a keen head for business. And I agreed. I certainly expected she would be one of my directors. I just expected my namesake to take over. I groomed you for that role, Liam."

"And you can groom Leiliana for that role too. It's not too late. She's eager, and I think she would be a great fit."

"What about Ben?"

Liam rubbed his chin. "Benjamin will be an important part of your business for sure, but I see him more as a techie kind of guy. You remember how he used to pick apart and then put together every piece of electronic equipment you ever gave him?"

"He still does," William observed wryly.

"I get the sense that he's more of a hands-on kind of guy rather than one to get caught up with the business side of things. Why? Are you considering him, rather than Leila?"

"No, I'm considering *you* rather than Leila."

"Dad, I believe a career in Christian music is where God is leading me. I need to be obedient."

Those were apparently the transformational words. William Lamport's expression grew to one of wonder. He rose from behind his desk and came to stand over Liam. Placing a hand on his shoulder, he said. "If that's the case, you need to follow. Go with my blessing. Whatever resources you need, whatever connections need to be made, will be provided."

"Thanks, Dad, for your support. But I want to do this on my own. I'm actually going to launch my own label with our band as the first artist. I don't plan to touch my inheritance to do it either. I will invest the money I've saved working for Lamport Holdings over the last two years. If God is leading me, He will take care of me. He will pave the way."

When Liam spotted the mathematics school teacher coming his way, he pushed off his car where he had been leaning and waiting.

"I thought you would never leave work. My goodness. School finished almost an hour ago."

Matthew McGregor smiled and pushed his glasses back up.

"I was working with a few of the slower kids, going over a few problems with them."

Liam folded his arms across his chest. "It sounds as though you really love teaching."

"It's not bad. I've come to enjoy it." He jiggled the car keys in his pocket and looked at the pavement. "It pays the bills at least. You know what I mean."

"No, I don't. When have I ever had to worry about paying bills?"

Matthew laughed. "What are you doing here anyway? I heard you were in Austria."

"Who'd you hear that from?"

"Reinhardt. He said he'd called for you and that's where your parents confided you'd gone."

"When was that?"

Matthew looked up in the air. "I think three weeks ago or so. Why?"

"Never mind." Liam clapped his hands and rubbed them together. It provided some warmth, but mainly it helped him to refocus. "Here's the thing. I know you like your teaching job. But tell me, is this your dream job?"

~*~*~*~

Sam sighed as he checked his social media page. He had just handed in his sales report that very morning, and he felt like he needed something to take his mind off what the report revealed. The numbers weren't good. He had known that even before it was confirmed in black and white, but there was nothing he could do about the state of the economy. Surely management would understand that.

Perhaps he needed more than a social media break. He needed to go get himself a cup of coffee. Maybe he would pass by HR and chat up that pretty Japanese assistant, Hana Ito, before coming back to his desk. She would be a welcome distraction.

He was about to stand when he spied the branch manager, Mr. Kochazek, thundering down the corridor. Sam straightened up and jiggled his keyboard's mouse. He quickly clicked the computer to a summary sheet and rubbed his chin, trying to look like he was actually reading the document instead of waiting for the man to pass.

He noticed from the corner of his eye how the manager paused to speak to his co-worker, Charles De Vecci, a brown-noser if ever there was one. And then Mr. Kochazek was on the move again.

Sam was holding his breath, waiting for him to pass by, when the man shouted, "Mr. Webber, in my office, now!"

Sam swallowed. This couldn't possibly have anything to do with that report, could it? He followed Mr. Kochazek into his office a few minutes later. The man threw a stack of papers across the desk at Sam.

"This performance report is abysmal! What do you have to say for yourself?"

"As I've tried to tell you, Mr. Kochazek, Sir, the economy is very bad. People are very cautious about taking on financial risks."

"Bull!" Mr. Kochazek barked, making Sam flinch. "Charles De Vecci is working in the same economy as you, and he has sold twice as many mortgages as you have." He leaned towards Sam. "You know what the real problem is? You're too lazy to get off your butt and go after business! You expect it to come to you."

Sam didn't bother to try to defend himself. Mr. Kochazek was probably right. The fact was he hated this job. A job offer directly out of college had found him working for the local bank, and he had quickly moved from teller to account manager. At first, it had been okay. It was within walking distance of his home, it paid the bills, and he got along well with his co-workers. But in the last twelve months, it had become stressful as the company directors began to put more pressure on its account managers to turn a profit.

Personally, he found it was a no-win situation. The targets were set high. And when he achieved them with great effort, like he had done last year, they were set higher the following year. Instead of being able simply to maintain the effort he had made, he was now being asked to surpass it. Predictably, he hadn't met the impossible target and was now being hauled across the coals.

He wanted to quit, but it didn't make sense to do that without having another job lined up and with student loans to repay. Truth be told, the most fun he had these days was when he played with the worship team at church.

"I am giving you one last chance to do better, Webber. Simply, because I have the world of respect for your father. If you do not meet your targets by the end of this quarter, you are out of a job."

"Why wait 'til then?" Sam muttered.

"Excuse me?"

Look. The truth is I hate this job. It sucks. The targets are completely unrealistic and inhumane. You make us work like slaves here while you lot get fat off our profits. I'm sick of it. You can just take your job and shove it.

"I'm waiting, Mr. Webber."

Sam blinked. He would love to allow those words to slip off the tip of his tongue and hit Mr. Kochazek between the eyes, but that was a luxury he couldn't yet afford.

"I'll work harder to improve the numbers, sir."

"You had better. Dismissed."

"Dismissed," Sam muttered as he closed the office door behind him. He would love to dismiss this job, but then what?

Just then his phone vibrated. He pulled it out of his pocket and checked the name. Liam Lamport. Perhaps Liam could give him a job. But doing what? It would be back to working behind a desk.

"Hi, Liam, what's up?"

"Does your job bring you satisfaction and fulfillment?"

"What?"

"I'm asking if you would like to continue doing a job you complain about ad nauseum or do something you love and make money while doing it."

Sam straightened. "Keep talking."

Chapter 24

He had left Reinhardt the last for a reason. He needed to discuss more than a career change. In the last couple of years, he had gotten busy with his job, and they hardly spoke. Heidi had become closer to him than Reinhardt. Unlike Matthew and Sam whom he interacted with often, he wasn't sure just how passionate Reinhardt was about music.

He met with him at a café. After they'd been served and had exchanged small talk for a few minutes, Liam got to the thing that had been on his mind for a little while.

"I was in Austria recently. Heidi showed up. How did she know I was going to be there?"

Reinhardt's raised a brow. "I told her. Was that a problem?"

"How did you know?"

"I called your parents."

"Why did you need to contact me so urgently?"

Reinhardt shifted in his seat and stared at Liam as he slowly sipped his drink. "What's wrong, Liam?"

"I'm just trying to understand why you thought it necessary to reveal to your sister that I was in Austria alone."

Reinhart carefully placed his mug on the table.

"Heidi told me she was trying to get in contact with you and asked if I had heard from you. I tried your phone. It went to voicemail. I called your parents to find out where I could reach you.

Your parents did not tell me to keep your location a secret. Did Heidi do something wrong?"

Liam ran a hand along his jaw and glanced around the coffee shop. It was around lunchtime, and traffic in the coffee shop was beginning to pick up. He considered how much he should reveal to Reinhardt.

"Are you aware that Nia left me?"

Reinhardt's mouth dropped open. "No. I was not aware of this. Why did she leave?"

Again Liam glanced around the shop. This wasn't the most private place to be sharing such information. "Let's take a walk," he suggested.

They finished their drink, paid for their things and left.

As they walked down the street, Liam thought that it was too bad he was only now talking to his friend after such a tragedy had occurred in his life. Reinhardt, despite his stiff manner, had always been a sensible person who offered sound advice. These days Liam hardly knew what was happening in Reinhardt's life.

"So, to get back to Nia. She left to go to L.A. to launch her music career."

Reinhardt gave him a sidelong glance. "No surprise there. She has always said that was what she planned to do."

Liam chewed that for a while. Was he the only one who hadn't seen this coming?

"But she will return, yes?"

"It's been three months, Reinhardt. She left without telling me and never even returned my calls."

Reinhardt's hand landed on his shoulder. "I'm so sorry. What are you going to do?"

Liam slowed to a stop. He had pondered that for so many hours, yet all he could come up with was to leave it in God's hands.

"Pray."

"Pray, yes. Act as well. Maybe she expects you to chase after her."

He hadn't told Reinhardt everything, but he would have to now.

"Listen, I tried contacting her a week ago. As I told you she hasn't returned my calls. But there's more. I messaged her to say I wanted to talk. She sent me a terse response that said it was over between us and please not to contact her again."

Reinhardt's mouth fell open. "Heavens, that was cold."

"Exactly. What do you do after a statement like that? I sense I need to leave this with God, Reinhardt."

Liam resumed walking, and Reinhardt fell into step beside him.

"And Heidi? How does she figure in all this?"

Liam took a deep breath. They had arrived at the messy part of the story.

"She came up to the chalet. It was the worst possible time. I was quite ill fighting off a flu bug. She took care of me. I didn't know she had it in her."

Reinhardt chuckled. "Heidi is very efficient. If there is a task to be done, she will see it done."

Liam smiled thinly. Sleeping with him had probably featured high on her task list.

They crossed the street into a park. He sat on a nearby bench and Reinhardt joined him.

"I was grateful to Heidi, and I think I let my guard down. I confided to her what had happened with Nia and shared my anger and disappointment. She was very sympathetic."

Liam leaned over and placed his head in his hands. He drew a deep breath then sat up and met Reinhardt's eyes.

"One night I indulged in too much alcohol. We ended up sleeping together."

Reinhardt pursed his lips and looked away. There was silence for some time.

"Don't be too hard on yourself. These things can happen," Reinhardt muttered.

Before Liam could ask him what he meant, he continued. "I always knew Heidi had feelings for you. I could sense you didn't feel the same way about her, but I knew she was hopeful that, eventually, you'd come to see her as more than my sister. When the two of you became close, I think it really heightened her expectations. When you married Nia, she was devastated."

Liam turned to stare at Reinhardt in shock. He hadn't recognized Heidi had such strong feelings for him. It was true that when they were younger, he'd been aware of her crush but after she had gone to college, they had gone their separate ways and for the next four years, their paths rarely crossed.

When she began her career at the investment company, she contacted him over a business matter, and he assisted her. From that time she would occasionally call for advice or help, and he rendered both happily. He was always warm toward her, not only because she was Reinhardt's sister, but also because he no longer perceived her as a nuisance. She never made any overt advances toward him, and he appreciated that.

When he married Nia, he had thought nothing of Heidi. He recalled now that she had seemed a little cold at the party to celebrate their wedding. At the time he had chalked it up to her being offended he hadn't told her he had gotten married.

Shortly after that night, Heidi declared to him she had gotten engaged to Henry Guinness, a man she had dated a few times in the past. He had congratulated her and later when he and Nia had run into her and Guinness at a party she had seemed happy.

He was stunned by the news now that she had been devastated.

"Are you sure about that? I never got the indication that was the case."

Reinhardt slowly nodded. "She told me so herself. Guinness had been begging her to marry him for the last year and a half. She kept telling him no. She only accepted after you married Nia."

Liam ran a hand down his neck as the pieces suddenly seemed to fall into place. Nia's suspicion about Heidi and all the signs he had missed were spot on, like the way she would conveniently ditch Guinness whenever he showed up. Even that night they were at the gala, as soon as Nia went to the ladies room, Heidi had asked Guinness to go and get her a drink. Immediately, she had begged Liam to dance with her seeing how much she loved to waltz to Fur Elïse.

He had felt a moment of discomfort but had obliged, deciding it was just harmless fun. Now he believed it had been a deliberate attempt on Heidi's part to anger Nia. Her confession to him in Austria about being there for him all along was the final piece of the puzzle. She had been carrying a torch for him all these years. How had he been so blind?

Liam put both hands on his face. "No wonder Nia left me. I am a blind fool."

Reinhardt looked down at his hands. "I always thought you knew, but were just humoring Heidi."

Liam turned to him suddenly. "Is this why you've been so distant over the last few years? Did you believe I was playing with your sister's emotions? Did you think I was some heartless fiend?"

Reinhardt looked a bit sheepish, and then he laughed uneasily.

"Not a fiend. I didn't think you were cruel, just indifferent."

"I genuinely liked Heidi though, and I regret the loss of our friendship."

"Lost? Why do you say it is lost?"

Liam bit his lip, not sure how the other man would take his next words.

"I rejected her," he admitted frankly. "I'm still in love with Nia, Reinhardt. She is still my wife for better or for worse. I made a mistake with Heidi, and I deeply regret that. In retaliation, she tried to lay the blame for what happened solely at my feet. I wasn't going to allow that. She has to face up to the role she played. She practically threw herself at me. Anyway, we had a falling out that I'm not sure will be repaired. I've forgiven her for what she did, but I'm not sure she has forgiven me or will forgive me when she finally comes to accept that nothing will ever develop between us."

Reinhardt had been looking down at his trousers during the conversation. When he met Liam's gaze, there was none of the anger he expected to see. Instead, there was sadness and understanding.

"I will talk to her. I will help her through this as best I can. I have never seen you look at another girl the way you look at Nia. I knew that night at your reception that Heidi didn't stand a chance. She can have tunnel vision when she wants something. That's our Heidi for you. It works well in business. Not so much in relationships."

"Speaking of which, I thought she was engaged to Guinness?"

Reinhardt shook his head sadly. "He broke things off after she ran off to Austria. I didn't understand why he would do that. She was very tightlipped about it. I now think she may have led him to believe she was romantically involved with you."

Liam grabbed his hair and groaned. Just what he needed, another enemy in this world. Guinness would no doubt blame him for his break up with Heidi if what Reinhardt was saying was true.

"Back to your comment about you not hearing from me, though. It had nothing to do with Heidi. I just got busy with study, and then work. I was trying to establish a name for myself in the architectural world, you know."

Liam had a suspicion there was more to it than that, but he didn't have the energy right now to press Reinhardt. Instead, he asked, "So, you really love what you do?"

Reinhardt looked surprised. "Of course. Don't you?"

Liam smiled and looked away for a moment. "I like it. I don't love it."

"Ah."

"Which is why I'm working on changing that."

"How?"

"I'm restarting our band."

Reinhardt's eyebrows shot up. "Really. You mean recreationally, like for fun?"

"No. As a career."

Reinhardt leaned back against the park bench hard and stared at Liam as though he had grown two heads.

"I don't understand."

"I've always loved singing and writing music. It's my passion. I've prayed about it, and that's what I feel God is leading me to do. I've resigned from my job at Lamport Holdings, and I'm launching a full-time music career."

"How do your parents feel about this?"

"They are supportive. Are you interested in joining us?"

He was sure the question was superfluous and that he already knew the answer.

One corner of Reinhardt's mouth tilted. "I'm happy for you. It is good that you can do this but, no, I have found what I enjoy doing as a career. Music I reserve for fun." His eyes turned serious. "Your father will help you, then?"

"I'm going to do this on my own, Reinhardt. I'll call on my father from time to time for business advice, but that is all. This is my dream, my venture, not Lamport Holdings'."

Reinhardt looked skeptical for a moment. "There's nothing wrong with using your connections to launch your business."

Liam laughed. "I'm not going to sit here and act as though I am pulling myself up by my bootstraps. I'm already starting out with a tremendous advantage for a variety of reasons. However, I'm not prepared to ride on the coattails of my family all my life. I will go out and take my own risks, and with God's help I will succeed."

A huge smile broke out over Reinhardt's face, and he held out a hand to him.

"I wish you all the very best, my friend. I hope maybe this venture brings you closer to what you have lost."

Liam knew he was referring to Nia. He took his friend's hand. "Thank you. Anytime you're interested in playing with us we'd welcome you. Until then, take great care of yourself."

~*~*~*~

"So, what do you think of my plan?"

Liam looked at the other two men and awaited their response to his question. He had just outlined to Sam and Matthew the business plan for a music label of their own. It involved them taking charge of their own careers rather than going the traditional route of being signed to a label. It meant more hard work on their part, but in the end, it would be worth it. They would be masters of their fate, captains of their souls.

He knew that was what he wanted. Now to find out if it was what the others wanted too.

Sam looked up from the document that set out the entire five-year plan from writing and composing their own songs to recording, packaging and marketing them. It even involved merchandising of brand products once they had established a name for themselves by the end of a three-year period.

"What I find interesting is how you sat down and detailed all this in just a week's time. After we agreed to leave our jobs and run off to form a band I assumed this would be a fly by the seat of your pants operation. Isn't this supposed to be a reckless adventure?" Sam asked with a grin.

Liam grinned back. "Adventure, yes. Reckless, no. Besides, you know I've got to plan. I don't do anything without thinking it through first."

The one time he had deviated from that model it hadn't turned out well. But he would rather not dwell on his marriage to Nia at this moment.

Matthew pushed up his glasses with his index finger and turned to Sam.

"He's a businessman. That's his training, which is good for us."

He turned to Liam. "But are you sure this isn't a bit reckless, Liam. It seems risky. Wouldn't it be easier to just send our demos to an established label? With your parents' connections, it would be easy to at least get an audition and take it from there."

Liam glanced at Sam who hid his smirk behind his cup of coffee. Sam told him yesterday that Matthew had not resigned his job but had instead taken an extended leave without pay. Liam tried not to take offense. He knew that Matthew was cautious, mainly due to the influence of practical parents who had sacrificed so that he could have the type of life they had not.

In Matthew's words, he did not intend to throw it in their faces by embarking on a risky singing career that might not pay the bills without a backup plan if it didn't work out. He had stopped short of saying that Liam had a trust fund to cushion any fall while he did not. But Liam knew he was probably thinking it.

Liam propped his arm on the top of his seat and shook his head. "If I wanted to play it safe I would still be Director of Operations at Lamport Holdings Head Office right now."

He sat forward, placing his forearms on the table. "We are going to do this the right way or not at all. There is risk involved with every business venture, but my plan is what would be termed in the business world as an acceptable risk. I have done my research. This can work. It will mean we have to work harder. We will need to be more involved in the business side of things. I understand that it may seem easier to just sign over our rights for the ease of just going into the studio and making music. But with my way we don't just become assets to a recording company. We aren't selling our souls for a bit of fame. I know how these recording companies exploit artists. They take and take and take. Yes, the artist gets a piece of the pie but at a tremendous cost to their identity. They have very little say in how their work is being marketed and promoted."

"But surely all recording companies aren't that way," Matthew argued.

Liam held up his hands. "You're right they aren't. There are a few out there that actually care about the artists. I would like us to one day be that recording company for other artists who may not want to go it alone. However, I've got the drive and the determination to go it alone. I'm not willing to sign over our rights to someone else. We have a great product to offer that will appeal to more than just people's carnal nature; it will minister to their souls. That is why I know we will succeed because God is blessing this venture. You have nothing to fear, Matt. Trust me."

Matthew nodded thoughtfully.

Sam sat forward and looked over at Mathew.

"You know I was sold from the get go but like you, I assumed we'd go the route of getting signed up to someone's label. But listening to Liam now I realize that while in the short term it would be easier to accept a record deal, in the long term it would mean we would be slaves to a label."

"Don't be so dramatic," Matthew said scowling at Sam, "We would have some say."

"Hear what you just said? *Some* say. Why should we only have *some* say? And that *some* may be more like *little* say or *ten percent* of the say. It will mean that when the record company says jump we ask how high."

"But it's a symbiotic relationship…" Matthew protested.

"How so?" Liam asked in earnest, encouraged that Sam at least understood what he was trying to achieve.

"The producers are dependent on us. If we don't perform, they have nothing to sell. So, we do have bargaining power," Matthew replied.

"We may have that power at some point in the future, but as an unknown band, we do not. They will be aware of our vulnerable position and exploit us." Liam's expression softened. "I know this is risky, but as you pointed out before, I'm a businessman. I weigh everything. I'm not reckless, and I'm not crazy."

"Who thinks you're crazy? Quitting your seven-figure a year job and deciding to become the lead singer of a fledgling band is totally sane," Matthew said with a smirk.

Liam felt his heart ease. He was making progress. He pressed on.

"This is not just about our music. It's about making a statement. For years, record labels have made their money by exploiting artists in millions of ways. They make money off every aspect of an artist's career like touring, merchandising, their name, their image, every single action. It's a real rip off. The public sees this artist with all the glamour and all the fame but not the sharks in the background pulling strings, wheeling the deals and making all the money. No lads, this will not happen to us. We will retain full control."

He sat back. Sam pounded the table in agreement. Matthew nodded. "One more question."

Liam cocked a brow.

"Where do we find a keyboardist?"

Liam smiled. "I'm glad you asked." He pulled his phone out of his pocket, located the image he wanted then passed his phone to the other guys.

"His name is Hans Nillson."

"Another German?" Matthew asked.

"Actually, he's Swedish. He was formerly a lead keyboardist for the Christian band *Great Commission,* but they broke up last year, and he has been looking for a new band ever since. He's very keen on meeting with us. I've prayed, and I've got a good feeling about him."

"He's got tattoos," Matthew murmured with distaste.

Liam nodded. "I asked about that. He told me it happened before he got saved. I don't think God wants us to discriminate against him because of his past. If God held our past mistakes against us none of us would be sitting here."

Sam nodded. "Here! Here!"

"So when do we get to meet him?" Matthew asked.

Liam looked at his watch. "I told him to meet us here this morning so he should arrive in another five minutes or so."

At that moment he looked up as Mr. Nillson, all six feet six of him entered the shop.

Liam jutted his jaw towards the door. "He's here."

Sam did a double take. "I thought you said he was Swedish?"

In the photo Hans was wearing a cap; now his curly afro was displayed in all its glory.

"He is. His father is Swedish. His mother is African."

Liam waved the man over and smiled. Even though the others had not yet agreed, he knew in his spirit that Hans would be a perfect fit for them. He felt excitement race through him at what they were birthing.

Chapter 25

*H*er debut album was finally finished!

As Nia moved around the room greeting industry folks at the glamorous launch event, she felt a sense of euphoria. The past four months of intense work had paid off. Damon had said he wanted to ensure he had the right material and producers for her debut album and it looked like he had achieved that.

Just as he'd promised, her first song had been a duet with Byron Brown. When it was released a few months ago, it gave Nia her first taste of success by becoming a top five pop hit. It led to her national televised debut alongside Byron on the *Today Show*.

She could still remember the excitement of going on national television and performing her first song next to the star. She had been captivated by the awe he inspired, the way people treated him wherever he went. She knew that this was the life she wanted and was now convinced she had made the right decision.

Damon kept pestering her to get a divorce, suggesting that she should cut ties with Liam lest he tried to stake a claim to her money in the future. She had barely restrained herself from laughing in his face when he had first suggested it. Liam was worth a fortune. What would he want with her money?

But over the last couple of months, she had begun to think of it more and more. It was not for the reasons Damon had mentioned, of course, but to put emotional closure to that part of her life and start over fresh. She had an upcoming tour planned to support her album. Once that was over she would seriously consider filing for divorce.

Liam rubbed a hand over tired eyes and glanced at the wall clock. It was just after 11 p.m. When he had started reviewing the band's marketing and PR plan it had been around eight. Hard to think three hours had passed so quickly. He got up to pour himself a cup of coffee and returned to his computer.

When the label had first been established, the band had started recording in a room in his penthouse which he had outfitted as a studio. It soon became obvious that such an arrangement was unsustainable. Not only did it reach a point where it seemed as though Sam, Matthew, and Hans were practically living in his home, but people who came to discuss business were also traipsing in. Soon the lines between his private life and work became blurred. He had no place to retreat to at the end of the day, and he began feeling stressed. That tension was not good for his creative flow. Song writing slowed to a trickle.

At that point, he met with the band. They agreed that the label needed to have an official home. They leased space in one of the Lamport Holdings properties in London. It was outfitted appropriately and even had a fancy label at the front. It was called LWM Records, named after the three who had invested a portion in the start-up enterprise.

Liam glanced around the office now. It was functional, if not entirely fancy, certainly nothing like what he had been used to at his old office at Lamport Holdings. But they had decided that their money in these initial stages would be plowed into the product and marketing and salaries for the essential employees they had hired. The frills would come later when they had finally realized a profit.

Liam leaned forward over the desk and made a few final comments on the document in preparation for the meeting with the marketing team the following day. When he was done, he moved the document to one side of his desk and opened his laptop. He immediately went to the band's website.

It had been updated just yesterday by the new social media consultant they had hired a month ago after the first one quit to pursue greener pastures. At the time, Liam had been sorry to see her go but now he was glad. This new man, an Indian named Suresh Patel, was brilliant. He brought things to Liam's attention, and came up with ideas, that the previous consultant had not. Not that he was blaming her. Lindsay had been fresh out of university when he had hired her, and while she was bright and enthusiastic, she hadn't a lot of experience. When the job was vacated, he saw it as an opportunity to hire someone with more savvy and know-how.

That decision had paid off big time. In the last three weeks alone they had received at least five times the amount of traffic on their website and the social media sites. Their followers had increased tenfold. Suresh was proving to be well worth the high fees he demanded.

Within the last month, the band also had made the decision to hire a business manager. It had meant that for the first time since embarking on this venture, Liam had a little more time to concentrate on writing music instead of running a business. It was hard to focus on being creative when you were bogged down with paying bills and reviewing contracts. He had to grudgingly concede that there were benefits to being managed. So, he had hired Sophie Kerr.

Sophie was middle-aged and savvy, and Liam felt comfortable with her. Perhaps it was because she reminded him of his mother. She had the same honey blonde hair and intelligent brown eyes, and she was smart, down-to-earth, and hard working. All of which worked well for him.

Liam nodded with satisfaction as he perused the site. The homepage featured a photo of the band as it appeared on their second album which had been shot in Covent Garden. Almost a year and a half after they had made this career move, he could finally say they were getting somewhere. He clicked on a tab that featured where their music could be purchased, and then onto the music videos they had made to accompany the hits from the albums.

Satisfied with the website, he switched focus and began composing an email to their marketer. According to Suresh, they needed to capitalize on the social media traffic by lining up more appearances on television shows to maximize their reach. Sophie was working on setting up meetings with leading Christian bands about *Redeemed* opening for them on their tours. Once this third album they were working on was finished, the band needed to promote it with a domestic tour. Just like Nia was doing in promotion of her albums right now.

Liam paused and rubbed the back of his neck. He wished he could blame fatigue for that name slipping into his thoughts, but he couldn't. To his eternal shame, he couldn't seem to stop himself from tracking Nia's rise to stardom. It felt like a lifetime had passed since she had left him.

Since that time, a year and a half now, she had launched two albums-- *Nia* and *Star*. The reviews had been great. *Rolling Stone* praised her as one of the most exciting voices in years. *New York Times* called her talent exceptional. *The Chicago Tribune* declared that she was an impressive whirlwind of energy and emotion.

He wasn't surprised at the praise. He was well aware of Nia's vocal talents. He had purchased the albums and over time had been able to listen to each song without plummeting into a pit of nostalgia. What had surprised him was that even though a few of them were certainly suggestive, most of them were sweet, breezy songs about love and the challenges of youth. He had been sure Deverre would have her belting out salacious lyrics like those of his popular stars.

Still, he couldn't shake his distrust of the man and his intentions for Nia.

What was certain, though, was that he was expending a great deal of money on marketing his latest pop star. Nia was everywhere. Wherever Liam went, he saw her image emblazoned on something or caught her speaking on one of the talk shows. No doubt, it was paying off. Last he had heard both albums combined had sold over three million copies worldwide.

At first, it was jolting to see her image. Every time he saw her his heart would skip a beat, and a deep regret would settle over him at the demise of their relationship. But just as he had schooled himself to listen to her songs without blubbering like an idiot, he managed to discipline his emotions over time to dispassionately view her image and move on.

"It's about time you put that in your past."

Nia swiveled around to stare at Damon as she dropped her hand guiltily to her side. She immediately regretted the gesture knowing there was nothing to feel guilty about. To prove it, she crossed her arms to expose the wedding ring she had just been twisting.

Immediately after her domestic tour had come to an end, Nia resolved to finally contemplate filing for divorce from Liam. She had taken out her wedding ring from where she had stuck it deep in her drawer almost two years ago and without thinking had fitted it on her finger. That act had seemed to fling open a portal into memories of her life with Liam.

She had blamed him for the break-up of their marriage, but she had been at fault too. He had tried to apologize. She had ignored him. Was it any wonder he had run into the arms of another woman? It hardly mattered now though. The last message she had sent him about not contacting her again had seemed to cut him to the quick. He had not tried since then.

She was now back in the studio working on her third album, and she was still wearing the ring. She had not been able to take it off, and she wasn't sure why. Liam clearly wanted nothing more to do with her.

A few minutes ago, she had taken a break from recording to grab some coffee when Damon had walked into the room. Apparently, the presence of her wedding band bothered him. He strode forward, stopping just a few inches in front of her. He lifted her hand and frowned at her wedding band.

"This is a farce. You need to get rid of it and get rid of Will-eee-um by way of divorce."

Nia's back stiffened. Ever since she had begun recording her first album in earnest, she and Damon had developed a relationship that most people found fascinating. For some reason, *El Honcho* treated Nia differently than his other artists; even esteemed stars like Sheba. He showed up to see Nia when he didn't need to. He applauded her every little success and was there at every event. He hovered and indulged her in a way he did for no one else.

People told her she had him eating out of her hands. She didn't comment because she knew better. While it was true she had some influence over Damon, she had never forgotten how she had to fight tooth and nail to get that fifteen percent of royalties. It proved to her like nothing else that when it came down to crunch time, Damon was all about the money.

She gave him the once-over as she wondered how she should respond to his latest attempt to cross the line between boss and confidante. He was a handsome man. He looked sharp as usual with his hair cut in a trendy style, trim beard, and manicured fingernails. He wore an expensive wool suit and well-polished leather shoes. Success covered him like a cloak, and it looked good on him. Still, she didn't trust him. That made for a tiring relationship. How could she ever relax completely around someone she didn't trust?

She tilted her head back to meet his eyes. She was one of the few people who seemed willing to meet his intense gaze head-on.

"My personal life is none of your business," she said.

He smiled in that annoying way of his that suggested she was totally naïve.

"Your personal life *is* my business. I am heavily invested in the brand that is Nia Carmichael. Everything you do and everything you say is a reflection on me."

Nia refused to reveal to him how much his words unnerved her. Even the suggestion that she was no longer her own person made her feel sick.

"That's not my interpretation. And it's not what I signed up for. If that's what you think, you are sadly disillusioned."

She pushed her index finger into his chest and felt a rush when she saw his eyes widen for a moment at her boldness. She didn't stop.

"You trespass if you think for one moment that I'm going to allow you or anyone else to tell me how to live my life. And if you push me too far, I will not be renewing this contract when it expires in three months."

She felt a surge of satisfaction when shock registered briefly in his eyes. It was short-lived, however, because the next words out of his mouth sent a chill up her spine.

"How do you know I'm going to offer to renew your contract?" he asked,

Nia felt her throat tighten. She willed herself not to break his gaze knowing that was exactly what he wanted. He couldn't be serious. He had never expressed any dissatisfaction with her performance. He turned away and drifted to the window and looked through the panes down into the L.A. city streets. She scrambled frantically in her mind for a response, but he wasn't finished.

"Your performance to date hasn't been bad, don't get me wrong."

Not bad! She had been getting rave reviews from both critics and the public alike. Her albums had sold millions, and her songs were still in the top ten on the Billboard charts. How could he say it was 'not bad'?

"The thing is we invested heavily in you. PR, marketing, wardrobe. You know I got the best producers and songwriters for those albums."

He turned around, staring at her thoughtfully as he rubbed his chin.

"So, I expected the sales figures to be better."

"Better?" she sputtered. "But Damon..."

He kept talking as though she hadn't opened her mouth.

"On the face of it, yeah, it seemed fine, but my finance people, you know the number crunchers, they are ultimately the ones who can tell me what the true picture is and Nia...," he shook his head, "I'm disappointed."

Nia felt like attacking Damon and scratching his eyes out. She had learned, though, that attempting such a thing would not only be futile but also foolish.

Several months ago she witnessed Damon get into a fight with a man bigger than himself. The man was a bouncer in a club who had dared to rest his hand on Damon's shoulder after Damon had caused a scene by threatening another record producer. Damon had floored the bouncer. She had never seen someone pummel another human being before and it had terrified her.

If Damon hadn't been pulled off the man, she was sure he would have killed him. For the first time, she had truly understood just how dangerous he was. Since then, she hadn't raised a hand to him. She knew he could easily flick her away like a flea.

If nothing else, the last several months had taught her that to be effective with this man she needed to stay cool. So now, she swallowed and met his eyes. She forced her lips to lift in a smile as she leaned her head to the right and sighed.

"Well then, Damon, it looks like it's time for us to part ways. I've had some offers from other studios. Perhaps it's time I explore them."

She saw his eyes flicker. It was barely perceptible, but she noticed, and it gave her the impetus to continue.

"There will be no hard feelings. You were the first one to believe in me, and I won't forget that."

She held her breath as she began walking towards the door, hoping he would not call her bluff.

"I never said I would not renew your contract. I simply mentioned the challenges we are facing. This is a discussion on how we can move forward together, Nia," he said softly.

She paused in her stride. Moments later she felt his hand on her shoulder. She spun around to face him and forced herself to smile.

"Oh, is that what that was? Good. Because I'd be happy to consider going forward with you, Damon, but we need to get one thing clear. My personal life is my business, and the moment you try to transgress that I walk."

He stared at her. "Here's a bit of professional advice, then. As we move forward together, your marriage to Lamport is going to prove a stumbling block."

"How on earth did you come to that conclusion?"

"As your spouse, he would be entitled to what you own and as your assets grow Nia so will what he owns of yours."

Nia shook her head. "As I mentioned before he is the heir to a fortune that makes your empire look like chump change."

"Doesn't matter. He will have ownership of your brand. He will have a say in all that. And heaven forbid that you say or do something he doesn't like. He can bring an injunction against you."

Nia hesitated, uncertain. "Is that true?"

"Ask your lawyer. If he's worth his salt, he'll know. I am telling you this as a friend. There is nothing between the two of you anymore. Make a clean break, or it will come back to haunt you."

Chapter 26

" Mr. Lamport was served notice."

"And?"

"He contacted my office today and said he will be contesting the divorce."

Nia jerked forward in her chair. "He did?"

Mr. Manzini, her lawyer, looked up at her above the bifocals perched on his nose and said, "Regrettably, yes. His action will not deter us, but it will delay things."

Nia felt hope stir in her chest. Was it possible that Liam still wanted her, or was he just being spiteful?

"Why?" she wondered out loud.

"You're worth a fortune now, Ms. Carmichael. You're also a star."

She had recently released her third album and was now working on the fourth. She had negotiated a new contract with Damon which saw her with still no more than fifteen percent but at least she had managed to acquire greater creative control.

This third album, *Nana Nia* was already a success. Several of its songs had peaked on the charts, and she now had the honor of being the first woman to generate four number one hits from one album. At the Grammy's that year, she was nominated for three awards including album of the year. She won a Grammy for best female pop vocal performance.

It was good to be doing so well. But every time she received another accolade, Damon took pleasure in reminding her that she was still hitched to William Lamport or Will-eee-um as he loved to stress in that annoying, demeaning way. She could not figure out what he could possibly have against Liam. If anything, Liam should be the one resentful of Damon. After all, from all appearances, Damon had stolen her away. Not that it was true. She had made the decision on her own.

"Perhaps Mr. Lamport hopes to capitalize on his association with you," Mr. Manzini continued.

"You haven't properly done your research, Mr. Manzini. William Lamport the fourth stands to inherit a title and an estate worth billions. Given all that he and his family stand for, marriage to me does him more harm than good."

She turned her head to gaze out the window. "No, there must be some other reason."

"Perhaps you should speak to him yourself and find out."

Nia startled. As bold as she was, she was scared to confront Liam. It was easier to avoid him rather than to hear the disapproval in his voice or see the coldness in his eyes.

While she told herself during the day that she was finally living the life she wanted, it was less easy to do on cold, lonely nights when sleep did not come easily. She would whisper in the dark that she was used to fractured relationships and this was no different.

She had left friends and made new ones. She had stepmothers who had disappeared, and new ones appeared. Her own father was hardly present. Her grandparents had died one by one. Friends she had known when she was younger she didn't keep in touch with now. Except for Bianca who was still her buddy and who she had hired to be her personal assistant.

But sometimes, she felt real regret for her past errors. She had not meant things to end like they had. She had meant to apologize and seek reconciliation, but after suspecting Liam had been carrying on with Heidi, it had deflated her. Then as weeks had turned into months and months had turned into years it had just gotten harder and harder to reach out to him.

Except now, she had a little hope. Liam didn't want the divorce. And unless he was being spiteful or difficult, there must be something positive in that.

"I understand that Mr. Lamport is here," Mr. Manzini commented.

Nia startled for the second time in as many minutes. "Here in L.A.?"

"No. Here in the USA. I think he's in Nashville. He's residing there based on what the courier was told."

"What's he doing in Nashville?"

Mr. Manzini took off his glasses and formed a steeple with his hands.

"It seems that he has established a record company."

"Get out of here!" Nia exclaimed.

"His band is the only one signed to it at the moment I heard."

Nia shook her head. "You're kidding!" How had she missed this? Why hadn't anyone told her? More to the point, had Liam decided to quit his job and pursue his passion? Was this something he was doing on the side? What was going on?

Suddenly, she wasn't so afraid to meet with him. She was curious about what had happened. In fact, she was burning with curiosity. She sat forward eagerly.

"Can you contact him and request a meeting between the two of us?"

Mr. Manzini nodded and made a notation on his paper.

"Any particular time?"

She was still working on her fourth album, but surely she could take a few days off. It was her due anyway. Ever since she had signed up with Double D Records all she had done was work.

"This week if possible. I'll clear my calendar and make myself available. I can fly down to Nashville. We can meet for dinner."

"Do not forget that it was you who left me. That it was you who threw our vows in my face. Don't expect me to be overjoyed to see you."

Nia halted at the words flung at her back by Liam as she headed for the door.

She should have known that this meeting would not have gone well from the moment Mr. Manzini had told her Liam would rather meet at his office than at a restaurant as she had suggested.

Then on her arrival, Liam had made her wait outside his door for twenty minutes. And when he had finally allowed her in, instead of greeting her with an apology, he had barked at her to make it quick because he had a busy schedule.

She could not believe that Liam could be so rude. The spark of joy she had felt at seeing his handsome face had been instantly extinguished.

She had grabbed her bag and muttered as she headed for the door, "I see this was a mistake."

But his words stopped her in her tracks. She turned to him. It was true she had been the one to leave. It had been foolish of her not to anticipate he would still be angry, but she had assumed, based on the speed at which he had agreed to meet with her, he was on his way to reconciliation. Clearly, she had misjudged him. But how did she make this right? She couldn't undo the past and the word 'sorry' seemed so inadequate.

He continued to watch her with cool blue eyes, and she was tempted again to walk away, but she hesitated. She had come so far. She needed to suck it up and deal with this.

She returned to her seat and lowered herself into the chair.

Taking a deep breath, she said, "Liam, I don't know how to make things right between us. You are correct, I did leave you, but all I can say at this point is that I'm sincerely sorry for the way things ended."

She dared to look at him and noticed a softening in his gaze.

He nodded. "I was surprised to receive your invitation," he said.

"When I received your response, I didn't understand what it meant," she said carefully, not wanting to antagonize him again.

He cocked a brow. "I thought I was clear. I'm contesting the divorce."

"But why?"

He seemed surprised. "Why? Did you forget the vows we said to each other? To God? I didn't take those lightly, Nia."

She was baffled. "But we've not been a couple for the last two years, Liam."

He drew in a deep breath. "I'm well aware of that. But that was your decision. Not mine. I never asked you to leave. I never left you."

"But you told me if I left not to bother coming back."

For the first time, he looked ashamed.

"Yes, and I'm sorry about that. But I did try to call you back and apologize. Your phone kept going to voicemail, and in frustration, I left message after message. You never called me back. I assumed you weren't interested in my apology. And the last message I sent you. Well, you made your feelings about my contacting you quite clear."

Nia looked down at her hands. He was right. She hadn't been interested in what he had to say until that day when Damon had acted like an idiot, and she had had a change of heart. She had listened to his messages then, and she had tried to contact him.

"I did call you back," she murmured.

He cocked his head to one side. "What's that?"

"I said I called you back."

He sat up a little straighter. "When was that?"

"It was about a month after I'd left…September 11th, I think."

She could almost see the wheels turning in his head. "I didn't receive a call from you," he said eventually.

"Heidi answered your phone," she said softly, observing him closely. The way the color drained from his face spoke volumes.

"What did she say to you?" he ground out between clenched teeth.

"She said the two of you were in Austria together. She told me you were asleep. What were the two of you doing up there alone, Liam?"

The way he couldn't meet her gaze was confirmation of what she had suspected.

Silence reigned for a while and was broken by the harsh bark of laughter that Nia was surprised came from her mouth. When Liam's startled expression found hers, she smiled bitterly.

"I just realized it wasn't just me who broke vows, was it?"

His gaze flickered, and for a moment she saw regret reflected in their depths.

"How long did it take you to recover in her arms, Liam?"

He fidgeted with something on his desk and didn't respond.

She was enraged. Here her heart was breaking, and he sat there like a stone. She sat forward abruptly and slapped her hand on the desk.

"Answer me!"

He glanced up at her and narrowed his eyes. After a moment he said, "I slept with Heidi once. I deeply regretted it. It has never happened again. In fact, I haven't seen Heidi since that day, and I have no intention of doing so either. There has been no one else since then."

Nia sank back against the seat. To hear him admit to sleeping with Heidi was not easy but there was a strange sense of relief in recognizing that he was straight with her, that Heidi was no longer in his life, and that she had not been the only one who had messed up.

He cleared his throat. "Are you happy, Nia?"

For a moment she thought he was asking if his confession had made her happy, but then she realized he was asking if she was happy with her life. She did not know how to respond, so she told a lie.

"Very happy," she said, forcing brightness into her voice.

"I'm glad." He looked a little sad when he said it though.

"Are you really?"

He chuckled mirthlessly. "Truthfully, I'm not. I still believe there's a better way."

"After all this time you still believe that your way was the best way."

"Of course I believe it. I'm living it."

"What do you mean?"

"Let's move on then to what really brought you to Nashville. To see what I was up to out here. Well, I decided to pursue a music career. That was one thing you were right about, and I thank you for that. I was not living my passion, so I decided to do something about it."

His mouth lifted in a grin that reached his eyes for a moment.

"And as it would have been hypocritical of me to do otherwise, I formed a recording company."

She was impressed but not surprised. Liam had been trained and groomed to be a businessman. Considering that both of his parents were business people, it was probably a part of his genetic makeup.

"I only became aware last week. I didn't know."

He shrugged. "We are fledgling and the first year was spent setting up the company and recording songs at every available moment. Fortunately, a lot of old songs I wrote I was able to use, so we had great material going in."

He stopped talking suddenly, perhaps thinking he was revealing too much. She wanted him to continue and leaned forward to touch his hand.

"I understand you've finished your third album and that it's scheduled for release next month."

"Where did you hear that?"

"It's on your website. I did an Internet search after I spoke with my lawyer."

His expression flickered with something that almost took her breath away. It looked like vulnerability. In the blink of an eye, it was gone, and he was all business again.

"Yes. It will be released soon. But our work is nothing like what you have been up to. Two albums in two years. A domestic tour and three Grammy nominations. Plus, I can't turn on the TV or pass by a magazine stand without seeing your image. I can see why it seems you made the right choice. My independent company wouldn't have been able to give you that kind of exposure. Certainly not in that kind of timeframe."

She couldn't let on that it wasn't all it had been cracked up to be. Two years in she was feeling pretty tired of Damon telling her what to do. And the fame had not filled her with contentment like she had thought it would. Sure, she buried herself in work and told herself that was all that mattered, but sometimes she felt so lonely, even in a crowd. At those moments she longed for more. She craved more. She craved relationship.

She missed the nights lying in Liam's arms where they would converse about every little thing. There were secrets she would share with him about her past, about her aspirations and her fears that she had never shared with anyone else. She missed that intimacy so much. Nothing she had experienced over the last couple of years could compare with that.

But she couldn't confess that now. She couldn't leave herself bare like that. It was too risky.

Involuntarily, her gaze flew to his, and she felt her heart ache at the sight of him. She closed her eyes briefly to regain her composure. She swallowed.

"Will you forgive me?"

"Forgive you for what?"

"For leaving?"

He smiled gently. "Some days it feels as if I have. When I see your image, I feel happy for you and what you've been able to achieve. Other days, I blast you to hell for what you put me through. I rue the day I ever met you, and I wish I could erase you from my memory."

She sucked in a breath and felt as though he had slapped her.

"But then I remember my indiscretion with Heidi, and I see that I'm not perfect either. So, yes, I do forgive you, but I also need you to forgive me my trespasses. Will you?"

The way he said it showed her he was still hurting. For all his nonchalance he still felt shame from his act of adultery.

"Yes, I do."

He released a breath.

Liam was wrong about the real reason she had come. It hadn't just been out of curiosity about his company, it also had been to find out why he didn't want a divorce. He had told her he didn't want to go through with the divorce because of the vows he had made, not because he loved her still and wanted her back. It was just because of vows made. For her, that wasn't enough.

She reached into her bag and took out her wedding band. She placed it on the table between them. She didn't miss how his eyes fastened on it as though it was a rattlesnake.

She clasped her hands. "I want to return this to you. And I want you to sign the divorce papers. This is not a marriage, Liam. We need to legally separate."

His head lifted. She couldn't read what was in the depth of his eyes, but it seemed to be a draught of emotions. She was unsure of what he would do.-To her surprise, he picked up the ring and turned it over in his hand.

"You want me to break our vows?"

She was tempted to say it wouldn't be the first time, but who was she to throw stones, particularly after she had granted forgiveness. Instead, she drew in a breath.

"How are we keeping our vows now? We live separate lives."

"Is there no chance you'll come back to me then?"

Her heart thudded. The offer was unexpectedly tempting, so tempting in fact that she felt tears form. She glanced away and blinked rapidly. She did not want to do this.

"Why would you want me after I flung our vows in your face as you put it?"

He seemed to think on this for a long time. "I don't know," he answered with a helpless shrug. He gave a bitter-sounding laugh and looked up at the ceiling as though the answers were held there.

"Mercy, I do not know why I still want you." He looked across at her and gazed into her eyes, "But, heaven help me, I still do."

It was said with so much emotion Nia felt her heart clench.

When he reached across the table for her hand, she didn't resist. She felt things she didn't want to feel. He lifted it to his mouth and grazed it with his lips.

"You're still my woman, Nia. Aren't you?"

She found herself nodding helplessly as though in a trance. She wanted to be his woman. In that moment, she didn't care what tomorrow brought them. She ached to return to the past.

"Liam," she whispered, and a moment later he vaulted from behind his desk and was pulling her to her feet and into his arms.

"I've missed you," he whispered in her ear and on a cry their lips met.

Nia felt such longing. All she could do was melt into him. She didn't even think she breathed through the whole kiss. When they came up for air, he whispered on her lips. "Let's get out of here."

Chapter 27

Liam knew that it was risky heading over to his apartment with Nia in the passenger seat of his car, but his head wasn't the one in charge anymore. From the moment he had seen Nia in the flesh again his heart had taken over. He reasoned that she was still his wife so this was in no way inappropriate. He was tired holding his emotions in check pretending that he wasn't hurting. He was tired of being a throbbing mass of numbness. He wanted to feel something like happiness again, and that was how he felt when he was with her.

In the apartment, he made them both a quick dinner of Thai vegetable curry with quinoa and a green salad. As they ate, they conversed on everything from politics to music to current affairs. After the meal, Liam made them a pot of tea, and they settled on the living room sofa and continued their conversation.

"Why Nashville?" Nia asked as Liam moved across the room to pull the curtains closed.

The evening was beginning to darken, revealing the lateness of the hour. He knew he should take Nia back to the hotel. Her flight left in the morning and she probably needed to pack, but he kept hoping she wouldn't leave. Not tonight. Not tomorrow. Not ever.

"Because Nashville is the Christian music capital of the world."

He came to sit down beside her. She slid off her shoes and placed her feet in his lap, and he began caressing them in a move that felt as natural as rain.

"When we first began, our base was in London, and we achieved modest success. Soon we launched a website, got a social media consultant, and we began to increase our visibility via social media. But when I asked our business manager to get us opportunities to tour with more established bands to increase our visibility in Christian circles, she advised us that no Christian band thrived in London. Nashville, she said, was the place to establish linkages, increase visibility, and make important connections in Christian circles."

When he had made the decision to leave London and relocate to Tennessee in a quest to cement the presence of *Redeemed* in the Christian music world, it had not been without doubts. Just as the decision to embark on a music career had come after much prayer and fasting, so did the decision to move to America.

He left the familiar for the unfamiliar. He abandoned the warm cocoon and protection of family and friends for a world where no one cared about him.

In an amazingly short time, however, *Redeemed* began to make strides. Doors opened. Opportunities knocked. Things happened. Liam also knew that it was God's intervention. They did meet challenges along the way. Sometimes they had disappointments, but through it all they could see God working on their behalf, paving the way. Just as He had parted the Red Sea for the Israelites to cross over to The Promised Land, He had not brought them there to leave them to flounder.

Although they were still considered by many to be new to the music scene, the band had met with undeniable success. Liam credited God with it all. He knew the Lord was the one who guided their decisions on everything from the songs Liam wrote to the music compilations. He was there in everything from their venues and set designs to merchandising of their products.

He glanced at Nia and found he had her rapt attention.

She looked so appealing with her hair tumbling all over her head, and her eyes lit with interest that he had to glance away to remember what he had been saying.

"After that, we decided to relocate to Nashville."

He chuckled. "It was like the British invasion because there were a couple of other British artists arriving in Nashville looking to make a name for themselves as well. There were no screaming girls, but we got us some great opportunities as opening acts for popular bands. Things have really looked up since then."

"No screaming girls?" She winked. "Hard to believe with that Swedish hunk you've got on your team now."

"How did you know about Hans?"

"Website, remember?"

He held a hand to his heart. "I'm gutted. I thought for you I was the only hunk who existed."

She laughed. "I just wanted to see what your reaction to that statement would be. You know you're utterly gorgeous, and no one compares to you."

"Not even Damon Deverre?"

She lost her smile, and he regretted the foolish comment that revealed his jealousy. He had not had the heart to ask her if her relationship with the man went beyond business, but he still wondered.

To his surprise though, instead of getting angry, she leaned forward and whispered in his ear, "Especially, not Damon Deverre."

He resumed rubbing her bare feet. This time applying more pressure to the instep. She closed her eyes and moaned in ecstasy, "Oh, that feels so good. Don't stop."

He held his breath as a surge of desire ripped through him. The air between them became charged. He was acutely aware of her, of how she felt, how she smelled, how lovely she looked, of her throaty laugh and silky voice.

Before he could think it through, Liam leaned forward and captured Nia's plump lips. Even though a voice in his head said this was not going to solve any problems just complicate things further, he silenced it. He drew her closer, and his mind almost exploded when she moaned softly and clung to him.

~*~*~*~

She gazed down at him and traced his cheek with her index finger. She had missed him, had missed this intimacy so much. She had spent the last ten or fifteen minutes watching Liam sleep even though she needed to get to the airport for her flight. At that moment, she simply did not care.

She leaned down and kissed his lips. His mouth twitched. She kept kissing him until he began to respond. He moaned. His arms reached around her back and tightened around her.

"My wife," he whispered.

She smiled. "My husband."

"Are we going to spend the day in bed?" he asked.

"We could."

A smile curved his mouth. He reached up and fingered strands of her hair.

"I meant to ask yesterday," he moaned, "What happened to my curls?"

As innocent as the comment was it reminded her of Damon and of her duties and responsibilities to the label. Damon would be expecting her to return to L.A. later today. They were still in the middle of recording songs for the album.

She resolutely stamped down thoughts of Damon and returned her gaze to Liam.

"The curls can return. They have only been tamed for now."

He lifted an eyebrow. "My wildcat tamed? Who could do that?"

Again they were moving into dangerous territory. Such talk led to thoughts of Damon. She propped up on an elbow and settled her face over his.

"I'm not tame, and I'd like to show you I'm not."

His hand reached around her curtain of hair to run down her neck.

"I'd like you too as well," he whispered, and then he sighed. "Unfortunately, I've got some meetings scheduled today."

He turned his head to gaze at the clock, "And already I have failed to show up for one of them."

She followed his gaze. It was now ten o'clock in the morning. She couldn't believe they had spent that much time in bed. It had been a long night for both of them. Liam had woke her up at least twice in a haze of passion, and she had eagerly responded each time. Still, disappointment flowed through her now that they had to return to real life again so soon. As she turned to get out of bed, Liam pulled her onto her back.

"What difference can one more hour make, right? I can always make the excuse that I simply was unable to get out of bed this morning. That would not be a lie," he said with a throaty chuckle.

She smiled and ran her finger on his chest. "If you're sure."

"I'm sure that I want you."

Was that all? Was this just about lust?

"What else," she asked just before his mouth descended. She felt him hesitate then he raised his head and stared into her eyes.

"I want us to be together again. I want you to come back to me."

How did she respond to that? Did she dare make promises to him? They had spoken about all kinds of things last night, but by some unspoken code, they had not spoken of the future. Until now.

"Isn't that what you want?" From the urgency of his question, she realized he had read the conflicted emotions on her face.

She raised her head from the pillow and pressed her mouth to his. She didn't want to think now. She didn't want to talk. She just wanted to feel. Again she sensed Liam's hesitation but then a moment later he devoured her mouth.

The voice bellowed through the phone, "Where are you?"

Nia held the phone at arm's length and glared at it for a moment before putting it back to her ear.

"What do you mean?" she asked, annoyed. "I told you I missed my flight."

"Bull! I am here at the reception desk at your hotel, Nia. They told me you checked out yesterday. Where are you?"

Nia flinched. Damon was here in Nashville. How had he even found out where she was staying? Did she have no privacy at all? She glanced around Liam's spacious apartment. He was on the phone discussing business.

This was her second day here. They had spent the previous day together like old times. In the evening she had checked out of the hotel and brought her things over. She hadn't thought of the implications of her actions.

The fact was that she had been due back in L.A. and that Damon would be fit to be tied if he knew what she was up to. She had texted him and told him she'd missed her flight and would be there the next day. Of course, she hadn't shown up that morning either. She couldn't believe that he had hopped on a plane and come thundering over there three hours later. It must mean he thought something was up.

"I am not your hostage nor am I your little child," she hissed. "Where I am is none of your business."

"You're with *him* aren't you?"

She sucked in a breath. So, this was why he had come after her. He felt threatened. He probably had not believed her story about missing the flight.

"Who I am with isn't any of your business either."

"We have a deadline by which to finish this album. You said you would be gone for one day and be back in the studio recording the next day. You did not show up. It was expected you would be there the following day and again you were a no-show. It became my business the moment that happened."

"For heaven's sake, Damon. It has only been two days. Just two."

"We're on a tight schedule. *Everything* that we do has been planned down to the nth degree. These are busy people, who also have schedules; who also have other artists to serve and other contracts to fulfill. They are not waiting around to record your songs, Nia Carmichael. This is not professional, and this is not the kind of thing I expect from artists signed to my label."

She felt like she was getting a scolding from the principal. She had been there and done that. She hadn't liked it then, and she hated it worse now. He was making out as though the world would come to a crashing halt because recording had been delayed by two days. She wasn't buying it for one second. This was just another attempt by him to control her and keep her from Liam.

"I will return as soon as my business here is done."

"You will return today," he corrected. "You will meet me at this hotel in one hour or your contract with Double D Records is in serious jeopardy."

Dread seeped into Nia. She wished she had the luxury of telling Damon to go jump in a lake, but she didn't. She had made many strides, but she was not well established enough at this point to jeopardize her contract with Double D Records. Damon knew he had her over a barrel.

Surely, Liam would understand. What they had shared had brought back so many feelings. He couldn't possibly turn his back on that just because she had to fulfill her commitment to Damon. Perhaps when the contract expired in two years, she could consider doing things Liam's way. By then, she would be a household name and could take the risk.

"I'll be there," she said and didn't wait for Damon to respond when she disconnected the call.

When Liam walked into the room, he was all smiles.

"I'm sorry about that, my love. I just had to speak to my manager about some upcoming gigs."

He dropped down beside her on the couch and caressed her leg. "So now I'm completely yours."

She produced a weak smile. "That's nice," she said, but couldn't meet his eyes.

Liam had always been sensitive to her moods. Not surprisingly, he sensed the change. Placing a hand under her chin and tilting her head upward he asked, "What's wrong?"

"Seems I'm needed in L.A. and can't take off the time I thought I could. I didn't tell you, but I'm in the middle of recording my third album."

"You don't have to return to California," he countered, nailing her with his intense blue gaze.

She began to get lost in the assurance of his eyes, but caught herself just in time.

"I have a contract, Liam. Airtight. They will sue me if I try to walk away right now."

She took his hand in hers to feel the reassurance of his touch even as she could see the warmth receding from his eyes.

"I'm just going to finish out this contract. It ends in two years. Then I can walk aw—"

"You can walk away right now."

He didn't shout but the slight edge to his words and the firm, uncompromising tone in which he said them made her flinch. Then he took her face in his hands, and his expression softened.

"Trust me, Nia, there has to be an exit clause in the contract. I'm certain Thomas wouldn't have let you sign it if it didn't. It will no doubt be expensive to walk away, but you know that finding that money is no problem for me. I would happily pay out Double D Records if it means freeing you from Damon Deverre's tyranny."

Nia shook her head. "Liam, I'm not being exploited. At least that's not how I feel. I know that we've talked about this before and you have your views on things, and I have mine. I don't have a problem with Damon's company profiting from my talent. I see it as a win-win. They invest in me, market me, provide me all I need to be a successful and in turn, I pay them a part of my earnings."

She forced a smile. "Of course I'm only getting the mean cuss to give me fifteen percent, but I've done my research. I'm actually doing better than most new artists who start at ten percent."

When Liam's eyes began to harden once more, she held up a hand.

"Look I'm not saying he's perfect. I know he's deeply flawed. But he has done nothing but work on my behalf to help me achieve my dream. He believed in me, and he put his money where his mouth is. I am earning more money and greater fame and recognition in these few years with him than I believed possible."

She reached out to caress Liam's cheek, but he jerked away, then stood abruptly and went over to the window.

"Liam, I know that's not what you want to hear, but I want to be honest with you."

He turned to her and the wariness, resignation, and regret she saw in his eyes scared her.

"Thanks for your honesty. It seems as though it was me who was misled, not you. You knew exactly what you wanted, what you signed up for. Far from having an issue with it, you relish it."

The way he said it sounded as though she was a pig wallowing in mud. Her stomach clenched.

"Just because I don't want to do things your way doesn't mean I'm a terrible person."

He shrugged nonchalantly. "If you say so."

She glared at him. "What about us?"

"*What* about us?" he asked.

She took a deep breath and forced lightness into her voice when she answered.

"Now that you're living here in the US, we need not be physically apart for long. We can commute on weekends. At least until we work out everything."

Her words fell away as his face twisted with a bitter sneer.

"Nia, you have made your choice."

"But yesterday you told me you wanted us to be together..."

"Not like what you're proposing." He drew a hand through his hair. "Listen, I made a mistake. I got carried away. I assumed that after you decided to keep the ring, it meant you were going to come back to me. That you were going to leave this life behind. I see that isn't the case."

He was unrecognizable as the passionate man who had held her in his arms the previous night and early that morning. She began to feel anger build in her.

"You are a selfish brute. And you call yourself a Christian!"

He seemed taken aback, but she didn't pause.

"After all this time it is still your way or the highway. Well, you know what? I didn't walk away from our marriage, as you are so fond of saying. I was kicked out by your unyielding, uncompromising attitude. You don't love me. You love yourself."

She slid the ring off her finger and tossed it at him. He caught it with one hand. "I'm leaving right now."

He cleared his throat. "I can take you back to the—"

"I'll call a taxi. Don't trouble yourself," she flung over her shoulder as she tore out of the room.

It was hard to believe that she had spent so many months agonizing over him and feeling regret.

Well, no more. She was done.

Chapter 28

Five Years Later

The moment Nia finished the final song, she waved to her fans and made her way backstage. She ignored their screams for her and for another encore.

Her manager, Raúl Fernandez, held out a towel for her. She grabbed it and began dabbing her face. Then she took the bottle of water he offered and immediately started gulping the liquid. She was incredibly thirsty as she was every night. Performing took a toll on her body. The combination of the hot strobe lights, her energetic performance, and tight outfits like the leather catsuit she wore tonight, made her lose fluids and become dehydrated fast.

The liquid she was drinking now contained electrolytes geared to replenish her body with essential minerals. She had learned the hard way after collapsing on stage four years ago from exhaustion. That was the last time she allowed such a thing to happen. Not only had it been embarrassing, but the rumors it had fueled about it being drug or alcohol-related, a bald face lie, had inspired her to take every caution to prevent a recurrence. She now traveled everywhere with her doctor and her personal chef.

The former was to monitor how her immune system was holding up under the pressure of live performances and constant travel. He was to ensure she was sleeping well, getting enough fluids, and that she wasn't picking up any nasty germs from the hundreds of VIP fans she greeted at each stop. The chef was there to see to it that she had freshly prepared nutritious meals.

These additions to her staff had not been made a moment too soon. The stakes had never been higher for ensuring that she remained healthy enough to maintain the arduous tour schedules and didn't miss a single performance. With CDs declining due to the advent of digital streaming, she relied more heavily on concert ticket sales and merchandising sales to generate income. At the same time Double D Records and their sponsors were pumping more and more money into bigger shows that would attract larger audiences.

It had been almost seven years since she had signed the first contract. During that time she had released seven albums, had been on one domestic tour and was now on her third world tour. She had won countless awards and graced the covers of numerous magazines. She had appeared in three motion pictures and endorsed more products than she could count on both hands. By anyone's standards, she had arrived. And still, it felt as though it wasn't enough. Something was missing, and she couldn't figure out what it could possibly be.

Raúl began rattling off the names of all the VIP fans waiting to see her at the after party. Not surprisingly, Damon was still there. Tonight, he had joined her on stage as the surprise performer on her hit song in which he rapped a couple verses. It had been a last minute decision he had made but had been well worth it for the effect it had had on the crowd. She hadn't seen Damon since she began the tour three months ago and he had called to say he would be with her in Cologne and perform for that song alone.

When she reached the changing room, people began buzzing around her to offer congratulations on her performance. Damon was there holding court as he sipped his peppermint tea. He stood and embraced her.

"You were amazing," he said simply.

Those gathered repeated the sentiment. Nia thanked them and turned to Damon with a tired smile.

"You weren't bad yourself."

He smiled back and squeezed her arm. "Well, I'll let you go and freshen up."

She nodded and followed her doctor and her personal assistant to the dressing room for her nightly ritual. As Dr. Nielsen checked her vitals and asked his usual questions to ascertain her state, she thought about Damon's last minute decision to make a guest appearance.

Just before she had started the tour, he had confessed that he had feelings for her and wanted to take their professional relationship to another level. It didn't entirely come as a surprise. Ever since her divorce from Liam, the atmosphere had changed between Damon and her. Instead of being a tyrant, he had become almost like a besotted lover.

The first time she had realized the change in Damon had come after the divorce had been finalized. In the act of rebellion against all men, she had cut off her hair. She could remember like it was yesterday the hush that had swept across the room when she had shown up at the recording studio. Everyone looked at her in horror as though she had gone stark raving mad.

Damon was out of town on business, but she had been warned that when he got back, there would be hell to pay. Questions were fired at her like, "Did you ask his permission to do this?" "Do you have a death wish" "What were you thinking?"

She was told that Damon liked his female performers to have long, flowing hair, Sheba being a classic example. Everyone advised her to go get hair extensions quickly before he came back and went crazy. They told her what had happened to the last artiste who had crossed Damon and that he was now living as a bum on the streets because after Damon dumped him no other recording company would even touch him. That was the influence Damon Deverre had in this town. Never mind his thin veneer of charm, they said, he was lethal.

At that moment, Nia really did not care. She was tired of being emotionally abused by the men in her life. Tired of people telling her what to do and feeling like they owned her. As far as she was concerned if Damon wanted to dump her, he could try. It didn't matter. She knew how to land on her feet, and she would more than survive. She would thrive.

By the time Damon was due back in town, her resolve had weakened. While on the outside she appeared completely in control, she was actually dreading a confrontation. When he walked into the room, she felt the change even before she heard his voice. It was in the way conversation died and nervous looks were darted between her and the door. When she turned around, Damon was there staring at her hair.

She held her breath.

Based on the lack of surprise in his expression she knew that the news of what she had done had reached him. He slowly ran his gaze over her head. Then he came up to her, took her by the shoulders and gently turned her around. She remained silent as she awaited his reaction, forcing herself to stay calm.

"I hear all the young women are rushing into their salons clutching photos of you and begging their stylists to give them the 'Nia' cut. We won't tell them it takes more than that to become Nia."

Relieved laughter filled the room. Nia herself released an inward sigh of relief. It seemed all the naysayers had been wrong.

"You look amazing. Who would have thought you could pull off something so risky?"

She grinned and poked him in the chest. "You need to trust my instincts more."

"I'm learning that," he muttered.

And to her surprise, he did trust her more. He marketed her new look. The promotional photos for the third album featured an edgier looking Nia. It proved fitting because the songs were also edgier.

She had moved away from the innocence of the first two albums into a more mature version of herself. She knew that some of the lyrics were suggestive, but she didn't care. If she wanted to move up to another level, she would have to take risks, not just with her physical appearance but also with her songs. Sure, she might lose a few fans, but she believed her music would appeal to a whole lot more people who were looking for a more visceral experience.

Over that time she and Damon became more like partners than master-slave. She was careful, though, to keep their relationship strictly professional. She never accompanied him to an event unless they were part of a large group and she never allowed him into her home when she was alone; neither did she visit his under those circumstances. It was crucial to her that people recognized her talent and didn't think she had gotten where she was by sleeping with *El Honcho*.

She did an emotional dance with him which vaguely resembled what had happened when she was at Julliard. She kept him interested enough to be of use to her but not so interested to make demands.

The payoff had been that most of what she requested was granted. Her royalties had moved from fifteen percent to eighteen percent and finally to the twenty percent only enjoyed by songwriters or composers. She also had been able to persuade him to yield creative control of her fourth, fifth, sixth and seventh albums. Not only that, but she had been able to boldly change her look for as many times as she had launched a new album.

But the dance was becoming more dangerous. They had spent a lot of time together collaborating on the last album in which Damon had appeared on two of the tracks. The track to the title song had been an instant hit, confirming that he still had widespread appeal as a singer even though he now focused mainly on the business side of the industry. It had demonstrated that they made a good team in business.

In as much as Nia had let down her guard over the last year and gotten close to Damon sometimes out of sheer loneliness but also because he was an undeniably attractive man, she still didn't entirely trust him. She had the feeling that if she ever moved out of his favor, he would prove a lethal enemy. Furthermore, she had seen all sides of him, and there were some sides she simply could not tolerate. Most important, though, she wasn't in love with him. This was why she had to think seriously about moving into a romantic relationship with Damon. She had to process his offer and would have a response for him when her nine-month tour was over. But Damon was not a patient man. She suspected he was really here to push her to give him an answer now.

As Nia greeted the VIP guests, she ignored the tiredness that tugged at her. She forced herself to smile and stay on her aching feet as she shared small talk, signed autographs and posed for photos with the fans who had paid hundreds extra just for the privilege of a few minutes in her company.

She felt Damon's eyes on her as she worked. She realized that she no longer felt the discomfort she had felt years ago at his attraction. In fact, it was thrilling to have someone who knew her to feel this way about her. It was not like these fans who raved and gushed and stammered in her presence and fancied themselves enamored with her. They had no idea who she was. What they saw in the media perhaps made them feel as though they did know her, but it wasn't true. It was just snapshots of her life carefully staged to create loyal fans. But Damon knew. He had seen all sides of her, and he was still there – dangerous, for sure – but there.

Nia sipped her drink and nodded as she listened to the heavily accented English of the German minister of cultural affairs. His blue eyes and blond hair caused him to morph into the image of Liam. She stared, and then blinked. She really needed to get some rest. Now she was hallucinating. She had no business thinking about Liam Lamport.

She had, of course, followed his band from their humble beginnings to being an important player in the gospel music industry. She wasn't a big listener of gospel music, but she was aware of *Redeemed* and had even spied their names in the last year or so creeping into the mainstream awards, like the Grammys.

She hadn't been surprised at Liam's success. She had known from the moment she had met that confident boy that he would succeed no matter what he attempted. It was good he was finally living his dream. She was thrilled if she had played a small part in that.

Nia excused herself from the minister and greeted a billionaire developer who began gushing in rapid German about how much he loved her music. She politely responded through the interpreter, posed for a photograph with him, and then went over to the bar to refill her fluids.

She mounted a bar stool as fatigue threatened to topple her. She reached for the glass while Damon took a seat opposite her.

"You look tired. Let's go back to the hotel."

She glanced at her watch. "My tour of duty has ten more minutes remaining," she pointed out.

He shrugged. "What's ten minutes?"

She quirked a brow at him. "This from the man who used to tell me that if I cheated people out of even one minute of my time, I would, in essence, be cheating myself because I could lose the lifetime devotion of that person."

"That was before you became a megastar and media darling who could do no wrong."

She took another sip of her water and wagged a finger at him. "You're only as good as your last performance," she mimicked him.

"I've created a monster." He placed his hands over his ears. "Stop quoting me."

She laughed genuinely for the first time this evening. She had been surprised to find that Damon Deverre had a playful side. It was rarely seen, especially by employees or artists signed to his label, but with Nia it was different. People had noticed that. People like Sheba who had seemed to sense that it was better to form a truce with Nia than to be her enemy and risk inciting Damon's wrath.

So, they were civil to each other and often exchanged pleasantries, but they could never be called friends. Even though Nia now had even more pop culture influence than Sheba, particularly among the younger set, there was no longer any rivalry between them. It might also have helped that Sheba had moved on from her failed romance with Damon, married an actor last year, and produced twins in February of this year.

Nia drained her glass. "Okay. You win. I'm going to the ladies' room and when I return my ten minutes should be up anyway, and we will be free to exit."

In the limousine on their way to the hotel, Nia resisted the urge to stretch out on one of the seats. Instead, she sunk low and snuggled in a corner as the car rolled through the streets. Aside from Damon, there was Dr. Nielsen, Bianca, Cassandra Dear, and two bodyguards.

Damon sat next to her. He leaned forward and whispered in her ear, "I missed you. That's why I came."

Nia smiled slightly but kept her eyes trained on his big hands resting on his legs.

"Have you got an answer for me yet?" he asked.

She raised her head and met his gaze. The glow from a streetlight illuminated inside the car for a moment and Damon's handsome face could be clearly seen. Nia was tempted to trace his thin mustache and beard but thought it would be foolhardy to touch him right now and spur on his hopes, particularly in light of what she had to say.

"Damon, I have been much too busy to think deeply about that. You know how intense this tour is. I go back to the hotel now, grab a few winks, and then I'm up preparing again for another big night here, and then tomorrow night I'm on a plane to Zurich."

"I'm well aware of your touring schedule, Nia. I signed off on it, remember?"

He caressed her leg, and she felt a twinge of discomfort. She glanced up at the others in the limo and noticed that a few pairs of eyes scuttled away. She gently removed Damon's hand and placed it back on his leg.

"I haven't decided yet, so easy there, cowboy," she murmured. "That is not a decision I take lightly. If I say yes, our relationship will change forever. There will be no turning back. I don't know if I want to risk a business relationship that has been profitable for both of us for a romance that may go south and end up ruining everything."

He shook his head. "No need for you to be concerned. I was involved with Sheba. We're no longer together romantically, but she's still with the label and doing great. It is possible."

She sighed. Why was he so relentless?

"If pressed right now I'm inclined to say no, Damon."

"Then give it some more thought, Nia. I've waited for years. What're another three months?"

There was thinly veiled frustration in his voice, and she could feel the annoyance radiating off him. While she regretted the tension, she wasn't going to allow Damon Deverre to pressure her into a decision that could have life-long negative consequences. She had already been there and done that.

Chapter 29

"Of all the places I thought we could run into each other, this was not one."

Nia froze.

She would know that deep, sexy voice anywhere. She slowly turned to face him.

"Liam, what are you doing here?"

"Shopping for jeans. You?"

She was too stunned to do more than stare for several minutes. Had she not just a week ago on what would have been the date of their wedding anniversary gotten all teary-eyed and nostalgic and then admonished herself for being a fool. And now for him to just show up out of the blue? Well, this was quite literally too much for her heart to take.

"Nia?"

She blinked. "Sh…shopping for jeans," she stammered again.

It seemed as though since the last time she had seen the man in person, almost five years ago, he had gotten more heart-stopping handsome. Even now, she could see from her peripheral vision how two of the store clerks had abandoned what they were doing to stare at him. They were probably trying to place him, figuring he was so gorgeous he must be a movie star.

He wore blue jeans, an off-white linen button-down shirt, black blazer, and black square-toed boots. His blond hair was windblown but still managed to look perfect, and his deep blue eyes just captivated her.

"*Gap* does sell some good jeans," he said.

"But what are you doing here in China?" Nia asked him.

She had just three nights previously completed a performance in Beijing and was now spending a few days catching up on some much-needed rest and recreation before continuing on to the Philippines tomorrow.

"I'm here because my parents are here. They are celebrating their thirtieth anniversary with a party tonight."

"And they had to come all the way to China to do it?"

"Apparently, it has something to do with this city playing a significant role in their courtship."

"Sounds very romantic."

It still embarrassed Nia when she thought of Liam's parents. She had genuinely liked and respected Lord and Lady Lamport, and she couldn't imagine what they thought of her now. They probably thought she was a horrible person and were relieved she was out of their son's life. She tried not to let it get to her, but she must have been wearing her emotions on her face because Liam's eyebrows drew together and he asked, "Are you okay?"

She took a deep breath and forced a smile. She nodded vigorously. "It's a real surprise seeing you though." She looked around him. "You're alone?"

He looked around her. "I am. *You* are not."

She was about to contradict him when she realized by his pointed gaze that he was referring to her security detail who stood on alert, watching him as she shopped. She had asked them to give her space. She hated to feel as though someone was constantly looking over her shoulder. But Damon insisted on it, stating he was just protecting his investment from crazed fans and homicidal maniacs. In fact, ever since she had begun getting death threats from some deranged fan a couple of weeks ago, he had ramped up the security even more. Now four men were standing around watching her shop.

It was beyond ridiculous. She didn't believe the threats for a moment. People got it into their heads to write things to create panic and to get attention. She was not willing to play along. Besides, why would someone seriously want to harm her? She was very likable if her ratings on social media were anything to go by. She had millions of followers.

"I'm still floored. Like you, I never expected to run into you in China of all places. It's like something out of a sci-fi movie," she commented, mainly to hide her nervousness and appear at ease.

"I actually think it's rather fortuitous."

"Why do you say that?"

"Because for the last few months I've done covers of a couple of your songs. They have been doing quite well. I wondered if you were aware."

She looked at him aghast. Liam Lamport, the Christian singer, had done covers of her songs? She searched her brain to think which songs on her last album would be appropriate for a Christian to sing and to her stinging embarrassment could only come up with three.

"Which songs?"

He rattled off the names. With each one, her eyes widened.

"Those songs? But you sing gospel."

Surprise covered his face, and then he burst out laughing.

"I'm sorry I didn't explain. I did covers of the tune. The lyrics I substituted with Christian ones. I would never feel comfortable singing your songs."

She winced at the slight but pretended it hadn't hurt. She feigned a bored expression and with a dismissive wave of her hand said, "Well that doesn't involve me. The music is copyrighted as you well know. As long as you paid the license fee, you're free to use it."

Nia turned away and began going through the racks once more. She was impressed with the ease with which she appeared to be ignoring him. The fact was it felt like every nerve was standing on end. Why had she thought she had gotten over this man? She clearly had not. She needed to put some distance between him and herself as soon as possible before she said or did something to reveal she was still carrying a torch. The humiliation would be too much to bear.

"So, you're buying jeans?" he asked casually following behind.

"Uh huh," Nia said slowly as she moved down the row of jeans.

Liam was shadowing her. Moving in for the kill, so to speak, and the moment this thought formed, she looked up and caught her bodyguards inching closer as well. She caught their attention and shook her head. Liam followed her gaze and continued talking as though he had not been almost intercepted.

"But this is the men's section," Liam pointed out in a conversational tone.

She stopped abruptly and turned around to face him. She had not realized he was so close behind her because now there was just the space of a breath between them and she was staring straight into the irises of his deep blue eyes.

Be still my beating heart.

"Just looking for a gift for a friend," she breathed.

"You look incredible," he whispered. He reached out and took a strand of her hair in his hand. "This remains my favorite look. I have always loved your curls."

This was the second time in the last five years that she had returned to her natural look. Damon had long ago conceded that it didn't matter what Nia did with her hair, her fans loved it, and her performances still sold out. But she changed her look because it went with her public image of being an iconoclast. She was someone who bucked tradition and what was expected, and she did the unconventional like dying her hair completely purple last year.

"Thanks," she muttered.

She knew she should take a step backward and put a little distance between them, but for some reason, she couldn't bring herself to do it. She felt so safe and warm in this electrically charged space. And the feel of his fingers in her hair was like sweet ecstasy and almost too painful to bear.

"Will you help me choose?" he asked softly.

"Choose?" she asked, feeling as though her mind was in a fog.

"A pair of jeans. You have excellent taste. 'Fashion icon' they call you."

Nia blinked and forced herself to focus on his statement and then frowned when she wondered if he was laughing at her. The twinkle in his eyes suggested he was.

The annoyance she felt broke the spell. She took a step back.

"You look just fine and very fashionable yourself. I'm sure you can select your own jeans," she said briskly.

He took a step closer once more eliminating the space she had placed between them. Now he was even closer, and she had to tilt her head up to look at him. He accommodated her by leaning down. He spoke so low she could feel his sweet breath on her face.

"But you were great at selecting my clothes." He placed a hand over his heart." Those couple of months we shared together as man and wife was the best-dressed era of my life."

Nia felt a warm flush spread over her body. Yes, he was definitely laughing at her. *So much for her shopping therapy.*

She turned to go, but not before Liam captured her arm and swung her around to face him. Nia shifted her head and saw the bodyguards making their way toward her. She shook her head at them once more.

Liam smiled. "Thanks for calling off your guard dogs – again."

"I shouldn't," she hissed. "You're taunting me."

"That's not true. I do remember that brief time with you more often than I care to admit."

She searched his face and realized that all the tease was gone from his eyes. He was serious.

"I miss you," he whispered.

Nia couldn't explain the feeling that went through her. It began in the center of her belly and radiated through her entire body. Was it possible that Liam still wanted her after everything that had passed between them? If he had not been holding on to her right then, she was sure she would have crumpled into a heap on the floor.

"This is my last night here," she blurted.

"Have dinner with me, tonight," he said caressing her bare arms. To her surprise, she agreed, but then she remembered something.

"Didn't you just say your parents' party is tonight?"

He shrugged. "They'll understand if I miss the party. Dinner with you is an opportunity I can't let pass by."

Liam felt sorry that he had to miss his parents' party but seeing Nia earlier that day had unleashed something in him that was not willing to be caged again. He felt like he had been in an emotional coma for the last five years and suddenly someone had shocked him awake. Now he was once again experiencing what it was like to be truly alive.

He couldn't figure out why she had that effect on him, but it had always been so. It seemed unlikely it would ever change, which was why he had begun flirting with her. It had been the most natural move in the world. Of course, worse than flirting with her had been his touching her. That had been his undoing. He had felt as though he would combust. It had taken remarkable restraint not to hold her tight and kiss her until she passed out.

As he was explaining to his parents why he would be missing out on the party, Leiliana walked into the room. She glanced at him suspiciously. "Why are you dressed so early?"

"I'm meeting with an old friend for dinner."

"Who's this old friend?" she asked.

"None of your business, that's who."

"Someone more important than Mum and Dad? Now, who could that be?" She smiled "Must be a woman."

"Will you shut up?"

"Let's see. Who do you know in China?"

She looked over to their parents as she flopped down on the couch, drawing her feet up under her. She turned to their father.

"Dad, does Liam have any former love interests in the Beijing office or at the hotel?"

Liam shook his head and rose to leave. "That would have been highly unprofessional."

She shrugged. "You don't work for Lamport Holdings anymore. Well, not technically anyway, unless you count your music label."

Two years ago, LWM Records had sold forty percent of its shares to Lamport Holdings. It had been the best move, financially. Liam had done things his way and succeeded. He, Sam, and Matthew who had become millionaires overnight now had access to unlimited capital and Lamport Holdings resources which had allowed their label to shift into the big time. In addition to *Redeemed*, LWM Records now had three more Christian artists signed to the label.

Liam smirked at his sister. Sure, she was whip-smart, but not even she could figure out who his date was for tonight. And that was for the best. Leiliana had been hurt when Nia had left him because the two had formed something of a friendship. While they had not really discussed it, he felt that Leiliana blamed Nia for the breakup. He had done nothing to dispel her feelings, but he knew there was plenty of blame to go around on both sides.

He took up the keys to his rental and started toward the foyer when Leiliana exclaimed, "Oh, my gosh! I know who Liam is having dinner with!"

The way she said it made him freeze.

"Nia Carmichael is in China. She performed here three nights ago, and I hear she is leaving for the Philippines tomorrow. Is it her? Liam, are you meeting her?"

Liam didn't know why he should feel annoyed. He was a grown man. He could dine with whomever he wanted. He whirled around and glared at Leiliana.

"Again, it's none of your business with whom I dine. You need to get a life, Leiliana, and stop trying to live vicariously through me."

Her jaw dropped open. He saw the hurt flash in her eyes before she slid her gaze away. Leiliana worked hard, too hard he sometimes thought. She had been involved with a guy a few years back, but after that relationship abruptly ended, it seemed as though she had submerged herself in work to the point where she had no social life. Since then, any guy with an interest was soon sent scurrying for cover under the glare of her rejection. Knowing his remark had probably hit home, Liam felt a pang of guilt.

"Listen, I'm sorry. I didn't mean to bark at you. That was uncalled for. I'll see you guys later."

Chapter 30

W hen Liam arrived at the restaurant, Nia was already seated at the table. As he took his seat, he heard the waiter say to her, "Your iced tea, Madam."

Liam shuddered and saw Nia's lips tip to reveal pearly white teeth in response. "I know. Abominable," she mouthed to him behind her hand.

Involuntarily, he returned the smile. He had once told her that iced tea was an abomination as tea was meant to be taken hot, not cold. He was surprised to find himself pleased she had remembered.

He gave his drink order to the waiter and then turned to Nia. "Sorry to be late. I miscalculated the time a bit," he apologized.

She gave a small groan of laughter. "You are always late, Liam."

"I wasn't late for our wedding."

Why had he started out with such a topic? He wondered if she remembered that their anniversary would have been a week ago. They had never celebrated not even one anniversary.

To his relief, she simply shook her head at him and smiled indulgently.

"That was because we went to the marriage office and then the church together."

It seemed as if, unlike him, the significance of this month had not registered with her.

Soon they had their menus in hand and turned their attention to perusing them.

"Thanks for inviting me to dinner," Nia said in a soft voice.

"My pleasure," he said, and genuinely meant it. Being here with her like this almost felt like old times.

She carefully placed her menu on the table and sighed. "I never liked how things ended between us five years ago. It has always bothered me that we who were so close ended up enemies. When I saw you today, it seemed like a chance to build bridges."

"Is that what you think? That we ended as enemies? Was that how you saw it?"

She felt compelled to explain her view.

"As soon as I returned to L.A. you sent over the signed copies of the divorce papers, Liam. That was after you had been so adamant that you weren't going to sign. That was proof that you strongly disapproved of my choice and wanted nothing more to do with me. Was I wrong in assuming that?"

When the waiter returned with Liam's mineral water, they ordered their meals. As he took a sip of his drink, he thought about Nia's question. He couldn't deny it. He had been hurting so badly and had felt so betrayed when she had made a choice that day in Nashville to return to Damon Deverre. He had lashed out, and she had lashed back. When she had left, he had felt completely hopeless as though there was no point in trying to revive something that was dead.

He slowly exhaled. He had spent months after the divorce resenting Nia. Instead of praying that God would save her soul, he had prayed that all her plans would crumble and that she'd come running back to him. Instead, she had reaped success after success. He'd gotten angry at God for allowing her to triumph after turning her back on him.

Like Asaph had lamented in Psalm 73, Liam had asked God why He allowed the wicked to prosper. Nia seemed to be blessed even though her music was ungodly. Yet he, who was glorifying God, was unable to have the kind of impact she had. He had simmered for a while, refusing to view or listen to anything that was connected with her.

Then one day, a year to the day of the divorce, as he mulled over how his life had reached such a point the Holy Spirit led him back to that Psalm. He had read it again but this time with new insight.

Yes, Asaph had begun the Psalm lamenting, but eventually, he had gone to the sanctuary of God and gained a perspective on his problem he had not had before. Asaph had recognized that while it might appear that the ungodly were prospering, they were not. In reality, they were on a slippery slope.

Liam realized with something like dread that while Nia might have found fame and fortune and it might appear she was living the good life, she was actually poised for destruction, desolation, and terrors. This new awareness brought him to his knees. His salvation was assured. Nia's wasn't. His prayer changed in that instant. He first asked God to forgive him for his sinful thoughts and then asked Him to save Nia from physical as well as spiritual harm. He asked Him not to bring judgment on her but rather redemption to her.

As he looked at her across the table now, he could truly say that they were no longer enemies. He prayed for her every single day.

"I know you don't approve of the way I'm living my life, Liam, but I'd still like it if we could be friends. I miss you. I miss talking to you about…everything."

His smile was genuine. "I thank you for your offer of friendship Nia. I humbly accept it."

She reached down beside her and a minute later was holding out a gift bag to him across the table. "Here you go," she said.

He was stunned. He hadn't expected Nia to bring him a present. He hadn't brought her any and felt a little awkward taking hers. A few seconds later when he opened the bag and saw its contents, he understood the reason for the gift and broke out in a laugh.

"Jeans!" Liam took them out of the bag and held them up briefly, and then he peered at the tag inside. "They look great. My size, my style. Perfect."

He folded the light blue jeans and placed them back in the bag.

"I must say, I did not expect you to take my request seriously. And…"

He feigned shock.

"…these are normal jeans, Nia. Not distressed. Not ripped. Not punk. Sophisticated Selvedge."

When Nia laughed, he was reminded of how much he loved the sound.

"Well, first off I felt duty bound to buy jeans for you. After all, you came to the Gap to buy jeans. At least that was the impression you gave me. Then you happened upon me, declared that I should help you pick them out, invited me to dinner and took off. All I could conclude was that it was now my responsibility to make sure that you got your jeans. I don't understand this comment about not expecting normal jeans, though. Weren't all those clothes I picked out for you when we were married, the ones you were raving about, stylish and sophisticated?"

By heaven, he adored this woman. Who else could match wits with him the way Nia could? Even after all these years apart they fell into conversation as easily as they had when they had first met.

"You're right, they were. But in recent times…" He looked her up and down and shook his head, "…really, Nia, the things you wear. I'm truly appalled at how your fashion sense just took a nosedive the moment you left me. It leaves me to believe that I was really your inspiration."

Nia burst out laughing, and Liam continued as he struggled to keep a straight face.

"I helped you to channel your fashion sense in the right direction. Now it has just spiraled out of control."

Actually, she looked quite stunning. Nia just had this ability to make even rags look glorious. Take what she was wearing now. On any other woman, the one-shoulder lilac top would have been a disaster. But on Nia, it was quite attractive. Her crown of beautiful hair was parted in the middle and pulled back into a messy knot at the back of her neck. And even though the only jewelry she wore was a large tanzanite cocktail ring and the tiniest pair of tanzanite earrings, she shone like a diamond. She smelled good too, like some kind of spice, and for a short while he forgot the real reason behind his invitation as he sat admiring her.

She pointed a purple coated talon at him, fighting to speak through her giggles.

"You've got this thing wrong, Lamport. When I was with you, I was very conscious that as the wife of a British aristocrat I did not have the luxury of wearing something say, like this." She made a sweeping motion down her front. "So while I flirted with unconventional styles and colors on the odd occasion, mostly I ensured that I did nothing to invite the disapproval of the British upper crust."

He sobered. Was this how she had really felt…as though she had to conform to someone's image of who she should be? And why was he only now hearing about it?

"Are you saying that you didn't feel socially at ease when we were married?"

"I can't say I was entirely comfortable. I was different from what your set is used to. Naturally, they didn't gravitate towards me. I was an outsider. I told myself I didn't care what anyone thought of me. Deep down it hurt. Now, because of my fame and success, everyone treats me as an equal, In fact, most people treat me like royalty. I don't have to worry about being accepted any longer. I am more than enough now. It gives me the luxury of being more creative and distinctive in my dress. I finally feel like I have the freedom to be completely myself and do whatever I want."

She took a sip of her drink and watched him through her lashes. He felt as though she had just played her first move and was waiting for him to play his.

"Did that extend to me? Did you feel as though you couldn't be yourself when you were with me?"

She shrugged the bare shoulder and replied, "There were so many rules. It was stifling."

She fanned herself and smiled in that Cheshire cat way of hers. Her glib response annoyed him but he told himself not to get angry, this was not about him. He should not take offense at her suggestion that their marriage had been a farce, or feel injured that she wanted to live lawlessly. This night was about engaging Nia in such a way that he could share God's love for her.

He waited until the waiter had set down their starters before them before speaking.

"But there are rules in the world you live in now, I am certain," he said casually sitting back in his seat and taking a sip of his water. "As much as you'd like to convince me you are completely free we know that you probably have more schedule planners than even I do right now. This tour of yours has to work like a fine-tuned machine. You are expected to be at a particular city singing at a particular venue on a certain night at a specific hour. You have to show up on time and be ready to perform at your maximum whether you feel like it or not. If you do not, the consequences will be dire."

Her smile thinned, and the playful light went out of her eyes. When she bent her head down to take a sip of her soup, it was clear to him that she wasn't sure how to respond to that.

"Tell me about these covers of my songs. Why are you doing them?" she asked. She raised her head as she placed the spoon back in the bowl and licked her lips to catch a spill.

She was clearly changing the subject, which meant he had impacted her. With satisfaction, Liam smiled and answered her query.

"I've heard some of your songs. They are very catchy. The messages, however, are not...wholesome."

He watched her face remain impassive as she stared at him with her cool light brown eyes.

"I got an idea that it would be interesting to rewrite the words to correct that error. You know, speak the truth rather than tell a lie." At this point, he saw a reaction. She took a deep breath and looked away as she sipped her drink.

Ever since her debut and sophomore albums, Liam had noticed that the messages in Nia's songs had gotten more and more edgy and provocative. It had reached the point that he had stopped listening to her music rather than run the risk of leaving his heart unguarded.

One day he had been having lunch at a restaurant with a group of young people from his church when he heard one of Nia's songs playing in the background. He recognized her distinctive voice instantly and had to consciously prevent himself from tapping his feet to the infectious beat. He noticed that the young people had no such inhibitions. A number of them were moving to the music, some even mouthing the lyrics word for word.

He glanced around the restaurant and noticed the song was having a similar effect on other diners. What was happening confirmed in his mind the influence Nia had. But as he listened to the suggestive lyrics of the song he knew that they weren't the type of messages that should be embraced by anyone, the young and impressionable, in particular. That was when he heard the Holy Spirit urge him to rewrite the song with the truth of God. At first, he had dismissed the idea. Why would he want to put himself through the emotional discomfort of wading through Nia's songs? God would not ask such a thing of him; he must have heard wrong.

It soon became clear, however, that God had a mission for him, and like He had pursued Jonah, He wasn't going to let Liam off the hook. After the restaurant incident, he attended a function where one of Nia's songs featured prominently. As he listened to the sinful message coated in an enticing beat, he felt as though a new song was being downloaded to his brain, replacing each verse with a spirit-filled version. Try as he might to ignore it he awoke in the night and had to scribble the new song so he could finally get some sleep.

What had begun as his first cover was so well received by his congregation and on social media that it inspired him to do two more covers of her songs over the last few months. What surprised him now was that she was completely oblivious. It forced him to acknowledge that even though he and Nia both had similar careers, they existed in two different realms. She in the world of popular secular music, he in the world of popular Christian music. Even though in recent times a few of his songs had crossed over, that had not been his intention. It had just happened that they had gone mainstream. For the most part, though, his songs were unmistakably, unapologetically, Christian. So, it would have been unlikely that his covers would have captured the attention of either her or her management team unless he was using them without the appropriate copyright license which, of course, he hadn't been.

Lately, he had begun to think that maybe this effort was about more than just providing Christian alternatives to Nia's popular songs. In his quiet time, as he prayed for Nia, he sensed the Holy Spirit telling him that the songs were also meant to minister to her. Again, he had argued with God. Why would his covers of Nia's songs minister to her more than he had tried to do in person? Had he not always shared his faith with her? What would be different now? Why would she even want to listen to the covers?

God's answer was immediate. Liam felt that He told him not to be like Naaman. He had turned that over in his mind. Of course, he was familiar with the story of Naaman, the commander of the guards of the Syrian army who had leprosy. He had gone to Elijah expecting to be healed. When Elijah had told him to dip seven times in the river Jordan the man had become outraged. Liam realized in that moment that in the same way Naaman was waiting for the miracle to come as he expected, he, Liam, was looking for Nia's conversion in a way he understood. He was not acknowledging the power of almighty God to choose whatever way he wanted to save her.

Liam had then humbly accepted what God was telling him. However, there remained the issue of how he was going to get into close enough proximity to her to share what God was asking him to do. He thought about ways to contact her but eventually decided to do nothing. This was God's plan. He would create the opportunity.

Running into her in the most unlikely place in the world, then, served as confirmation that God wanted him to speak to her about this. That was the only reason he had asked her to dinner. At least that was what he told himself.

"I think we should do a song together."

Her eyes widened. "Me? Sing gospel? I don't think so, Liam."

"Why not? You believe in God don't you?"

"Of course."

"So what's the problem then?"

"I don't want to that's all."

"Really comfortable with the unwholesome lyrics, huh? No room in your life for anything clean and pure?"

She sat back and folded her arms across her chest. She glared at him.

"Why did you invite me to dinner? Was it to take me to task for my music. Because all you've been doing all night is sending these barbs my way."

"Is that how you see it? I thought I was just trying to be honest."

"I was under the impression that this was about us or I wouldn't have come."

"There is no longer an 'us,' Nia. You saw to that."

She heaved a sigh and picked up her bag to leave.

"Here we go again," she muttered.

He reached across the table, and his hand closed around her wrist. She tried to shake it free, but he held on.

"I'm sorry. I shouldn't have said that. I did invite you to dinner. And even though I've been trying to tell myself otherwise, it was because seeing you made me feel things I haven't felt in years. It reminded me how much you still mean to me."

His confession surprised him and Nia too, based on the way her eyes flickered with emotion.

"It's interesting that you should say that," she said in a throaty whisper. "Because when I saw you, I felt the same. I don't know why we can't just be free to love each other and allow everything else to work itself out. When I was with you was the happiest time of my life. Why be miserable apart when we can be happy together?"

He caressed her hand. "You are so beautiful."

She was not simply beautiful, she was captivating and bewitching. It was why she was one of the top female performers of all time. And it was why he needed to be very careful, or he would fall into temptation like he had five years ago only to wake up the next morning and find that the same old issues were still between them.

He withdrew his hand and sat back. "Sorry," he muttered.

She looked angry. "What are you apologizing for? No one has more right to touch me than you."

He shook his head. "That's not true. I have no right to touch you; you're no longer my wife. You're not even my girlfriend."

She sat back in defeat. "What do you want, Liam? What is the point in this?" she shook a hand into the air. "This is never going to work. We have different values and different views on life. We have proven that the attraction, the pull, we feel for each other, can only get us so far. It takes us to a place that feels good for a while but then…" she drew her shoulders up to her ears. "…I can't give you what you want."

"And what do I want?"

"A perfect robot," she spat angrily.

He cocked an eyebrow and waited, refusing to take the bait.

She took a few calming breaths and then pasted on a smile. "You want me to believe everything you do and be this perfect Christian. Well, I can't do that."

"Why not? What is so terrible about what I believe?"

"There is nothing terrible about it. I just can't believe it."

"You believed it when we were married. What changed?"

"Look, I was never really sure I believed it. At least I believed some of it but not all."

"Have you departed so far from the faith you were raised in Nia?"

"What are you talking about? The first few years of my life were spent with parents who had no religious beliefs as far as I could tell. My mother had rebelled against her Baptist roots and run away to become a singer. In the heyday of her fame, she met up with my father and fell in love with one of the most hedonistic men on the planet. And that was the religion the two of them practiced until things between them got so bad that the only thing that made sense was for them to part ways. After that, my mother's recreational drug use got completely out of control, and I was sent to live with my grandmother. Yes, Grandmama was a Bible-thumping Baptist preacher. And, yes, I enjoyed going to church with her on Sundays. And, yes, I even got saved a couple of times. But, guess what?"

She looked off for a moment and then continued.

"It didn't stick, because my prayers never came true. God didn't answer my prayers to help my parents get back together, or help my father to love me more, or my mother to spend more time with me. They all went unanswered. And the last prayer I prayed was when Grandmama, the only one who seemed to care about me, was sick and all I wanted was for her to get healed, and the whole church prayed. And you know what? Nothing happened. She died anyway. That proved to me that the only thing you're going to get in life are the things you work hard for yourself. So, that's what I did. I began to plan what I wanted and how I was going to get it. I don't care who approves or who disapproves, Liam. Not even you. Because if I don't do this, if I don't make my life work, if I don't achieve my dreams, then who will? No one else will achieve them for me. I have to make it happen."

She poked herself in the chest repeatedly to emphasize her point.

Liam remained speechless as Nia vented. He had been tempted to interrupt a few times, but the Holy Spirit had urged him to be quiet. Now he saw why. He was finally getting valuable insight into why she was the way she was.

When she was finished, she was heaving with emotion. He felt both sad and excited at the same time because even though it was terrible to think that Nia had this twisted view of God, it was good to finally have some clarity on why she did. She blamed God for all that had happened in her life, and she didn't trust Him to take control now. She felt that she needed to be in charge, and if she didn't trust God then how could she trust anyone else, including Liam.

She wiped her face with a tissue.

"Thanks for dinner." She picked up her bag and stood.

"But we're not done," he said, "I want to take you somewhere else. And you'll love it. Promise."

He was almost sure she was going to decline, but after a brief hesitation, she nodded. Five minutes later, they were walking down the street on their way to the National Art Museum of China.

Because it was summer, it was still light out even though it was after 7 pm. It meant that Nia was spotted instantly and people started pointing and whispering about them. As some whipped out their phones to photograph them, something suddenly occurred to Liam.

"Hey, you're without your security detail," he said.

She smiled enigmatically. "Not really. It's just that I asked them to remain at a very discreet distance."

He glanced around and didn't see the guys from yesterday, and then Nia said, "Look up to your right."

He did so and spotted the man reading a paper on the park bench. He was dressed like a tourist, complete with camera and all. Another was leaning against a tree, sipping something from a paper cup and apparently trying to appear inconspicuous.

Liam shook his head. "Tell them that if they really want to blend in, they need to whip out their phones and photograph you. That would be realistic."

She slanted a glance at him. "You are insufferable."

"And yet you continue to suffer me, even though I'm about to ruin your reputation."

She watched him askance. "*You*? Ruin *my* reputation?"

"Of course. These photos of us are bound to be splashed across the cover of some tabloid. They will be wondering who the mystery man is with Nia. Then they will discover it is me, the Christian guy. Not good for your bad girl image, Nia." He wagged his index finger in her face.

She grabbed hold of it and made a motion as though to bite it. He tugged it away and pulled her to his side. In a move that was completely natural, she slipped an arm around his waist.

"It's a risk I guess I'm going to have to take," she said, sighing dramatically.

He leaned down and whispered in her ear, "How about I kiss you and increase the stakes?"

She looked like a deer caught in headlights. "You wouldn't dare," she breathed.

"I would," he corrected. "But I won't on this occasion."

He noticed her shy smile. She wouldn't know how much it cost him not to kiss her at that moment.

"So, why the security, though? You always hated that sort of thing. Now they are everywhere."

"Increased fame brings increased risks. I've got some weirdo sending me death threats now."

He stopped cold and tugged her back when she tried to move off. "What did you say?"

"Death threats. No big deal."

"No big deal? Nia, are you listening to yourself?"

"Liam, it happens, okay? Famous people do get threatened every once in a while."

"I don't understand how you can be so blasé about this. When did they begin?"

"They started a couple of weeks ago when I tweeted my support of Israel."

He got distracted for a moment because he had Jewish ancestry on his mother's side and it warmed his heart somehow to think that Nia supported his people, as he considered them.

"Why did you do that?"

She shrugged. "After Hamas militants launched a rocket on Israel and the Jews were fighting back, there were people online criticizing the Jews. I remembered Grandmama Carmichael saying that God gave that land to the Jewish people. I simply tweeted 'Jews have a right to defend themselves.' You would think I'd blasphemed the way these people carried on."

"What people? Carry on how?"

"Some of my followers. They started tweeting back things like 'you are a disgrace' 'you need to educate yourself, dumb a**.' Then there were the ones who got vicious. One tweeted, 'go kill yourself' and there was one in particular that really made me angry that said, 'You will soon join the other murdering Jewish scum in Hell.' Maybe I shouldn't have responded, but I hate it when people try to tell me what I should and should not do."

Didn't he know it?

Nia continued, "I tweeted back. 'The Jews are God's chosen people, so YOU can go to hell.' Since then the death threats have been coming in every form and on all my social media sites. Even in the mail now. I just think the guy or gal is a freak looking for attention. I can support who I want. I swear some of these fans think they own me."

Liam held Nia by the arm and brought her to an abrupt stop.

"There are times I want to shake you. This is one of them. Don't just dismiss this, Nia."

"So, what should I do? Live in fear? I thought you admired my bravery."

"There is a fine line between bravery and stupidity. I just want you to take this more seriously. I know I made a comment earlier about you calling off your guard dogs. Now I'm concerned they're too far away."

"You are over-reacting. Just like Damon is."

"For once he and I see eye to eye. You need to be cautious."

"I think I liked you better when you were the detached ex."

"That's not even funny, Nia."

"We're here!" she announced in a relieved tone of voice. He allowed her to change the subject as they continued into the building. She would have a roasting for him once she found out why he'd brought her there, so it was best to focus on what lay ahead and deal with her revelation later.

Chapter 31

s they entered the museum, Nia glanced around.

"What's happening here? Looks like there is some kind of party going on," she commented to Liam as they were waved in by security.

Guests were mingling as they drank wine and ate hors d'oeuvres.

"Hey, I'm seeing some familiar faces. Like friends of your pa…"

Her tone drifted, and she glanced up at Liam as something began to dawn on her. He was staring resolutely ahead as they strode forward and was clasping her hand tightly as though she might decide to bolt at any moment. Which she would do if this were what she suspected.

"Liam Lamport!" she said between clenched teeth. "I am going to kill you if this celebration is what I think it is."

"And what would that be," he asked, feigning innocence as they turned a corner.

"Your parents' anniv–"

"Liam…" There was his father's voice. "Nia…"

She stiffened when she saw the surprised look on Liam's parents' face. It was worse than she could have imagined. They hadn't even known she was coming. She felt like wrenching her hand out of Liam's and clobbering him. But that would make things worse.

Instead, she relaxed her posture, squeezed his hand as tightly as she could manage to evince her displeasure and smiled as broadly as she could.

For their part, his parents recovered quickly. They smiled and took turns hugging and kissing her on both cheeks.

"Look who I found today," Liam said

His mother wagged a finger at him. "You could have told us you were bringing Nia, Liam. There was no need to be so mysterious."

Liam had told her in the store that he wouldn't be attending the anniversary celebration. He was many things, but a liar wasn't one. Perhaps it had been a spur of the moment decision.

Nia relaxed a little and when she laughed it was genuine. "Well, he didn't tell me either. I guess it was meant to be a surprise on both sides," she said, slanting him a questioning look.

He didn't respond but just smiled in that maddening way of his as though he was keeping an important secret.

"You look amazing," Lady Lamport commented.

"Really? Your son told me that my fashion sense leaves a lot to be desired," Nia said sliding her eyes over to Liam.

"Liam! You didn't," his mother admonished, swatting his arm.

Nia smirked as twin red spots appeared on Liam's cheeks.

"It's okay, Lady Lamport. He's a man. What do they know about ladies fashions, right?"

"Is that Nia?" a booming voice called.

Nia's head whipped around, and she looked in shock at the handsome young man with the twinkling blue eyes striding up to them with a pretty Asian girl on his arm.

"Benjamin!" she exclaimed just before he picked her up and whirled her around.

The last time she had seen Benjamin had been seven years ago when he was sixteen. Those seven years had sure made a difference.

He was now tall and broad, and his boyish good looks were decidedly more manly.

"My, how you have grown! You make me feel shorter than ever," she said while looking up at him.

He grinned. "How is my favorite sister-in-law?"

"No longer your sister-in-law," she muttered feeling her cheeks warm.

He leaned down and whispered back, "You will always be my favorite sister-in-law no matter who Liam marries."

She forced a smile as she tried to imagine Liam marrying someone else. It was not a pleasant thought. Benjamin turned and introduced her to the girl standing by his side and wearing a shy awestruck expression.

"Nia, this is Mei Shiung. She's one of the artists featured here. Her work is phenomenal. Mei, this is the one and only Nia Carmichael. And of course, she needs no introduction."

Mei bowed slightly. "It is a pleasure to meet you, Miss Carmichael. I attended your concert. It was wonderful."

Nia smiled and bowed also. "Thanks, Mei, and please call me Nia. I look forward to viewing your work tonight."

A waiter came up to them bearing a tray of sweet potato and coconut maki. Nia declined. "Liam and I just had dinner," she explained. She noted how Lord Lamport's eyes lit with interest as his gazed moved between her and Liam.

Lady Lamport touched Nia's arm. "Nia, you've really become quite the business woman. All these brands of yours are wonderful. I'm actually wearing your latest perfume right now."

She held up her wrist for Nia to take a whiff. It was indeed *Divine Diva*. It was a spicy oriental fragrance. Nia had selected its notes herself. She now felt her chest brim with pride that a woman she admired so much was wearing the perfume she had a hand in creating. How gracious Barbara Dickson was. Nia was sure that she could not in good conscience say that Barbara listened to her songs or that she would ever attend her concerts, but the areas of Nia's career she felt comfortable supporting, she did. Nia could live with that.

"Guess what? I'm wearing it too," Nia said, beaming at Barbara.

To Nia's surprise, Liam leaned down and sniffed her neck. "Is that what I've been smelling all evening? The fragrance you created? It smells incredible on you."

He had caught Nia off guard, and she stared at him foolishly for a few minutes. She felt impossibly hot. How embarrassing to be blushing in front of Liam's parents, but she couldn't help it. His gesture and the hazy way he was watching her made her feel as though she would melt.

Perhaps Lord Lamport realized that it would be a good time to break the awkward silence. He cleared his throat and commented, "Nia, we understand that you're in the middle of a world tour right now."

Nia turned to her former father-in-law, grateful for the distraction from Liam's intense gaze.

"Yes, I am. I did North America, Africa, Europe, and now I've reached this part of the world. And it's not close to being over yet. I might just be the hardest working gal in show business," she said with a laugh.

The others laughed along with her. "So you're bound for the Philippines next?" Lord Lamport asked.

"I am. Have you been following my tour?"

His blue eyes, so like Liam's, twinkled. "I must confess that I have not. But Leiliana seems to be. She's the one who told us."

"Speaking of Leiliana, where is she?"

At that moment Lord Lamport looked up. "Ah, here she is now."

Nia looked around. Leiliana Lamport was gliding towards them like a queen. Like Benjamin, Leiliana had matured. She was no longer a skinny teenage girl. She was now a full grown woman with the curves that went along with it. The girl had always been very attractive with her long dark blond hair and pretty amber eyes. She was now even more so. The difference between her and Benjamin, though, was in their attitude towards Nia. While he had been warm, Nia found Leiliana's gaze cool.

"We were just talking about you," Lord Lamport said when Leiliana came to stand beside him.

"Were you speaking about how accurate I was regarding Liam's destination tonight, even though I almost got torched for suggesting it?" She gave Nia the once over. "Nia, how are you?"

Nia felt uncomfortable, but she wasn't going to let Leiliana know this. She raised her chin and met the girl's gaze head-on. "I'm wonderful. Yourself?"

"Tired. I'm supposed to be on holiday. Yet, I'm getting calls from the office every day."

"I've warned you about that, Leia. You need to delegate more," Lord Lamport said with a frown.

"She doesn't delegate because she's a control freak. Isn't that right, Leia?" Liam said.

Leiliana stuck out her tongue at him, and Nia burst into laughter at the image of this elegant girl in her silk and diamonds making a face like a little girl.

This seemed to break the ice. Leiliana turned to Nia and started giggling.

"He is so annoying, Nia! Sometimes I want to strangle him, I swear."

Nia nodded in agreement. "I know the feeling."

Liam rolled his eyes at them. "So glad you two have found common ground again. At my expense of course, but never mind that," he said dryly.

Leiliana took Nia's hand. "It's great seeing you again. This outfit is so unique. I love how bold you are with fashion."

Nia smiled. She had been attracted to the unorthodox top the moment she laid eyes on it. It had an asymmetrical hem with one side which was short and the other dropping way past her hip. She had paired it with a black full-length opera skirt and black stilettos.

"And you are really rocking this dress, girl," she commented to Leiliana.

Both Lamport women looked quite smashing, Barbara in her fuchsia cheongsam gown and Leiliana in her sapphire blue silk dress.

Other guests came over to greet the family, and after a short while, Liam excused himself saying he and Nia wanted to view the exhibits. As they walked away, Liam fixed Nia's arm in the crook of his.

"Now that wasn't so bad was it?" he asked giving her hand a pat.

She sighed. Actually, it wasn't as bad as she would have imagined it. She was so sure for years that the Lamports hated her. Instead, they had treated her with affection. It almost made her want to return to the fold of this family.

"No, it wasn't. But why did you do it, Liam?"

He kissed the back of her hand. The gesture was so unexpectedly intimate and tender it made her feel instantly light-headed.

"Because I wanted you to see that my parents still adore you, Nia. You can love someone even though you don't agree with some of the things they have done."

"They were gracious," she agreed, and then she looked across at him. "Is that the way you feel about me?" she asked in a small voice.

"Of course it is, Carmichael. I still adore you. You know that," he replied softly. He cleared his throat before changing the subject.

"Now, my parent's paid good money so their guests could view these exhibits. Let's not let it go to waste."

For the first time that night, Nia began to take an interest in her surroundings. Although her heart was still buzzing with Liam's words, she was able to focus on the tour.

What made the experience so rich was that Liam, fluent in Mandarin, was the perfect guide, translating everything they saw and heard. As they moved from one exhibit to another, it occurred to her that she would have missed a trip to this place if Liam hadn't brought her here. That was one of the things she admired about him, how much he enjoyed cultural experiences.

She remembered how when they were dating, he had expanded her horizons by taking her to places she had never been in all her years studying in New York. They'd been to many off-beat museums, like the Louis Armstrong Museum and the Museum of Interesting things. Also, there were the popular places like the outdoor theatre in Socrates Park, art galleries, photography exhibits, the opera, the ballet, and the theatre. She had experienced all these things at Liam's behest, and she had enjoyed every one of them.

It was so different with Damon. His interest lay in making money, being in the media and partying, clubbing, and gambling. Those were the things that appealed to him. How could she settle for a life like that with Damon after she had enjoyed such a different life with Liam?

Liam took her over to a series of abstract paintings. She looked at the name and realized there were all by the same artist, Mei Shiung.

"So, are Benjamin and Mei an item?"

Liam shrugged. "Benjamin is quite charming. The ladies love him, and he seems unwilling to resist the temptation to flirt. He only met Mei on this trip. It's very likely he won't see her again when he leaves here. He's been leaving a string of broken hearts in his wake ever since he turned sixteen."

Nia nudged Liam playfully with her elbow. "Hard to believe the two of you are brothers, Liam."

"I know, but I'm working on him," he said with a grin.

After the tour, she and Liam sat side by side on a huge sofa in one of the exhibit rooms.

"Tell me more about your childhood, Nia."

"Why?" she asked cautiously. She didn't feel like reliving it, and she certainly didn't want his pity.

He leaned close and nudged her with his shoulder. "Didn't you a little while ago agree to be my friend? Isn't that what friends do? Share their past?"

She couldn't help but smile a little. He really was quite persuasive. If she was going to pour out her heart to someone, who better than Liam. She took a deep breath, and for the first time, Nia completely shared just how chaotic her life had been. She told how sometimes she would find herself with as little as ten minutes notice before she was put on a plane and sent to spend time with either her grandmother in France or her grandmother in Georgia because neither of her parents had time to deal with her. She shared with him how this had taught her to be independent and resourceful at an early age.

As she spoke, all the memories came to the fore. Looking back, she had had such a tumultuous childhood. There had been so much uncertainty. This was why after a while it became important for her to do things her way; to call the shots. Yes, she had had to make compromises, including forgetting some of the values her Grandmother Carmichael had taught her. Even when she felt guilt over some of her actions, she buried it and justified them as being a means to an end. The end was to be rich and powerful and in control of her own destiny.

When Liam reached for her hand, she was pulled back to the present. He was staring at her and, instead of condemnation or even pity, all she saw was compassion in his eyes.

"I won't pretend to understand what you went through all those years, Nia. My life was completely different to yours, as you know. But I can tell you with utmost sincerity that through all of that God loved you. I don't know why God allows evil to run rampant, but mankind was the one to set it into motion. When Adam and Eve chose to disobey God they allowed sin into the world and mankind has been suffering the ill effects ever since."

He didn't want to sound like he was preaching, but this was information she needed to know. He took a breath and continued.

"God is not to blame. It wasn't his fault. He had a perfect world created for us, but we rejected His way and sought our own. Yet he didn't abandon us. He had a plan. He has been holding our hands throughout all history. He is still looking out for us. He is still turning our sorrow into joy and making good out of our bad choices and negative experiences. He sent Jesus to die for our sins so that we won't have to pay the ultimate price ourselves, which is everlasting death."

She used her free hand to swat a tear away. She didn't want to hear this. It would mean she would have to own up to making a mistake. That couldn't possibly be true. To turn her back on this life would mean risking it all. She couldn't afford to do that. She turned away from him.

"Stop. I don't want to hear any more."

"Why not? Am I making you uncomfortable?"

"Yes, you are. I want to be angry. I don't want to trust a God who allows me to feel pain."

Liam shook his head. "You know there was a period in my life when I was angry at God too."

Her gaze flew to his in surprise. It was hard to believe that Liam's faith had ever taken a hit. He seemed so sure; so secure.

"It occurred after you left me the second time around."

She felt shaken as she stared into his eyes.

"I was responsible?"

He nodded and tapped her nose. "Yes, you caused me to question my beliefs. I asked God to let everything you touched turn to dust and instead he allowed it to turn to gold."

Nia couldn't believe Liam was admitting to her that he had wished ill on her dreams. She began to shrink away, but then his next words caused her to get still.

"I questioned what kind of God allowed ungodly people to flourish. I questioned the point in me seeking to live a good life, a life of obedience when others could do as they pleased with no repercussions. Well, His response to me was clear: All that glitters isn't gold, and pray for the people I want Him to save. I realized that if I couldn't trust Him, who could I trust? Could I trust the devil? I knew I could not. Everything he offered was fake. It seemed like the real thing, but upon closer inspection, it wasn't. So if I couldn't trust the devil, it meant I had to trust God. I decided then and there that I would trust Him even when I didn't understand Him. Even when He didn't make sense to me, I would choose to trust."

He took her hand. "Nia, my life has not been perfect. I have had challenges and trials. But that decision I made has never wavered. I still don't always understand Him. But I know with unshakeable faith that He loves me. Why else would He have died for me? In Romans chapter five it says that at just the right time when we were still powerless Christ died for the ungodly. It goes on to say that very rarely will anyone die for a righteous person, although perhaps someone might possibly dare to die for a good person. But God demonstrates his love for us in this. While we were still sinners, Christ died for us."

Liam paused to gauge her interest. She had remained very quiet, so he plowed on and prayed he was planting seeds.

"Now, tell me, does that sound to you like a God you cannot trust, that you cannot depend on? He has already saved your life. He has gone to prepare a place for you. He has planned forward for you. So, why do you think he wouldn't care about your immediate provision? He is still caring for you, Nia. He is still protecting you from harm. He has blessed you with this amazing talent, and even though you have not chosen to use it for His glory, He has not taken it away. Let go of all this anger and bitterness and let Him be the loving father you never had. Let Him wrap His loving arms around you. Surrender to Him."

She turned her face into Liam's chest as tears flowed down her face. Liam's arms tightened around her as she sighed and her body sagged against his.

Eventually, they left the party and took a taxi over to the hotel. She sensed his disappointment that she hadn't repented of her sins then and there, but this was a decision she had to carefully weigh. The word 'surrender' scared her. It made her feel vulnerable and panic-stricken. She had always been a fighter. She didn't know how else to live. She was not used to surrendering to anyone.

When Liam brought the car to a stop at the hotel entrance, he turned to her.

"I hope we can keep in touch this time."

She looked at him as disappointment flowed through her.

"You're not coming up?" She didn't want this time with him to end so soon.

He smiled wryly. "The last time I made a similar decision we both know how it turned out. I can't come up to your room. It would be way too tempting, and we're no longer a married couple are we?"

She felt hurt and oddly angry. Damon would give his eyeteeth to spend the night with her but not Liam Lamport. He was too honorable for that. Even though it irked her, she grudgingly acknowledged that this was another thing she loved about him; how principled he was. She ran the back of her hand over his cheek and sighed deeply.

"But we need to talk about our relationship. I miss you, Liam. I want us to try again."

She saw a look pass over his eyes that she couldn't interpret. Then he glanced down as he took her hand in his and skimmed the knuckles with his thumb. He remained silent for a while, and then he finally met her eyes.

"Nothing would make me happier than for you to be a part of my life. I have always wanted you. But I have come to realize that unless we believe the same thing; unless you are as devoted to Christianity as I am then all we will end up doing is making each other miserable."

This was not what she wanted to hear. She snatched her hand away and wrenched the door open. Liam grasped her shoulders and pulled her to face him.

"Nia, don't you think I want this? I want you. I have never stopped wanting you. I have struggled for so many years to accept that we couldn't be together and it was hard. That divorce nearly tore me apart. Don't look so surprised. It was not a light decision. But I realized I couldn't hold onto you. When you rejected my God, you rejected me too, Nia, and there can be no compromise. You have to come to Him first before you can come to me."

"So you can finally accept me? I have to do things your way, Liam? Well, no! Just leave me alone. You make yourself out to be this good person, but you're not. *You* are a control freak. You have never loved me. You love this vision of who I can be."

"That is not true–" he began.

But she was no longer listening. "It is true! You have broken my heart so many times. You act like you're the only one who suffered. Well, I have too. You know what? We cannot be friends. We simply can't. A real friend would not give me an ultimatum."

When she reached for the door this time, he didn't stop her. She slammed out of the car not even looking back. Vaguely, she heard the car drive away as she pushed through the glass doors.

She realized she needed someone to numb the pain. The moment she reached her room she dialed Damon.

"Damon, I've been thinking about your proposal, and I accept. It is time to move our relationship to the next level."

Chapter 32

Seven months later

Nia was driving up the Pacific Coast highway singing along with the radio. It was one of the rare days she was driving herself. Ever since those death threats had started, Damon had insisted that she have security to shadow her every move. She knew the death threats were still coming. She didn't answer her own mail, so she didn't know the details. Bianca did that, and after the first few notes, Nia had told her that she didn't want to see any more. From then on Bianca would call the police if a threat was received by mail. Anything on social media was reported to the host site.

A week ago, Bianca opened a letter and then went pale.

"Nia, I think you should see this."

"No!" Nia had said, backing away. "I do not want anyone messing with my head. Just call the police."

She didn't know what the letter had said, but after that, the police agreed with Damon's position that she should be extra careful and that tightening security was not a bad idea. They also promised to increase patrol to her area. Damon had demanded she take a security detail with her everywhere she went. He had even directed them to keep her fans away from her in public places.

It had become so stifling she had simply had enough and had lost her temper with security this morning. She had told the security chief, Mike Seale, she was leaving home to go to the hair salon, unaccompanied. He had apologetically said, "I'm sorry, but my orders are that you are not to go anywhere alone."

"I give the orders around here, not Damon Deverre. And if you don't move out of my way right now, I'm going to snatch the gun out of your holster and shoot you with it!"

In Response, he had stepped back with his hands held up high. She knew he was angry and quite possibly hurt. After all, he put his life on the line every day to protect hers. Seale was a good man, a Christian, who once had told her that he took his duty to keep her safe very seriously. She felt a tug of guilt at treating him this way, but she didn't back down. If she didn't have some time alone, she would surely go mad.

When she left, she saw Seale on the phone arguing with someone. She figured it was probably Damon. Her phone rang just as she was pulling out of her driveway and the hands-free device announced it was Damon calling. Yes, Seale had definitely called Damon. She had refused to answer. To think that she was only dating the man and he could be so possessive. It was even worse than when she had been just his employee.

Nia brushed back her windblown hair with one hand as she checked her side mirror and switched lanes. Damon had called the entire time she was at the salon, but she had kept declining the call. If he knew she also was driving a convertible, he probably would have a conniption. Of course, he probably did know because Mike would have informed him.

When a man in a black Porsche suddenly zoomed alongside her car, horn honking, Nia startled and almost swerved into oncoming traffic.

"Hey, Nia. Nia Carmichael," the man yelled out his window, "I love all your songs! I love you! I want to marry you!"

Nia swallowed and placed a hand over her heart. The man had almost scared the living daylights out of her. She took a minute to catch her breath as he started singing one of her songs. He sounded terrible. Nia felt her tension drain away as she broke out in loud laughter.

"What's your name?" she called out.

"Luis Miguel Hontiveros, your future husband."

Laughter spilled from Nia's lips again as she struggled to keep her eyes on the road.

"Where are you from, future husband?"

"Right here, but I was born in Cuba. Can't you just come have a drink with me?"

Just then her phone started ringing again. Her hands-free device announced that Damon Deverre was calling. Nia sighed. This man defined the word relentless.

With a final look at the Cuban hunk, she yelled out, "You're very sweet. But I don't think so," just before doing the California version of the brush off, changing lanes and dropping behind another car. She immediately told the device to answer the call.

"Nia, where are you?" Damon asked. Nia was about to snap his head off when she realized he didn't sound angry.

"I'm on the highway, heading home," she said.

Another driver honked and waved, and she waved back. It felt so good to be free to engage with her fans.

"I'm calling to remind you about the party tonight at my place."

As if she could forget. For the whole week, he had been messaging her and asking her opinion on everything from the décor to the entertainment, to the food stations. The way he was acting one would think he didn't have at least four parties at his house in any given month.

"I haven't forgotten."

"I was trying to reach you all day," he said. He sounded more concerned than annoyed.

"I was at the salon."

"The salon, huh? A new look for tonight?"

Not *that* new. Her hair was straight again, and she had added blonde highlights. Cleary, it was an attractive look since she had just received a marriage proposal from Mr. Luis What's-His-Name.

"Yes, you'll love it."

"I'm sure I will. It's impossible for you to look anything but gorgeous."

She smiled at the compliment, but still, she was suspicious he hadn't lit into her about dumping her security team. There was no doubt that he knew. Damon knew everything, but for some reason, he wasn't trying to pick a fight with her. Maybe this was one of those rare phenomena that occurred around a summer solstice or something, only it wasn't summer, and she didn't believe in any of that nonsense. Maybe he was just in a good mood. Probably he just got a great return on an investment he'd made or was anticipating one. Perhaps, this would be a good time to ask for another five percent in royalties.

An hour later, Nia sat looking out from her ivory and glass penthouse onto the Malibu coast as she sipped a virgin daiquiri and classical music flowed through the house. She felt off-kilter and mildly discontented, but she didn't know why. She was young, beautiful, rich, powerful and loved. Well, not loved by *everyone.* There was some crazed person out there who had it in for her, but apart from that, she had millions of loyal fans.

When the doorbell rang, she sighed as she got up and lowered the volume on the radio. Maybe she needed to take a real break; a break from the public, the press, Damon. Just to rest and recover for a few weeks. Perhaps that would help to fill this hole inside of her.

She opened the door to a blonde woman who stepped through and extended a slim hand. "Namona Venton-Ross," she said with a Canadian accent.

Nia briefly clasped her hand.

She led the woman further into the house.

"Have a seat," she said, waving to the bar stool in front of her.

She joined Ms. Venton-Ross on the seat beside her and took a sip of the daiquiri.

"Want one?" she asked as she watched the woman fix her bag and a recorder on the bar top.

"No, thank you. I could use a glass of water though."

Nia slid off the stool and strode behind the bar. She reached in the fridge and removed a bottle of Evian then she went over to the cupboard and took down a crystal glass. She placed both in front of the reporter.

"Ice?" she asked.

The woman shook her head no.

Nia went back to her seat and took another sip of the drink. She ran her tongue over her teeth as the woman twisted off the cap of the water bottle and poured some of the liquid into the glass.

"Thanks for granting the interview."

Nia nodded.

The woman held up the recorder. "Do you mind if I use this?"

Nia shook her head.

Ms. Venton-Ross turned it on and placed it back on the counter. She reached for the book beside it.

"On my way over here I was listening to Christian radio–"

"Are you a Christian?" Nia interrupted.

The woman blinked, clearly not expecting the question.

"As a matter of fact, I am."

Nia swung gently from left to right on the stool and took another sip of her drink as she stared at the woman with new eyes. She looked fashionable enough in her white blouse and slim fitting black pants. She wore a single gold band on her left hand suggesting she was married. Nia absently ran a finger over her own finger, bare now for over seven years.

"So, how come you don't write for Christian magazines?"

"Well, I've decided to be a light in this dark world, wherever that finds me."

"That's an interesting perspective. But don't you find that there are stories you have to cover that conflict with your Christian values?"

Again Mrs. Venton-Ross blinked. Nia resisted the urge to smirk. She was enjoying asking the questions for a change. Maybe she should consider a second career as a reporter.

"I…Miss Carmichael…"

"Nia's fine."

"Nia…with all due respect, this isn't about me." She smiled to soften the words.

Nia shrugged. "I thought this was a two-way street. You learn about me, and I learn about you. Guess I was wrong. Be careful, though, I only give as good as I get."

The woman's eyes grew round. "Well, then. Let me see. To answer your question yes, there are times my values conflict with the articles I'm asked to write."

"What do you do then?"

"I pray and ask God's guidance about whether I should go through with a particular thing."

"And how do you know it's Him answering you and not your own desires."

"If I don't feel comfortable about something then it's probably because He doesn't want me to do it."

"How do you know it's just not your own unwillingness to be open-minded and try something different?"

"I sometimes struggle with that," she admitted. She was silent for a short while, and then she said, "I search His word to see if it lines up with what I believe He's saying to me."

Nia shook her head. "Such Christianese. What's *searching His word* mean? Do you start from Genesis and end at Revelation to see if something jumps out?"

"It's hard to explain."

"Give me an example."

"Let's see," the reporter pressed an index finger on her lower lip. "Okay. Last month the magazine asked me to do a story on a man who'd had a sex change. I was to share his experience with readers."

Nia sat back in her seat. This was going to be interesting.

"I prayed about whether to do the story. The editor knows that I became a Christian a few years ago and even though I haven't publicized it, he knows my view on certain topics. When he asked me to do the story I sensed he was trying to gauge my reaction. Would I be willing to interview this person without judgment?"

Nia watched her. "And?"

"My gut reaction was that no way would I want to subject myself to that. But I didn't respond initially. I asked him if I could be given a little time to think about it. You see, one of the things I've come to fear is that standing up for my faith is going to make me come across as a bigot."

"I can see how that would happen."

"I recognized at that moment that if I refused to interview this person because of their choices, I would be a hypocrite. After all, I have interviewed all types of people who are involved in all types of sinful behavior including fornication. No sin is greater than the other in the eyes of God. Then during my Bible study the next morning, as I was praying about what to do I felt the Holy Spirit direct me to the story of Jesus speaking with the woman at the well. Do you know what that was about?" she asked.

Nia searched her brain. "I don't quite remember what she had done wrong, but I do know she had five husbands or something. Was that even legal back then?"

Ms. Venton-Ross smiled. Nia noticed she had kind eyes.

"Actually, Jesus told her that she had had five husbands and the man she was now living with was not her husband. The suggestion was that her husbands were living, so either they had divorced her or she them and the man she was living with at the time was not her husband. He might have been someone else's husband, but the point was she was either committing adultery or fornicating. Either way, she was living in sin."

Nia nodded. "Go on."

"So, I read that story and it seemed to me as though God was telling me that in the same way Jesus did not shy away from talking not only to a woman but a Samaritan woman, and not only a Samaritan woman but one who was blatantly living in sin, I should not shy away from this man. I should go and hear what he had to say."

Nia was riveted. "Then what happened?"

"I interviewed him."

"Her, you mean. She'd had the sex change by then."

"No, Miss Carmichael, God created him a man. Even though he changed his sexual organs and injected female hormones, it doesn't mean he is a woman. God determines our gender; we do not. Just like coloring my hair blonde doesn't make me a natural blonde. I may appear to be one, I may even fool some people, but I've still got mouse-colored hair under this and when I'm late getting to the salon for my dye job everyone knows the truth."

Nia found herself nodding. What this woman said was true. She never would have known unless she looked closely that Ms. Venton-Ross wasn't a natural blonde. But it didn't change facts. She was a brunette.

"I take your point. Please continue with your story. I'm very interested in what happened next."

"I interviewed him and found out that the surgery had not brought him the peace and happiness he craved. He shared with me that having the sex change hadn't been all it was cut out to be. He said that he had been teased as a boy and berated by his stepfather for being effeminate. He entered into many homosexual relationships and eventually he decided to just come out and become who he wanted to be, a woman. The whole process was painful and uncomfortable, but now he had finally done it, and the happiness he had expected continued to elude him. It made him feel as though there was no point to life."

"What did you do then?" Nia prompted, now on the edge of her seat. She could relate to wanting something so badly, and when you finally got it, you still were not happy or didn't feel the satisfaction you were so sure it would have brought you.

The woman smiled wryly. "I did what Jesus would do. I offered him the Living Water. I told him that there was One who could bring that peace he craved. One who made him, who loved him completely and who had a perfect plan for his life. He just had to surrender."

Nia sucked in a sharp breath and jerked upright. She felt goose bumps on her skin. *Those words.*

"Are you all right?" the woman asked. Concern was reflected on her face.

Nia waved a hand in the air. "I'm fine. Please continue."

"Well, he broke down and cried. I held him. The thing is that when I used to see him on TV talking about his lifestyle all I felt was disgust. But at that moment, I felt such love for him. That was God! He made me see him through His eyes as one of His precious children who needed Him. The man was a sinner in need of a Savior the same as all of us. Anyway, he asked God to forgive him of his sins. I pray for him every day. He messages me sometimes to let me know how he's doing."

"That's sad in a way. He's had his body changed. How can he undo that?"

"He can. It won't be easy, but God is able to heal and restore."

Nia nodded then realized the story wasn't over yet. "What about your article? What did your editor say?"

"The article was not well received by the magazine. I wrote the truth. I also included research done in Sweden where the culture is strongly supportive of transgender persons. It followed people for over thirty years after sexual reassignment and found that ten to fifteen years after the reassignment the suicide rate of those persons rose twenty times higher than their peers. The conclusion was that sex change is physically impossible. You can change your *body parts*, but it doesn't change who you really are. As a Christian, I know it's because God is the one who assigns gender, not human beings. Gender identity has become the new buzzword, but true identity can only be found in who we are in Christ."

"So, they didn't publish the article."

"Sadly, no. In fact, I was read the riot act for 'bias', as they called it."

Nia raised an eyebrow. "Yet, you're still here."

She shrugged. "God is in charge of my destiny, not mankind."

Nia smiled. The interview continued.

"Now, back to *my* question. I was listening to the radio and Liam Lamport's song, *I am yours, and you are mine* has gone to number one. It's a Christian remake of your number one hit song *I am Yours, Baby*. How does that news make you feel?"

Nia's smile instantly died, but she managed to keep her voice casual as she responded. "It's a cover of *my* hit song, so I feel great. The royalty fees keep coming. His success is my success."

She drained the glass, the contents of which had long since melted, and then resumed twisting from side to side on the stool.

One skeptical dark blonde-looking brow climbed. Nia wondered if the woman dyed her eyebrows as well.

"Yes, but he's been doing it more and more. Every time you bring out a hit song he makes a Christian cover. Doesn't that strike you as a little purposeful? Like he's out to prove a point."

Nia crossed her arms and straightened her back. She leveled her gaze at the reporter. "Listen, I like you. I really do, but if you continue to question me about Liam Lamport, this interview is over."

The woman cleared her throat. "I'm sorry, Miss Ca - Nia - I didn't realize Liam Lamport was a sensitive topic for you. Let's move on, then."

Nia almost rolled her eyes. Just then her phone rang. She decided to let the voicemail cut in. Mrs. Venton-Ross began asking her another question, but Nia held up a hand for a moment as her lawyer's voice came over the machine urgently asking that she call him.

It sounded very important. For some unknown reason, she felt anxiety creep up her spine. She excused herself and walked over to the phone in the corner of the family room. She took a seat and called Mr. Manzini, keeping an eye on Namona Venton-Ross.

"It's Nia. What's up?"

"Nia, I've got some news you won't be happy about."

"I'm listening."

"The court called this afternoon to say that your divorce was never finalized. You are still married to William Lamport."

Chapter 33

Despite the dull ache in her head, Nia was momentarily distracted from her thoughts by how magnificent Damon's mansion and its grounds looked. From the moment she stepped out of the limo, she could see the way the estate was lit with thousands of tiny lights not to mention the sparkling lights draped through the trees which surrounded the vast property.

Immediately, a few cameramen stepped up and snapped off pictures of her. She automatically smiled and posed, satisfied that she was camera ready. She wore a brown snakeskin leather dress with a jeweled neck and jeweled belted waist. An arctic marble frost fox coat and matching white stilettos completed the look. She could be quite confident that no other woman would be dressed like her tonight as the dress had been custom made. She had no doubt, though, that the moment the photos hit the press, the next morning designers would be busy creating copies.

Come to think of it, why was the press here? She had thought this was just a party. Why would Damon invite the press? What was up?

Then Damon appeared to escort her up the steps and into his home. Nia accepted the kiss on her cheek and nodded in appreciation as she gave him the once over. He did cut a fine figure in his dark navy blue suit, white button-down shirt, wine-colored tie, and shiny slim toe tan boots. And of course, he wore his diamond tie pin, diamond stud earrings and matching cufflinks with flair. Damon was nothing if not flashy.

At the door, he helped her out of her coat and handed it to a waiting attendant. Again, a photographer took some more shots of them.

Nia paused in admiration. The inside was even more stunning with beautiful floral creations everywhere. Someone was singing jazzy music. There were neatly dressed wait-staff weaving through, balancing trays of champagne. Others carried canapés. What was going on? This was very different from Damon's usual rowdy affairs.

In fact, it reminded her of something Liam would do. She swallowed hard at that name. Her mind began drifting to her conversation with Manzini earlier. She had almost collapsed. She didn't know what she had told the reporter after that, but the woman asked her if she wanted to continue the interview another time and she had gratefully agreed. Nia told her she'd received unexpected news and the woman had nodded in understanding. Then, to Nia's surprise, she had prayed for her there and then.

Nia and Damon were quickly surrounded by several of his guests. She greeted them affably but kept wondering what the occasion was. Before she could question him, he excused himself to check on something.

She spotted him several minutes later and disengaged from a group of people to join him.

"This party is great, Damon. What's the occasion?"

He kissed her temple. "I'm glad you approve."

"Yeah, but what's it for?"

He winked. "It's a surprise."

She almost groaned. She wanted to be informed, not surprised. No matter how she pressed him he kept his lips sealed.

It was well after 10 p.m. when he shared the surprise. Standing before a room of over one hundred people, Damon flipped open a black box to reveal a ring with the largest diamond she had ever seen.

Nia was stunned. This could not be happening. Especially not after the news she had received today. She watched helplessly as Damon fell on one knee and said, "Nia Carmichael, will you marry me."

All she could do was stare. Without waiting for her assent, Damon slid the ring on her finger, pulled her into a hug and then placed a kiss on her lips. All the while cameras were shooting off like machine guns.

Nia checked her watch again and resisted the urge to call Liam. She was limiting communication with him as far as possible. In fact, it had been her lawyer who had called him at her behest to come to his office in L.A. and sign the hastily drawn up divorce papers.

It was now four days since Damon's proposal. She hadn't said yes to Damon, no matter what the world might think; but she hadn't said no either. This mess with the divorce papers just made things worse. The last thing she needed was for it to come to light that she was still married to Liam while planning to marry another man. Even though, she actually had not yet agreed to marry Damon.

Liam was now half an hour late.

Nia reached for her bag to call him when the door opened. She looked up, and there was the man himself led in by Mr. Manzini's secretary.

Nia quickly glanced away. She did not want to look at him. She wanted him to sign and exit her life forever. So why did that last thought cause her stomach to tighten?

She kept her eyes on the hands in her lap, but when he sat beside her, she got a whiff of his cologne and had to close her eyes briefly as unwanted emotions swept over her.

"Sorry to be late," he muttered.

She rolled her eyes. He was always late which meant he wasn't really sorry.

Mr. Manzini began, "The reason we are here is–"

"You found out Nia and I are still married, and she's anxious to get a real divorce this time," Liam finished for him.

After a brief hesitation Mr. Manzini said, "Yes, the paperwork is all here. You can peruse it to check if everything is in order and then sign."

Nia lifted her head and fixed her gaze on Mr. Manzini's framed degree. From the corner of her eyes, she could see Liam watching her. She wished she knew what was going through his head at this very moment. Was it a replay of their last conversation when she had accused him of being a dictator? She sure hoped so. If he were still smarting from their angry exchange, then he'd sign the papers fast, and she could resume her systematic attempt to purge him from her consciousness.

He turned back to the lawyer. "When you contacted me you said that due to an administrative mistake the divorce wasn't finalized. Can you tell me a little more about that?"

"It seems as though there was some fraudulent activity. The judge who signed the papers does not even exist. This rendered them null and void."

"Remarkable," Liam said slowly, as though this was some great mystery he was trying to solve. "Do you think someone in the office perhaps wanted to cut down on their workload and decided to sign it themselves?"

"Perhaps."

Liam gave a little laugh.

She began to get exasperated. What was there to laugh about and why didn't he just sign the stupid papers. "Aren't you going to sign?" she asked, shaking her foot and keeping her gaze averted.

"I'll need to read all of it first."

"Go ahead then." She snuck a glance at him. It was maddening that even with wind-tousled hair he still looked gorgeous.

"Oh, not now. I don't have the time. Besides, my lawyer also needs to see them."

Her eyes flew to his. "For Pete's sake! It's the same thing you signed last time."

"I don't know that. That's what you're saying. I still need my lawyer to see it to be sure."

She sighed with dramatic exaggeration and slumped against the back of the seat.

"What's the rush?" he asked almost conversationally. "Are you planning to get married?"

The blood receded from her face. Did he know? Damon had only proposed four days ago, but that was a lifetime on the information superhighway.

"I…I…that's none of your business," she snapped, sitting up and glaring at him.

He ran the back of his hand along his chin and watched her with a self-satisfied smile.

"Of course it's my business, Carmichael. You asked me to come to see you. I accommodated your request because I had business in L.A. anyway. Frankly, though, it puzzled me why you couldn't have sent the documents by priority mail."

"Because I want to expedite things."

His eyes flickered over her as she picked up the documents and the pen beside them and handed them to him.

"Liam, please sign and let us be done with this business. You know it's over between us."

Liam held them in front of him and began to read. A few minutes later, he lowered them and turned to her.

"You know, when I first signed the divorce papers, I did so against my better judgment. And then, amazingly, something totally bizarre happens to make the divorce not legally valid." He shook his head and pocketed the pen. "I don't know, Nia. I just don't feel right about this."

"You are such a wicked man."

His head jerked backward. "Wicked? I never thought I'd hear that term used to describe me. I mean I've been told I've got a wickedly sexy smile. I've been called devilishly handsome. It's even been said I've got a naughty sense of humor and a bad sense of style. But wicked?"

She put up a hand. "Stop. I'm not joking with you. You will sign this, Liam. Or, I will…I will…I will take you to the cleaners!"

"Take me to the what?"

"I never asked for anything when we supposedly divorced the first time. If you contest this again Liam so help me I will take half of what you own."

His eyes narrowed. "Why just half? You didn't take half my heart when you left me. You took the whole thing, so why stop at just half of my possessions?"

He pushed away from the table abruptly, causing it to shake, and took up the papers.

"Where are you going?" she asked, sitting forward in alarm.

"Away from here. I'll get back to you on these in due course."

"HE POPPED THE QUESTION AND SHE SAID YES!" the headline screamed.

Liam slowly lowered the tabloid magazine he had taken up in the waiting room of the distributor with whom he was meeting and sat back. So this was why Nia was in such a hurry to get a divorce; because she wanted to marry Damon Deverre.

He shouldn't be surprised. The two had been an item for the last few months. He had been hurt when he first learned they were seeing each other. No, *hurt* was not the word. That was way too mild to describe the raw sense of grief that had ripped through him when he found out.

He glanced at the photo of the two again. Deverre was smiling wide enough for both of them. He looked euphoric.

Liam brought the magazine up to his face. The diamond on that ring was huge and gaudy. Strange, he never thought Nia would go for something like that. He saw her as having more refined taste despite her outlandish sense of style, but maybe he had just been fooling himself. After all, the man she had gone for was not subtle. He was flashy.

Liam took another look at the man who seemed to have been pursuing Nia since the day Liam had met her. And now he had her. Damon Deverre finally had what he had wanted all these years. Under other circumstances, Liam–might concede that he had been bested. But his congratulations to his opponent seemed to be quite late in coming. In reality, he had been bested when Nia had first left him and accompanied Damon to Los Angeles. This latest move was just Damon confirming his win.

Liam leaned forward and placed his aching head in his hands. Perhaps he should just sign the papers and be done with the thing. She was right. It was over. Or was it?

Liam lifted his head. That was defeatist talk. It was not too late for them. It wouldn't be too late until she either went along with the divorce without his consent or until she and Deverre exchanged vows. He at least had bargaining power. She had admitted to wanting the divorce expedited. He could promise to do so if she was prepared to do something for him. He had not given up on his dream of them singing together. He felt deep in his soul that if he could get her to sing Amazing Grace with him again like she had all those years ago, it would bring her to her knees. If that didn't work, he would concede defeat and sign the documents.

~*~*~*~

Nia absently gnawed the inside of her cheek as she listened to her mother distractedly. She had decided to pay Nikki a visit. It gave her a break from Damon and an opportunity to think clearly without him hounding her twenty-four seven about making wedding plans. Was it possible his megalomania had finally gone to his head? He was behaving as though it was a given she would marry him. Just yesterday when she was leaving Malibu for Holmby Hills after he had done freaking out about her driving herself alone for almost an hour, he proceeded to tell her he needed her back by the following Tuesday as they were being interviewed by a famous talk show host.

It was more than she could take. When she told him she wasn't wearing the ring he had replied that it was a good idea given its value and the fact that she would be driving alone. He didn't even allow her to explain that it was because she hadn't yet said yes to his proposal. Dealing with him was exasperating, and she had finally given up and driven away.

While the long drive cleared her thoughts of Damon, it filled her mind with thoughts of Liam. Five days had passed. Five whole days since she'd asked that man to sign the papers. And instead of signed documents, all she had received was a call a day later from his manager, requesting that Nia sing a song with him on his new album.

Nia had tried to be gracious to the woman. After all, it wasn't her fault she worked for such an unreasonable person. Nia had explained to Ms. Kerr that she would sing anything once Liam signed the documents he had in his possession. A day later, the manager called her back to confirm that Liam had agreed to her proposal and would contact her shortly regarding when and where they would record the song.

She had felt like pulling her hair out by the roots. What an infuriating man! *He* had accepted *her* proposal? He was the one blackmailing her. The brute had gone from doing covers of her songs to now demanding that she sing his songs. Why couldn't he just sign the documents and leave her alone?

Oh, the pressure she was under. Between Liam and Damon, she just might wind up in a nut house.

Nia chewed on a thumbnail and stared off into space. She still couldn't believe the mess she was in with Damon. As he had knelt before her holding out the ring she had kept telling herself to say something; to say she wasn't sure and she needed time. But she just couldn't seem to bring herself to say that to him in front of all his friends and industry colleagues. It had seemed so cruel, so unkind. And then he had slid on the ring and kissed and hugged her as though it were a fait accompli that she would accept.

Nia looked up at her mother as she placed the steaming dish of Potatoes à la Nikki, baked lamb chops and vegetables in front of her then returned to the kitchen to bring in her own plate.

"Looks great, Mama."

Nikki nodded with a smile and then reached her hands across the table.

"Let's say grace."

Nia squeezed her eyes closed and said "Amen" when her mother was done. She took a bite of the potatoes first and then sighed with contentment. Yep, nothing like mama's cooking.

"This is good. Just like I remember. No Michelin star restaurant I've ever been to could compare to this stuff," she said, jabbing her fork in the direction of her plate.

Her mother beamed. "You say the sweetest things," Nikki said in her Georgia peach accent.

"It's the truth."

Nikki Carmichael had always loved to cook. She liked to say that she had been a momma's girl, a shy child who preferred to stay indoors around her mother's skirts than play with her other siblings outdoors. That's where she'd learned to cook. It was hard to believe that the famed best-selling music artist had ever been shy, but Nikki said that she just came to life on stage. Deep down, she was really an introvert.

Nia remembered that her mother had always cooked for their family on the few occasions when she was at home, even though they had domestic help. She understood from others that even on the tour bus she had cooked for her band. She said cooking was an inspiration and frequently she'd find herself humming and then would have a song in her head. In fact, she had once attempted to cook when she was high and almost burned down the house. Nia always remembered that because she was sent to live with Grandmama Carmichael for the most extended period after that incident.

Nia's gaze drifted to her mother's face. She had surely come a long way. She didn't even take aspirin now; that was how clean she was. And she still loved to cook. Two years ago she had published a celebrity cookbook which quickly became a best seller.

It didn't seem as though she had passed the cooking gene on to Nia, though. Nia didn't attempt anything beyond toast and scrambled eggs. She remembered now the one time she had cooked for Liam. He had been so gracious, even though the meal hadn't been very good. He had gently taken over cooking duties after that.

Nia frowned. How many times had she thought of that infuriating man in the space of an hour? She had been doing so well since Beijing. She had managed to push him into the recesses of her brain. Now, this matter with the divorce had resurfaced, and she could not seem to stop thinking of the man. This must have been how Pharaoh felt about Moses.

She pulled her thoughts back to the food before her. She really appreciated a home-cooked meal. Her meals were always prepared by other people these days. Of course, she'd missed out on this treat for a few years after she had left Liam. She and her mother had been in a terrible fight over her decision. At that time, Nia had been enraged. She had accused Nikki of being the biggest hypocrite because she had pursued her career and made it a god all the years

Nia had been growing up. How could she who had achieved superstardom want to deny Nia that experience herself?

Her mother had been hurt by her thoughtless words. Nia had been too angry to apologize. Later, shame had kept her from contacting her mother. Nia had buried herself in her career and convinced herself she didn't need anyone, her mother least of all. Then a year and a half later, she had run into her mother at an award show. Nikki was being nominated for her new gospel album. When they embraced, the dam had broken, and Nia was unable to stop the floodgate of tears. They had gone back to Nia's hotel and spent the night talking and catching up.

Nikki confessed to Nia that she didn't approve of some of her choices but had to accept that she was now an adult and had to live her own life. It was during that time that for the first time Nikki had a heart-to-heart talk with Nia about her life. She told Nia that she had been raised in the church. Her father had been a pastor, but after he had died her mother took over pastoring. Nikki had been in the choir but, one day a friend of hers sent her demo to a record producer in Los Angeles. When she got a visit from the man, her mother had told her in no uncertain terms that she did not support this devil's music and had sent the man packing. Months later, Nikki packed her bags and followed the man to L.A.

With her beauty and amazing vocal talents, Nikki Carmichael quickly rose to stardom. But through it all, Nikki was concealing a terrible secret. When she had started out, her label had been running her ragged by exploiting the eighteen-year-old and trying to get as much mileage out of her as possible. She soon found she couldn't keep up the frantic pace. Her manager offered her a questionable solution. It was a small pill that would allow her to stay awake and keep working. The problem was that she then needed another type of pill to help her get to sleep. She quickly became dependent on the drugs.

It was a secret she kept from Jacques Annuad. He had no idea when he married the glamorous twenty-three-year-old R&B star that his wife was well on her way to becoming a drug addict. Soon after Nia was born the habit had gotten worst, but Jacques didn't know because Nikki was always on the road touring and when she was home for a few months, he was out shooting a movie. By the time Nia was four years old, the two were pretty much leading separate lives. The rumors reached Nikki that Jacques was sleeping with other women, often times the leading actress of his latest movie.

Niki's response was to book another tour to escape from real life. Eventually, she couldn't ignore the truth any longer when several photos were published in the press with Jacques on a secluded beach in the South of France kissing a topless woman.

But leaving Jacques did not solve the problem of Nikki's drug addiction. By then it was apparent to everyone she was a full-blown addict. She checked herself into rehab for the first time after she had fallen into a downer-induced coma and woke up to realize she had almost burned down the house with Nia in it. She had passed out while preparing a meal.

Nia remembered that as one of the scariest moments of her life. The smoke detector was blaring, and she was trying to wake her mother as smoke began to fill the house. But Nikki didn't move. Eventually, the fire department had broken down the door and gotten them out. She didn't see her mother for a year after that and didn't know why at the time. She had thought she'd done something wrong and maybe her mother had sent her away. It was only years later she had realized Nikki had gone to rehab. Nikki revealed to Nia that she had also been filled with guilt and couldn't bear to keep Nia until she felt strong enough emotionally to take care of her eight-year-old.

That was the first time Nikki had gone to rehab. She had stayed drug-free for so long she felt confident she could be a mother to Nia once more, but a year later she relapsed. There was a repeat of the scenario two more times and for all the world to see. The tabloids delighted in reporting her mother's struggle.

And then Nikki found God.

Nia sat forward abruptly. "Mama, how did you recover from your drug addiction?"

Nikki smiled slowly. "I just did, baby. I met Thomas on a flight to Crossroads Center in Antigua. I had tried every other rehab clinic in California. I figured maybe I needed to experience a totally different country and then it would stick. I don't know what I was thinking. Anyway, on the plane, I was seated next to this tall guy. I noticed that he was cute, especially when he turned those hazel eyes on me and smiled. I was so nervous about whether this rehab would really work that I didn't smile back. He asked if I was okay. I don't know why I confided in a total stranger, but maybe I figured the whole world knew about my struggle, so what difference did it make."

Nikki stopped for a few seconds before continuing to share with her daughter.

"I told him everything, expecting the usual sympathetic babble about being sure it would work this time. But he shocked me when he quietly told me that God could heal me if I were prepared to surrender my life to Him. At that moment he reminded me of my daddy. I swear I got goose bumps. I remembered once when I was a little girl seeing my daddy ministering to a man who had an alcohol problem and saying that same thing."

Nikki's eyes took on a far off look. "Nia, I don't know how to describe it. I just felt like a dam had broken. I started to bawl. That man put an arm around my shoulders while I just cried and cried and when I was done, he asked me if he could pray for me. I could only nod. And after that Nia, my craving was just gone. I just knew it was gone. I could feel the difference. I felt like a new woman. That was when I knew without a shadow of a doubt how real God is; how personal He is, and how much He cares for us."

It sounded so much like what Liam had said to her, she placed her fork back in her plate and sat back.

"Everything all right with you?" her mother asked.

"I guess," she muttered.

"What's wrong?"

"Who says something's wrong," Nia rebutted attempting a smile, which faltered when she met her mother's concern eyes.

"Come on, Nia. I can see all's not well."

"Liam," Nia said with a sigh.

A hopeful look seemed to sparkle in Nikki's eyes.

"What about Liam?"

Nia was about to tell her about the fact that she and Liam were still married, but that look stopped her in her tracks. She didn't want her mother pressuring her about reconciliation. She thought about the other thing that was annoying her about him lately.

"He's been doing these covers of my songs."

"Yes, I heard."

"You heard? You never mentioned it."

"When it comes to Liam I like to follow your lead."

"So what do you think?"

"About?"

"The covers."

"Do you really want to know?"

Nia folded her hands over her chest, sat back. "Sure."

Nikki glanced at Nia's plate. "Don't let your lamb get cold. There's nothing worse than cold lamb."

Nia picked up her knife and fork and dutifully took a small bite of lamb. She rarely ate meat. It was Liam's influence. Although she'd tried to start eating meat again to get all things Liam out of her life, it still didn't feel right.

"Well, I thought his versions were very good. You know he's an extremely talented songwriter. I've always said so."

"Better than my versions."

"Don't take it so personally. You didn't write your songs after all."

"No, just sang them. And to hear my own mother thinks someone else's version is better. Well…"

Nikki waved a hand dismissively. "Oh, stop it, Nia. It's not a matter of the voice. You know I'd choose your voice over his any day because you're my daughter and I think you've been blessed immeasurably with a great voice. However, this is not just any old cover. It's his substitution of your lyrics with his. The tune's the same. The words are different. His glorify God. Yours don't. That's why I prefer his, and I won't apologize for it."

Nikki stood to take her plate to the kitchen.

"Fine." Nia's voice followed her. "His people are asking me to appear on his next album."

"You? Really?" Nikki glanced over her shoulder at her in surprise.

Nia rolled her eyes. "What? You think I can't sing gospel?"

"I know you can sing gospel. You used to sing at Mama's church. I've still got those little videos she sent me of you up there with your two pigtails and singing your little heart out."

Nikki sighed wistfully and then sobered. "I'm just surprised you would be willing to sing gospel considerin' that you've gone in a completely different direction in your career."

"First of all, I'm not an atheist, Mama. I know there is a God."

Her mother seemed about to say something then thought better of it. She turned her back to her as she faced the kitchen sink. Over the sound of running water, she only said, "Hmm."

"Second of all, I haven't said I'm willing to sing gospel."

Nia sat brooding as her mother finished up then returned to the table.

"Let's go into the family room where we can be more comfortable."

When they were seated on a big taupe leather sofa with scattered throw cushions facing toward a large window with a view of the well-manicured grounds, Nikki returned to the conversation.

"I think it would be a great idea for you to sing with him."

"Of course you do."

"I've always liked Liam," Nikki murmured wistfully, staring out through the window. "I'll never forget the impression he made on me that morning he marched up to the chalet in Austria and proposed that I release you into his care. And to think I actually complied to a teenage boy's request. He was unlike any teenager I'd ever met. I never had cause to regret that decis–"

"Damon proposed."

Her mother visibly startled, and then she actually shuddered. "I see."

Nia pursed her lips. Not a surprising reaction but still…

"What did you say to him?"

"Not much."

"What do you mean?"

Nia sighed. The moment of truth. This was not going to go over well.

"He proposed to me in front of a hundred guests at his home. He proposed and then he slid the ring on my finger, Mama. Before I could even get over my shock, he was kissing me, hugging me. I never replied. Everyone just assumed I said yes. Cameras were flashing around us, people were clapping. What could I do? I couldn't embarrass him by saying no, could I?"

Her mother watched her in shock. There was silence for a short while as Nikki's mouth stayed agape.

"I can't believe what I'm hearin'. You're goin' to marry a man 'cause you didn't want to publicly embarrass him?"

Nia glanced away.

"That would have served him right for being so arrogant. He assumed you would say yes." Then Nikki paused. "You know what? I wouldn't put it past him to have set you up to make it impossible for you to say no. He knew you wouldn't want to embarrass him. He manipulated you!"

Nikki's voice had risen higher with each sentence. She now sat up straight in her chair, her body turned towards Nia.

Nia regretted confessing to Nikki. Her mother was making her feel foolish and naïve.

"Who said I'm going to marry him? I simply said he proposed and you fly off on a tangent."

Nikki glanced down at Nia's finger and noted it was bare. She flopped back against the pillows. "Well, at least you haven't decided to go through with it yet. I know what to add to my prayer list."

She sounded relieved. Nia knew what Nikki *wouldn't* be praying for.

Chapter 34

"People are beginning to talk."

Liam took his time responding to Sophie. He had a fair idea what she was referring to given that their last conversation had been about the cover he was doing of Nia's latest hit.

He took another sip of his tea then placed the teacup carefully into the saucer. He dabbed the corner of his mouth with a napkin.

"About what?" he asked, meeting and holding her gaze.

"You and Nia Carmichael. The only covers you do are of her songs."

"I only did seven covers."

"All of her songs. The only covers you have ever done. You don't think that's drawing attention? Now tongues are wagging. They want to know if something is going on between the pop star and the Christian music star."

Liam sighed. The covers had started out innocently enough, now it almost seemed as though he was baiting her. The other band members, specifically Matthew and Sam, had even questioned him about it recently.

"You know it's no secret that Nia's my wife...I mean *ex*-wife."

He hoped that Sophie hadn't noticed his slip of the tongue. He always had difficulty thinking of Nia as his *ex*. The recent knowledge that they weren't even divorced only made it worse.

"Precisely. *Ex*-wife. They consider that there is a great moral divide between you two. They figure that maybe you two split because of it."

"They should *consider* minding their own business," he said, thinking wryly how that was something Nia would say.

"Oh, Liam, you know that's not going to happen. You're a public figure. Your life is the public's business. Remember when those photos of you two in China during her tour were published? You recall all the speculation it generated."

"It died down, didn't it?"

"Yes, when it was revealed soon after that she was now dating Damon Deverre. Even then some sleazy tabloid newspaper hinted at a love triangle. All that sensationalism is not good for your image as a Christian artist."

"What are you suggesting, Sophie?"

"Don't release this next cover. Concentrate on finishing the album. Keep your head down until this blows over."

He took his lower lip between his teeth. He acknowledged she could have a point, but he felt like he was on a mission. "But this cover is *sooo* good. When you hear it you will be blown away," he teased.

"Are you becoming a cover, no…a Nia-cover, junkie?" she asked half-jokingly.

He pursed his lips and looked down at the amber liquid in his cup.

"People appreciate what I'm doing," he muttered.

"Yeah, some do. Others argue you're opening her to a new audience who are going to listen to her originals to compare with your remakes and may be taken in."

He shook his head. "No matter what you do you'll have your naysayers. Like those who felt my music was too upbeat and might give Christian kids a taste for pop songs."

"Liam, my point is you need to tread carefully here. You don't want to lose your supporters."

"Have you gotten back to her yet about the fact that I will expedite things if she does the song?" he asked, abruptly changing the subject.

She nodded. "I have."

"What was her response?"

"She said she will think about it. Maybe you should approach her yourself. It might be more persuasive if it came straight from you."

"I like how you think I've got influence with her."

"You must have. She hasn't said no outright."

Liam looked into his cup. Well, he was attending the Grammy's next week. Nia would be there, nominated as she was in several categories. He would also be attending as the band had garnered two nominations. Perhaps he would run into her at that time and maybe if he played his cards right, he could convince her to come sing with him.

Liam took a sip of the glass of champagne and nodded, listening to Sam, Hans, and Matthew with one ear as he surveyed the room of glittering stars. He had been looking the whole evening and still he had not spotted Nia. She had to appear at some point. Not only was she a multiple awards nominee, but she was also set to perform, according to the program. *Redeemed* had been nominated in the Best Contemporary Christian Song/Performance and Best Contemporary Christian Album category. Originally, he'd had every intention of absenting himself as he had done last year and the year before that, but now he welcomed the opportunity to see her.

He scanned the room once more. Suddenly, his breath seemed suspended. Nia had arrived. There she was with her fiancé and their entourage. Liam scrutinized her face and noticed that she didn't look too happy. She looked tense and uptight. Did she and Deverre perhaps have a fight on their way over there? Not that he cared. His gaze shifted to Deverre who seemed to be in a relaxed, jovial mood.

Liam wished he could get Nia alone. He really wanted to talk to her, but he didn't want to have to interact with Deverre to do so. As if wishes came true, Deverre was soon called away, and Nia stood chatting with a small group of people. Now was his chance.

Liam excused himself from the members of his band and made his way towards Nia.

Nia was fuming. She had told Damon in the limo as they drove over to the Staples Centre for the Grammy Award Ceremony that she couldn't marry him and he had told her not to be ridiculous. She had taken his ring out of her handbag and handed it over to him. He had laughed, removed it out of its box, and tried to slide it on her finger.

When she had resisted, he had sighed as though dealing with an errant child and said, "Nia, now is not the time for theatrics."

"Theatrics! You should know after the stunt you pulled two weeks ago."

"What stunt?"

"You gave everyone the impression I'd said yes to you when I had not."

He shook his head. "I don't know what you're talking about. I just assumed you were too overcome to speak. I took it for granted you'd say yes. Why wouldn't you? Isn't that what you were blackmailing me with when you told me a few months ago that you aren't sleeping with me because we're not married? I've never thought of you as particularly religious, so I figured you were just holding out for a ring."

Nia was insulted although she wasn't sure why she was. Might it be because it sounded as though Damon was saying she had no morals? She didn't know what to believe. Damon was a master deceiver. Perhaps he was trying to distract her by turning things around on her. Well, two could play that game.

"So, what you are really saying is that you only proposed so that you could get me into bed. Am I to be flattered by that admission?"

"You're overreacting. It doesn't matter why I want to marry you. The point is that I do. If you have concerns, we'll discuss them but let's not make it an issue tonight of all nights. Everyone thinks we're engaged. If you show up tonight without the ring on, it'll look like we broke our engagement off and it will draw attention from your win. And we all know you'll be taking home some of those Grammys tonight."

Nia had sat back and sulked. She couldn't argue with his logic. Her mama was right, he was a master manipulator.

He stood next to her acting as though everything was right as rain between them and all she could feel was the weight of the ridiculously large gemstone on her finger.

When Damon was called away to deal with an issue regarding one of the artists on his label she was relieved to be free of his presence. It would be great if he disappeared for the rest of the evening altogether. She didn't even listen to the people chatting like magpies around her and trying without success to draw her into the conversation. She just sipped her tonic water and stared off into surly silence.

If Damon thought he could keep his ruse up for much longer, he had another think coming. She decided that the moment she was back in the limo with him, she was placing this rock in his hands. He could spin it however he wanted.

Nia saw the woman in front of her with the ridiculous fascinator on her head turn around in annoyance to confront whoever had tapped her and then Nia idly noted the woman's enraptured expression. Who had captured her attention? Then a man stepped into her line of vision.

Oh my!

Michelangelo's David had nothing on Liam Lamport. He wore a slim fit tuxedo and was sporting a thin mustache and a beard. And he had never looked sexier.

What was he doing here? Was it possible he had been nominated for a Grammy? She wracked her brain and drew a blank. He hardly looked at the woman. He was staring straight at his almost ex-wife as he made his way over to stand in front of her.

"Hi, Nia."

"What are you doing here?" she blurted.

"My band's a nominee. May we speak in private?"

At this moment she almost wished Damon was here rather than have to deal with Liam. He leaned down and whispered in her ear.

"I want to speak to you about the divorce but if you'd rather me discuss it here among your friends."

She gulped. That was the last thing she wanted. She hadn't even broken the news to Damon yet, not that she owed him an explanation given that she wasn't sure she wanted to marry him. The more she became aware of his tactics, the more convinced she was that she did not want to be his wife.

Even if Liam didn't know this, he at least knew that she wouldn't want such an embarrassing thing publicized when the whole world thought she and Damon were engaged to be married. Clearly, Damon wasn't the only one who knew how to manipulate. She felt like she was a chess pawn.

She gave her glass to Bianca and turned to Liam. "Lead the way."

He led her to a secluded area of the lobby. Leaning against a pillar, he folded his arms across his chest and watched her with mild amusement.

"Very nice dress, Miz Carmichael. You look just like a debutante," he commented.

Nia rolled her eyes and glanced away. The dress was quite a departure from her usual unorthodox style, which was why she had selected it. She hated being predictable. It was a fifties-inspired black ball gown featuring a tight strapless silk bodice and a flowing full-length taffeta skirt. Her hair was pinned back from her face in a bun. Her lips were ruby red to match her shoes and nails. The only jewelry she wore apart from pearl bob earrings was the ridiculously heavy ring.

"And *you* look like you need a shave," she said to get a rise out of him.

To her further annoyance instead of taking offense, he laughed and rubbed a hand over the beard. "Are you trying to make me believe you don't like my beard? Come on, Nia, admit it, you find it terribly attractive."

She glanced away. She would eat nails before she admitted that the look sent a thrill through her. "What do you want to discuss, Liam? I've got to get back."

To her surprise, he grabbed her left hand and brought it up to his face. He ran his thumb over the huge diamond.

"You know, bigamy is still illegal in the U.S."

She tried to tug her hand away, but his grip tightened.

"I'll have you know William Lamport, that I have no intention of marrying Damon Deverre…" He looked stunned for a moment. But several heartbeats later she continued. "…while I'm married to you."

Something like regret flickered in his eyes. "Have the two of you set a date? Is that why you're rushing me to get a divorce?"

"No, we haven't, although I don't know why I'm telling you this. It isn't any of your business."

"Of course it's my business. You are still my wife. I remain very interested in your affairs."

She stamped her little foot. "Will you stop this? For all we knew we were divorced, and that didn't seem to bother you."

For the first time, he seemed to lose his cool. "That's a lie! It bothered me very much."

"Not enough for you to take me up on my offer when we were in Beijing that we start over," she blurted unintentionally.

Why had she told him that? Now he would think his rejection had hurt her, which it certainly had not.

"Do you love him?" he asked, staring deep into her eyes as though daring her to lie to his face.

She felt a flash of anger at his gall. He didn't want her but didn't want anyone else to either. "I don't need to be in love with Damon to marry him. I was in love with you and look how far it got me."

"What are you saying?"

"Love can only take a person so far."

He straightened and released her hand. "Have you given any more thought to singing with me on my album?"

She blinked at the change in conversation. "Have we finally gotten to the reason you brought me over here?"

He nodded.

"Well, the answer is that I don't like being blackmailed."

"I don't see it as blackmail. I see it as us both getting what we want, win-win."

"Whatever."

"Have you thought about it, Nia?"

"I have."

She had been thinking about it more and more lately. She had finally brought herself to listen to those infernal covers and found to her dismay that they made her feel uneasy; they tugged at her conscience. But she didn't want that to happen. She didn't want to be confronted with her sin. It was too uncomfortable. Furthermore, she could see no advantage in being holed up with Liam for two days, or however long, recording a song together. That sounded like the stage would be set for her to fall for him again and then have him reject her.

"And?"

"And, I can't do it."

Liam drew in a sharp breath. He seemed genuinely stunned as though he never expected her to turn him down.

She continued. "If you don't want to sign the papers that's your prerogative. I will get the divorce without your consent. It will take longer, but I'm prepared to live with that."

With that, she turned away from his overpowering presence and left the lobby.

What did he do now? Where did he go from here? Liam brooded and mainly tuned out the award show host who made one colorless joke after another.

It wasn't like he had any hold over Nia. She was right. He didn't have to sign the papers for the divorce to be granted. It might take a little more time if he didn't sign, but it would be granted eventually. Maybe he was wrong, though, but he was getting a distinct impression that Nia might not be as eager to marry Deverre as Deverre was to marry her.

Liam sat up straighter in his chair as the award host asked the crowd to welcome Nia and Damon singing their hit song. Not that he had needed to ask them. As soon as he mentioned the names of the two stars the room erupted in head-splitting applause.

As Nia and Damon and the dancers moved across the stage in a tightly choreographed performance shrouded in intimate lighting and smoke, Liam felt as though he was watching a seduction. Like the highly suggestive lyrics of Nia's hit song, the performance was designed to titillate. And it was effective if the audience's screams of rapture and energetic hand moves were anything to go by.

The way she was dressed in that sequined body suit that really resembled a one-piece swimsuit from the fifties and the way she shimmied her hips in front of Deverre caused Liam to clench and unclench his hands and wish that he was anywhere but here.

What was he playing at by trying to get this girl to sing gospel music? Clearly, she preferred to wallow in filth and sinful conduct. She was comfortable with this life. He needed to give up on her and forget her forever.

Then one line in the song grabbed his attention. *"You and me forever we'll be…forever, we'll be… forever, we'll be…you vowed forever."*

Lima felt his heart race. Yes, he had vowed forever. She had vowed forever. He couldn't just give up on her. She was his wife. He had made a vow to love, protect and cherish her. That must mean that he would do all he could to save her and that included continuing to petition God for her soul.

The performance was ending, and for a moment just before the lights dimmed, Liam thought he caught a look of wistfulness on her face. Or was it his imagination? Either way, it caused him to reconsider his position that she was comfortable with her life. He remembered the seventy-seventh Psalm. Nia was on a slippery slope and if she wasn't uncomfortable, if she didn't see the real danger, then it must mean she was blind. And if she was comfortable and blind, it must mean he wasn't praying hard enough.

In that moment he placed his head in his hands and prayed.

"Lord, You have said in Your word that the prayers of a righteous man avail much. Lord, I come to You then on the strength of that prayer to petition for Nia. For her soul. O Lord, I want You to take the scales off her eyes and the wool out of her ears and make her very uncomfortable in her lifestyle. Help her, Lord, to see what she is doing wrong. Not only putting her own soul in jeopardy but those of the millions who idolize her. Dear Lord, I pray this prayer in the precious name of Jesus. Amen."

~*~*~*~

Nia slid the ring off her finger and dropped it on her vanity. She braced herself against the edge of the table and stared at the ring for a long time.

Damon had left before the ceremony had ended. One of his hip-hop stars had had an overdose and had to be rushed to the hospital.

This night should have been a happy one. She had won three awards, but she was miserable. She couldn't get Liam out of her mind. She couldn't stop thinking of him. He also had been a winner that night. His band had won in the Best Contemporary Christian pop song/performance category.

She had watched in rapt attention as he had stepped on stage to quite a few catcalls. Most likely that was because of his looks since it was doubtful that most in the crowd cared about or even listened to Christian music. She had been surprised at first when he had started evangelizing in the minute he had, telling people to remember that life meant nothing unless it was lived for God and to His glory.

She had shifted uncomfortably in her seat and glanced down at her hands, telling herself that she was embarrassed for him. This sort of thing was just not done. But she knew deep down the embarrassment was really for her and all that she had lost of herself to become a pop culture queen. She had sold her soul, but it was surely too late for someone like her.

Nia pushed off the table and crawled into bed and curled herself into a ball. She felt like a hollowed out shell. Why was it that she had achieved everything she ever could have wanted and yet at that moment she felt like she would give it all up for joy and peace?

Chapter 35

"Why are you giving that to me?" he asked as though she had not told him already that she didn't want it.

"I can't marry you, Damon. I'm sorry."

"You're sorry? Nia, I know I seem to be pressuring you by pushing for a date. I promise I won't do that any longer. Take your time."

She bit her lip. Why was he so obtuse? She didn't want to hurt him, but he was forcing her to say things she'd rather not.

"Damon, that's not the problem. I've thought about this long and hard and I realize that I don't want to get married again."

He sat back in his seat and nodded slowly. His face even looked sympathetic. "I understand. That farce of a marriage you had would make anybody shy away from going there again."

He abruptly sat forward. "But it'll be different with us." He waved his hand in the space between the two of them. "We are so good together." He laughed suddenly. "We even sound good together. Our last song is still number one, baby, after a record ten weeks on the Billboard charts."

She didn't even crack a smile in response. She literally was becoming weary of the way he ignored her position on this and treated her as though she were a naïve child.

She stood abruptly and held out the ring. "Damon, if you don't take this I swear I will drive to the nearest pawn shop and sell it."

Anger blazed across his face. He jumped to his feet and snatched it out of her hand. He looked enraged as he glowered at her with blood in his eyes. She began to feel apprehensive even though she held his gaze unflinchingly.

His chest heaved as though he had been running a marathon. Eventually, he calmed enough to spit out. "You really think you're something great, don't you?"

Her chin went up a notch. No, she didn't think she was anything great at all. She had managed to wreck her marriage to the only one who had really seemed to love her. She had made one selfish, self-serving decision after another. And while she had no doubts that she could sing, and that she could put on a good show, she didn't think she was anything wonderful as a person.

But Damon didn't have to know that.

"If I don't, then who will?" she said as she shrugged and turned away from him.

He grabbed her by the arm and yanked her around to face him. She raised her hand to slap him, but he was lightning fast and caught her wrist in his other hand.

She tried to bring up her knee between them, but he spun her around and trapped her body against his, pinning her hands to her sides.

She felt his breath on her ear as he said in a menacing tone, "I made you, Nia Carmichael. You are the work of my hands. You don't just throw my ring in my face and tell me to get lost like I'm the yard boy. I will make you pay for even thinking you can dump me."

She began to struggle against him and then stilled. What was she doing? She was alone with Damon in her home. This was the angry person she had seen almost beat to death a man twice his size. Did she really want to antagonize him?

Of course, she could scream. Security would come running. They might possibly restrain Damon Deverre, even though he was the boss. Maybe. And if they did, then what? It would be all over the papers. Did she need bad publicity to overshadow her Grammy win last night?

Nia took a deep breath and forced herself to speak evenly. "I'm sorry," she said quietly.

Eventually, his breathing slowed and his hold on her eased.

She continued in the soft tone. "Damon, I'm not throwing your ring in your face. I told you I needed to think about your proposal. I thought about it. I don't want to get married again; plain and simple. You need to accept that."

He straightened and seemed to be forcing himself back under control. Finally, he released her and stepped back. "So, what happens now? Are you still my girlfriend?"

She hadn't thought out that part but if she wasn't willing to marry him where did that leave them. She sighed before delivering the final verdict.

"I think it's best that we take a break."

Anger flared again, but this time it was ice cold anger.

He shook his head. "When I heard that you and that man disappeared together just before the Grammy ceremony began I knew that wasn't a good sign. What did he do? Convince you to come back to him? Is that it? You going to go back to England and become a lady of the manor; or are you going to join his troupe of performing clowns?"

"Liam has nothing to do with this."

"For someone who lies so often you stink at it. You know what? You are welcome to return to your Will-eee-um. See if he can bring you the success I have."

With that, he slammed out of her house.

~*~*~*~

"I heard that the engagement between Nia and Damon Deverre is off."

Liam resolutely kept his eyes on the documents before him and pretended that Sam had not just whispered that to him as he took the adjoining seat.

"So, Sophie, from what you've outlined here, we'll take the plane to our destination and then we'll rent a tour bus for the trips to the cities."

The band was preparing to commence its third concert tour, one of which had been worldwide. This one would be launched in support of their fourth album *Unapologetically Apologetic*. It would be even bigger than the first worldwide tour two and a half years ago. It was a sixty-city arena tour with seventy-five shows.

"Yes, Liam, that's the plan. But we'll need a bigger plane. Your jet won't be able to fit all the passengers as well as the equipment."

He nodded. "That's not a problem." Lamport Holdings had bought out Cessna several years ago. They would simply lease one of the larger jets from the company.

When they took a break a few minutes later so that Sophie could make a few calls, Sam nudged him.

"Did you hear what I said before?"

He looked across at Sam with a raised eyebrow. "About?"

"Nia and Dam–..."

"I already know," he said abruptly.

"How do you feel?" Matthew asked beside him.

Liam tapped his pen on the sheet in front of him.

"I feel that we need to focus on this upcoming tour and not get sidetracked with Hollywood gossip."

Hans howled with laughter and Sam held up his hands.

"I don't get why you're so annoyed, bloke. I thought that was good news."

Liam threw down his pen and pushed away from the table. He needed a cup of freshly brewed tea.

What *he* couldn't get was why his love life or lack thereof was a source of interest for Sam and Matthew. Of late it seemed like they were on a crusade to reunite him and Nia. It had started when he had unwittingly – or was it dimwittedly – shared with them that he and Nia were actually still married due to an administrative error. From that time, they seemed compelled to bring him frequent news bulletins. For example, Nia had shown up at a recent event unaccompanied, or she had been photographed recently at a fashion show without wearing her ring. And now, Nia and Deverre were no longer getting married.

He knew his friends probably thought that it augured well for the two of them, but they hadn't seen her the way he had that night. She had told him in no uncertain terms that not only would she *not be singing* with him but that she was getting the divorce with or without his agreement. He hadn't had the heart to tell them that bit of news. It was still too painful to contemplate, so he had stuffed it down and concentrated on preparing for the upcoming tour.

He still prayed for Nia every day, but he had lost hope that there was a future for the two of them. The fact that she and Deverre had broken up changed nothing. Nia had made it quite clear she did not want Liam back on his terms. While he knew that if he accepted her way of life she would be willing to give things a go again, he just couldn't do that.

He had been called by God to live a life of purpose, one where God got all the glory. He needed a woman by his side who understood that and supported it. Nia was not that woman. He couldn't help the way he felt about her. He would love her until the day he died, he knew that now. But to please himself in this, he knew he would be displeasing God, and pleasing God was his ultimate goal.

Liam took his cup of hot tea back to the table.

Sophie was back and sharing a bit of news. At the break in conversation, he held up a hand.

"I need to announce that Nia and I met about two weeks ago. She told me she will go through with the divorce whether or not I agree to it. So, if we're not divorced by now, we soon will be. What I'm trying to say is that I don't want to speak about our relationship, and I would thank the lot of you to respect that. Sophie, sorry for interrupting. You were just about to name the arenas at which tickets have already sold out…"

Damon had not been kidding when he'd told her she would pay for dumping him. The last three months had been the most uncomfortable of Nia's career. It had reminded her of what had happened just after she had married Liam. While Damon couldn't completely ignore her seeing that they now had a business relationship, he made it as difficult for her as possible.

The irony was that this was one of the main reasons she had been reluctant to get involved with him in the first place. She had told him that if things went south, it would impact negatively on their business relationship. He had brushed it off and now look what was happening.

First, he stopped responding to her calls or her text messages, forcing her to go through his personal assistant for every little thing. Next, he held parties and events and did not invite her. She would hear about them after the fact, like in the media the next day. Or, sometimes, industry people would message her and ask where she had been during the event.

The third insult was when he started squiring some new upstart songstress named Genevieve around town. It didn't bother her on a personal level because she didn't care who Damon took up with, but it was the message he was giving the press, making statements like, "it's a relief to be with a woman who is not a drama queen," or

"Genevieve has got a sound that's so fresh and vibrant. She reminds me of Nia in the early days," the implication being that she had grown stale.

But the fourth and worst insult came when he had dared to pull some of the best songwriters and producers in the industry off her latest album to work on the new girl's. That was when she realized she had to show Damon Deverre that she was no longer his little chess piece.

She fired Raúl, who she was convinced was working more on Damon's behalf than hers, hired a new manager and promptly instructed the woman to set up meetings with all the top record company CEOs and to ensure that was leaked to the press.

At that point, she hadn't cared what she had to lose. While she enjoyed twenty percent royalties and creative control with Damon's company, she was now a major star with worldwide influence and knew she could demand the same thing from another label. It was a risk she had to take. She couldn't just sit around and allow Damon to destroy the reputation she had spent so many years building up.

Her negotiations were successful. The CEOs hadn't taken much convincing. In fact, they were licking their chops, having tried unsuccessfully to court her away from Damon for years. She had gotten all she had asked for which meant she could comfortably leave Damon. The only problem was that Damon really was the best in the business. However, she was prepared to go with second best if that was what it took to teach him a lesson.

She was still considering her options when she agreed to meet with Damon. He had been trying to reach her unsuccessfully for over a week. He had first tried to contact her just after news of her first meeting with the CEO of Sony Music broke in the press. She remembered glancing at her phone and swiping to reject his call. He had begun messaging and calling in earnest after that. She found it quite interesting that he didn't seem to like the taste of his own medicine.

It was when she had instructed her lawyer to send Damon a letter terminating her contract with Double D Records on the grounds that he was failing to fulfill his obligations towards her that things began to heat up.

Damon showed up at her house demanding to speak to her, and she watched with interest how the very guards that he had insisted she hire denied him entry. As she observed him curse and carry on, instead of feeling smugness and satisfaction, Nia began to feel a little guilty. It was true that she owed Damon nothing; *he* had received eighty percent of the royalties *she* had worked hard to earn. However, he had been generous with her over the years and believed in her unreservedly, even when others hadn't. He at least deserved to be given an ear. So, she had agreed to meet with him for lunch.

They were meeting at a swanky diner on Rodeo drive. Nia had done a little shopping first to relax her. Now, two hours later, she was feeling no pain.

She sipped a glass of iced tea and watched through her aviator sunglasses as Damon strode toward her looking like Mr. Cool. Only, she knew he was not cool. Right now she had him hot under the collar, but he had brought it on himself.

She allowed him to kiss her cheek and followed him with her eyes as he took a seat opposite her and pulled in his chair.

He gave the waiter his drink order, the usual herb tea, and took up the menu, commenting as he perused it. "The weather's nice today."

Nia quirked a brow. Damon never talked about anything as mundane as the weather. What was he up to?

She took a sip of her cool drink and lifted her hair off her neck. It was, in fact, *not* a nice day. It was insufferably hot, and the summer had barely begun.

He looked up at her suddenly and nailed her with his gaze.

"I want you back, Nia," he said and tossed the menu on the table.

She released her hair and sat up straight. "Damon, do not start that again."

He shook his head. "I don't mean romantically. I'm speaking about your attempt to try to end our contract. This charge that you're not getting what was promised under our agreement is bogus, and you know it."

"What I know is that you pulled a vendetta on me when I turned down your marriage proposal, and you have been systematically trying to destroy my career ever since."

He looked shocked. "Why would I do something so stupid to an artist who is making me money hand over fist?"

"I wondered the same thing. Then I remembered a recent news story of a machete-wielding man who chopped a woman to death, set fire to the woman and then himself. You wanted to hurt me even if it meant hurting yourself in the process. By linking up with this Genevieve character, who I've got to say Damon is really too young for you, the girl is barely nineteen, you are trying to create a new star for yourself so that you still ensure the viability of your company."

For a moment it seemed like he would try to deny it when he suddenly fell back against his chair and began to chuckle helplessly.

If she didn't know better, she would think he was under the influence.

Finally, he scrubbed a hand over his face and watched her with a mixture of admiration, amusement, and defeat.

"You see why I love you? There is no one like you in the world. That's why I'm not giving you up without a fight."

She signaled to a waiter and asked him to refresh her drink. Then she smiled at Damon.

"I'm so glad to hear you say that because after that fiasco you pulled you're going to have to do a lot of fighting to win back my confidence in Double D Records."

Chapter 36

"*L*ord, we ask You to bless this music; bless our performance. Help us to bring honor and glory to Your matchless name, dear Lord, and not in any way seek to glorify ourselves. We pray that You will touch this crowd today. Help the words of our songs to minister to the souls of everyone gathered here. It doesn't matter why they are here. You have ordained that they be here this day and, Lord, we know that You have promised in Your Word that nothing that we do in Your name will be wasted. And so we want to pray that it will just touch the crowd in a way that leads them to You. In Jesus' name, amen."

Liam dropped the hands of the group members and then hugged each man. It was their ritual before every performance. What good were all their efforts if God wasn't a part of it?

Redeemed was performing in London. For Liam, London featured highly on the tour the band had embarked on six months ago. They had covered North America and were now moving through Europe. He had left England for last because he wanted to savor the time in this part of the world and visit with his parents before returning to Tennessee. They had five more arenas in England to cover before the tour ended.

The entire tour had been grueling, but for them it was like missionary work, spreading the Gospel of Christ through music. Their interaction with fans remained, for him, one of the most meaningful aspects of the outreach. Hearing personal testimonies from people across all walks of life of how the music had impacted them made every sacrifice, every discomfort, and every sleep-deprived trip worth it.

A few minutes after the group prayed, the band walked onto the London stage at the O2 Arena to thundering cheers and applause. The energy from the crowd was overpowering. Liam just soaked it in like a sponge. It felt good to return home to such a reception.

After hailing the homegrown crowd, he began to speak the truth of Psalm 96 into the atmosphere.

"Sing to the Lord a new song; sing to the Lord, all the earth. Sing to the Lord, praise His name. Proclaim His salvation day after day. Declare His glory among the nations, His marvelous deeds among all peoples. For great is the Lord and most worthy of praise; He is to be feared above all gods. For all the gods of the nations are idols, but the Lord made the heavens. Splendor and majesty are before Him; strength and glory are in His sanctuary."

Liam swung to the left and shouted, "Ascribe to the Lord, all you families of nations, ascribe to the Lord glory and strength. Ascribe to the Lord the glory due His name; bring an offering and come into His courts. Worship the Lord in the splendor of His holiness; tremble before Him, all the earth. Say among the nations, 'The Lord reigns.'"

He ran to the right and declared, "The world is firmly established, it cannot be moved; He will judge the peoples with equity. Let the heavens rejoice, let the earth be glad; let the sea resound, and all that is in it. Let the fields be jubilant, and everything in them; let all the trees of the forest sing for joy. Let all creation rejoice before the Lord, for He comes, He comes to judge the earth."

Liam returned to center stage and lifted his hands in worship as he exclaimed, "He will judge the world in righteousness and the peoples in His faithfulness!"

As the crowd roared, Liam began strumming his guitar. Sam and Hans began to clap, and the audience soon joined them as the three guys moved around the stage. From the moment Liam began to sing he could see how the enraptured crowd sang every word along with him. Sam began playing his guitar, and at the next verse Hans and Matthew picked up the rhythm on the keyboard and the drums.

The euphoria riding the audience was contagious. It lent positive energy to the experience. Every color and creed under the sun was clapping, singing, jumping and jamming as they participated in songs of praise to God for what He had done for them by bringing them out of the darkness into His glorious light.

Liam grabbed the cordless microphone. As he sang, he was hopping and skipping and dancing around the stage to the song with the rest of the band and the audience. The huge screens above them tracked his every move. He knew that no matter where they were located, the audience could see them, thanks to technology. When the song ended, the sound of applause and cheering was deafening. Liam fisted his mic in the air. This was what it was all about. Raising a joyful noise unto the Lord!

The band sang twelve more songs before the night was over, each one even better received than the last. At the end of it all they prayed, and as they had done in every city, Liam extended an invitation to those present.

"I just want to say, you've been a great crowd tonight, so enthusiastic, so passionate. I want to tell you that God is looking for people who will worship Him not only with their mouths but also with their hearts. The Word of God says He wants people who will worship Him in spirit and in truth. Christian worship engages the heart and the head. It requires true doctrine about God and His plan to rescue sinners, and it requires true emotion about that doctrine. There must be both spirit and truth. Truth without emotion produces dead doctrine and a church full of admirers, not doers."

As Liam spoke, Hans lightly played on the keyboard.

"On the other hand, emotion without truth produces empty worship, people who get excited about the idea of God but who are not willing to discipline themselves to live holy lives that foster and deepen their relationship with a Holy God. Strong affection for God rooted in sound doctrine is what is required to worship Him in spirit and in truth. If there is anyone here today seeking to go deeper in their relationship with God and worship Him in spirit and in truth, I invite you to just raise your hand where you are or come to the front of the stage where there will be people who will pray for you. Thank you."

Liam could see hands go up. He could see people making their way to the front. He knew some were probably just caught up in the euphoria and the seed would be falling on rocky ground. Since it had no root, it would last only a short time. When trouble or persecution came that shallow planted seed would fall away.

He also knew that there would be some for whom the seed was falling on good soil. They would hear the Word and understand it, and it would produce good fruit. In that moment he prayed that the majority were in that category. And he prayed for Nia, that she also one day soon would be among those accepting the Word and that it would produce good fruit in her life.

"Are you all set for the performance?"

"Yes, I am. I'm going on stage in another few minutes," Nia said to Damon over the phone.

"Well, then, break a leg," he said.

She chuckled as she hung up. Imagine Damon using cutesy terms like that. They had indeed settled back into a routine of sorts. He seemed to be trying to court her again, in every way. He had agreed to all her terms including having full creative control over her next album. He had also put in writing that when her contract came up for renewal in a year's time, she would get twenty-five percent He had even stopped seeing Genevieve.

Nia was glad about that part because the girl really was too young for Damon, but she wished he would pursue someone other than her.

Notwithstanding the fact that she didn't love him, she also didn't think she wanted to subject herself to romance again. She was in full protective mode these days. Allowing her heart to feel again was a risk she could not afford.

She checked her appearance one final time. She was dressed in a strapless white bodysuit tucked into a high-waist, slim-fit white pants with black crossed suspenders. Her straight hair was pulled completely off her face to dangle in a low ponytail at the base of her neck. She wore matching silver cuffs on each wrist and silver hoops in her ears. On her feet were black stilettos.

She was about to go onstage in Wembley Stadium in London to perform a couple of songs for a charity event to fight world hunger. She reflected with a wry smile that her mother-in-law would be proud.

Nia stilled and looked at herself in the mirror. *Mother-in-law.* Yes, Barbara Dickson was still her mother-in-law. Nia had not proceeded with the divorce. Mr. Manzini had advised her that she didn't need to wait until Liam signed for the divorce to be finalized. She didn't bother to tell him she knew all of this already. All she had said was that she was too busy to deal with any of that right now and he was to await her instructions. That had been five months ago. What was she waiting on? Why didn't she go through with it? She had absolutely nothing to lose and everything to gain from emotionally freeing herself of William Lamport IV.

As she made her way backstage, Nia stopped and covered her eyes with her hand. She was not going to cry like a fool and ruin her makeup. This had been a long day, coming to the center as she had straight from the airport. Someone placed a hand on her shoulder and handed her a mic. She straightened her back, took a deep breath and walked on stage.

~*~*~*~

"Did you know that Nia's here performing at Wembley Stadium tonight?" Sam asked. A moment later he was holding a sheet of paper before Liam's face.

Liam didn't break his stride towards the elevator as he read the promotional flyer advertising a charity event to end extreme poverty. Nia was listed as one of four prominent musical acts headlining the event.

"Where did you get this?" Liam asked, giving it back to Sam and jabbing the elevator button.

Sam folded up the flyer and stuffed it in his pocket. "The hotel front desk."

They boarded the elevator and Liam selected their floor number. He glanced at Sam who was watching him cautiously.

"What?" he asked holding out both hands.

"She's appearing in this city tonight, bloke. Aren't you going to see her?"

"I already know what she looks like and what she sounds like. So, no, I'm not going to see Nia perform one of her R-rated songs."

Sam chuckled. "They're not all R-rated."

Liam glared at Sam. "What's that supposed to mean? Do you listen to her songs?"

Sam made a face. "Not really. Though sometimes it's hard not to hear them if one's in a public place. That's all they play these days, and they are quite catchy so you can find yourself–"

Liam held up a hand as the elevator lurched to a stop.

"Enough. I get the picture."

"I think you should go see her. It can't be a coincidence that your paths are intersecting like this…"

Liam had thought the same thing when he had seen Nia in Beijing. And look how that had turned out. Far from her singing with him as he had hoped, they had ended up having a fight and she had no doubt divorced him by now.

384

Sam kept pushing. "It's not far away. If you leave now, you could probably get the tail end of the concert. You may not see her perform, but you should at least try to see her."

As they walked towards their rooms, Liam slanted a look at Sam.

"I must say, ever since you and Hana Ito tied the knot I believe you think the whole world should pair off."

Sam had gotten married three years ago to the HR assistant from his old job.

"Can I help it if I want everyone to be as happy as I am?"

Liam took in a deep breath. He was genuinely happy for his friend. Marriage looked good on Sam. It had settled him. Even though he was still carefree, Liam sensed a new maturity in Sam brought on by the added responsibility of a wife, and a two-year-old son, Haruto. Their marriage seemed to be surviving the separation caused by the tour. Hana and Haruto had even met up with the band in one of the tour cities.

Watching the loving family interact had only made Liam feel a deep sense of regret for what he and Nia had lost. He wondered if Sam really understood that his and Nia's problems would not be simple to solve. Hana was a Christian. She shared Sam's values. It didn't mean that their marriage was perfect, but it did help when problems arose.

Sam wasn't finished talking.

"…my matchmaking has been going quite well too I might add. If it weren't for me getting Matthew the telephone number of that cute photographer from *Christianity Today* who kept giving him cow eyes through the entire shoot, he would not now be engaged to her."

"Is that what you fancy yourself doing by insisting I go see Nia, matchmaking? Sam, I asked you not to pursue this. I love her, but she doesn't want a life with me. Not on my terms. In fact, she is divorcing me without my consent. As hard as it is to admit, I don't think there is any hope for us as a couple."

Sam continued as if Liam hadn't spoken. "I still think you should try to see her. The last time you saw her was six months ago. That's a long time. Perhaps she's changed her outlook."

Liam took the key card from his jacket pocket. "We have to leave here early tomorrow to travel to Manchester. I need to get to sleep. Have a good night."

The moment Nia walked on stage, jubilant screams of joy from the audience filled the arena. Finally, they died down sufficiently for her to be heard above the din as she began to sing her song. It was just her and her band for this one. No dancers. No pyrotechnics. This was a love song that was full of longing, promise, and heart. She felt every word as she sang it. She couldn't help it as Liam's face loomed in her mind's eye.

She sang that she would remain by her lover's side through good and bad, thick and thin. But she hadn't done that, had she? She had left him. Blessedly, her voice stayed strong throughout the performance, even though she felt overcome by the song's lyrics. Those words seemed to point to her own heartbreaking romance with a boy who was too good for her. She could never reach Liam's standard of goodness. But had she ever even tried? It had always been about her and what she wanted.

As Nia poured out her voice, it seemed as though every member of the audience was pouring out theirs too as they sang in concert with her. At the end of the song the crowd cheered, yelled and cat whistled.

Nia waited for them to die down just a bit, then said, "I just want to say thank–"

Nia never finished her sentence. A moment later there was a massive explosion that rocked the arena to its very foundation.

She felt as though the blast had hit her in the chest. One moment she was standing and the next she was lifted off the ground by an invisible force and then knocked to the ground by the aftershock.

Intense heat covered her like an inferno. As screams of terror filled the air, Nia felt her body and realized that she was not on fire, but she knew she had to get out of there. She began to crawl with no destination in mind, just trying to get away from the smoke and heat. Mayhem and havoc had taken over.

Blindly, she felt around until her hand touched something strong like steel. Perhaps she could pull herself to her feet. The steel frame shook as feet thundered. The noise was horrific. She wanted to put her hands over her ears to drown out the screams of torment. It sounded as though people were hurting, even dying. She could hear wailing; terrible, tortured wails.

"Oh God," she pleaded. "Please help me. Don't let me die this way. Please!"

Suddenly she heard someone scream her name. It sounded like Liam, but she must be hallucinating. What would Liam be doing here? No, it was most likely the attacker. Maybe the bomb had been targeted at her. The whole world knew she was going to be here right now. She suddenly remembered the death threats. The person had said some terrible things like her body would be in so many pieces they wouldn't be able to scrape together enough to put her in a box. She had refused to read any more of the letters since that one.

She felt bile build in her throat and clamped a hand over her mouth as her stomach convulsed. This had to be the work of that maniac. She couldn't stay here like a sitting duck. She had to find somewhere to hide. She pushed off the spot and instantly fell to her knees as intense pain lanced through her foot. One of the stiletto heels had broken off, and now she was lopsided, not that she could walk anyway.

She couldn't think about that now. That man was still after her. As if on cue she heard a male voice calling out her name to the top of his lungs. She shivered all over and felt as though she was going to be sick. It sounded like Liam, but it was a trick. The bomber was trying to trap her.

"God, please help," she frantically pleaded as she started to crawl away. Just as she made it to the edge of the stage and relief began to pour through her, hands seized her from behind.

Nia screamed and screamed until she was hoarse as she kicked and flailed out her arms at her attacker. Still, the hands held on, and then her attacker pushed her arms down and secured them before raising her into his arms. She gathered breath again to scream for help. When she opened her eyes and focused, the breath went out of her.

It was Liam. It really was Liam. He was a bedraggled mess. His hair was blown all over his head. His face was smudged in soot, his eyes looked red, but he was the sweetest sight she had ever seen. Choking back tears, Nia turned her face into his chest.

"Liam, thank God," she said.

Nia felt as though she was overcome, then the strength left her body.

~*~*~*~

Liam sat in a room at the police station. His arm was around Nia as she spoke about the attack.

He watched her with a combination of worry and relief. He felt relieved that she had not suffered any substantial injuries except for a sprained ankle which the paramedics had treated on site and then released her so that the police could take a statement.

But what worried him was how relaxed she was. Nia had just suffered a traumatic experience, and no one could convince him that she was taking it as well as she seemed to be.

In his opinion, all that had happened hadn't sunk in yet. But once it did, once Nia understood the enormity of what had taken place, she would break down. As strong as she was, she was only human.

She made a joke about being told to break a leg before her performance, and she'd almost fulfilled it. As she laughed, the police darted a worried glance at Liam. His heart contracted.

While the paramedics had been tending to Nia, the officer had explained to Liam that the man was a suicide bomber. He went on to say that the only thing that had saved Nia was that he had been intercepted at the last minute by one of her security guards. That man had given his life for her. Nia didn't yet know that her chief of security, Mike Seale, had given his life to save hers.

Liam could have been in the same position if he had arrived just a few minutes earlier. While he had insisted to Sam that he was going to get some rest, the Holy Spirit had other ideas. Liam was unable to sleep. He could not shake the urgency in his spirit that he needed to be at that charity concert.

He had pleaded, "God, why? You know I don't listen to that type of music. Why are you making me go somewhere I don't feel comfortable?"

"So, it's about your comfort then, Liam? Is this what you were speaking about when you encouraged those people to worship me in spirit and in truth? In truth, I wouldn't let you go to an unsavory place unless I had a purpose for doing so."

He remembered Jesus spending time at a tax collector's house. It would have appeared to many people that He was consorting with a thief, but Jesus ignored them because He had a purpose in mind.

Finally convinced, Liam got out of bed and got dressed, firm in his conviction that there was a purpose in him going to Wembley Stadium to see Nia perform her song. Even if he didn't know yet what that purpose was.

He got there just before she came on stage. As he purchased his ticket and was passing the security checkpoint, he heard Nia begin to sing her soulful love song. It was a song about loyalty, about a forever kind of love. She promised not to leave his side, not to leave him down on his knees. She promised to be there to hold him tight. He had to stop walking for a minute as a wave of emotion washed over him and threatened to drown him in past sorrows. He almost turned around and walked out of the arena, but he heard the still small voice say, 'Stay, Liam.'

He prayed for strength and headed down front. It was at that moment he saw the man move quickly toward the stage with purpose. It might have been the sinister smile on his face or the way he reached into his jacket, but for some unknown reason, Liam knew that he had ill intent.

Liam took off running toward him seconds before the man was being intercepted by Nia's bodyguard. A moment later, there was a loud explosion that sent Liam hurling onto his back. It stunned him for a minute, but he stumbled to his feet. When he saw the impenetrable cloud of smoke in front of him, terror gripped him. It was unlike anything he had ever known.

He had rushed forward, screaming Nia's name until he felt his lungs would burst, praying he was heading the right way and praying harder still that she was alive. He was pushing past people who were fleeing in the opposite direction.

Mercifully, as the smoke began to clear, he was able to bulldoze his way past the chaos, vaulting over obstacles as he raced toward the stage. He kept hollering her name, praying she could hear him over the dreadful screams. He called to her until his throat felt raw. When he saw her crawling away, he had almost collapsed with relief. She was alive! Nia was alive!

When she began to fight him, he was momentarily stunned but quickly realized she didn't know who it was that held her. She was just reacting out of fear.

It was now two hours since they had been at the police station. During that time he had called her family and friends to let them know she was safe, although the press who were camped outside no doubt already had broadcast the news.

The Police were still conducting investigations. The preliminary evidence seemed to suggest that the attacker had died at the scene from the bomb he had detonated. Whether it was the man responsible for sending the death threats to Nia or if the incident was unrelated was yet to be determined.

Nia asked, "How many people were injured?"

The event had been declared a mass casualty based on the reports Liam had been receiving from Sam, Hans, and Matthew. It had also been confirmed that young people attending the concert, some of them in their early teens, were among the many dead. But he would not share this with Nia right now. She'd been through enough for one night. He hoped the policeman wouldn't either.

When the man Nia had questioned glanced at him, Liam gave an infinitesimal shake of his head.

Mercifully, all the man said was, "We can't say at this point."

Before Nia could ask any more questions, Liam stood. "Are we all done here? She needs to get some rest."

The policeman nodded. He just asked that Nia sign the statement she had given.

The moment they stepped out of the station Liam almost wished he had enquired whether there was a back door. The press descended like a flock of vultures. They began tossing questions at Nia. With the help of her three remaining bodyguards and her manager, Liam managed to elbow his way through the crowd and guide her into the waiting car. The manager said that they had found Nia's things including her phone which she passed to her.

Liam felt like snatching the phone out of her hands and flinging it out the window because the moment Nia turned it on it began to vibrate. It was Damon Deverre.

If the one-sided conversation Liam could hear was anything to go by, Nia was reassuring Deverre that she was fine apart from a slightly sprained ankle. Suddenly, her face crumpled. Liam was seized with the desire once again to grab the phone from her hands, but he restrained himself. The last thing Nia needed was for him to lose his cool. What was the man saying to her?

Soon she was telling him he didn't need to do that and that she would be returning home soon anyway. This seemed to suggest that

Deverre was on his way to jolly old England to make it *less* jolly. From the little he knew of the man he doubted Damon Deverre would be deterred by Nia's assurances that he need not come.

Liam dropped off the manager to her hotel and despite her protests, declared that he was taking Nia home with him. He then instructed the driver to take them to the nearest and safest place, the London Waldorf.

She glanced at him. "You look terrible, Lamport," she said with a shaky smile.

She was trying to lighten the mood, and he decided to play along.

"Me? Clearly, you have not looked in a mirror lately, Carmichael. You've just taken grunge to a whole new level."

She looked down at the grimy, formerly white ensemble, the torn pants, shorn where the paramedics had worked to bandage her ankle. Her shoulders suddenly rounded, and she covered her face with her hands. In an instant, Liam's arms were around her as he pulled her to him.

"What is it?" he asked in her smoky smelling hair.

She turned her head. "Damon said that Mike Seale died trying to prevent the man from getting to me. Is that true, Liam?"

He would love to deny his knowledge of it or even say it wasn't true but that wasn't the case. He wanted to punch Deverres' lights out. What value was there in burdening Nia with that devastating news right now?

He sighed deeply. "Yes, Nia. It's true."

"He said many people, including teenagers, were killed in the blast and countless more were injured."

"I heard something like that."

"This is all my fault," she said in a small voice.

He took her chin in his hand and tilted her head to meet his gaze. "That is not true. This is the fault of that sick, evil man who detonated that bomb, not you, Nia. You were as much of a victim as they were."

She shook her head as tears streamed. "So why am I still alive? Why am I not dead? What makes me so special, Liam?"

He couldn't answer those questions. All he could do was watch her as he prayed to God to give him the right words.

"Nia, I don't know why this happened. I can't tell you why evil continues to run rampant. Why some people die, and others live. I can only tell you that it's not your fault. You were not to blame."

"You're wrong, Liam. It is my fault. They came to see me. All those happy young people, who sang every word of my songs, came to that concert because of me. And Mike gave up his life to save mine. Yes, it is my fault they are all dead."

He continued to protest, but he found to his frustration that Nia was no longer listening. She appeared to have crawled into a shell.

Chapter 37

iam awoke with a start. He turned to reach for Nia, but there was only empty space. She wasn't beside him. His feet hit the floor, but before he rushed for the open door, he heard Nia singing. His heartbeat stabilized as the events of the previous night flooded his memory, but he felt concern. Why was Nia singing?

Then he noticed the aroma of food cooking. He wrinkled his nose. Nia was cooking? But Nia never cooked. He glanced at his watch. Eight-twenty. The last time he had checked the time it had been two-thirty. That was when Nia had finally fallen asleep in his arms. Now, it seemed she was up and cooking.

A feeling of nostalgia hit him, and for a moment he felt an intense sense of longing. When they had lived together for that brief time after their marriage, she had cooked for him once. It hadn't been very good, and clearly she hadn't liked doing it, but she had done it out of love for him. He had taken over cooking duties after that to relieve her of something she disliked. He had wanted to reassure her that he had not married her for anything she could do for him. He had married her because he loved her and wanted to share his life with her, pure and simple. How had that simple desire to just love her morph into this desire to change her? That wasn't really his job, was it? It was the Holy Spirit's.

He pushed to his feet and reached for his phone but stopped. He could find out what was happening in the world later. For now, he needed some sustenance. He felt quite starved and wondered if it was related to the excitement of the previous evening, for lack of a better word.

When he reached the kitchen, Liam leaned against the doorframe and watched Nia as she moved around with her back to him. She took something out of the oven and then hobbled a little as she moved to the sink to wash her hands.

Liam thought that she should probably try to keep off her ankle although her limp was not very defined right now. Elevating and icing it during the night must have helped.

His eyes traveled over her form again. She looked so alluring in his old college jersey and nothing else. He had offered it to her after she had showered the previous night. He no longer had any of her previous clothes. He had boxed everything of hers up soon after she had left. Even though he had been tempted to donate all of it to charity, he had instead mailed them to her in Los Angeles.

Only his clothes were available. The Waldorf boutiques were all closed now, but he would go shopping for her this morning immediately after breakfast. While it was unlikely she would choose to stay here much longer, she would need something to wear when she did leave.

His eyes ran down her form once more. For someone so short her legs seemed to go on forever in that make-do attire. Her hair had been pulled into a high ponytail which made her look like a college freshman. He felt his body tighten as unbidden memories of their intimate moments engulfed him.

She turned around, jumping when she saw him.

"How long were you standing there?"

He didn't move. "Not long."

"Are you hungry?"

He pushed off the door frame and moved towards her. He was hungry. Very hungry. But no longer for food. For something else that he couldn't have.

"Ravenous," he said.

"Good." She smiled and turned back to the stove. "I made hash browns and black bean patties, and I've got some tea brewing in the teapot."

"You didn't have to go to this trouble, Nia."

She gave a little laugh. "I wouldn't say it was trouble. These are frozen hash browns and frozen black bean patties. Just bake at 400 degrees for twenty minutes."

"Nonetheless, I didn't expect any of this. Besides you should probably stay off that ankle." He came up to her and took her by the shoulders. "Aren't you shaken up about what happened last night?"

She shrugged matter-of-factly. "I've come to terms with it. Don't worry it will all be taken care of."

Liam blinked. This was even more worrisome than her laughing last night and her singing just now. He pulled out a chair and took a seat at the table as he observed her bustle about. She looked fine, but he knew she was not. Not even he was fine. He had not quite come to grips with the fact that he had been a hair's breath away from losing her.

She looked over her shoulder at him as she fixed a plate with hash browns and black bean patties.

"I don't think I've properly thanked you for rescuing me last night. So, thank you, Liam, for being there. For saving me."

He didn't know how to respond to that.

You could tell her I was the one who really saved her and not you.

She placed the plates on the table, and before he knew her intention, she leaned forward and kissed his cheek.

When she drew back, he caught a whiff of his body-wash on her. As she moved away, he grabbed her wrist. She turned her pretty face to him, but he resisted the urge to tug her down into his lap. He knew where that could lead.

"I wish I could take the credit, Nia, but that was God. It was He who saved you from that maniac. If it weren't for His intervention, I would not have been there. You need to thank Him."

She appeared to consider this for a moment, and then she sat.

"So, if God saved me, Liam, why didn't He save the others? Are you saying that they deserved to die?"

He bowed his head and quickly blessed his meal. When he looked up, she was watching him as she placed a tiny bite in her mouth.

It would be great if he could get some nourishment in his body before he tackled these deep philosophical questions. He reached for the teapot and poured some tea into a cup.

He took several sips as she continued to watch him.

"I don't know why God saved you and not countless others, Nia," he eventually said honestly. "I do know that there is a plan for each and every one of us. Your plan was not to die yesterday."

"Why? I've done nothing particularly great with my life. Not according to you anyway. Why would God want to preserve me of all people? Mike was a good man, and he died trying to save me. How is that even fair?"

As he chewed and swallowed his food, she seemed to be waiting patiently for an answer. He decided he would pray while he ate. Clearly, Nia was in a mood. She was searching for answers he couldn't immediately provide.

Eventually, he was done and felt satiated. He dabbed his mouth with a napkin and took a deep breath.

"Nia, you seem to be asking why bad things happen to good people. The fact is that none of us is immune to bad things happening, whether we're good or bad, as you put it. But I get that you're asking why someone like Mike, who you told me last night was a Christian, should have died instead of you. All I can tell you is that God has His reasons for allowing evil and suffering.

For one thing, He can use these circumstances to grow our faith. It can make us more Christ-like. What happened was terrible, but it may bring some of the survivors closer to God. The thing is, Nia, I can't sit here and tell you honestly that I know why God allowed that terrible event to take place. But as a Christian, I know that God has a plan."

Liam paused to take a sip of tea and pray for wisdom before he continued.

"Oswald Chambers said that one day there will come a personal and direct touch from God when every tear and perplexity, every oppression and distress, every suffering and pain and wrong and injustice will have a complete and an ample and overwhelming explanation."

As Nia looked off into a corner of the room, seemingly pondering his words, Liam noticed for the first time that she had hardly touched her food.

"You haven't eaten," he said.

"I'm not hungry."

"Still, you should eat something."

"So that you would have the pleasure of cleaning up my vomit. No thank you," she said it with the wisp of a smile to take the edge off her retort.

"By the way, Damon is on his way over."

Liam froze. "Coming where? Here? To my apartment?"

She nodded somberly.

"He suggested we make things right. I need to hold a charity fundraiser for the families of the victims to show that terrorists do not win and that we are not afraid."

She sounded as though she was reading off a script. He was very concerned about the vacant look in her eyes.

Liam pushed his plate away and leaned back in his chair. "Is this what you meant earlier when you said things were being taken care of?"

"Yes."

"Nia, I don't think you're ready to go back on stage."

"Damon says I am."

"Well, then, Damon is a fool," he thundered. A moment later the telephone rang. He got up to answer it. He listened to the voice on the other end and drew a deep breath. Damon Deverre had arrived.

Nia languished on the couch wearing Liam's jersey and workout shorts with the string drawn tight to prevent them from falling off. He had insisted she wear the latter if she wanted him to let Deverre come up to his suite.

Deverre sat forward as he laid out his plan of action to Nia.

Liam stood staring out the window, his anger building the more Deverre spoke. Eventually, he couldn't take it anymore.

"Are you nuts?" he asked Deverre, trying without success to keep the edge from his tone.

Deverre proceeded to ignore him as though he had not uttered a word.

Liam tramped over to him. "I am talking to you!"

Deverre looked him up and down.

"You are not talking to me, Will-eee-um. You would not dare to address me in that manner."

"Get out of my home!"

Nia held up her hands. "Please the two of you, don't fight. Liam, come sit next to me."

He didn't want to, but the way she looked, so vulnerable curled up in the corner of the big sofa in his clothes, sizes too large, made his heart go out to her.

He sunk down next to her and saw Deverre's eyes narrow when Nia scooted close to nestle against him.

"Now, Liam, if you would listen to Damon, you would see why it's a good idea."

Deverre made a rude sound with his teeth. "Why are you discussing it with him? Is he a PR person? I'm advising you based on the professional advice I was given by my PR consultant."

"PR consultant?" Liam interjected. "Really? Did you also speak to a mental health professional? Because that is who you should be speaking to."

"Mental health? There is nothing wrong with her. Look at her. She's perfectly fine."

"Perfectly fine? Does it make sense to you that she would be perfectly fine after almost being blown to bits and having dozens of her fans suffer that fate? Do you think she's made of stone?"

"You underestimate her. She is a strong, beautiful woman."

"Post Traumatic Syndrome Disorder does not have anything to do with being strong or weak. It can happen to anyone."

"Including you? Because you seem really stressed out, man. You need to chill and let me take over here."

"You need to leave, right now," Liam said as he stood up, hands on hips.

Deverre stood too, and they faced off.

Nia screamed.

They both startled and turned to her in alarm.

"What's wrong, baby?" Deverre asked.

Liam took her arm and stared at her. "Nia, talk to me. What's the matter?"

Chest heaving, she answered, "I did that to get your attention. To remind you that I am still here and that I am capable of making my own decisions."

She turned to Liam. "I appreciate all that you have done for me. I really do. But Damon's right. I have to get back out there even though I don't want to. It's like falling off a bicycle or something."

"It's nothing like falling off a bicycle, Nia. Listen to me–"

She held up a hand to stop Liam's sensible observations. She swallowed and continued, "Liam, let me finish. I feel like I need to do this. I need to show people that I'm fine and that I support them. It'll help raise money for them."

"I can give them the money. I can set up a fund for them right now with a donation of a million dollars and invite other people to contribute."

"You can't throw your money at every problem, Liam," she said softly.

That hurt, particularly because he had the impression she was making allusions to the conversation they'd had about her career. He felt deflated. Why did he always find himself in this same foolish trap? Nia inevitably did what she wanted. It didn't matter what he thought or said.

He wearily got to his feet. "You're right, Nia. I can't throw my money at everything. I'll go downstairs and get something from the boutiques for you to wear."

As he turned away, Deverre stopped him in his tracks.

"No need," he said, "Nia told me she needed something to wear. I did some shopping just before I got here."

Liam affixed a smile before he turned to face the two again.

"Well, it looks like between the two of you everything is covered."

Deverre looked as smug as the cat that had eaten the canary. He now reached over on the seat beside him and took up a black bag which he handed over to Nia. Liam concluded that it contained the clothing he had purchased.

"I'll wait downstairs for you, Nia," Deverre said as he threw a self-satisfied smile Liam's way and then strode in the direction from whence he had come.

The moment Deverre was gone, Nia fitted the bag in the crook of her arm, got up, and hobbled toward him. Ignoring the hands folded across his chest, she wrapped her arms around his waist and hugged him.

"Thanks for understanding. I'll go get dressed," she said.

"Do you need help?"

"No, I'm fine. I made my way around the kitchen when you were asleep, remember. I've got this."

As he watched her limp away, he shook his head. He would love to sweep her into his arms and take her to what had once been their bedroom. Did she even remember or acknowledge that this was the place they had lived the short while before their marriage unraveled? If he could he would not only take her there he would lock her away to keep her safe from every bad and evil thing. But that wasn't his call. Nia had to make her own decisions.

He sighed and dropped his hands to his side. He in no way agreed with what had just transpired. He would wait to see how it would play out. In the meantime, he had a sold out concert in Manchester that evening to get to, and he was already behind time.

Nia pulled on the beige and black burlap dress. It had an unusual design that looked like it had been stitched on the wrong side. She had worn it once before, during a performance in Paris that had gone very well. It had been magical. She had chosen it now because she needed something to remind her of that happy time. It would work as a talisman to ward off the evil spirits that were threatening her every time she laid down her head. They were whispering to her even now about that night – that dreadful night.

She looked at the dress again. It would help. This was fine. That horrible man was dead. He could no longer harm her.

There was a loud knock at the door that startled her.

Get it together, Nia.

She stepped out of the room with her smile pasted on so broad her cheeks ached.

"I'm ready," she said in a high pitched voice.

Her manager held her arm, "Are you sure about this?" she asked.

"Of course she's sure, Petra," Damon said behind her. "She's is one tough cookie. My hero. You know, social media has been ablaze with praise for you doing this. Baby, far from causing you to lose, that incident is causing you to gain."

Nia felt like she would throw up all over his pristine white motorcycle jacket. Was he trying to say that the horrific incident that had taken place in London a few nights ago had worked in her favor? Perhaps she had misunderstood. Not even Damon could be so insensitive.

She ran a hand down her neck.

"Are you okay, Nia?" Petra asked.

"I just need some water, that's all."

Damon snapped his fingers, and instantly a chilled bottle of water was pressed into her hand. She gulped and still couldn't get the taste of smoke and death from her mouth.

She swallowed and straightened her back. She could do this. She had to do this. She stepped out on to the stage. The bright lights came on and instantly she was transported back to that night.

Nia cast a nervous glance around. This wasn't right. It was the same place. But it couldn't be. They had told her that place had been designated a crime scene so this couldn't be the same place.

Someone screamed her name, and she took a step back. Other voices added to theirs, chanting her name. Suddenly, the chant morphed into screams of terror. No! Not again! Nia's nostrils burned with the smell of the smoke. She began to shake uncontrollably.

A hand closed around her arm. It was him! He was going to kill her!

Nia frantically tried to get away. She kicked and scratched and bit as she screamed. She was not going down without a fight. Not today. But he was lifting her. He was abducting her to kill her. She kept screaming until her voice was reduced to a rasping sound. Then she was flung into a vehicle. Someone slapped her in the face. She caught her breath and blinked as Damon's horrified face came into focus.

She had just had a nightmare while fully awake.

Chapter 38

Redeemed was a couple of minutes away from mounting the stage at Glasgow when Liam's phone vibrated in the pocket of his leather jacket. He pulled it out and looked at the screen.

Nia?

His thumb hovered. Should he answer? He was about to perform and did not need the distraction. Deciding to ignore it and return the call later, he swiped "reject" and placed the phone in his pocket.

He could hear the MC announcing the band. A moment later the phone started to vibrate again. He looked at the number. Nia was calling once more. What if she was in trouble? His heart skipped a beat. His thumb shot across the screen.

"Nia?" he whispered, slowing his steps and pressing the phone to his ears so he could hear above the din of the eager crowd.

"Liam." It came out a combination sob and relieved sigh. "Liam…I need you. I need you to come."

He pressed his hand to his left ear so he could hear her better.

"Nia? Can you repeat yourself? I can barely hear you."

"I need you to come," she whispered again.

"Come? Where? Where are you?" he asked urgently.

"In the bathroom."

"Bathroom where?"

She was making this very difficult for him. He felt a hand on his arm and glanced around to meet Matthew's eyes.

"We need to go on now," Matthew said, gesturing wildly.

Holding up a hand to him, Liam turned back to the phone.

"Bathroom where, Nia? What's going on? Are you in some kind of trouble?"

"I'm at the Waldorf."

"Which Waldorf?"

He was beginning to get impatient. Sam had joined Matthew and was asking what he was doing that was so urgent. He turned his back on them.

"The London Waldorf. I need you to come."

"What's wrong?" he repeated. "Why do you need me to come?"

"I'm falling apart...I need you...Please!"

The last word caught on a sob, and he felt his chest tighten. Nia needed him. He ran a hand through his hair.

"Liam," he heard Matthew impatiently hiss, "come on, the crowd is getting restless. We were announced two minutes ago."

He covered the bottom half of the phone. "Will you hold on a minute? This is important."

He propped an arm on the wall in front of him and leaned his head on it.

"Nia, I'm about to go on stage. I'm performing in Glasgow tonight. I'll call you the minute we come off, okay."

When he heard her begin to quietly sob he felt as though his heart was cracking in pieces.

"Nia, Nia!" he called until her sobs slowed to hiccups. "I'll leave now to come get you. It's going to take an hour and a half by plane. Can you hold on until then?"

She sniffed but said nothing.

"Nia! Speak to me."

"Okay...yes. Okay, I can."

Liam disconnected the phone and placed both palms against the wall. He breathed long and deep before he turned to face bewilderment and annoyance.

"Nia is in trouble. I need to go to her," he said quietly.

Matthew and Hans began to protest. Only Sam nodded and watched him thoughtfully.

"Listen to me," Liam said, raising his voice, "we are canceling tonight's performance. Speak to the MC. Tell him to let the fans know there is an emergency I need to deal with. Tell them they will be fully reimbursed and that we will reschedule this concert at the earliest opportunity. That's all he needs to say."

Sam stepped forward and squeezed his shoulders. "Keep us posted, okay. We'll be praying for you both."

Liam nodded gratefully, and with that, he ran out of the arena.

~*~*~*~

Liam studied Damon Deverre, steely-eyed. He clenched his jaw so tight he felt it would crack.

"What do you want, Will-eee-um?" Damon scoffed. "I hope you're not here to see Nia because she doesn't want to see you."

For a moment Liam was taken aback, and then he remembered that he couldn't trust anything Damon Deverre said. The man had an ulterior motive.

"Are you quite certain of that?"

"I sure am," Deverre said in a mocking tone and attempted to close the door but Liam jammed his foot in between the door and its frame.

"Listen, Deverre. I have no beef with you. Nia called me. She sounded–"

"She called you?" Damon asked, shock covering his face.

"Yes, she asked me to come get her. She sounded like she was in some kind of trouble."

After a brief hesitation, Damon stepped back from the door.

"She told you to come get her, and you came, after all she did to you?" he asked shaking his head.

Liam told himself to ignore the man. He knew that Damon was just trying to get under his skin.

"Where is she?" he asked evenly, now standing in the foyer. He could hear voices coming from inside. It seemed as though Nia's entourage was there also.

Damon gestured with the cup of some minty smelling tea in his hand.

"She's in the bathroom. That's where she locked herself two hours ago."

Liam was alarmed for a moment. She had assured him she would hold on, but two hours was a long time to be in the bathroom. Suppose she had harmed herself during that time. She hadn't sounded too stable when she had called him.

"How do you know she's all right?"

"Because every time I knock she screams at me to go away and leave her alone," Damon said. He stared at Liam through angry eyes. "I can't believe she called you."

Deverre shook his head in disgust as his face contorted with bitterness.

"I've been trying to get her from in there for the last two hours." He shrugged. "But, hey, if you can get her out, be my guest," he said grudgingly.

"Where is it?"

Again Damon's angry eyes watched him defiantly, Liam was about to turn away and search for the room himself. He knew the layouts of Waldorf rooms so locating the bathroom wouldn't be hard.

As he turned to go, Damon mumbled, "Down the passage and to the right, through the bedroom."

"Thank you," Liam said automatically, reflecting a second later that he wasn't completely insincere. The mere fact that Damon had shared that with him, had allowed him to come in when he regarded him as a rival for Nia's affection had to mean that the man really did care for her in his own twisted way.

Liam didn't even acknowledge the sea of faces that stood around talking when he passed the living room. He saw them from the corner of his eye and noted how conversation ceased when he turned up and vaguely noted how it increased in hushed tones when he was out of sight. But he hardly cared. His only interest was in getting to Nia.

Nia rocked back and forth on the bathroom floor, hugging her legs. She had cried for so long she didn't think she had any tears left. She felt drained and empty, but she didn't want to leave this room. She had no energy to move. She didn't know what to do. She felt scared and hopeless and lonely. Yes, very lonely. But wasn't that her own fault? She had chosen this life, had she not? She had thought the adoration of millions of fans would fill the void, but it had not. How was it possible to be loved and to be worshipped by so many, and yet to feel so hollow inside. She knew what Liam would say. He would say that God loved her and, if she allowed Him to, His love would fill the hollowness inside. But it couldn't be so. She had strayed so far away from God it wasn't possible He would forgive all her terrible sins. If it were her, she wouldn't be so forgiving.

And her sins were even greater now. It was because of her all those people were dead. They had paid for whatever she had done to enrage that maniac. And yet, she lived. She had thought she was ready to perform again, but Liam had been right. She was far from ready.

Liam.

She sniffed and placed her finger on her lips. Just hearing his voice earlier had been so comforting. He had said he would come. Would he? Or had he finally grown fed up with her and her issues? Even if he hadn't completely given up on her, he wasn't just waiting around for Nia Carmichael to call him. He had a busy life. He had responsibilities and commitments. Liam was nothing if not committed; if not responsible. It was she who was reckless, irresponsible, and rebellious.

She could feel tears well up again. Unlovable. Those so-called fans didn't love her. Not really. They didn't really know her. If she no longer entertained and titillated them, they would soon lose interest in her and turn their backs on her.

Even Damon had grown tired of asking her to come out to talk to him. Not that she cared. Anyway, it was his fault she was in this scary emotional state.

Nia sniffed. No, it wasn't. Not really. She had made her choice. It always came back to her. The fact that she gave in to her desires without thinking things through. The tears came again. She thought she'd had none left, but she was wrong.

"Jesus loves me this I know for the Bible tells me so," she sang softly on a hiccup. Was it possible that Jesus loved her still? Nia's breath hitched.

"No!" a voice screamed in her head. "He does not! No one loves you!"

She sobbed quietly in her hands. Then she heard a sound at the door. It was a knock. She drew a finger under her nose. Damon again. Why didn't he just leave her alone?

"Go away!" she yelled. She took off her shoe and threw it against the door for emphasis.

There was silence for a minute. The only sound was her sniffles until she heard the one voice in the world she wanted to hear...

"Nia, it's me. Please open up."

That was not Damon. It was Liam. He had come.

Nia scrambled to her feet. Liam had come. Liam had come. Wait. Was it really him? Was it a trick? She paused at the door, pressed her ear to it and her hand to the knob.

"Liam?" she called. Was that scratchy shaky voice that sounded like it had come from beneath the earth really hers?

"Yes, darling. It's me. Please open the door."

Her heart skipped a beat. *Darling.* He had called her darling.

Nia's hand moved with lightning speed to unlock and throw open the door in one fluid motion. And then he was there in front of her. Liam. She hungrily devoured his beautiful face for one moment before she collapsed in his arms.

"You came," she murmured as he enveloped her in a hug.

"Of course I came. You said you needed me."

She sniffed. "I do need you," she said in a muffled voice.

"What's that?" He eased back so he could see her.

She looked into his face. "I do need you, Liam. Take me away from here. I need to leave. I need you to take me away."

She buried her face in his jacket and deeply inhaled his spicy cologne. She clutched him as she closed her eyes and sagged against him. He grabbed her and held her against him.

"Where do you want to go?"

"Anywhere. I just want to leave."

She knew she was acting like a child, but she didn't care. Her knees folded under her. Liam didn't disappoint, he slid an arm around her back, another beneath her knees and lifted her into his arms. She looped an arm around his neck, closed her eyes and breathed deeply of him.

She could feel herself being carried and she could hear voices getting closer. They were all her handlers and minders and so-called friends. When she heard Damon's angry voice, she closed her eyes tighter.

"Where do you think you're taking her?"

"That's none of your business, Deverre. Now move out of my way," Liam said with a voice so sharp it could cut through steel.

To her surprise and relief, Damon did not challenge Liam.

"She's set to perform in Abu Dhabi in one week. Wherever you're taking her, she'd better be back in time for that or she'll have to answer to a stadium of 300,000 fans. Already she's disappointed the bunch tonight. We've been doing damage control for that. If you want to be party to destroying her career and aiding in her financial ruin, you go ahead. But when the suing starts, I'll ensure that you get named in the suit."

She felt Liam stop. He wasn't considering Damon's words, was he? He swung around.

"I just canceled a show I was doing in Glasgow tonight. I will lose revenue on that show. But that's okay. I will stop at nothing to save Nia. If I have to personally compensate each and every one who has lost out on her performance tonight and those who will lose out in Abu Dhabi you can be assured I will. Because there is no way I'm letting Nia perform in one week. No way!"

Nia felt as though all the breath was instantly stolen from her. Liam had made that sacrifice for her? She hadn't even been aware that he had to cancel his show tonight because of her. He had made a huge sacrifice on her account. Turning his back on all those fans could not have been an easy decision for someone like him, not to mention the financial hit he would take because of it. Now he was promising to bear the financial burden of her non-performance if she didn't show up next week, which she wasn't sure she would. She felt like weeping all over again. She did not deserve someone like him in her life.

Damon had no answer, but as they got to the door, he laughed bitterly and called out, "You're a bigger fool than I could have imagined. She left you! Don't you remember? She ran off with me. And she left you, your royal highness, not once but twice. When will you wake up and realize that Nia only cares about one person and it ain't you and it ain't me? It's Nia."

Just before they walked through the door, Nia heard Damon shout, "You know what? You're welcome to the ungrateful–"

The rest of his angry barrage of swear words became muted as Liam slammed the door firmly behind them. But Damon's words had hit their mark. She could feel Liam tense as he held her. He was no doubt pondering them. But it wasn't true. Damon was a liar. She did care about Liam. She had never ever stopped loving him, but she had no credibility with him. There was no way he would believe anything she had to say. She would just have to prove it to him.

As Liam held Nia in his arms in the elevator, he thought of the exchange with Damon Deverre. The man had known what buttons to push, no doubt about it. It was true that Nia had left Liam. Twice. And both times she had left with Damon Deverre. Was Deverre right? Was she really the only one she cared about...just herself? Seeds of doubt began to germinate. Why had she called Liam now? Was it because she knew that she was his Achilles heel? That he would do most anything for her? Wasn't it time that he cut her loose?

He looked down at her. Her eyes were closed, but he knew she wasn't sleeping. Her breathing was too shallow. Whether he liked it or not, the sight of her just filled him. What was it about her? She was undeniably beautiful, but there was more to it than that. He was drawn to her. He had always been drawn to her. From the moment he had met her that night in Austria he had been captivated. And no matter the missteps she had taken since then, he still was. When would he be free of her? Would this act of rescuing her now finally free him?

He shook her gently. She opened her eyes to peer up to him, and he felt his heart contract. Why was she the only woman to have this effect on him?

The elevator reached the basement. Liam knew he could not leave via the hotel lobby with Nia in his arms and go unnoticed. On arrival, he had seen the throng of reporters and had headed directly to the basement to avoid them. Fortunately, he had a special pass to every area of this hotel.

He used the key fob to unlock the car and then gently placed Nia in the passenger seat. As he leaned over to draw the seatbelt across her body, she shuddered.

He drew back and looked in her face. "Are you cold?"

She nodded. He took off his jacket and draped it around her shoulders.

"Thank you," she murmured.

He headed over to the driver's side. After he had strapped in, he turned to her and rested his arm over the back of her seat.

"Why did you call me, Nia?"

She looked surprised at the question then her eyes dropped to her hands, and she said softly, "I believed you still cared about me. I hoped you cared enough to come."

He swallowed and rested both hands on the steering wheel as he stared through the windshield. "You knew I'd come."

"I...I couldn't be sure. Not after everything."

He turned to watch her. He wanted to be detached, but it was a battle. He loved her still. Passionately. And he always would. No matter what Nia did, he would always love her. Damon was right. He was a fool.

What he should really do was drop her wherever she wanted to go and, having done his duty and rescued her, fly off like Superman.

"Where do you want to go?"

She shrugged and played with a seam of what he now noticed was one of the ugliest dresses he had ever seen.

"Nia, I need to know. Do you want me to check you into another hotel?"

"Do you know what happened, Liam? Do you know why I called you?"

"No. I don't know. But I'm getting the impression it has something to do with the performance tonight."

She nodded and continued making tiny folds with her garment on her leg.

"I stepped out on that stage, so confident I could do this and then suddenly it was like I was back there, and everything came back to me, the smell of smoke and burning flesh, the screams of terror, the pain, the sight of people running, falling over each other as panic seized them, my own feeling of helplessness and fear. I froze. I simply couldn't do it. Damon had to come and take me off the stage, and then I began to fight him. Like I thought maybe he was the attacker returned to finish me off."

She placed her elbows on her legs and held her head in her hands.

"Oh, Liam, it was awful. When I came to my senses, I was already being hustled into the limo. On our way, I heard Damon on the phone with my publicist talking about damage control. I was horrified at what I had done and what would be all over the media this very night."

Liam rubbed her back. "It sounds as though you're suffering from Post-traumatic Stress Disorder. It's no indictment of you, Nia. You just need some help."

"You mean like a psychologist?"

He nodded. "Or a counselor. Someone trained in this type of thing who can listen to you and give you useful advice."

Her face contorted and he realized with a jolt of alarm that Nia was about to cry again.

"You tried to warn me about this, and I wouldn't listen. This is all my fault," she blubbered.

Liam immediately reached over and pulled her into his arms.

"Darling, please, don't cry."

She caught her breath on a sob and lifted her head to watch him in surprise.

"You called me darling again," she whispered.

He froze. Yes, he had. Thoughtlessly. Instinctively. But she wasn't his darling was she? She wasn't his sweetheart nor was she his…wife. Or was she? Now didn't seem to be the best time to quiz her on whether the divorce had been finalized.

Liam briefly closed his eyes to regain clarity and focus. He felt fingers on his lips and his eyes startled wide open.

"Don't," he said huskily.

"Liam," she whispered. Their gazes met. He could feel himself drowning in the depths of her eyes. His body's response was almost primal. He should resist. He had to resist. Nia was just feeling vulnerable right now. He should not take advantage of that. But before he knew it, his lips were on hers.

Those soft lips. Liam sighed. Oh, how he had missed them. Nia's arms crept around his neck. He ignored the discomfort of the armrest between them and drew closer to her. She seemed to sigh into him, and he sipped and sipped of her nectar, and still, he did not get his fill.

It was the jarring sound of a distant car horn that eventually drew them apart.

He cleared his throat. "Where to?"

She shrugged, watching him with hazy eyes. "I don't care, so long as I'm with you."

Chapter 39

*I*n the plane, Liam watched Nia sleep in the cockpit beside him.

When she had told him she didn't care where she was going as long as she was with him, he was immediately conflicted. The band had concerts scheduled at three more arenas before the tour ended. There was no way he was taking Nia near a concert venue until she had dealt with her trauma. If he couldn't take her with them, it meant he would have to bring the tour to an end.

The remaining arenas were sold out. He knew he would be disappointing tens of thousands of ardent fans if he canceled, but he had taken one look into Nia's eyes and knew that was what he had to do. The band, Hans and Matthew, in particular, would not be pleased but they would just have to deal with his decision. Nia needed him and for right now she was his first human priority.

But where would he take her? It occurred to him that a relaxed tropical environment might be just what the doctor ordered. And what better tropical island than the one in which they had been so happy.

Nia opened her eyes and glanced around her owlishly. She was aboard a plane and Liam was in the pilot seat. How had she gotten here? Her last memory was of being in the passenger seat of Liam's car, staring over at him dreamily as he drove, closing her eyes for a moment...

"You're awake," he observed. "Good. We're soon there."

Nia glanced at her watch. It was saying 6:10, which had to be a.m. based on the way the sun shone through the windows of the plane.

"Where are we going?" she asked.

"Barbados," he answered so softly she would have missed it if she hadn't been watching his lips.

Barbados? Why would Liam take her back to the place where they had gotten married? Was he trying to send her a message?

"Why?" she asked, breath suspended.

He kept his gaze center forward. "I think the atmosphere and the environment would be good for you. The warm sunshine, calm sea water, cool tropical breeze. I think that combined will help you heal."

"What about your tour?"

He began the descent into the Grantley Adams International Airport.

"The tour is over. We only had a few more cities to do anyway. I canceled the shows."

Nia was speechless. Canceling one of his shows was one thing, but the remaining tour? She couldn't fathom how much money the band would lose because of her. She felt like bawling. She didn't deserve this. She didn't deserve his faithfulness and devotion.

Her throat constricted. She swallowed and turned her head so he wouldn't see her tears.

Finally, she whispered, "Thank you."

He shrugged. "It's no big deal, Nia."

It was very much a big deal to her. And one way or another she would prove to him how much.

It was the same villa.

Nia remembered it the moment the vehicle turned down the street. Their visit had been over eight years ago, but she remembered.

When the car came to a stop, Liam turned to her. "I need to go shopping for you," he declared.

Yes, indeed. She looked down at her dress. It was literally the only thing she had to wear.

His eyes traveled over her form. "I've got to say, Carmichael, that is one ugly dress."

She genuinely laughed for the first time in days. "I'll have you know that this is a Bottega Veneta gown that set me back a cool $2,000."

He shook his head. "So, it's an *expensive,* ugly dress. I stand corrected."

She slapped his arm. "I'm on to you, Lamport. You just want to go shopping for me. You've been chomping at the bit to do it for days."

He held up his hands in surrender. "You got me."

~*~*~*~

Nia showered and changed into the clothes Liam had purchased for her. Then she sat and ate the light lunch he'd prepared. Now they lounged on the patio with a cool drink made from a local fruit called golden apple.

Liam was satisfied that his decision to come to the island had been a good one. For the first time, Nia's face looked relaxed and happy.

Suddenly, she turned to him and asked, "Why are you doing this?"

He was caught off guard for a moment. "Doing what?"

"Helping me. Why did you come when I called? Why did you cancel your shows?"

He stalled. "You didn't want me to?"

She laughed a little. "Of course I did."

"In the car back in London you said you hoped I'd come, but you weren't sure, not after everything. What did you mean by that?"

There was silence for a spell as she stared out into the ocean. Finally, she sighed deeply.

"I have consistently made a choice to pursue life my way instead of the way you suggested. I have always told you my terms. I've never been prepared to try things your way. I was afraid you had gotten tired of bailing me out of situations of my own making."

She dragged a hand through her long hair and met his gaze. "But maybe you haven't quite given up on me."

Was she on a fishing expedition? If so, he was not going to bite. He crossed his arms over his chest and leaned back in the lounge chair.

"Are you feeling any better?"

She looked a little disappointed he had changed the subject, but she nodded and managed a small smile.

"Yes, I feel a lot better. It was a great idea to bring me here."

He stared at her a long moment before returning her smile.

"The pleasure is mine."

Nia retired for bed early that evening. As silence fell and Liam sat alone on the terrace, watching the sunset, he felt God call his name. He was calling him into communion with Him. Liam answered and began to share his feelings about Nia.

He confessed to God that while he had resolved to put her in the past, he still yearned for her. He shared with his Father his soul's desire to be with this woman who was not where she needed to be spiritually. He explained that it made him feel as though he was dishonoring God by desiring someone who did not love Him the way he, Liam, did.

He felt God was saying, 'just lay your burdens and care at My feet. I will deal with them. Just lay them down, son.'

So, he prayed for Nia. He prayed for her soul as he always did but he added her emotional well-being to his plea now. He prayed for those who had been injured and the families of those who had been killed in the terrorist attack. He prayed for God to turn the tragedy into something positive by helping people to recognize the fragility of life and the importance of living it with eternity in view.

He even prayed for Damon Deverre that God would help him to see that he was building his life on the shaky ground of riches and fame that would sink and slip away, rather than the firm foundation of Christ alone. Finally, he asked God to enable him to resist the urge to bring glory to himself by becoming Nia's hero, but instead to bring glory to God so that He could become her hero.

When he was done, he felt a peace and joy wash over him as though everything would be alright. He felt the assurance from the Holy Spirit that no matter what he went through in life, whether fire or flood, he was loved. God had not wasted his time. All he had been through in life, with Nia, with his career choices, finding his way spiritually, every challenge and disappointment, God had been there beside him molding him, step by step, breath by breath into the man He wanted him to become.

The journey was far from over, but he was assured that through it all God would be by his side. He felt as though God was singing over him and that song filled his pores and his innermost parts until he felt like he had to open his mouth and sing it to the world. He raced back inside, grabbed a pen and notepad, and settled again on the terrace as he filled page after page with raw emotion.

When Liam had poured everything out on paper, he began the process of reviewing and editing the material. Soon he was sure he had the words of a new song. He picked up his guitar and began to strum out music to go with the words of the song, but it didn't feel quite right, so he propped up the guitar and went to sit at the piano in the living room. He began to tickle the ivories and sing the words of his newly penned song. As he repeated the verses, the music came to him and seemed to fit.

Nia's eyelids fluttered open. When she heard the music and the singing she knew what had awoken her. It wasn't loud but the night was still, so the sound, as faint as it was, had traveled. She stayed quiet, enjoying the song. She knew it was Liam singing. She would know that beautiful, grainy voice anywhere.

The words were muffled, but she could hear the emotion in his voice as he sang. Then the music stopped again. Soon it started up. She could just imagine Liam sitting there at the piano and making notes as he sang to get the music and lyrics just right. That was the way he and the band had worked when she watched them play during that brief time in Austria.

She got out of bed and quietly crept down the corridor. She wanted to see Liam at work, but she didn't want to disturb him. She peeped around the corner, and her heart sighed when she saw him. He was so beautiful it almost hurt to gaze upon him. He was bent over the piano and scribbling on a notepad. As moonlight streamed through the sunroof and shone on his head, it almost gave the appearance of a halo.

Nia smiled wryly. Liam might look like an angel, but he was no saint. He had made mistakes, like sleeping with Heidi Wolffe, like his harsh words to her, and his often high-handed attitude. But he was an undeniably good man. He had strong moral convictions, which he stood by. He had integrity and principles. He was a man of honor and unspeakable loyalty. Even after everything, he was still here for her and taking care of her even though he didn't agree with her lifestyle.

She knew he didn't expect her to be perfect either, even though she had unfairly charged him with such. All he had asked was that she submit all her imperfections to the One who *was* perfect. She had never even tried. She had accused him of wanting things his way, but she had been just as guilty of that.

When he looked up, she darted back behind the wall. She held her breath but released it slowly when he began to play the piano again and sing the words. She could now hear them clearly. He was declaring that God stilled his soul with joy. He sang that even through trials he knew that he was loved. He had that assurance. He spoke of a God who was great enough to simply speak the earth into being and yet was personal enough to walk right beside him and commune with him every moment of the day.

The song tore at Nia's heart. She sank to her knees. Liam declared that God was his Father. God loved him like a son. He talked with him. He walked with him. They were in relationship. She buried her face in her hands and her body wracked with sobs.

"God, are You there? Are You listening? Do You love me too? After all I've done, do You love me still? Am I Your daughter?"

She fell over on her side and curled up in a ball as she finally, after all these years, cracked open the door to her heart.

Liam twisted his head from side to side to get out the kink. He stretched. He felt like he finally had it. The song was finished. When he got to Nashville, he would play it for the band and see if they had any changes to propose. He felt in his spirit that this was going to be the runaway hit on their new album.

A slow smile spread across his face. "Thank you, God," he said as he always did when a new song was downloaded onto his heart.

It happened like this sometimes. He'd just be there praying, and suddenly a song would come to him, and in short order, he had penned a new song. Often, after he reviewed it, he couldn't believe he had written something so profound, but then he was reminded it wasn't him. He was just a channel. It was all God's doing, and this song was a prime example. It had power... power that could only come from the Holy Spirit. He sensed it would touch many lives.

He ran a hand over his tired face and glanced at the clock. It was late. Hard to believe six hours had passed since Nia had gone to bed. Time ceased to have meaning when he was immersed in songwriting and composing.

He made his way to his bedroom and jumped back in alarm as his foot connected with something on the floor. Liam looked down and was surprised to see Nia lying there curled in a ball, hands tucked under her head. He lowered to his haunches, wondering fleetingly if she was hurt, dismissing it a moment later when he listened and realized she was just sleeping. What was she doing here? Had she been listening to him play?

His heartstrings pulled at him as he brushed a few wayward strands of hair from her face. *His Nia.* It didn't matter if they were no longer man and wife, she would always be *His Nia.*

With a sigh, he gathered her to him and stood. She stirred, muttered something and turned her face into his chest. It reminded him of when he had carried her from the hotel just last night, and when he had carried her from that arena, and the many times he had carried her to their bedroom during their brief period as man and wife.

He almost felt like a superhero rescuing the damsel. He sobered as he remembered his prayer. No, he wasn't the real superhero. He wasn't the one Nia needed. Nia needed Jesus. *He* was the one to rescue her. He was the only one who could save her and give her hope and a future. He was the only one who could give her eternal life.

When Liam reached the bedroom, he placed Nia gently on the bed, retrieved a light duvet from the cupboard and covered her. He leaned forward and kissed her brow then slid to his knees beside her. As he would do for a patient on her deathbed, he interceded for Nia. He prayed for the woman he loved that God would bring her back to Himself before it was too late.

When Nia opened her eyes, the first thing she felt was Liam. He was lying next to her on the bed. For a moment she wondered how she had gotten there.

Then she remembered the last place she'd been was in the corridor listening to him play. She'd probably fallen asleep there. Then he had brought her to bed. And fallen asleep next to her? Why had he stayed with her through the night? She had understood it in London after the bombing. She had begged him not to leave her that night, and he had agreed not to. But why had he done it last night?

Her eyes roamed his handsome face. *Her Liam.* A smile tugged at the corner of her mouth. He was at her mercy now. She reached out a hand to run over his stubble. It was seriously sexy, this new bearded look. But before her hand could reach the prickly destination, she paused.

No, she shouldn't. She recalled the last time they were together in Beijing when she had tried to get him up to her hotel room. She remembered what he had told her. It was too tempting. He hadn't been willing to give in to the temptation then because they were no longer married. While she could now reveal they still were, she didn't believe it would matter too much to him.

Liam had told her in not so many words that he couldn't renew their relationship unless she was prepared to turn away from the life she was leading. Her Grandmama Carmichael used to say that light did not have communion with darkness. It was true. He was light, and she was darkness.

She took a deep breath and sat up, allowing the duvet to fall from her. Placing her head in her hands, she quietly sobbed. She felt a touch on her back and startled.

"What's wrong?" Liam asked quietly.

She looked up, wiping her face with the back of her hand. She felt no shame in front of Liam. He'd seen her at her worst before.

She shrugged. "Nothing you can help with."

"I know who can help though," he offered quietly.

"The psychologist?"

A corner of his mouth lifted. "No. Jesus can help."

"I'm a lost cause."

"No, you're not. Do you know that many of the great men and women of the Bible were all deeply flawed? David was an adulterer and a murderer. Moses was also a murderer and a coward. Let's see, Abraham was a liar, Jacob was also a liar and a trickster. Mary Magdalene was a woman with a checkered past. Rahab was a prostitute. And I could go on and on. But God was able to clean them up and use them all in a mighty way. He won't ever give up on you, Nia."

Another sob escaped. Liam sat up and drew her to him.

"There's a war on between guilt and grace. There's nothing you've done, there's no place you've been, there's nothing you've thought, Nia, that our Lord won't forgive. Romans chapter eight says that nothing separates us from His love. Not death, nor life, nor angels or demons; not things present or things in the future. Not powers, heights, depths. Nothing in all creation can separate us from His love."

Now she was bawling.

"Is that why I feel the way I do, Liam? So empty without Him?" she hiccuped when her tears had died down. "I don't want to feel like this anymore. I want to give it all up. What can I do?"

He lifted a hand and cupped her jaw. "Surrender. Surrender everything to Him – your past, your present, your future. Give it to Him. Repent of your sins. Ask Him to forgive you and accept His forgiveness and His grace. Resolve to live only for Him from now on."

She was so tempted to sink into Liam. But this wasn't about her and Liam. This was about her and God. If she didn't get that part right then, she would never get the relationship with Liam right.

"Just like that? Can it be so simple?"

"First John 1:9 says if we confess our sins He is faithful and just to forgive our sins and cleanse us from all unrighteousness."

She looked up at him. "That's what I want to do. I am tired of this burden of guilt and shame. I want to be free."

He gathered her in his arms. "Tell him. Just tell him."

"Lord, I'm so sorry, so sorry for all the bad things I've done. Forgive me for turning my back on You and for caring more about the things of this world than the things of God. Please forgive me. Please cleanse me of my sins. Help me to do Your will, dearest precious Savior. Thank you."

"Thank you, God," Liam prayed, "Thank you."

Chapter 40

Mia half sat, half lay on a chaise lounge clutching the Holy Bible in her hands. Her eyes raced over the pages as she hungrily devoured her Father's love note to her and all His children. Ever since her conversion one week ago, she had felt an unquenchable thirst for the Living Water. She wanted to learn more about the One who had saved her. Liam had presented her with a Bible, well-used, and told her to begin at the Gospel of John.

That was what she had been doing every day since – reading, meditating and crying. She had been so eager to share with Liam all that she was learning. Like a child telling her friends about a trip to Disneyland. To her surprise, Liam listened, as though fascinated. When she commented that if she didn't know better, she would think he was hearing a particular passage for the first time, he responded that because God's word was alive, it was dynamic. It never got old or stale, it was always current and as such verses previously read could take on fresh meaning in a new circumstance.

He sat beside her now strumming a tune on his guitar and intermittently pausing to make notes. His creative juices certainly appeared to be flowing. Ever since their first night here, he had penned something like a song every other day.

As she watched him, she couldn't help remembering that he had proposed to her beside this same pool eight years ago. Now, here they were again. Married, yet apart. She had yet to enlighten him on their marital status. She was a little apprehensive over what his reaction was likely to be.

On the one hand, if he was disappointed that would hurt. On the other hand, if he was happy she might get her hopes up and cause her to want something she couldn't have.

He lightly played the introduction to a song. When he paused to make a note, she leaned toward him. "I want you to write a song for me."

He titled his head to one side. "A song for you?"

She nodded. "I'm not a gifted songwriter like you. But I would like my words fashioned into a song. The way I feel. I just want a song I can sing about that feeling."

He nodded thoughtfully. "Okay, let's do that. Tell me how you're feeling. Tell me everything and I'll write it down, and then we'll see how we can take parts of that and create poetry."

She told him of how when she had read about Jesus' crucifixion that she had felt like she was the one who was driving those nails through His hands. As though every time she had rebelled against Him she had been hurting Him, crucifying Him. She shared how when she read of Peter's denial she felt as though she was also guilty of the same thing. The way she lived her life and the lyrics of her songs all denied the truth of God and even told people it was all right to follow their own passions and desires and care nothing for His ways. She confessed, with tears, that she had done things she now wished she hadn't. She had seen things she wished she could erase from her memory; had spoken and sang words that she was now ashamed of.

And to think that in spite of all this, God, looked at her, arms wide open and told her it was all forgiven. Forgiven! Just like that. He, who she'd wronged time and time again, had told her that there was freedom from all she had done. That her slate was wiped clean.

Such grace. His amazing grace. This was the grace that had made a man sacrifice His life to save hers because He knew that His life was already assured in heaven.

After that horrific explosion, she could have been dead and buried and awaiting judgment for her sins. She could have been lost forever in everlasting hellfire. Instead, she was forgiven. His blood had made her innocent.

Three hours later, Nia watched in fascination as Liam took all the disjointed ramble that represented the way she felt at this moment and put it into a song. Even though it would need some refining, she could picture herself pouring out her heart as she sang that song on stage.

They took a break and then spent the rest of the night putting music to the words. Liam seemed to think it was important that they finish it that very day. He never once complained about getting tired. In an unspoken agreement, they knew they would press on until it was finished because it had significance for Nia. It was her testimony.

Liam watched Nia happily over breakfast the next morning. He still was on a high. He had prayed for Nia's salvation for so long it was almost hard to believe it had finally happened. He had waited over the coming days to see if it would stick or if she would lose interest or get bored but to his great joy, he could feel her sincerity.

As they were washing the breakfast dishes side by side, she began to sing "her" song.

"I didn't tell you this yesterday," he said as he soaped a dish and passed it to her to rinse, "but the words of your song reminds me of one on our band's album, called *Glorious Light*."

She rinsed a mug and placed it in the dish dryer and turned to him. "I want to hear you sing it to me as soon as we're done here."

Several minutes later he stood in front of her by the pool, strumming the strings of his guitar with a pick. Then he began to sing. It was one of his favorite songs on this last album. As he plucked the guitar strings and sang he moved around the pool and Nia hopped up to move with him.

She started singing the refrain. Nia was a natural. Soon she was singing the entire song in concert with him. As he played, they were jumping, shaking, dancing, and making a joyful noise to the Lord like two carefree teenagers. Liam felt such joy he was sure he would explode into a million brilliant lights.

When they finally stopped they were panting from the exertion, their chests heaving. He collapsed into the lounge chaise, and Nia fell on him. Eventually, their laughter eased, and their labored breathing abated. Then they became very aware of each other. Nia lifted her head to stare down at Liam. He shifted his body to stare up at her. He moved strands out of her face and traced his thumb down her cheeks to her lips. When he placed a hand at the back of her head and pulled her mouth down to meet his, a tremor flowed from her into him. He allowed himself the luxury of kissing her for a few moments. Then he shifted, so they were both lying on their sides, gazing at each other.

"What happens next?" he whispered.

He didn't anticipate that they could hide out in a villa in Barbados forever. The real world and all their responsibilities still beckoned.

"I feel such joy."

He nodded in understanding.

"I feel an urgency to share this news with the world, Liam."

"Then share, you must."

"Have you seen the news?"

Damon looked over at Cassandra as she bounded into his office holding up her phone, her bleached platinum blond hair flying around her head.

Damon was not in a good mood. He was still coming to grips with the fact that Nia had left him. Just like that. For the first time, he was truly terrified that she was gone for good. She had not returned any of his calls or messages for the last week. It was like she no longer cared about the empire he had helped her build. Perhaps she had simply gone stark, raving mad.

"What?

"It's about Nia. Look." She shoved her phone in front of his face.

Damon squinted and reached for his reading glasses. He took the phone.

The article said, *"Pop queen Nia has canceled all her events including an upcoming sold out concert and declared that she has become a Christian. Yesterday, the megastar took to social media with the revelation, posting on Instagram, 'I've given my life to Jesus. I am now a follower of Christ. All my pop shows will be canceled because He (God) has other work for me to do. I encourage my fans to also seek Christ. The reward is eternal life. I love all of you. You have always followed me throughout my career. Follow me on this new and better path."*

A swear word burst from Damon's lips.

"Do you think it is a gimmick?" Cassandra asked.

"It's him. He's to blame for this."

He swore again and would have dashed Cassandra's phone to the ground if she hadn't snatched it from his hand just in time.

Oh, how he hated William Lamport! He had hated him from the moment he had met him. The man was the epitome of everything Damon resented. Rich, white privilege. And it didn't matter that he had a few drops of black blood in his genes. The point was that he looked white and he was treated with all the respect and opportunities that went with that. He had been born into a loving home with every luxury at his fingertips. He had never known what it was like to be so hungry that even rodents began to look tempting. He didn't know what it was like to grow up with a father who didn't care about anything except the contents of a bottle. He didn't know what it was to grow up in a place where only the toughest and meanest survived. William Lamport knew *nothing* about survival; he had not had to work like a slave for every piece of wealth, power and nod of respect like Damon had.

Everything William Lamport had ever wanted had been handed to him on a silver platter! His money, his power, even his recording company. So why on earth should he get the girl too? Damon had taken extreme pleasure in stealing Nia away from William Lamport, and even though he had suspected over the years that she still carried a torch for the blue-eyed boy, he never had once eased up on his pursuit. It didn't matter if he fully had her heart as long as he had *her*. That would be enough. And now all this was being threatened because of that bomb attack. He brought down his fist on the desk so hard it made the items jump.

Cassandra was used to his outbursts and didn't react. She asked, "What are you going to do?"

"I want you to find out where she is. I'm going to get her back."

When the desire to sing with Nia had come to him months ago, Liam had no idea at the time it would play out the way it was doing right now.

Nia was sitting next to him at the piano, as planned. She was singing with him, but instead of the words impacting her and setting her on redemption road as he had initially expected, she was inspiring the words they were singing because she truly believed them.

They currently had their phones shut off. He had sent identical emails to the band and to his family telling them he was taking a leave of absence for an unspecified period. They had heard the news about Nia so they no doubt understood.

He suspected that social media was ablaze with the events of her breakdown at the fundraising concert and then her recent posting about becoming a Christian. The two of them were avoiding social media right now. In fact, they were avoiding the outside world, period.

Before she turned off her phone, Nia had spoken to a few people. Liam had noted that Damon Deverre was not one of them. He couldn't explain how relieved that made him feel. He had an irrational fear that if that man contacted her too soon, he might convince her to abandon the hope she had found and return to her previous life.

Nia turned to him. "I really like your covers, Liam," she said almost shyly. "Can we sing one together?"

So, that was how it began. The first was one of Nia's most popular songs. He had changed it from a ballad about two lovers to a song about how God had given His all to him, and he would do the same as he gave God all the glory and the praise.

To hear Nia singing this Christian version of her popular song touched Liam down to his core.

As she turned toward Liam and hitched one foot on the stool leaving the other dangling down, she said, "How about we rewrite one together?"

He was speechless. This was even more than he had hoped for.

"S…sure," he stammered.

She burst out laughing. "You should see the expression on your face. One would think I just asked you to go bull riding."

He quirked a brow as his mouth twitched. He remembered when he had made the joke at his parents' country home.

"What do you mean? Bull riding is nothing. Frankly, it's mild compared to the roller coaster ride I've been on since the day I met you, Nia Carmichael."

He expected her to make some witty comeback. Instead, her next words almost made him choke on his saliva.

"It's Nia Lamport, still," she said softly.

He startled. "What?"

She nodded, her gaze never leaving his. "I couldn't go through with it, Liam. I simply couldn't."

His mouth fell open. "You mean to say that all this time we've still been married? Why didn't you say something?"

She shrugged. "I don't know. I wasn't sure how you would take the news. We're so happy I was afraid it would change things."

"It does. We're married." He dragged a hand through his hair and looked heavenward. "We're married," he said louder, with a buoyant laugh. He grabbed her arms and kissed her hard. "I love you!"

Her breath caught on a sob.

"I've been exercising restraint like you can't imagine thinking I didn't have the right to touch you. Now I realize I do."

He leaned towards her, his intentions clear. Then he halted an inch from her face, his expression changing.

He sat back. "No, this isn't right."

She looked alarmed. "What isn't right?"

"Nia, we have made so many missteps. We have broken our vows to each other."

He glanced at her and realized the color had begun to recede from her face. He hastened to explain.

"What I'm trying to say, darling, is that before we go forward, a re-commitment is necessary."

She blinked. "What?"

He vaulted off the piano stool to grab his guitar and was back in record time.

"I'll let the song say it all."

Liam sang the song he had written for her the night before their wedding reception. It took on new meaning for him. He now understood what it truly meant to speak of a forever love. They were both flawed, but the point was that they were now committed to God and His love covered a multitude of sins. As long as they sought to love each other the way He loved them they would be all right.

He ended on a grin a mile wide. Then he leaned toward her and whispered, "Your turn, Mrs. Lamport."

She turned to face the piano. She knew some basics thanks to her Julliard piano training, although she had confided in him that she rarely played these days. While he vaguely noted that her playing was good enough, it was really the words of her song that captured his attention. It was the love song she had sung the night of the bombing. The fact that she could sing that song with all the memories associated with it must mean that some healing had taken place over the last couple of weeks.

She didn't finish though. She stopped midway and turned to him. She whispered, "I can't sing it. Not yet."

He pulled her into his arms. "It's okay, darling. I understand."

She turned her head and pulled back slightly to look into his eyes.

"Whenever I sang that song all I could think of was you; of how much I loved you and how much you meant to me. The last time I sang it, I realized I had broken my promise to you to never leave your side. I did fling our vows in your face to pursue my own dreams. I was so selfish, Liam. Will you forgive me?"

"Nia, I do forgive you. Will you forgive me for being so unyielding and uncompromising as you once put it so eloquently?"

She laughed a little and then sobered. "Yes, Liam, I forgive you."

"Nia, I vow to spend the rest of my life showing you how much I love you and how much you mean to me."

Her lips trembled as she smiled. As she was about to open her mouth, a loud knock startled them and caused them to look at each other in confusion.

"Who on earth is that?" Liam asked as he rose to go to the door.

Chapter 41

L iam peered through the peephole and had to rub his eyes and look again.

This was not possible. Damon Deverre again!

He walked back to where Nia still sat in front of the piano.

"Damon Deverre is here! He's outside. How did he know where you were?"

She looked stunned. "I don't know. I didn't tell him if that's what you think."

He didn't know what to think. They had just recommitted to each other. Was it going to be tested so soon?

He didn't want to answer the door. He was tempted, in fact, to call the police and ask them to get this man off his property, but something kept him back. Rather, some*one*, the Holy Spirit, told him it wasn't his decision to make.

He couldn't start over fresh with Nia if he continued to make the same mistakes. He had to let her decide what she wanted to do and be prepared to accept it even if he didn't agree.

He took a deep breath and asked calmly, "Should I let him in?"

There came a rap again, louder this time with the yell, or was it a war cry, "Nia, it's me, Damon. Open up!"

FOREVER YOURS (A ROYAL DESCENDANTS NOVEL)

Liam could feel a surge of anger. The nerve of that man. He had no couth whatsoever. To show up uninvited on his property and then proceed to call out for Nia as though he fancied himself Ben yelling for Elaine in *The Graduate's* wedding scene. He would love to open the door and fit his fist to the center of the man's face.

Again Liam told himself to hold strain. He took another deep calming breath.

"Nia? What should I do?"

She squared her shoulders. "Let him in. I need to talk to him, might as well do it now."

He nodded once and when he pulled open the door Deverre's arm was raised as though he was about to pound on it for the third time.

Liam smiled brightly. "Good morning, Mr. Deverre. How can I help you?"

The man peered into the villa, and his gaze found Nia.

"Nia!" he exclaimed, shouldering past Liam without a greeting.

Liam gritted his teeth as he closed the door.

Deverre walked up to Nia. "What's going on, baby? Are you feeling all right?"

She smiled serenely. "I'm doing so much better, Damon. Thanks for asking."

He sighed. "You have a lot of people worried. You've been gone for so long."

"Only nine days."

"Nine days is a long time for someone like you to be…"

He stopped suddenly. "I saw your social media messages. What are you doing, Nia? Is this about the attack? Your mental breakdown? Is that what that claim about finding Jesus is about?" He asked the questions soothingly as though speaking to someone who was not quite stable.

Nia laughed lightly. "Damon, why don't we sit so we can talk," she said, leading Deverre over to the living area with its picturesque view of the aquamarine ocean.

Liam took a seat at the piano and observed the two from a distance that gave Nia a little privacy while allowing him to be close enough to be of assistance if the man tried to pull anything.

"Can I get you anything to drink?" Nia offered politely.

Deverre took a seat and shook his head while still watching her cautiously.

"Damon, I'm the best I've ever been. I'm finally happy."

Shock followed by annoyance flashed across his face. "You canceled your shows. Why would you do that? You never even discussed that with me."

With each sentence, his voice rose in frustration.

"I didn't need to. This is a personal decision."

"Yeah, one that will cost me, Nia. Our contract is clear…"

"Don't worry about the contract, Damon. I'm through. I'm not making that type of music anymore."

"What type of music is that?"

"The kind that glorifies created things rather than the One who created them," she said patiently.

Liam observed how peaceful she looked and felt his heart swell with pride. Why did he ever doubt that this woman could hold her own?

When she leaned forward and squeezed his hand, Deverre jerked away and yelled, "This is crap!"

He shot to his feet and turned to jab an accusatory finger at Liam. "This is your fault! You are the one who led her down this stupid path that will destroy her career and reputation. I hope you are happy. You finally got all you wanted these years – to ruin her."

Before Liam could think of a response, Nia was on her feet touching Deverre's arm. When he turned toward her, she placed a hand on his cheek. Liam couldn't help the surge of jealousy he felt at seeing her touch this man, once her fiancé, with such tenderness. He glanced away, but her next words soothed all his discomfort.

"Damon, this has nothing to do with Liam. It has everything to do with God. He saved me. I feel free, there's nothing you can offer me, or that the world can offer me, that can compare to that."

"God!" Deverre bellowed.

Liam was surprised he didn't spit on the ground for emphasis.

"I'll tell you about your God. I had a drunken father who would come home and beat the stuffing out of my mother. She prayed night and day for him to change but he never did, and one day the useless bum came home and beat her to within an inch of her life. When I got home from school that day and found out what had happened, I waited for him by the door and when he entered I split his head open with a baseball bat. I was sent to a juvenile center for that, even though I didn't succeed in killing him. My mother never fully recovered from that last beating he gave her. She lived for another few years, but she was never of any use to herself. She had brain damage. He did that to her. And your God did nothing about it."

Nia touched his arm again. "Damon, I don't know why God allowed that evil to happen. But I do know that He loves you and your mother and your father too–"

Deverre held his head and exploded with indignation. "That's love? Well, if that's love I don't want it. Enough of this foolish talk, okay? I've come to take you back with me."

Liam resisted the urge to surge to his feet and announce to Deverre that Nia was not going anywhere with him. He bit his lip and concentrated on his breathing. This was not his decision to make. If the last eight years had taught him anything, it was that.

When Liam saw Nia turn away to look out the window he held his breath and waited.

Finally, she faced Deverre.

"Damon, like you, my family life was nothing to crow about. I had a drug addict for a mother and a self-centered womanizer for a father. As a child, I was constantly moved around. I felt for a long time, most of my life actually, that God didn't care about me and I could only rely on myself. But even that false claim didn't make me happy. This notion that I was on my own was not comforting. Even though I told myself I was fine, I really wasn't. Yes, I did things my own way. Yes, I reaped success and fame. But you know what? Happiness was fleeting moments. It was defined by achievements and accolades and approval of others. It was fragile. Throughout it all, I felt empty. I tried to fill up the spaces with parties and travel and the adoration of fans. Even my relationship with you was an attempt to feel like someone powerful and successful had accepted me for the way I was."

Her eyes skittered to Liam. He understood that Deverre had been an antidote to him and his refusal to take her back unless she surrendered to God. But her look was one of gratitude, not accusation.

She turned back to Deverre. "But, Damon, there was this hole, and I couldn't figure out why. It made no sense. Then I began to feel as though God was trying to get my attention. I think the terrorist attack shocked me into finally realizing that if I had died right then, I would have been doomed to spend the rest of eternity in Hell. I had built up treasures on earth and none in Heaven. I had turned my back on God, rejected Him, told lies about who He is, and encouraged others to do the same through the lyrics of my songs. How could I even face Him on Judgment Day knowing my life had been a waste? I don't want to live like that anymore. I didn't know what it felt like to be free. I know now. There is no way I'm going back to that prison I once called living life. Fame, fortune…I don't want it anymore. I don't care about it. It doesn't define who I am. I am a child of God. There is nothing anyone can say to trump that. There is no follower of my music who can give me a greater thrill. There is no award that means more than that."

If Liam felt he was proud of her before it was impossible to describe the way he felt now. He felt like his heart was bursting with joy.

She turned to him, and he met her gaze across the room. She still was talking to Deverre, but this was meant for him it seemed.

"Trust was not something I was used to. Trusting meant being hurt. So I decided to only trust in myself and my abilities."

She gave a harsh laugh and looked to Deverre. "You once told me that I thought I was something. The truth is deep down I knew I was nothing. I knew I was just keeping it together with chewing gum and duct tape, putting on a façade. My identity came from my talent and my looks and my charm, so it was fragile. I lived in constant fear that one of those things might just disappear. When that man attacked me, I could have been burned, scarred, crippled, maimed like some were. I could have damaged my vocal cords and then where would I be? But, Damon, I now know I'm something. And it has nothing to do with my abilities, my looks, or my charm. It has to do with being a child of the King of the universe."

Liam smiled as her eyes found his once more and he knew she was referencing how he had described himself when they had met in Austria. He had said he was a prince, the son of the King of the universe. She hadn't understood then what that meant. Clearly, she understood now.

She continued. "I'm a princess. I like this new status. I love the way it makes me feel. I love being free."

"But your fans..." Deverre sputtered, and Liam noted he no longer sounded sure of himself. He sounded deflated.

"I don't care if they deride me. I don't care if they refuse to follow me. I'm not going back to that life."

She suddenly choked up. "Damon, when I look at Him, the feeling I get I can't describe to you. It's just amazing. I've never known such grace, such love."

Damon Deverre looked confused for a moment. "Him?" he pointed at Liam. "You mean him?"

Nia grasped Deverre's face and swung it to her. She looked fierce.

"Damon, look at me! I'm speaking about Christ, my Savior. He can be yours too. Don't reject him. Your life is about as empty as mine was. All your material riches will rust away when you die. Your soul will live, forever. Store up riches in heaven instead."

Deverre grabbed her hands and thrust her from him. As Nia stumbled backward, Liam shot to his feet and began to close the space between them. When Nia threw up her hand to stop him, he reluctantly halted a few feet from the two.

Her attention returned to Deverre. "You are not happy."

"You know nothing about me! Just because I went out with you a few times you think you know me?" he spat. "If you want to follow this clown, fine. Go ahead. What do you have to lose anyway? As you enjoyed reminding me, he's loaded. But you know what? You will just become an insignificant little cog in his family's machinery, an exotic bird that amuses people like him."

Nia shook her head. "Damon, God loves you. He *loooves* you! Your earthly father let you down, but your Everlasting Father has not! You could be dead. He is preserving your life right now because He has a plan for your life still. And while you are alive, there is hope that you can live out your purpose before you leave this world."

"I *am* living my purpose! My purpose is to become rich and famous by any means necessary. And I've done it. You don't know the half of what I've done to get to where I am, little girl. I have practically sold my soul to the devil. It's too late for me. I'm in too deep. I'm not willing to lose everything I worked for tooth and nail, sacrificed for, sold my conscience and my heart to have, for someone in the sky I've never seen, who *you* have never seen. I know now that you have gone crazy!"

Nia stepped up to him and got right into his face, Liam braced himself in case Deverre pushed her again. He would not stand by another time and allow the woman he loved to get shoved around.

"You claimed to love me. Was that even true?" Nia asked softly.

Deverre looked uncomfortable for a moment. "I do love you. But not more than I love myself. I'm not going to give up my life for you if that's what you're asking."

She settled back on her heels and watched him with a faint smile.

"That's not true love, Damon. I know all about that kind of love. It's the selfish kind, where you're only willing to love when there is no cost to yourself. True love gives everything, empties itself of everything. That's the love God has shown me. Even though I turned on Him, was against Him, He still loves me. He still wants me. He has forgiven my every sin. Where else in the universe can I, can you, can Liam, find that kind of love? Do not reject the One who gave up everything so you might have a chance to have life. Please."

She looked at Deverre with moist, shiny, pleading eyes. Liam felt like he would cry too.

When Damon Deverre released a cry that sounded as though it was coming from a wounded animal, Liam took a step back in shock. The man doubled over, fell on his knees and held his head. His body convulsed, and for a moment Liam thought he was having some kind of epileptic seizure until he realized he was wailing.

Liam felt his chest tighten. Such emotion as he could not describe filled him. He didn't even realize when he rushed to the man's side and fell down on his knees beside him. He didn't stop to think as his hand went around Deverre's shoulders. Then he began praying, interceding, for the one who should be his enemy but for whom he now only felt compassion.

Nia had sunk to the ground in front of Damon. She held his hand and lent her voice in supplication to Liam's. Damon Deverre rocked back and forth and cried for heaven only knew how long.

Sometime later, Damon sat back on his haunches, wiping his face on the back of his arm. Silence reigned for a while, and then he looked at Liam as though he was seeing him for the first time.

"I've been angry for so long. I feel like I can't exist without that anger. I've trusted in myself for so long."

He held out a shaky hand to Nia. "Do you think there is really hope for someone like me? Do you really believe that?"

She nodded with a small smile. "Yes, Damon. There was hope for me. There is hope for you."

She sat cross-legged in front of him.

"Damon, there was a thief on the cross being crucified beside Jesus. He had done so many bad things, he knew he deserved to die, but all he had to do was believe in Jesus. That's what he did, and he was forgiven of his sins and got to spend eternity with Jesus. There is no doubt in my mind you have done many bad things. There is also no doubt that no matter what they were you can be forgiven. But, Damon, you have to repent. You have to give up this life."

Damon glanced away, rubbed his nose with his hand and struggled to get to his feet. Liam also stood. Damon watched him a long time then he held out a hand. "Take care of her, William."

Liam inclined his head as he shook Damon's hand. "I will."

Deverre looked down at Nia and looped a smile. "You know, Double D Records does not produce Christian music, so it looks like this is the end of the road for us."

She got to her feet and hugged him. When she drew back, she said, "I pray that one day soon Double D Records will *only* produce Christian music. In any case, I'll be joining my husband's troupe."

"You will?" Liam asked in wonder.

She turned to him with a hint of vulnerability in her eyes. "Only if you'll have me, of course."

He didn't respond. He was too overcome. He just stared into her eyes.

As Damon headed for the door, the movement broke their eye contact.

"Sorry for disturbing you, folks. I'll let you get back. We can discuss the contract later."

"Hey..." Nia called.

Damon looked back with his hand on the door.

"I'll be praying for you."

He looked conflicted for a moment and then he took a deep breath and nodded slowly. "I would really appreciate that, Nia."

Epilogue

Nia stood backstage, clasping and unclasping her hands as she prepared to mount the stage with *Redeemed*.

It was now eight months after the tragedy; several months since she had joined the band. They had spent months recording their new album and had launched a domestic tour to support its recent release. This tour would only be three months long with performances at twenty-seven arenas given that Nia was now three and a half months pregnant with her and Liam's first child.

It would be the first time she was performing in public since the bombing.

Liam kissed her temple and pulled her into a side hug. "Philippians 4:13," he whispered just before they moved onto the stage.

Nia held on to the promise of that Scripture verse as the floodlights came on and the delighted crowd welcomed the band with screams of jubilation.

"I can do all things through Christ who gives me strength. I can do all things through Christ who gives me strength," she said over and over again in her mind.

As her gaze anxiously swept the crowd, she began to feel her palms sweat. The music began, and Liam started to sing the first verse. Even though she was wearing her in-ear monitor, allowing her to drown out most of the sounds, she felt as though the noises around her were ramped up. Her heart pounded in anxiety. Her eyes darted from left to right. She had no bodyguards. Liam had persuaded her that they didn't need them. He had reminded her of Psalm 91.

He who dwells in the secret place of the most high shall abide under the shadow of the Almighty. I will say of the Lord He is our refuge and our fortress in Him we will trust. Surely He shall deliver us from the snare of the fowler and from the perilous pestilence. He shall cover us with His feathers and under His wings we shall take refuge. His truth shall be our shield and buckler.

It had sounded so right at the time. Now, she could feel the enemy whisper doubt in her ears.

She prayed, "Lord, heal me of this anxiety. Make me whole again. Help me not to be afraid but to put my trust in You."

Suddenly, she felt as though her fear was gone. She was free. Like her mother had been supernaturally healed of her addiction, she had been healed of her Post Traumatic Stress Disorder.

Nia moved across the stage now in free abandon as she sang that she was no longer a slave to fear. How apt those words were at that very moment, and how true they were.

After the concert was over and they were heading over to the hotel, she snuggled up next to Liam as the other band members chatted.

"I was praying for you tonight through the performance," he said, "that God would give you the strength you need to face your fears."

"I felt those prayers over me, Liam. God healed me. He touched me and made me whole."

Liam leaned down and kissed her, and then he lovingly ran a hand over her slight baby bump, barely noticeable at this stage.

"Yes, He is indeed the great restorer. He makes all that is broken whole again. I'm looking forward to what He has in store for us for the rest of our lives as we learn to trust Him more and more."

Nia leaned back against Liam with a contented sigh. She also was looking forward because she knew that no matter what, she had complete assurance that *God was in control!*

~*~*~THE END~*~*~

Glossary

Ma petite fille chérie – My darling daughter

Monsieur – Mister

Madame – Mistress

Ma chérie/Mon chéri – My dear/My darling

Pardon – Excuse me.

Non – no

Bien sur – of course

Grandmére – grandmother

Comme on fait son lit, on se couche - As you make your bed, so you must lie

Discussion Questions

1. Liam reveals his purity ring. He could have made the purity vow without a public symbol. Why do you think such a manifestation is significant? In what ways does this mirror marriage rings?

2. Liam and Nia make a split minute decision to get married. Do you think this was a good idea? Give the reason for your answer.

3. Why do you think it is important that a couple not be unequally yoked?

4. Liam says that everything belongs to God. What is your perspective on this? How might such an approach bring one closer to God?

5. Liam becomes hurt when Nia says she doesn't want or need his protection. Why might words like this wound a man? What is your definition of a husband's protection of his wife in this era of feminism? What do you think the biblical definition is?

6. At Liam's wedding reception, his father in his speech says 'Love is a constant act of forgiveness'. Do you agree? Explain the reason for your answer. Consider how 1 Corinthians 13 is applied here.

7. Liam resigns from his father's company because he feels led by God to make a career change. Have you ever felt led by God in this way? If yes, how did you respond and what was the outcome?

8. Nia accuses Liam of not acting very Christian when he only wants her back on his terms. Do you agree? How could he have been more Christ-like in his approach while still maintaining his integrity?

9. Liam feels led to pray for Nia instead of condemning her. How might you incorporate prayer for celebrities of popular culture into your intercessory prayer? Why would this please God?

10. Liam describes one of Nia's songs as a sinful message coated in an enticing beat. Does this describe any of the songs you listen to? Why is it important for Christians to be discerning in the music we listen to?

11. Nia says she got saved a couple of times and it didn't stick. Was there ever a time in your life you felt this way?

12. Liam tells the audience that God is looking for people who will worship Him not only with their mouths but also with their hearts. He says that strong affection for God rooted in sound doctrine is what is required to worship Him in spirit and in truth. Do you agree with this statement? Give the reason for your answer.

13. Liam responds to God's prompting and because of his obedience is able to rescue Nia. Can you cite an instance when you responded to God's prompting and in doing so were able to help someone?

14. What are your thoughts on why bad things happen to "good" people? How can tragedy serve a purpose in our lives?

15. Liam tells Nia, "Surrender. Surrender everything to Him – your past, your present, your future. Give it to Him. Repent of your sins. Ask Him to forgive you and accept His forgiveness and His grace. Resolve to live only for Him from now on." Have you surrendered your life to Christ? If not, what is preventing you from doing so now?

About the Author

NICOLE TAYLOR is the author of four romance novels and has been honored with the Christain Small Publishers Association (CSPA) Award. With a master's in human resource management and a bachelor's in sociology and psychology, she is a manager in the public sector by day and scribbles away on her next novel by night. Nicole lives with her husband and three children on the beautiful island of Barbados. You can visit her online at www.authornicoletaylor.com.

Books by Nicole Taylor

The Royal Couple
Second Chance
A Case For Love
Forever Yours

Contact

Please visit Nicole Taylor on the web!

Facebook: https://www.facebook.com/AuthorNicoleTaylor/

Twitter: https://twitter.com/Elocin_Rolyat

Website: http://www.authornicoletaylor.com/

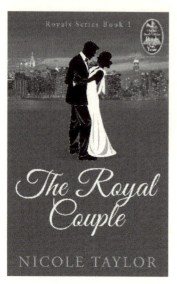

Winner of the 2016 Christian Small Publisher Book of the Year Award!

Movie star, BARBARA Dickson, tells herself she is fine being single. She has a successful career, enjoys her philanthropic pursuits and is growing in her relationship with the Lord. Then, the dashing billionaire who shattered her young heart walks back into her life and rocks her well-ordered existence.

Sparks fly when devastatingly handsome blue-blood heir WILLIAM Lamport III first sets eyes on Barbara at his family's estate. The two fall hard and fast for each other, but William's past comes back to haunt him and tear the two apart.

Now, nine years later, William has returned and is determined to reunite with the one woman he has never been able to forget. He hotly pursues Barbara in the hopes she'll give him another chance. He is bewildered that all she seems willing to offer him is friendship. William is used to getting what he wants, but this strong, amazing, woman of faith is no easy conquest.

Will this journey teach William to surrender to God's will and not seek his own? And will Barbara trust God with her future or will she allow fear to keep her from giving her heart to the only man she has ever loved?

Most people would say she leads a charmed life.

DANA Dickson is beautiful, rich, famous, and married to a gorgeous movie star. Yet, she is desperately unhappy.

When Dana marries actor ROBERT Cortelli, she is sure she has the loving, devoted husband she has always dreamed of.

Eleven years and three children later, Dana instead finds herself playing second fiddle to Robert's demanding film career.

Just when Dana thinks she's had enough, a catastrophic incident occurs that forces her to respond with faith and courage. But as the couple begins to rekindle their romance and discover God's plan and purpose for their lives, secrets are revealed that threaten to shatter their newfound intimacy.

Will Robert and Dana allow past mistakes to tear them apart? Or will love and forgiveness win out and give this couple the second chance they so desperately long for?

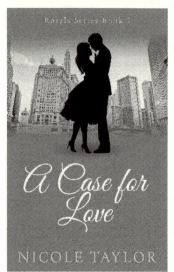

RONNIE Dickson is excited when she lands a coveted position with one of the country's leading law firms, Jones Law. Ronnie expects that this will be the job to help her discover her destiny. What she doesn't expect is to fall for the firm's handsome CEO, DAVID Jones, first day on the job.

Driven and focused, David Jones knows what he wants for his life. He wants to make his mark as the newest CEO of his family's legal dynasty and he wants to get elected state representative and bring positive change to Chicago. David also knows that to achieve his dreams he has to avoid another scandal at all costs.

But what is a man to do when the woman who captures his heart is also the one who is off limits. As David's intense feelings for Ronnie threaten to consume him, he must decide – should he give up the thing that could stand in the way of achieving his goals? Or should he sacrifice his ambitions for lasting love.

Made in the USA
Columbia, SC
08 November 2018